Set on the Navajo reservation and packed with Native American wisdom, Aimée and David Thurlos' Ella Clah novels are written with a sharp eye for the conflict between the traditionalist and modernist ways of life.

"The Thurlos provide Tony Hillerman with good company on the sunburnt sands and hills of the Southwest."
—*Cape Coral Daily Breeze*

Enemy Way

"The conflicts between the old ways and Ella's job as an investigator on the Navajo police force are at the core of this readable novel."
—*Dallas Morning News*

"A masterfully written, carefully plotted mystery featuring one of the genre's most believable and empathetic protagonists."
—*Booklist*

Bad Medicine

"This novel has it all: murder, sex, drugs, and racial tension on the Rez. The Thurlos know what keeps readers turning pages. Enough action to satisfy, dangling questions that have to be answered."
—*The New Mexican*

Death Walker

"Ella Clah is a complex, well-crafted character with both strengths and flaws that make her appealing to readers. I never wanted to quit reading. The story is steeped in authenticity. If Hillerman ever retires, [the Thurlos] will be the obvious heirs apparent."
—*Colorado Springs Gazette Telegraph*

Blackening Song

"The action moves swiftly in this well-written mystery. Highly recommended."
—*Library Journal*

Also by Aimée and David Thurlo

ELLA CLAH NOVELS
Blackening Song
Death Walker
Bad Medicine
Enemy Way
Shooting Chant
Red Mesa
Changing Woman
Tracking Bear

LEE NEZ NOVELS
Second Sunrise
Blood Retribution (coming)

SISTER AGATHA NOVELS
Bad Faith
Thief in Retreat (coming)

Plant Them Deep

ENEMY WAY

—✕—✕—✕—✕—✕—

AIMÉE & DAVID THURLO

A TOM DOHERTY ASSOCIATES BOOK
NEW YORK

This is a work of fiction. All the characters and events portrayed in this book are either products of the author's imagination or are used fictitiously.

ENEMY WAY

A Forge Book
Published by Tom Doherty Associates, LLC
175 Fifth Avenue
New York, NY 10010

www.tor.com

Forge® is a registered trademark of Tom Doherty Associates, LLC.

ISBN 0-812-56459-6
EAN 978-0812-56459-4
Library of Congress Catalog Card Number: 98-21192

First edition: September 1998
First mass market edition: August 1999

Printed in the United States of America

0 9 8 7 6 5

To Melissa Singer, Jen Hogan, and the folks at Forge who
believed in Ella and helped smooth out her path.

And to Meg Ruley, who believes in us.

ACKNOWLEDGMENTS

——— ✖ ✖ ✖ ———

To those people who have helped us but whose jobs or affiliations make it inappropriate for them to accept a public thank-you: You know who you are, and we're both deeply grateful for the kindness you've shown us.

ENEMY WAY

PROLOGUE

——————— ✖ ✖ ✖ ———————

Navajo Police Special Investigator Ella Clah bent down to the water fountain installed in the tiny alcove of the Shiprock bank lobby. The water was so cold it hurt her teeth, but at least it didn't have that metallic aftertaste like the fountain at the station.

It was her day off, but she needed to deposit her paycheck. She'd been carrying it around since yesterday. She hated making ATM deposits, so she'd rushed over this afternoon barely making it before closing time.

Straightening up, Ella noticed the bank manager standing behind his desk, key ring in hand, staring oddly toward the door.

"Nobody move! This is a robbery." A man's voice yelled from across the room. He sounded Anglo, with a trace of a southern accent, maybe Texan.

Ella ducked out of sight and took out her pistol, peeking around the corner of the alcove. Two masked perps were just inside the lobby door, brandishing a pistol and sawed-off shotgun.

"Everyone down on the floor. Now!" shouted the man with the accent. He was waving a pistol—a nine-millimeter Browning. Everyone quickly complied, including the old man and woman who'd been behind Ella earlier, and now were depositing their Social Security checks.

Nobody except the robbers made a sound, which was a good thing. Noise and excitement tended to make armed criminals even more nervous and apt to pull the trigger.

Ella watched the man with the Browning. He was a real cool customer. As she studied him, he grabbed Herbert, the bank manager, by the collar, and stuck the pistol to his head, forcing him out from behind his desk. "Give me the keys to the cash drawers!"

Ella ducked back out of sight as the perp with the shotgun took a quick look around the room. She had to consider her options carefully. If she made her move now and tried to make an arrest, two customers and at least three bank employees could get hit if the robbers decided to open fire. But there was another possibility. If she could avoid detection for a while longer, maybe the opportunity to get the drop on them would present itself, or she could follow them outside and try to make the arrest in the parking lot.

She still vividly remembered a heavily armed lunatic in a crowded L.A. diner. It had been a very close call for her and a bunch of other people. Hostages had been wounded. She'd finally put a stop to it by killing the gunman at point-blank range. She didn't want to have to do that here again today.

The leader, the one with the Browning, took a set of keys from Herbert and put the pistol to the back of his head. For a second Ella wondered if the perp was planning on pulling the trigger. She took aim, but Browning just laughed, then leaped over to the teller's side of the high counter. The employees over there had already disappeared, probably curled up on the floor, praying that a little cooperation would get them home alive tonight.

Shotgun continued to watch the room, sweeping the sawed-off pump around like a fire hose, making sure nobody else came into the bank. Ella kept low behind the corner of the alcove. Fortunately, one of those stand-alone counters was between her and the robbers, and there were none of those surveillance mirrors to show where she was hiding.

In another minute the leader filled a bank bag with cash. As he tossed over the money and climbed back across onto the customer side, Ella took advantage of his preoccupation and slipped out beside the island counter. If she had figured it right, it would be possible to edge around behind the robbers without being seen.

"Let's go. Keep watching for trouble." Browning yelled to Shotgun, then he turned around to the prone customers and employees. "Nobody gets up for five minutes. If I see one of you dipsticks so much as raise your head, I'll come back in and blow your brains out."

Shotgun stopped at the door and looked outside. "Looks clear. Here I go."

Ella inched closer, and saw the first robber disappear from view. When Browning passed by the counter, Ella saw her chance. She reached out and grabbed his pistol hand, putting her own nine-millimeter Sig into the small of his back. He flinched, but let her take the pistol without a word.

"Good choice, smart mouth," Ella whispered. "Now keep walking and don't make any sudden moves. I'm a cop, but I'll blow your spine in half without a thought to save these people's lives." Ella prodded the man forward, slipping the Browning into her jacket pocket while she walked toward the front entrance. "Call 911, Herbert," she said a bit louder, without looking away from her captive.

They made it to the door without incident, and with the perp in front of her, Ella was screened somewhat from the other man outside. "If you want to live, stay smart."

They stepped outside, her pistol still in the small of the man's back. Ella tried not to tense up. She knew she still had to confront the man with the shotgun less than twenty feet in front of her. He was carrying the weapon unobtrusively down at his side, and surveying the parking lot for cops when her makeshift strategy was suddenly put to the test.

"Cop!" a woman screamed. Ella looked to her right and saw a woman pointing a pistol at her from out the window of an old brown Chevy.

The man with the shotgun whirled and fired, dropping the money sack in the parking lot and doing some serious damage to the big blue mailbox just to her left. Ella shoved her prisoner down below the brick planter in front of the bank, following him behind cover just as the shotgun went off again. Chunks of brick and shreds of boxwood showered the wall above Ella's head, and her prisoner groaned in pain.

By then, the woman in the Chevy was firing too, screaming and yelling at the top of her lungs. Bullets struck the cinder-block wall in a half-dozen places above the planter, but Ella had already left the wounded robber and was moving toward the other end of the structure.

Fear left a bitter taste in her mouth, but training and instinct spurred her on. Ella rose slightly, risking a fast look, and saw Shotgun jump into the car with the bag of money. As she raised her pistol and took aim at the shooter, she spotted two people standing by a pickup a few vehicles farther down, right in her line of sight. She'd planned to hit the robber's front tire, but it was at the wrong angle. Shifting her aim, she fired two quick shots into the Chevy's engine block instead.

Shotgun fired, and she was forced to duck down again. Ella heard the squeal of tires and, in frustration, watched as the vehicle roared down the street, heading away past the grocery store. She couldn't even get one shot off without endangering civilians, but she smiled slowly as she saw smoke coming from underneath the hood. With luck, they wouldn't get too far.

Ella hurried back to her prisoner who was laying on the sidewalk behind the planter, cursing a blue streak. Blood oozed from buckshot wounds along his upper thigh. As she crouched beside him, Herbert poked his head out the door of the bank, and noticed the wounded man. "Want me to call an ambulance too, Officer Clah?"

"You better get them here fast. I'm bleeding to death!" the robber said, and moaned.

"You'll live," Ella assured him. Giving Herbert a nod, she read the perp his rights. "If I were you, I'd start thinking of a way to cut a deal. Life as you know it has just come to an end."

ONE

✖ ✖ ✖

Ella stood at the window, watching the last rays of the fading sun arc across the land in blood red sheets, changing the soft earth tones of the New Mexican desert into crimson hues. The rugged mesas floated among a soft haze created by the dust that lingered in the air, easing the stark outlines of the sagebrush- and juniper-dotted canyons.

At least the morning hours today had been hers to enjoy. Gathering medicinal herbs with her mother and learning about the Plant People, had left her with a sense of connectedness to the *Dineh*, one she hadn't felt in a long time. And while the late afternoon had been an adventure she didn't want to repeat again soon, it certainly could have gone a lot worse, as it had for the person she'd come to interview.

Now, as she waited in the hospital lobby for her crime scene officer, the rush of excitement and adrenalin she'd felt earlier finally started to vanish along with the sunlight.

There had been a time when serious crime had not been a problem here on the Rez, but those days were long gone. The outside world had crept in, leaving its mark on them all. Admittedly, crime often took a different form here, one unique to the Navajo Nation. The spiritual and material worlds were too intertwined in The People's thinking for it to be otherwise. Yet, lately it seemed that even that distinction was becoming less pronounced.

As round-faced Sergeant Tache came into the lobby, Ella turned and faced him. Like herself and a half dozen other specialists and detectives on the Tribal force, Tache wore civilian clothes, which in the Four Corners usually meant western boots, snaps instead of buttons on a colorful print shirt, and jeans. Big silver belt buckles were also almost standard. Only the sidearm and badge he wore clipped on his belt would identify him as a police sergeant, and even those would usually be hidden from casual view by his Levi jacket.

"I got your message from the dispatcher and came right over," she said. "We still haven't found the other two perps or that brown Chevy. Are the doctors finally going to let us interview the prisoner? I tried to get him to waive his right before, but he's a tough nut to crack."

"His attorney was here when he came out of recovery ten minutes ago and they've been talking ever since. The nurses had him moved upstairs to Room Two-oh-two, so I stationed an officer outside and cuffed the prisoner to the bed. I can tell you what else we've learned about him on the way up there."

"Then let's go."

Tache's expression was somber as he walked with her to the elevator. He stared ahead, organizing his thoughts, and when he spoke, his words were measured and well thought-out. Ella had expected no less from this man who was an integral part of their generally successful crime scene investigations team. Tache had been the first officer to arrive after the bank robbery that afternoon, and had been the last one to leave the crime scene two hours later.

"The County Sheriff wants to move the prisoner to the jail in Farmington as soon as possible, but that's up to Big Ed and the Tribal attorneys. It probably won't be for twenty-four hours anyway, according to the doctor who briefed me. By the way, the fingerprint results confirm the ID you made from the mug files. He's Joey Baker, all right."

"I also caught a glimpse of the female, who wasn't wearing a mask. I believe she's Baker's wife, Barbara," Ella added. "Anything on the man with the shotgun?"

Tache nodded. "According to Baker's file, another Anglo named Jim Shepherd was convicted along with Joey Baker and Barbara about five years ago for armed robbery. They've all been living in Farmington for the past year or so since their early good-time releases from prison."

Ella nodded to the officer in the tan uniform stationed by the hospital room door, then went inside with Tache. Baker, a muscular, dirty-blond man with several tattoos, was sitting up on the bed, resting against the elevated mattress and several pillows. He was handcuffed to the bed by his right wrist. The moment he saw Ella Baker swore, his stare filled with hatred. She ignored his mad-dogging, a move typical of criminals looking for someone to blame when the law caught up to them.

Ella shifted her gaze to the other Anglo man in the room. He was wearing an expensive gray suit and standing to the right of the bed. With one raised eyebrow, she silently asked him to identify himself. From the silk tie and sharkskin boots, she guessed he was a lawyer.

"I'm Martin Miller," he said fluidly. "I'm Mr. Baker's counsel, and you must be Special Investigator Ella Clah, the ex-FBI agent and arresting officer."

Ella nodded, and Miller continued. "Tread carefully, officer. My client and I fully expect to file a civil suit against your department. Mr. Baker has been threatened, shot, and harassed, all for having the misfortune of being in the wrong place at the wrong time."

"While threatening citizens with a loaded handgun,

wearing a ski mask, and robbing a bank," Ella added, amused. "You better find an attorney who can cut a deal, Baker, or at least someone with a stronger grip on reality. I hope that's not your whole story. That defense won't work on a five-year-old."

"My client has explained to me that the actual bank robber assaulted him outside the bank, and forced him to go inside at the barrel of a shotgun." Miller added.

"Then why was your client wearing a mask? Surely the 'real robber' wouldn't have cared if Baker's face was seen. Another point, your client was the one giving all the orders, waving around a pistol loaded with fourteen rounds of live ammunition," Ella countered smoothly. "And the pistol functions perfectly, right?" She turned to Tache, who nodded in agreement.

"I was told what to say," Baker said, a smug look on his face. "And he said the pistol didn't work."

Ella watched Baker. Something about this man was making her skin crawl. She knew from his behavior in the bank that he was calm and cruel, and enjoyed baiting people. But that, in itself, was not unusual for a criminal. There was something else about him, something more elusive, that was sending signals to her brain.

"I don't have to remind you that I certainly didn't shoot myself," Baker added with a confident grin. "It was the actual criminal who did that."

"Sergeant Tache has helped me identify the other two members of your gang," Ella said meeting his gaze and holding it. "You seem to share a history of crimes with them. Want to change your story any before I continue?"

"*My* gang? I have no idea what you're talking about."

"Your wife Barbara, who fired at me several times with a handgun, was the driver of the getaway car. The man with the shotgun was James Shepherd. They're the ones who shot you, remember? If I hadn't pulled you down behind that planter, you might be in the morgue now instead of that bed."

"My wife? Barb was the one who dropped me off, if that's what you mean," Baker said, his eyes never wavering from Ella's. "And Shepherd? Well, I do know him, he shares our rental home, but he's been busy lately looking for a job, and I haven't seen him all day. It's true we've made mistakes in the past, but that's behind us now. We all served our sentences. You can't pin this on us. I was a victim of a criminal today, just like the other people at that bank."

He was sticking to his lies, hoping to find anything to contradict so he could get them on the defensive. Ella felt Baker's open challenge, and figured it was time to try and rattle that composure a bit. "Your wife and your friend are out there on the run in a disabled car, with every officer within a hundred miles looking for them. You'd be better off helping us locate them before they come up against a group of well-armed officers. We already have enough physical evidence and testimony to convict you. Don't let the next piece of news you hear be an account of your wife's death."

"That's enough." Miller held up his hand. "You're badgering my client, and he's been nothing but patient with you, despite his life-threatening injuries. This interview is finished. If the district attorney has any charges to file against Mr. Baker, then I should be told about them now so I can have adequate time to prepare his defense."

"I'm aware of the law, counselor," Ella replied, forcing her tone to remain casual. She started to say more, when she caught a glimpse of Officer Justine Goodluck standing just inside the door. Two years ago, her second cousin had been assigned to her crime team, and since that time, Ella had never had reason to regret it.

Excusing herself, Ella sent Tache to check on hospital security while she met with her assistant in the hall. Justine's handgun, holstered at her belt beside the open front of a blue satin rodeo jacket, seemed disproportionately large for the slender young woman's figure. But, despite her youthful appearance, Justine was all business.

"Any more news on the two perps still at large?" Ella asked.

"Not yet, but you know we had roadblocks up within five minutes of the call, and extra officers are out searching every mile of road in the area. Hopefully, those two shots you put in their engine block screwed up something. Even if they didn't, there's no way they'll make it out of the county, much less the state. By now, I'm sure they know it, too." Justine's voice was confident.

Ella considered the matter silently for several moments before speaking. "It's possible they may not be trying to leave the Rez anyway. I'm certain that the woman who drove the getaway car is Baker's wife. She may yet decide to try and spring her husband. Have Tache stick close around here. He's seen the photos, so he should be able to recognize Shepherd and the woman. If he spots either of them, tell him to call for backup if at all possible before taking action."

"I'll have another guard posted here, too," Justine said, "and coordinate things with Sergeant Tache."

As her cell phone beeped, Ella reached for the unit clipped to her belt. The reception was poor from her location, so she moved farther down the corridor until the static cleared.

"The dispatcher asked me to notify you," came the voice of the on-duty officer. "Sergeant Neskahi has been patrolling along the Colorado state line. A few minutes ago, he requested that Angel Hawk, the air ambulance, be sent to the site of an auto accident on a side road just south of the Colorado border, a half mile off of Highway Six-six-six."

"Understood. But what's that got to do with me? That's hospital business."

"There's something fishy about the call. Neskahi has been with the department for years. It's not like him to screw up a ten code. But he kept referring to a ten–thirty-one as a trauma victim pickup."

"Which it isn't. That's the code for a suspicious person," Ella said mostly to herself, her mind racing.

"Of course he had the flu last week, and he's still feeling lousy. . . ."

"Hold on for a moment." Ella glanced at Justine. "Tell the hospital not to dispatch the air ambulance until I give the okay," she said, then turned her attention back to the officer on the phone. "What else? Did the dispatcher pick up on any other indications of trouble?"

"No. That's why we figured you'd want to make the call on this one."

"Thanks. I'll handle it from here." Ella weighed the information carefully. Sergeant Neskahi was an old hand at police work, and had worked with her on several investigations recently. Everyone made mistakes, but it didn't seem likely that the sergeant would make one of this nature. He'd worked dozens of accidents in his time as a patrol officer.

Justine jogged back from the ER desk. "Better hurry. The pilot is really pissed off. He's ready to fly and the medic is on board. The flyboy is demanding to know if we're going to accept responsibility for a delay that could end up costing lives."

Ella frowned. She had no proof that there was a problem, but she also couldn't send a civilian into a potentially dangerous situation. "I'm on my way."

Ella took a white coat from a hook by the nurse's station. Seeing what Ella had done, a young nurse by the supply cabinet came toward her and reached for the jacket. "That isn't yours."

"I'm just borrowing it. Consider it a police emergency." Ella said and glowered at her.

The woman backed up a step, then saw the badge pinned to Ella's belt and the pistol in her holster. "Bring it back, okay?"

Ella nodded once, and slipped the jacket on over her own. "I'm going along on this ride," she told Justine. "If Neskahi is in trouble, I'll be there to back him up. If it is a mistake, and there's a victim that needs to be transported, the helicopter crew can do their job and I'll ride back with the sergeant, quizzing him on the ten codes."

They hurried up the stairs to the roof and as they opened the door and stepped out, the helicopter's rotor blades picked up speed. The downwash 'whomp' seemed to send its vibrations right through Ella. "One more thing," she yelled at Justine. "Send two units to Neskahi's location right away. If there *is* trouble, I want to have plenty of backup."

Ella kept her head down and ran over to the shiny white and turquoise air ambulance. A silver hawk with a halo was painted on the pilot's door, and below it was the name "Angel Hawk."

The moment Ella climbed into the helicopter, she leaned forward to talk to the Navajo pilot. His jaw was set, and one look told her that this wasn't a man who liked sharing authority.

"You aren't a member of my crew, and this isn't a carnival ride. What makes you think you can go up in my chopper?" he shouted over the rotor noise.

She opened the white jacket she'd borrowed, and showed

him her badge and police ID. "I'm going with you on this run. There may be more to the situation than a medical emergency."

The lanky young medic sitting on a fold-down seat in the patient treatment area placed his hand on the pilot's shoulder. "We can't afford the time to argue, boss. We have a pickup to make."

The pilot gave Ella a quick nod. "I've heard about you, Investigator Clah, so okay, you can go. Climb up front and ride with me. As soon as you have that seat belt fastened, we're going to lift off. You can fill me in on the way. If I'm heading into trouble, I want to know exactly what I'm facing."

"Deal."

Fighting the sudden lurch in her stomach as they took off, Ella gave the pilot a long, sideways glance. She'd never met the man before, but, then again, the reservation was a large place and the air ambulance was a very recent addition to the hospital. Also, these days she was hardly ever sent on traffic accident calls.

Ella glanced at the pilot's name tag. Jeremiah Crow. She searched her memory for the name, but came up empty. "You must be new to this corner of the Rez."

Crow nodded. "My clan has always lived in the Tuba City area. After the military I flew tourists over the Grand Canyon before the job opened up here." He glanced over at her quickly, then focused back on his dimmed instrument panel. "Now you know about me. It's time to keep your side of the bargain. And talk fast. We'll be there in just a few minutes."

Ella filled him in on what she knew, then added, "When we get there, stay alert until I give you a thumbs-up. Any other sign will mean that you're to lift off immediately."

"We'll be sitting ducks inside this chopper on the ground,

even in the dark. I flew scout missions in the army. I've been shot at enough to know a little strategy pays for itself. I suggest we do a fast orbit first and illuminate the area with the spotlight. It's got an adjustable beam width, so you can assess the situation before we take action. From below it'll look as if we're searching for the best place to set this bird down."

"All right," Ella agreed. "It's a good plan. But, once we're down, if there's trouble, you stay out of it. Lift off immediately."

Ella watched the stark expanse of desert below them. The moon had risen from behind the cliffs, and a blend of dark and light shadows dotted the terrain making the familiar appear more sinister than it ever would in daylight.

As they drew close to the site of the accident, red flares burning on the highway marked the location. Jeremiah Crow looked at the scene below, then veered to the right for the promised low orbit of the area. "Looks like an accident, all right."

Ella followed the beam of the chopper's searchlight. A single black sports car was tipped over on its side, but there were no skid marks on the road leading up to it. There was no sign of spilled oil or gasoline on the pavement either. "No. There are several things that aren't quite right," she said, pointing out what she'd noticed.

Neskahi's police unit was parked a little farther down the road, and the sergeant was crouched by the figure lying on the asphalt. Just a few feet away were two civilians, both wearing jackets.

Ella fought the sudden chill that enveloped her. "There's trouble here. I can feel it."

"If I aim the searchlight right into their eyes, the people down there will never see you leave the chopper."

"Go for it." Ella took her pistol from its holster, and placed it in her jacket pocket. The feel of the cold metal against her hand was reassuring.

"I'll land between the civilians and the police car, but move fast. Whatever else is happening, the person on the ground appears to need some very real help. There's a lot of blood around the body."

"Just remember to stay in the aircraft, and keep the blades turning until I signal."

Just before the hovering copter touched down, Ella jumped out. As promised, the two civilians were pinned by the spotlight, trying to shield their eyes.

Ella circled, keeping below the road bed as much as possible. The sagebrush was taller downslope, fed by runoff from the asphalt. As she got close, she could see that the figure on the road was just a stuffed dummy made out of old clothes, and the blood was probably red paint or something like tomato sauce. Ella stepped out onto the road behind the pair.

The engine noise and prop wash from the chopper was drowning out the sounds she was making, but Ella still approached cautiously, her weapon out and ready. The civilians were both looking down toward Neskahi, and at the same time trying to shield their eyes from the glare of the spotlight.

"Why in the hell doesn't he turn off that light?" The person on the left, a woman, yelled. Ella recognized the voice from earlier that day. It was Barbara Baker.

Neskahi, who'd avoided looking at the helicopter with its blinding light, turned toward the voice, and saw Ella standing less than ten feet behind the couple. He avoided any expression of recognition, but his body tensed, a signal to Ella. "Maybe it was something I said. Why don't you set down your weapons and surrender now?"

The man cursed, bringing a sawed-off shotgun out of his

jacket. Neskahi leaped up, grabbing the man's weapon and yanking it up into the air as he kneed him in the groin. The shotgun went off with a roar and the man lost his grip on the weapon.

The woman yanked a pistol out of her pocket, but before she could bring it to bear, Ella was there. She kicked the weapon out of the woman's hand, spun around, and knocked the surprised woman down with a well-aimed kick to her sternum. When the woman looked up again, she was staring into the barrel of Ella's nine-millimeter pistol.

"Don't move. Don't even breathe," Ella hissed, her glance darting over to Neskahi, who now had the shotgun aimed at the woman's partner. The man lay groaning on the pavement. "You okay, Sergeant?"

"No problems here." The sergeant retrieved his own handgun from the man's jacket pocket, then handcuffed him and hauled him to his feet.

Ella turned and gave a thumbs-up toward the helicopter.

"Get that damn searchlight off me, will you?" The man turned his head away from the helicopter, which had finally shut down its engine.

"We should have known they were up to something," the woman complained as Ella handcuffed her wrists behind her back. "Your plan really sucked, you know that?"

"You were happy to tip my car over, Barb," he said, biting off the words.

Hearing the woman's identity confirmed brought a smile to Ella's lips. She quickly informed the two of their rights. "You'll be glad to know, Mrs. Baker, that your husband is going to recover. He's decided to end his life of crime and tell us everything, too." She glanced at Shepherd. "We already know, for example, that you're the one who put the Bakers up to this job, Mr. Shepherd," she added.

"Me?" Jim Shepherd's eyes grew wide. "Wait a minute—"

"Shut up, you moron," the woman yelled. "They're playing mind games." She gave Ella a hard look. "Nice try, but you're not getting any information from us."

Ella chuckled. "I have a hard time believing that. The only real question in my mind is which of you three is going to volunteer first to testify for the D.A. in exchange for reduced charges."

"They wanted Angel Hawk so they could fly to the hospital and rescue the perp you nailed at the bank," Neskahi said as they escorted the prisoners to his patrol car. "Barb is Joey Baker's wife. He told us she'd come for him. Baker, in fact, told us a great deal. This guy is Jim Shepherd. They've all served time for armed robbery as part of a losing team."

"Joey ratted us out! That piece of—" Shepherd leaned forward in his seat, cursing.

"Shut up, you idiot. If you keep talking, you'll send us all to prison until we're too old to chew solid food."

"Lady, you're headed for a cell no matter what he says," Ella said calmly. "But a little attitude adjustment of your own might help you reduce that sentence."

After they canceled the backup that was still on the way, Ella saw Jeremiah Crow and the young medic standing near the figure on the ground. Crow glanced over at her and shook his head in disgust.

Neskahi caught the gesture. "That's how they lured me into stopping. The woman caught me completely off guard with her little act. She was crouched down low, faking CPR on the dummy, yelling her head off like it was dying. From a distance it's hard to tell that's just a bunch of old clothes stuffed with weeds."

"Where was Shepherd hiding? In the brush?"

"He was beside the car, playing dead. It wasn't the same vehicle described in the robbery, so I thought it might be legit."

"They either hijacked this car or had it hidden on a back road, planning on making a switch after the robbery. Most Navajos could never afford one of these imported models," Ella said.

"Well, Sergeant, looks like you just caught yourself two bank robbers." Jeremiah Crow smiled.

"How did you know?" the woman asked Ella from inside the car. "I was listening to the officer's call, and he never gave us away."

"Oh, yes he did. In cop-speak he told us plenty," Ella answered, letting the robbers continue to wonder.

Ella walked with Jeremiah Crow and his medic back to the helicopter. "You guys can return now. I'll drive back with the sergeant and the prisoners. Thanks for your help and cooperation. And the ride."

"No problem." Jeremiah cracked a smile. "It was . . . interesting."

Ella stood back as Angel Hawk took off and quickly disappeared into the dark. In another minute, all she could see were the blue and red running lights, and then they, too, faded away.

Neskahi was already behind the wheel when she returned to the vehicle. As her gaze drifted over the somber pair in the backseat, she felt an incredible sense of satisfaction. It was at times like these that she realized how much she loved police work. It was a rush to know that she'd helped rid society of a few predators, if only for a few years at a time.

Although the trip back took half an hour to cover the distance that had taken ten minutes in the chopper, it was a lot quieter and easier on the stomach. Five minutes from Shiprock, Neskahi's radio crackled to life.

Hearing her call sign, Ella picked up the mike and depressed the button on the side. "Go ahead, PD."

"I'm patching through a transmission from Angel Hawk. There was a ten–forty-five the chief wants you to know about directly from the source. Go Channel six for this one."

Ella felt her skin grow clammy. A 10-45 was an auto accident with injuries. "Go ahead, Angel Hawk," she said, clutching the mike so hard her fingers tingled.

"Shortly after you released Angel Hawk, we were dispatched to transport an accident victim south of Shiprock on Highway Six-six-six." Jeremiah's voice was low, but clear. "Rose Destea is at the hospital now, getting prepped for emergency surgery. She's your mother, right?"

Ella couldn't breathe. It was as if her throat had suddenly locked. She fought a momentary feeling of vertigo. "What's her condition?" she managed in a whisper thin voice.

"Critical."

"I'm on my way."

Ella glanced at Neskahi as she replaced the mike. "Drop me off at the hospital on the way in. Then take these two on to the station."

"Done." Neskahi pressed down on the accelerator, and switched on the emergency lights and siren.

Collecting all the willpower she could muster, Ella forced her body to stop shaking. Her mother . . . in a traffic accident. Critical. Her mind raced, creating one hideous scenario after another.

She struggled to push the images away and succeeded. Yet, as her thoughts became still, fear, black and encompassing as the night surrounding them, engulfed her.

TWO

✳ ✳ ✳

Ella paced in the waiting room outside the ER, unable to sit for even a minute. On the badly tuned television set a late-night talk show host told jokes to a half-dozen empty chairs. Ella wasn't listening. This hospital visit was personal, and the minutes passed slowly, each marking their own eternity.

If only someone had been able to locate her brother Clifford. Ella knew that it would have meant the world to her mother to discover that her son had done a Come-to-Life ceremony while she lay unconscious. But Clifford was out of touch, off visiting the Sacred Mountains. He'd gone to teach his son about the four peaks that guarded and bordered their world. Each was alive and individual but, together, they acted as one, defining the borders of the land given to the *Dineh* by the gods. Since each peak was at a different point of the compass, and Clifford hadn't checked in, it was impossible to send out a search party to locate him. The Rez was larger than several of the smaller states.

Ella still hoped, however, that somehow she'd be able to tell Clifford about the accident before he heard about it from someone else. It would be hard enough news for him to face coming from family. At least she didn't have to worry that her brother would fight their mother's hospitalization. Although he was a traditionalist, in every sense of the word, Clifford was also a practical man. He was one of the tribe's most sought-after *hataaliis*, or medicine men, but like more and more of the followers of the old ways he had discovered they really could co-exist with the new. The People often went to doctors for surgery and for medical treatment, but then went to the *hataaliis* for help in mending the mind and spirit. A patient who'd been through surgery would often request a Life Way to restore the harmony that would heal his body. Clifford had played a major role in supporting such choices.

Ella forced herself to sit down, wishing Carolyn was there to keep her company. Doctor Roanhorse, Ella's best friend, had purposely stayed away out of respect for Rose and Clifford. Many of the *Dineh*, The People, believed the tribe's ME was contaminated with the *chindi*, the evil in a man that stayed earthbound after death. Even though Rose was tolerant of Ella's friendship with Carolyn, it was no secret that her mother was also a traditionalist.

During unconsciousness, tradition held that a person's 'wind breath,' or soul, was temporarily lost. No one was supposed to approach the body for fear of driving that living spirit away, and this rule applied even more strongly to someone like Carolyn whose work brought her in contact with *chindis*. Although Rose was in the operating room, Carolyn had even refrained from going to the observation post the interns used, or being anywhere in the area while the surgery was taking place.

In deference to her friendship with Ella, however, Carolyn had come by with coffee and for brief visits in the waiting room twice already. It was that support that had helped Ella deal with what haunted her thoughts.

As Ella stared across the room, lost in thought, she saw

Officer Michael Cloud appear. The barrel-chested cop and his family were longtime friends of her mother.

"Any news?" he asked, reaching over and turning the sound down on the television set.

"Not yet. She's still in surgery. Do you know what happened? I haven't received any reports yet."

Michael nodded. "That's why I'm here. I thought you'd want to hear this directly from me, since I was the first officer at the scene."

Ella sat up. "Go ahead."

"Dispatch sent me after a waitress at the Totah Cafe called the station. She saw a car veer over into the wrong lane and strike another vehicle, your mother's car, head on."

Ella felt the blood draining from her face. "Was it a murder attempt then?"

He shook his head. "DWI. The other driver was Leo Bekis, a tribal attorney. The breathalyzer showed he had twice the legal limit of alcohol in his system."

Anger darkened Ella's spirit, and she began to lose control. If Bekis had been there right now, she might have shot him. "You mean that my mother's fighting for her life because of a drunk driver?"

Michael nodded once.

"Was the drunk killed?"

"Minor cuts and bruises." Michael averted his gaze. "They've been keeping him under observation, just in case. He passed out on the way in, and they aren't sure if it was just the alcohol."

Ella's rage buzzed around her like a swarm of bees, overwhelming the flash of disappointment she'd felt for a second after learning that the drunk had not died. As she looked at Michael she noticed he was staring down at his boots. He was holding something back. A second later, she knew what it was. "Bekis has been arrested before for DWI, hasn't he?"

"Twice. Seems he always manages to make bail after a few hours in the tank, and avoid a suspended license."

Ella caught sight of a man being led out of an examining room by a police officer. A bandage was on his forehead and the back of his hand, and he had a black eye. He was barely able to stand on his feet. "Is that him?"

Michael nodded. "I remanded him into the custody of another officer as soon as my backup arrived at the scene. I didn't want to see this thrown out of court for any reason."

Ella started across the hall, and Michael put a hand on her shoulder, holding her back.

"Don't, Ella," he said. "You'll only make it easier for him in court."

"Why was that piece of garbage still driving a car?" she managed through clenched teeth.

"He's a lawyer with friends who are also lawyers—and judges. The most he's ever been forced to do is pay a fine and do a few hours of community service."

Ella looked at the man who had walked over to stand beside Bekis. It was Robert Kauley, who was known for accepting cases that a maggot couldn't stomach. It seemed particularly fitting in this situation. "I'm going to have a few words with Kauley."

"Why don't you cool off first—" Michael said, then stopped as a nurse hurried over to tell Ella that her mother was coming out of surgery.

Ella hurried down the hall, arriving just as the doors to the operating room swung open and Rose was wheeled out on a gurney.

Ella hurried to her mother, and fell into step beside the nurses taking her to the recovery room. Rose had IVs in both arms, and looked battered and bruised, as if someone had beaten her half to death. Her graying black hair was tucked into a white cap, and Ella could see a bandage beneath. "I'm here, Mom, and I'll take care of everything. You just get better."

"She can't hear you now, dear," the nurse wearing green scrubs told her gently as they walked down the hall. "She'll be unconscious for a while longer, but the doctor will be out to talk to you soon."

"Will my mother be okay?" Ella whispered the words, struggling to keep her voice from breaking.

"The doctor will explain all that to you," the nurse said obliquely, then disappeared, along with Ella's mother and an orderly, through the double doors leading to the recovery room.

Ella paced back down the hall, restless and afraid, sensing that the news wouldn't be good. What the hell was the doctor waiting for? She stared at the double doors leading to the operating room, tempted to go in. As she took a step toward them, Dr. Natoni came out.

He looked grim, and even worse, cautious. Ella suspected that, in this case, it meant that there'd be no absolutes as well as no positive good news. She braced herself.

"Mind if we sit down?" Natoni said, gesturing toward the sofa. "I don't know about you, but I'm beat."

She followed him wordlessly, impatience tearing at her restraint. "Don't string me along, Doc. Get to the bottom line."

He shrugged. "Okay. Your mom will live, Ella, you don't have to worry about that. It was a miracle and the seat belt, I suppose. There doesn't appear to be any brain damage, just a mild concussion, but her legs were badly broken, and there's some major nerve and tissue damage there. She'll need a wheelchair for a while until she starts to heal. But even though we have a good prognosis, it's possible she may never be able to walk again without crutches. The worst-case scenario would be a wheelchair, but I don't see that happening."

The relief that Ella had felt upon learning that her mother would survive was suddenly replaced with the disturbing news that Rose could face life on crutches, or even a wheelchair. Her mother was finally adjusting to widowhood and beginning to discover a new life for herself. She was active socially, taking comfort in old friendships now renewed. Yet once again she would have to adapt, rebuild, and find new ways to define herself. It was all so unfair. Her mother had been through enough.

"This isn't conclusive, you understand. The extent of her recovery depends on how her physical therapy goes and how she heals. I'm betting that eventually Rose will regain full mobility. She is such an active, positive person, I can't see her giving up."

Ella heard the reassurance in Dr. Natoni's voice, but his words seemed to come from a distance. Inside, she still felt the fear and anguish her mother had experienced from the accident.

"I think her belief in the old ways will really help her now. As an MD, I'm not a traditionalist. Far from it. But I do know that mental attitude can be crucial to the recovery process. Once she's over the initial trauma, your brother might be able to do more for her than we can at this facility."

Ella glanced across the hall into the waiting room where she'd spent the past few painful hours. Leo Bekis, in handcuffs, was being led over to a row of chairs along the far wall, where some of his relatives were waiting to see him. Bekis would most likely sleep the night away in jail, then wake up with nothing more than a few muscle aches and a bad hangover. Her mother, meanwhile, might face months or years of pain and frustration trying to learn to walk again unaided.

When Leo tried to talk to his visitors, his speech was so slurred and incoherent the family quickly stopped asking him questions. Ella noticed Gladys Bekis; they'd gone to high school together, though Gladys had been a senior when Ella had been a freshman. Gladys gave her a look filled with pity, then came over.

"I know that you must be really upset now," Gladys said. "But it was an accident, and Leo is sorry. He hasn't been feeling well lately."

The statement seemed almost laughable. Ella's hands clenched into fists. "How can you make excuses for that drunk?" she muttered, and turned away. "You're almost as pathetic as he is."

"Wait. You just don't understand," Gladys said, and reached for Ella's shoulder.

Ella spun around, staring coldly right into the shorter woman's face. Gladys turned white and stepped back. Ella got right back into her face. "My mother is going to live, which is damned lucky for you and for your drunken brother. But she may be on crutches the rest of her life. I'm going to make sure your brother pays for his crimes this time. Count on it."

Out of the corner of her eye, Ella became aware of Lulu Todea and another local reporter hurrying toward them with a camera. Bekis' family must have seen them at the same time, because Leo's brother, Paul, quickly came over and led the speechless Gladys away.

Lulu came directly up to Ella, while the second reporter targeted the Bekis family.

"I understand Leo Bekis had been drinking when the accident happened," Lulu said, holding a tape recorder up in front of Ella's face. "You probably know by now that this is the third time he's been arrested for DWI. How does that make you feel?"

Ella knew she shouldn't say anything, but she couldn't hold back. "That man went to college to learn the law. He knows right from wrong in legal terms better than most of us. Still, he chose to dishonor his profession and family by getting behind the wheel drunk. Look at his condition right now, and verify the facts for yourself. I intend to do everything I can to see that he suffers as much as my mother does." Ella took a deep breath, trying to calm down. That's when she heard Gladys speaking on behalf of her brother.

"He didn't do anything wrong. Yeah, he admits to having had one beer at a friend's, but that's it. The tests are incorrect. You'll see. He took a bump on the head, and that's what's making him dizzy."

Kauley stepped forward. "The Breathalyzer tests are notoriously inaccurate. My client was taking cough medicine. That's why the alcohol level tested high."

Fury ripped through her. Ella turned to cross the hall, but, before she could reach the attorney or his client, Michael Cloud intercepted her.

Another officer led the handcuffed Bekis away, allowing him to stagger down the hallway as the reporter took photographs.

Ella smiled mirthlessly as she turned to face Lulu. "You know how a drunk man walks. I think you can see where the truth lies."

Suddenly, Leo's brother Paul shoved the photographer and, as the man stumbled, the camera flew into the air, hitting the floor with a crunch. Paul moved in on the photographer, who was scrambling for the camera, but before Paul could land a punch, Officer Cloud stepped between them. Intercepting Paul's swing, he twisted his arm and pushed him against the wall hard.

"Paul Bekis, you're under arrest for assault."

Suddenly Gladys yelled and leaped on Michael's back, trying to pry him away from her brother. Ella grabbed her away roughly, and, forcing her to the floor, handcuffed her hands behind her back. Gladys struggled for a few moments, but Ella was bigger and stronger, and the other woman finally gave up.

A camera flash went off right in front of Ella's face. Through the dots of brilliant light that hung in front of her eyes, Ella saw Lulu had pulled out her own camera.

"Get that damn thing away from me before I cite you for interfering with an arrest," she snapped.

"I'm just doing my job," Lulu answered.

"And I'd be doing mine in arresting you. Now give us some room." Ella wasn't sure where he'd come from, but Officer Jimmy Frank appeared and reached for Lulu's camera. The reporter stepped back automatically to avoid Jimmy's grasp. "Thank you for stepping back, ma'am," Jimmy said, smiling coldly.

As Ella led Gladys down the hall, she heard Jimmy talking and taking control of the crowd before things continued their downward spiral.

Outside, Gladys started pleading to be released, but her words fell on deaf ears. Ella turned the sobbing woman over to Michael after he'd placed Paul in the back seat. "I'll be in soon to make a report. This is one disturbance I can't wait to see reach the courts. But right now, I have to stay here."

"Understood."

By the time Ella returned to the waiting room, Jimmy Frank was the only one there. "Good job," she said. "We needed another officer on the scene."

"I'm glad I decided to stop by. I heard about your mother and decided to take my sixty-one here."

Ella nodded. "I appreciate the help. Go have your dinner. You've earned it."

"Glad I could help out. If there's anything else I can do, just name it."

"Thanks. Right now, all anyone can do is wait. My mother is in recovery, still asleep. At least she didn't have to see this circus."

Ella returned to the waiting area, and bought a cup of hot cocoa from the vending machine. It tasted like cardboard, and the scalding liquid burned her throat, but it was better than nothing. It was good to feel something besides anger. She managed to stay seated for only a few moments before restlessness forced her to her feet and she began to pace again.

Carolyn Roanhorse came up as Ella tossed the empty cup into the trash with a vengeance.

"If you stay here, wearing a hole in the carpet with your pacing, you're going to go crazy."

Ella looked at her friend. "I feel so helpless. I'm a cop, for cripes sakes. It's my job to keep civilians safe, but we can't even keep drunks like Leo Bekis from getting behind the wheel time after time until they destroy someone else's life. The system really sucks."

"Yeah, but not all the time, and not on everything. Don't condemn all you've dedicated your life to, based on this one incident."

"I can't get it out of my mind. Do you know that my mother may be on crutches the rest of her life? Maybe even a wheelchair."

Carolyn exhaled softly. "But at least she's alive."

"You *know* my mother. These past three years she's worked hard to make a life for herself without my father.

She'd just reached that point where things were where she wanted them to be, and now, this happens."

"Don't sell Rose short. She's got a will made of iron, that's how she survived the murder of your father. She'll have a hard road ahead, but it won't be the first time."

Ella stared down the hall at the recovery room door. "That walking six-pack will have a million excuses for his actions, but none of those will be any help at all to my mother. She'll be dealing with the results of what he did long after he's forgotten all about it." Rage made her shake again, and she stuck her hands in her pockets to control them.

Carolyn looked at her, a worried expression on her face. "Go home. Look around your house to see what might need to be changed to accommodate a wheelchair, or run five miles across the mesa. Get busy and start working off that anger, or it will eat at you like a cancer. Staying here, waiting for your mother to regain consciousness, is not a good thing for you now."

Ella nodded, realizing that Carolyn was right, yet still feeling guilty about needing to leave. All her life she'd been the type to *make* things happen. Patience was one Navajo virtue she was able to practice only when she was expecting a big payoff, like having a trap slam shut on a criminal. The kind of waiting she was doing now led nowhere, except to the hope that no more bad news would follow when her mother finally awoke. Ella just wasn't suited for this.

She sighed. "I *can't* leave and take the chance she'll wake up alone, confused and surrounded by strangers."

"Then don't go for long. Come back in an hour. You'll be in better shape to deal with things then."

Ella took a deep breath and nodded slowly. Carolyn was right. She couldn't stay here, pacing endlessly, with Leo Bekis' drunken face flashing across her mind. She glanced back at the recovery room doors. "Yeah, maybe I should leave, just for a bit. I serve no function standing around here, and there are other things I need to do."

Saying good-bye to Carolyn, Ella strode down the hall. It was late now, but she knew that if she asked, her crime scene team would make a special trip to the site of the accident. They'd make sure the department had a case that would stick.

As Ella stepped out into the cold night air, the icy blast made her shudder and gather her jacket against her. It was early March, but it might as well have been January. Ella slipped into her Jeep and turned the heater controls up to max, trying to ignore the cold air coming through the vents. It would warm up soon.

As she sped down the dark highway, memories of her days as a young girl, of her relationship with her mother, flashed unbidden to her mind. She remembered cutting her own long black hair short because boys on the bus had been pulling it. The results had been disastrous and her mother had spent hours with a pair of scissors trying to even it out so it wouldn't look so bad for school pictures coming up.

Ella was given the choice of wearing a floppy hat, or going with short hair uncovered. To this day, her mom kept the photo of Ella in that hat on the wall. Ella remembered how the hat had set a brief fashion trend for the fourth grade, with all the other girls looking for hats of their own.

Her mother had not always approved of Ella's choices, but she had respected her daughter's right to follow her own path.

Tears welled up in Ella's eyes. Her path had been to become a law enforcement officer, but when it had come down to it, she hadn't been able to keep one pathetic drunk from almost taking her mother's life.

Approaching the Totah Cafe, Ella slowed down and looked for the orange paint sprayed on the road by the investigating officers. Once she saw the marks ahead, she pulled off onto the shoulder and stopped. Flashlight in hand, she stepped out and walked over to where the collision had occurred. The wreckage had been cleared. The investigating officers had already done their work here, measuring every mark and position as they reconstructed the accident on paper. She walked around, not really expecting to find anything, but needing to look for herself.

Her throat tightened as she saw the hundreds of small cubes of glass strewn across the asphalt. There were skid marks, but from their overlapping pattern it was apparent they were made as one vehicle shoved the other back, their front wheels locked up by twisted metal. Her mother probably hadn't had time to swerve or hit the brakes before the impact.

As she continued her methodical search, she saw small pools of blood on the pavement. Ella swallowed convulsively, determined to fight the tears of anger that stung her eyes. As she walked over to where a section of plastic grill lay at the side of the highway, the beam of her flashlight fell over some curious tracks in the dirt. Hauntingly familiar marks, about the size of quarters, dotted the ground in a trail that led away from the scene.

Ella knelt down, studying the tracks, ignoring the cold shudder that was running up her spine. Each circle had a smaller concentric circle inside it, and there was an indentation in the middle, like a dot. Last year she'd encountered marks like these, almost certainly left by the rubber tip of a cane, in places where people had been hurt, or lives threatened, including her own. The person leaving those marks had never been identified.

She stood up slowly. Finding these marks here, now, raised many questions in her mind. Before she could sort out her thoughts, she heard a vehicle slowing down behind her.

Its headlights half blinded her as it pulled off the highway fifty feet away.

Ella reached down, laying her hand over the butt of her pistol as she squinted, avoiding looking directly at the vehicle. Braced for trouble, she moved off the shoulder of the road into darkness, turning off her flashlight as she waited to see who the driver was.

He stepped out of the pickup, leaving the engine running. She recognized her neighbor Kevin Tolino as he appeared in the glow of the vehicle's headlights. Kevin was a tribal attorney, like Bekis, although, admittedly, he was one of the more respected members of the community and not just because he was of the same clan as the Tribal President. His standing had come as a result of his prowess in standing up for Navajo rights in the Anglo courts, not his political connections.

"Counselor," she greeted him coldly, stepping back up onto the road. She was not in the mood to deal with any more lawyers tonight. "What brings you here?"

"I was on my way home when I noticed you by the road. Is there a criminal investigation here? I can see there's been an accident, but I didn't think you normally handled traffic calls."

"This seems to be my day for it. Does your curiosity have something to do with two tribal attorneys who are now involved in this DWI case?"

"What DWI? I've been out of town for a week. What happened?"

"My mother was badly injured right here earlier tonight in a head-on Leo Bekis caused," Ella said. "The man was so drunk he could barely walk over an hour after the wreck. Robert Kauley is representing him, and is already trying to get the man off by discrediting the Breathalyzer test."

Something flashed in Kevin's eyes, an emotion that appeared and was gone before she could identify it. "Kauley is no paragon of virtue, but it's his job to dispute the evidence if he thinks it's appropriate to do so," Kevin said quietly. "I'm really sorry to hear about your mother, though. What can I do to help?"

"Nothing. I want no help, not from any lawyer, not ever. You ought to be ashamed of your profession, with people like Bekis and Kauley representing it. Lawyers prey on society like scavengers, cockroaches, casting aside any notion of justice and morality in exchange for money. I have no respect for anyone who manipulates and evades the law for any sleazeball with enough money to buy their conscience." Ella stepped away from Kevin as if he carried the plague.

"I know you're hurting," Kevin said quietly, "so I'll forget your angry words. You know sweeping statements like that have no basis in reality."

His calm demeanor only increased her anger, but, before she could vent it, Kevin strode back to his truck.

As she watched him drive away, she heard her call sign come over the radio. Ella went to the Jeep and answered the summons. It was Tache. The bank robbers had been processed, and were now in jail. Leo Bekis was locked up too, but they expected him to make bail and be released by morning.

Not trusting her voice, she answered only with a quick 10-4.

The lonely highway, and the darkness engulfing her vehicle, suited Ella's mood as she drove out into the emptiness that greeted her. There was no disputing that her mother's vehicle had been hit by a drunk driver, and surely that was something no one could have arranged. Still, intuition told her that there was more going on than what appeared on the surface.

Her thoughts circled like wolves sniffing the breeze. She

needed to talk to her brother and find a way to squelch the anger and the fear that was slowly taking her over, filling her with a numbing coldness that had nothing to do with the weather.

Although she didn't really expect Clifford to be home, she followed the impulse to drive by his house. She wasn't sure why, but she felt drawn there. Knowing her intuition had never steered her wrong, she turned onto the dirt track that led to her brother's home.

THREE

---— ✖ ✖ ✖ ——---

Ella maneuvered carefully, knowing by heart where each and every rut and pothole lay without the help of her headlights. She'd traveled this stretch many times, and might have done just as well driving by moonlight alone.

As she approached Clifford's home, she was surprised to see the lights were on in the kitchen. More important, as the blanket that covered the entrance to the ceremonial hogan behind the house fluttered in the breeze, she caught a glimpse of her brother inside, working.

Something unexpected must have come up if he'd cut his trip short. Ella didn't wait in the car as customary to be invited in, since the circumstances were far from normal.

As she got out of the Jeep, her brother came to meet her. "I had a feeling something was wrong," Clifford said. "It was as if you were calling to me, so I came back. What's happened?"

Ella told him everything, including the evidence she'd seen at the accident scene and the cane-like impressions she'd found on the ground nearby. Like her, he knew their significance.

"We'll discuss this on the way to the hospital," Clifford

said immediately. "I have to be there. Medical science has never truly understood the importance of treating the body and mind as a whole. They'll treat her body, but the rest will be up to us."

"You can go with me. It's time I was getting back, anyway."

"There are a few things I'll need from the house, and my wife and son need to be told about the accident. I won't be long." He ran inside. When he came out moments later, her Jeep was already running.

They rode in silence for a while, but throughout the trip she could feel her brother's gaze on her.

"I can sense the anger in you," he said at last. "If you don't control it, it will blind your thoughts and destroy your ability to function."

She took her eyes off the road for a moment and glared at him. "It's better to feel this anger than the nothingness I felt a short time ago. For a while, it was like being dead inside. Do you realize how close we came to losing our second parent to lawlessness on the Rez? I'm supposed to protect people from these scumbags, not come around later and pick up the pieces."

He exhaled softly. "Pride. That has always been your Achilles' heel, little sister."

"This isn't pride. It's a fact. Our mother is lying unconscious in a hospital bed right now, her legs shattered, because some drunk weaseled his way through the system."

"You can't be all things to all people. You don't want to be just a cop, you want to be Superwoman."

"Stuff it," she growled at him. He was partially right, but she had no patience for psychoanalytical babble right now. Her love for her mother was real, and the hurt and helplessness she felt because of what had happened was worse than a knife in her heart.

"Don't you see what's happening to you?" Clifford warned, as if reading her mind. "That darkness will destroy you if you let it. Right now, you want the power to change the wrongs. It's almost a need. That's a bad road to go down. Control and channel your emotions."

"I *do* want power. I want to be in a position to really change things for the better, but I can't do anything unless I can change the system." She shook her head. "Problem is I have the wrong temperament for rulemaking and politics. Tonight, for example, I met someone who really is in a position to change things. Yet, instead of challenging him to do just that, I nearly took his head off." She told him about her meeting with Kevin.

"Bad mistake. You should remain on good terms with the best lawyer around. Someday we may need his services. He's an honest man and you know it."

"Yeah, I do," she sighed.

As they passed a new low income housing area near the highway, Clifford sat up slowly, his body tense.

Ella nodded. "Yeah, I get an uneasy feeling whenever I drive through this area, too." She looked at the half-dozen teenagers standing beneath the yellow porch light in front of one of the houses. They were dressed in extremely baggy pants, with long military-style web belts with brass tips, and dark athletic sports jackets which promoted an Arizona college team.

They held their hands in front of their chests, making a peculiar half circle with thumb and forefinger with their left hand, connected with three downward fingers from their right.

"What are they doing?"

"They know my Jeep, most of the kids do. You can look at that as a hello, or a challenge. That's their version of sign language. They're identifying their gang with a crude

MD—Many Devils. They know there's nothing I can do about that, they're not breaking curfew yet, or causing a disturbance." She paused, gathering her thoughts. "I wonder if they're the reason we both get a strange feeling around here. Gangs are becoming all too common on the Rez with kids who don't get involved in school activities, or find something useful to do."

"Something bad *is* happening here, something that could shake the entire community. They're part of the problem, but not all of it," Clifford said, his voice distant and thoughtful.

Picking up the mike, Ella asked for a patrol car to make another pass through the neighborhood after curfew.

"Our mother's accident, the cane prints, this feeling I get in certain areas around here . . . it makes me wonder about skinwalkers. Our old enemies did swear to get their revenge." Ella checked in her rearview mirror as a chill ran down her spine.

"Yes, but how would they get a drunk to do their work for them?" Clifford shook his head. "This time I don't think they're to blame. Nobody can rely on an alcoholic. Drunk driving is a problem on the Rez, one of the biggest. Our mother is simply the latest victim."

By the time they arrived at the hospital, Ella had started to feel the first signs of weariness. It had been a very long day.

They checked at the desk and, verifying that their mother was still in the recovery room, sat down in the waiting area. Ella leaned back against the well-worn vinyl seat. It crackled as she shifted, trying to find a comfortable position.

A moment later, a young Navajo nurse came out and greeted them. "Mrs. Destea is going to be wheeled out shortly. She's awake, though still very groggy. We'll place her in Room One-oh-four, just down the hall. What she needs most of all right now is rest. Please don't visit for too long."

Ella nodded. "I understand. Thank you."

Ella and Clifford walked into their mother's room as soon as the nurse gave them the okay. Rose looked terribly pale, and old well beyond her years. It was a shock seeing her this weak and vulnerable, and Ella could tell that Clifford was equally moved, though he would never mention it.

"I'll stay with Mom tonight, little sister. Go home. You're asleep on your feet."

Ella shook her head. "We'll take turns sleeping and watching over her tonight. Once she's really awake, I want her to see us both here. I can't imagine anything worse than coming out of an experience like the one she's been through and finding only strangers."

"That's one area where Navajo ways are superior to Anglo medicine," Clifford nodded. "In the old time, a patient would have a Sing done for her while she was surrounded by family and friends. This support would help her get better. Hospitals make few concessions to the human needs of the patient. Of course a Sing is out of the question here because it's the wrong kind of atmosphere, and the elaborate preparations that are required would disrupt hospital procedures. To the staff there, those are paramount." He shook his head.

Ella smiled. "Progress isn't always a road without obstructions."

Clifford glanced at his mother, concern etched on his features. "No, it sure isn't."

Ella woke up in the armchair she'd brought into her mother's room, her entire body stiff and sore. Every few hours through the night she'd been awakened by a nurse coming in to check on her mom's vital signs. Rose had slept through each session.

As she sat up, Ella looked around and noticed her brother at the window, saying his prayers to the dawn. Sometimes she wished she could have been more like him. He had confidence and a strength that came from his beliefs. Those beliefs defined him in a way she envied. Clifford fit a very real need within the tribe, one that even modern medicine couldn't touch. And, unlike a cop, he had the respect of everyone.

As Ella glanced over to her mother's bed, she saw Rose open her eyes. "You're awake," Ella announced.

Clifford turned and smiled. "How are you, Mother?"

"Tired. I'm so tired," she said. "And my body hurts all over."

As she finished speaking, a nurse came into the room. "You two children will have to leave now. I need to examine your mother."

Ella glanced at Rose. "If you want me to stay, I will."

Rose's gaze rested on her daughter. "Just come back when the nurse is through."

Ella nodded, then walked out into the hall with Clifford. "I wonder when they'll tell Mother about her legs."

"She probably suspects already. Mother is very intuitive. Besides, I doubt she can even feel them, they're so wrapped up and braced."

Ella longed for the anger that had supported her the night before. There was greater strength there than in this sense of acute weariness she now felt. "She'll need the support of both of us getting, literally, back on her feet, and maybe you more than me, Brother," she said, wishing it wasn't true, but knowing it was. "Your knowledge of our ways will give her the courage she'll need to fight her way back to health."

He shrugged. "Regardless of what we do or say, the amount of progress she makes will be up to her."

"She'll also need our help around the house," Ella answered. "We'll have to make sure the place will be safe and functional for her on crutches. Maybe even for a wheelchair at first, which might require some construction-type work."

As the nurse left the room, Ella and Clifford went back inside. Rose was sitting up slightly now, propped up by pillows and the elevated mattress of the special bed. Her eyes did little to hide her pain, an injury that went far beyond the physical. There was a touch of defeat in her expression, too, and that alarmed Ella more than anything else could have.

Trying to compose herself, determined that her mother wouldn't see that she was afraid, Ella sat down slowly and managed a smile. Clifford stood by the window, silent.

"You are pretending for my benefit, Daughter, but I can see your concern." Rose looked over at her son. "Yours, too. You both know that my legs . . . don't work. Soon the rest of me will follow."

Ella felt an icy hand grip her heart. "What are you talking about? What did the nurse say to you?"

"She talked about exercises, and using crutches. They even insist on starting me out in a wheelchair. But all that won't matter, really. My time is coming soon."

Ella looked into her mother's eyes. This was not her mother's well known intuition, something Ella shared with Rose, this was despair and defeat. "You've been through a lot, Mom, but you'll come out of this. Your legs will heal. And we have the other driver in custody. He was drunk, and it was all his fault. He'll pay. Count on it."

Rose smiled. "My daughter, always concerned about justice. But sometimes there is no justice."

"There will be in this case," Ella said adamantly.

"You look tired, Daughter. You should go home. Your brother will stay with me for a while before he has to leave."

Ella glanced at Clifford and he nodded, confirming his willingness to take the first watch. Ella looked back at her mother and smiled gently. "I'll take care of myself, Mom, if you'll do the same. And I'll see that justice is done, too, but

I will need your help. Do you remember seeing someone with a cane walking by the side of the road around the time of the accident?"

Rose's expression grew pensive and she stared at an indeterminate spot across the room. "What made you ask that? I remember seeing an old Navajo woman, a traditionalist, wearing a long velvet skirt and a blanket wrapped around her upper body to keep warm. I don't know who she was, but I was thinking of offering her a ride. It was cold outside, and she was having a difficult time walking, in spite of the cane. But she wasn't in the road, if that's what you're asking. It must have been the alcohol that made the other driver weave over into my lane."

Ella nodded. "Okay. Thanks. We found some tracks and it was a loose end I wanted to tie up." She leaned over and gave her mother a kiss. "I'm going home now to shower and change, then go in to work. Is there anything you want me to bring when I come back later today?"

Rose thought about it, then shook her head. "My herbs won't do anything to help me now. Just make sure someone feeds Two," she said.

Ella smiled. At least her mother was concerned about the dog. That was a good sign. "I bet he's already missing you, but don't worry. I'll take good care of him."

Ella stepped aside as Clifford came toward the bed, nodding good-bye. A proper Sing would take days and couldn't be done here. For now, Clifford would do a brief pollen blessing. Next time, when Rose was stronger, a longer prayer would be done. Invoking the power of the gods, Clifford would recount the exploits of the Holy People and take their mother on a symbolic journey that would renew her strength. Ella wished there was something concrete like that that she could do to help her mother heal, other than just making sure the house was ready.

Ella went home, showered, and fed the dog. Two was a scraggly mutt that vaguely resembled a rusty collie, if one were to squint and had a good imagination. The dog had a face only a mother could love, but from the day Rose had let the hungry, shivering stray into the house, the mutt had been fiercely loyal to and protective of everyone in her family.

As Ella began to fix herself a quick sandwich, she paused for a moment, aware of the stillness. The total silence inside the house jarred her nerves. She'd lived alone before, but this was the only place she'd ever called home. The quiet that echoed around her seemed out of place and frightening. The refrigerator came on all of a sudden, and she jumped.

Ella turned on the Navajo station and listened to country western ballads while she wrote up a quick report on the incident with the Bekis family at the hospital. She was finished, about to turn off the radio, when the morning news came on. The capture of the bank robbers was the lead story, but her mother's accident and the facts surrounding the drunk driver responsible followed, with nearly as much coverage. Questions were being asked about the courts that had allowed the man to retain his license.

Ella nodded in approval. Too many drunks, their condition self-inflicted, were getting off with excuses, bending the law to suit themselves. She had no sympathy for anyone who drove intoxicated, but, then again, she'd never been one to ascribe to the philosophy that people were simply victims of their environment and therefore not responsible or accountable for their actions.

Poverty and the harsh living conditions on the Rez had led to a high rate of alcoholism. She understood that, but she also believed that anyone who knew right from wrong was as responsible for the choices they made, drunk or sober, as she was for hers.

Finished with her sandwich, she chugged a small glass of milk, checked her weapon, then walked out the door. She had no desire to linger here with only frustration over her mother's accident as company.

When Ella arrived at the station, she saw a large group of reporters hovering near the main entrance, despite the relatively early hour. Most weren't from the Rez. There were too many Anglo faces mingled in that crowd, faces she recognized from TV news shows.

Apparently they were waiting for her, and knew what she looked like. It couldn't be the uniform, because she was a plainclothes officer. They rushed toward her like a swarm of bees, cameras running and microphones raised. She swallowed her disgust. They were not there to right any wrongs, but to get a story, the more sensational the better. They were doing their jobs, but their own careers were probably their first priority, not justice.

Ella shook the bitter thoughts aside. While with the FBI, senior agents had always handled communication with the press, so she had never learned Bureau-speak. But now that she was the senior officer of her own police unit, the job of spokesperson had fallen on her shoulders more than once over the past few years.

Ella knew that despite their sometimes shallow perception, the press had power. At the moment that power was the only tool she had. She gave them short and abrasive sound bites, truthful quotes she was sure they'd print. She cited the facts of Bekis' arrest record, demonstrating how he'd used the system to elude justice, while continuing to violate the law. She then described her mother's condition, wanting to reach hearts she knew had long grown cold, calloused by the litany of violence that made up the daily news nowadays.

As she spoke, she noticed Big Ed at the open window of

his office, watching and listening. She refused to look directly at him. If he disapproved of what she was doing, he'd let her know soon enough. She had this one chance, and she wouldn't back away.

As Ella entered her office, she found Justine waiting. "That was some news conference you gave out there."

"You disapprove?"

"No, I don't, but Big Ed wants to see you. He may have another take on this."

Ella nodded. "I'll go talk to him." She looked through the phone messages, searching for something important enough to make her forget her problems, at least for a while, but everything was painfully routine.

This was the first time she'd ever felt the need to escape her own life. The revelation took her by surprise. Up to now, she would have been more likely to joke that she had *no* life of her own.

As she entered Big Ed's office she saw him standing by the window, watching the newspaper and television vans driving away. "Well, at least the reporters are leaving. That's one good thing about your impromptu statement out there."

"You don't approve of what I said?"

"Oh, I agree with what you said, but I don't think you should have said it the way you did. You were too blunt about our suspect, and as an officer of this department it's not your job, or ours, to take sides. The department has an established position on DWI that's well known and publicized. It's the job of the district attorney to prosecute criminals."

"But I'm also a human being and I have a right to my opinions. My mother isn't a cop, and I'm her daughter."

He held up a hand. "I'm not going to argue this with

you. I know that your mother's been badly injured. And all of us here are very sorry about that. Rose is well-liked by everyone, and we're worried about her, just like you are. But your statements out there are going to result in the press hounding our judges and politicians. What you said *will* be distorted by somebody along the line. Eventually, that will result in calls to me, and who knows, maybe even a lawsuit from Bekis or one of his family. Lawyers do that."

"I didn't say anything that couldn't be verified as factual, and if it results in any changes to the law, making it tougher for a person arrested for DWI to retain his license or vehicle despite his expensive lawyers, wouldn't it be worth it?"

"That's not the function of this department, nor is it your job. That's why we have legislators, judges, and tribal spokespeople like myself. I'm sure I'll be called upon soon enough to restate our department's position, probably as soon as the public reads or hears the news."

"Then if I make any more statements, I'll make sure that they are not linked to me as a tribal officer, but rather to me, as an individual. I'll be off duty, and away from this facility."

"I'll accept that for now."

Hearing a knock on the door, Ella followed the chief's gaze and turned around. "I hate to interrupt," Justine said, "but we have trouble. There's been what appears to be a homicide."

For one fleeting moment, Ella hoped it was Bekis. "Where, and do we know the identity of the victim?"

She nodded. "It's Lisa Aspass. Wilson Joe apparently found the body when he went to her home to find out why she hadn't shown up for work at the college."

At the mention of the familiar names, Ella felt her body grow cold. Wilson had been engaged to marry Lisa. Sorrow filled her as she realized the blow her friend had sustained.

Yesterday her life had seemed a challenge, but manageable. The future had held a myriad of possibilities. Now her mother was gravely injured and a good friend had just lost the woman he loved. It seemed as if only an expanse of darkness lay ahead, obscuring all the light.

FOUR

✖ ✖ ✖

Ella was worried about her
mother, but still there was work to do. She turned on the siren
as she sped down the highway. Justine rode with her, searching
her notes for the directions to Lisa's home. Neither of them had
been there before. Harry Ute, the crime scene investigator and
Ralph Tache, the photographer, were in the van behind them.

"Wilson called it in?" Ella asked her assistant.

"Right," Justine said. "He asked for you, and when I told
him you were in a meeting, he told me what had happened.
He sounded like a robot, everything he said was in a mono-
tone. It was eerie. Maybe it was shock, but . . ." Justine remained quiet for a moment. "I know he's your friend, boss.
Do you think you can keep focused on this case?"

Ella glared at her assistant. "I won't make nearly as many
assumptions as you're making, I guarantee that."

Justine looked away, and stared at the notebook on her
lap as if it had become the most interesting thing on the
planet. Finally, she spoke. "You told the reporters about
wanting to see justice done and how things get thrown out
of court over details that aren't relevant to the case. I just
want to make sure we don't have that happen to us on this
investigation."

"I didn't know you'd listened so closely to my impromptu press conference."

Justine shrugged. "There were a lot of us nearby."

Ella opened and closed her hands, flexing her fingers, though still careful not to completely let go of the wheel. Justine had a point, and she shouldn't have turned on her. "It's true that Wilson Joe is a longtime friend of mine, but I also know my job. He may end up as a suspect, but it's also quite possible he has a solid alibi for the time of death. He's not the kind of person to kill except to protect someone else. But we won't cut him any slack simply because I know him. This is a murder investigation. If at any time you feel anything is being done improperly, then say so right then. I may head our team, but it *is* a team."

"Okay. We'll take it one step at a time," Justine said.

Following Justine's directions, Ella turned and headed into the relatively new residential area she'd traveled through with Clifford the evening before. Her skin was crawling as she slowed down and nodded to the three gang members sitting on the hood of a beat-up old Chevy. It was as if they had never moved. Maybe hanging out *was* their job. As before, they flashed her their gang sign. It wasn't the young gangsters that bothered her today, though. What she felt was more elusive than that, and far more dangerous.

As they drove through the neighborhood, she was surprised to see how many of the small two- or three-bedroom houses had fresh graffiti sprayed on their walls. When they pulled up to one of the dwellings, a beige mass-produced home that was one of a few untouched by the tagging, Ella saw Wilson's familiar truck parked in the driveway beside a late-model compact car. Bracing herself, she stepped out of the Jeep. A strange, intense feeling of danger assailed her. She studied the houses around her, yet she saw nothing threatening. If anything, the street looked almost deserted, like an anthill in winter.

Justine glanced at Ella. "What's wrong? You've got that look on your face."

Ella knew that her intuition was well known among the members of the department, especially Justine, whom she'd worked with closely for nearly two years now. "It's a feeling, that's all. Stay on your guard," she said, knowing no further explanation was necessary.

They approached the house slowly, hands on the butts of their pistols. A neighbor across the street appeared at a window to satisfy her curiosity. Ella reached the front door first and found it ajar. One of the keys from a large brass ring was in the lock. Looking at the other keys closely without touching any, Ella could find only one car key, and it was to Lisa's make of vehicle, not Wilson's truck. The keys apparently belonged to the victim.

Ella knocked on the front door anyway to let Wilson, who she presumed was still inside, know someone was there. She reached up high to avoid smearing any potential fingerprints and, as she knocked, the force moved the door back another three inches. Ella bent down and studied the latch and the edge of the door, now easily viewed. Though she hadn't noticed it at first glance, the door had apparently been jimmied. Fresh indentations gouged the metal and the wood around it.

"It looks like somebody used a big screwdriver or a wrecking bar to force the lock. They didn't leave much in the way of marks, though. Make sure you get good photos of this," she said, turning to Tache and Ute, who were already putting on their skintight rubber gloves. Ella and Justine did the same, taking a pair each from Ute.

Once she was ready, Ella walked into the entryway and

looked around for Wilson. "We're police officers! Where are you?"

Wilson appeared from the kitchen, his steps halting. He looked devastated. The color had drained from his face, and his shoulders were slumped.

He gestured by pursing his lips, Navajo-style. "She's . . . the body . . . is in the living room."

When Ella stepped into the living room, the first thing that struck her was the chaos, a scene typical to residential burglaries. Drawers had been pulled open and their contents tossed on the floor, potted plants had been overturned and soil was everywhere. Two lamps had been smashed. The TV stand was empty, a dust-free spot where the television had rested left a telltale mark. Based upon the rectangular dust-free spot on the shelf beneath it, the VCR that belonged there was also gone.

As she took in the rest of the room, she saw Lisa's broken body just a few feet from the couch, on the far side. Blood had soaked into the carpet beneath her, where it had dried. More specks of blood could be found on items along the floor, including papers from a drawer and a teacher's grade book, indicating that she had been killed after at least part of the room had been tossed.

Mingling with more crimson splatter marks on the closest wall was a small smear of a transparent, gooey-looking substance. Ella drew nearer and studied it. A fleck of blood on it told her the goo hit the wall first. It appeared to be either petroleum jelly or maybe hair gel. Justine would know for sure once she tested it.

It was then she registered a faint but peculiar scent still lingering in the air. It was an acrid, burned-wool type of smell that seemed strongest near the corner. She studied the carpet and found traces of burnt cloth fibers. Perhaps the killers hadn't escaped unscathed. Maybe Lisa had managed to burn one or more of her assailants. It was also possible that when the body was turned over, she would find Lisa's clothing had been set on fire.

As Ella crouched by the victim's body, she caught a glimpse of Wilson out of the corner of her eye. He was standing near the doorway, looking on, his face ashen. Wordlessly, Ella gestured to Justine to take him out of the room.

Once he was out of earshot, Ella glanced at Ute, who had begun his initial walk-through of the scene. "Next time you go to the van, call the station and have someone check with the hospital and doctors in this area and see if anyone's treated a burn patient this morning. And while you're processing the scene, see if you can find a lighter or matches, or any flammable liquid that might have been used by the victim or her assailants."

Ute nodded, wrote down a few notes, then continued his initial survey.

Ella focused on the body again. It had been a brutal killing, almost certainly carried out to eliminate the witness to the burglary. Carolyn would have to make the final determination, but it looked to Ella as if Lisa had been beaten to death with a blunt object.

As Ella stood up slowly, searching for the weapon among the scattered drawer contents and debris, one thought niggled at the back of her mind. There had been a time when violence like this would have upset her greatly. Now all that was evoked in her was an incredible drive to find answers. Her reaction worried her. She'd heard of cops who had become so jaded by the crimes they were forced to deal with, that nothing ever touched them. She didn't want to become like that.

Justine came and touched her on the shoulder. "Carolyn's on her way. Wilson says he didn't touch anything except

when he pushed the door open, then closed it partially behind him. He said it was ajar when he got here, with the
owner's key in the lock. He made the call on his cell phone."

"Thanks." Ella stood up slowly and began a methodical
search from the victim out. A small, gray metal box lay on
the sofa just to the right of Lisa's head. Traces of hair and
blood were stuck to one of its dented corners. Tache, now in
the room with his camera, began taking photos while Ute
sketched the room in his notebook. Afterwards, they would
bag and tag all the evidence.

Leaving them to continue their work, Ella went to find
Wilson. She found him sitting in the kitchen, staring at his
hands. Ella searched him wordlessly for traces of blood, but
he was clean.

"What happened here?" she asked, sitting across
from him.

"I . . . I don't know. She didn't show up for her morning
classes, or leave a message to say she was ill. We were going
to discuss her grading system over lunch, so I decided to call
and see what was going on. I got worried when she didn't
answer the phone, so I came over. Her car was in the driveway, and I noticed her sack lunch was already on the seat
cushion, like she was getting ready to leave. The door was
open and the keys were still in the lock, so I called out to her.
When she didn't answer, I came inside." He paused for a moment. "I found her right where she is now."

Ella heard Carolyn's voice and looked up. Spotting her
friend the ME as she stepped through the kitchen, Ella excused herself for a moment and followed Dr. Roanhorse into
the living room.

The middle-aged, sturdily built ME stepped carefully
around objects on the carpet and arrived beside the body. Ella
cleared her throat, then asked softly so that Wilson wasn't
likely to hear her words. "When you turn her over, let me

know if you find any burns or burn marks on her or her clothing, will you?"

"Sure. It'll be a while, though. I want to look the body over very carefully first, and make sure Tache has every angle I need covered with photos."

"I'll leave you to it, then." Ella replied, then returned to Wilson, who hadn't seemed to have moved a muscle while she was out of the room.

"I'm sorry for the interruption. Did you see anyone around, or a car or van?"

"I . . . don't know. Kids, or maybe a neighbor driving by. But nobody was standing outside that I could see."

"Did she ever forget things when she left for work, and then have to come back?"

"Occasionally. Sometimes she'd leave her grade book here, or papers or a lesson plan she wanted to work on at school. Or she'd forget her lunch. First year teachers do that." Wilson's voice got a little stronger as he spoke of everyday things.

"That would explain the grade book in the living room and the keys in the door. She could have come back for it, since you were going to be working on grades with her later on. She probably didn't notice the door had already been jimmied. If she had, she wouldn't have tried her key. Does she have any friends or students who might have come by on a weekday morning, or has anybody been bothering her lately, following her or hanging around the house?" Ella asked gently.

"Not that I know of. She got along with everybody, but didn't really socialize. Her teaching schedule pretty much takes up the week, and for a new teacher, that's a lot. Face it, who has time for anything except work anymore?" Wilson looked up at Ella and shrugged. "You know what I mean. It's the same way for all of us."

She nodded. "Unfortunately, that's very true."

Justine came into the room and signalled for Ella.

Ella asked Wilson to try and remember anything Lisa had said to him recently that might be of help, then excused herself again and went to join Justine. "What's up?"

"We found some interesting things. Come take a look."

Ella excused herself again and walked back into the living room. At the entrance to the bedroom hall, Justine pointed out what they had found. A small bronze sculpture of a rearing mustang had been dropped near a pair of cheap yellow cleaning gloves. Both items were covered with blood.

"We lifted a partial print from the glove. The killer must have touched it while taking them off."

"Good job!" Ella said.

"Well, it's something, but it's only a partial, so I'm not sure how much will be useable. We need a certain number of points before the print can be used to ID anyone."

Ella nodded.

"I also lifted one smudged print from the small metal box near the victim but, again, I'm making no promises. There is one thing that I can tell you with certainty. From the footprints near the back porch we know that there were at least two thieves in the house, and they left through the rear door. The tracks there look like they came from expensive athletic shoes. You can see the brand's logo clearly in both sets."

"Like I've seen some of the gang kids around here wearing." Ella finished the thought for her. "I wonder why they didn't break in through the back door?"

"The lock on the back door is a big deadbolt. It looks like they tried to jimmy it first, failed, and moved around to the front. That lock was easy. They barely left a mark."

"Did you check in the back yard for tracks there, too?"

"Not beyond the porch yet."

"I'll go take a look at the back door, then look around in the yard."

Ella confirmed Justine's theory about the deadbolt, then followed the tracks leading from the house out into the grounds. One set belonged to size eight shoes, the other came from a slightly larger size. The trendy footwear, with its distinctive vinyl soles and the endorsement of a millionaire sports celebrity, was popular with teens everywhere. She doubted any local stores carried the expensive shoes, and outside the Rez, where they were available, they'd be too common to trace.

Ella kept searching. The yard here wasn't fenced, and there were no trees. The desert terrain came right up to the house. Landscaping, except for mostly fruit trees, wasn't that common on the Rez, where every dollar counted. Footprints were easier to distinguish in the dirt than on grass, so that was good for her.

She discovered car tracks where the footprints ended. The direction the house faced made it unlikely that either of the victim's neighbors to the sides had seen the vehicle as it approached, unless they had been staring out of their bedroom windows.

Lisa's house stood at the corner of a series of lots, and at an angle to an arroyo a few hundred yards away. Lisa would have had a great view, and privacy, which made her house more vulnerable to burglars.

Ella studied the ground, but the car had clearly circled around to the highway, less than a half mile away. As she worked her way back toward the house, she saw another set of tracks that made her blood turn cold. They appeared to be the same cane-like marks she's been finding around scenes of violence for several months now.

Justine came up from behind her. "I saw them, too."

"They were made before the killers arrived. The imprint of one athletic shoe is over one of the circles."

"I'll talk to the neighbors," Justine said. "Maybe someone can tell me if Lisa had any elderly or disabled visitors lately. You remember seeing marks like these when we were working on another case, don't you?"

Ella nodded. "But my theory regarding those tracks doesn't fit this case. This murder probably has nothing to do with skin . . . the evil ones. It looks like kids broke in to rip off the place, then got involved in more than they'd bargained for. I saw the victim's grade book in the living room, and noticed her car was parked only halfway up the drive. She must have left for work, then discovered along the way that she'd left her grade book behind. When she came back to get it, she walked in on the burglars."

"There *have* been a rash of residential burglaries all over these new areas lately. We suspect that they are the work of one or more of the gangs, but the department hasn't been able to prove anything or get a suspect they can take to court," Justine added.

"I want you to try to find out what kind of walking stick makes an impression like this one, with the two circles and that little indentation in the middle. I don't know if we can track that, we've never had much luck classifying cane prints, but it's worth a shot."

"The person who left this trail didn't bother being cautious," Justine said. "Maybe he or she didn't know what was about to happen."

"Or maybe the person knew, but taunting us held a special appeal." Ella pursed her lips, deep in thought. "There's one person I want you to check out for me. She uses a cane. Her name is Jane Clah."

Justine's eyebrows shot up. "A relative of our late unlamented police chief?"

"Yes. She was my father-in-law's aunt. I've met her before, on police business, in that case involving the senator's daughter and her boyfriend, and I should warn you, there's something . . . disturbing . . . about her." Ella searched her mind for another word, something that would describe her unsettling meeting with Jane Clah, but came up empty.

"Is she dangerous?" Justine asked.

"You don't have to worry about her pulling a gun and shooting you, if that's what you mean. But you should still be on your guard."

"You're being uncharacteristically vague, like when you're talking about the evil ones."

Ella took a deep breath then let it out. She didn't know if Jane Clah was a skinwalker, but it was certainly possible. "After you meet her, you'll understand. But, in all fairness, it's possible that my ties to that family have affected my judgement of her."

Justine nodded once. She had just started to say something more when she saw Carolyn gesturing from the back door. "I think you're wanted inside."

Ella excused herself and went to meet the ME. "Are you through here?"

"Yeah. I figured you'd want a preliminary, though." Seeing Ella nod, she continued. "My guess is that she was struck by the metal box, and then the bronze horse. The edge of the metal box caught her in the forehead, and might have stunned her. Maybe it was even thrown. But the horse was what did all the damage. Her skull is caved in, and there's blood and hair from the victim on its heavy base. The indentions in her skull seem to fit the base, too. But I can't verify all this until I'm back at the morgue."

"Did she die as a result of the beating?"

"I can't say for sure yet, but it sure looks that way. And there are no burns or burn marks on her hands, body, or clothes. I checked specifically, and can't find the source of those burned fibers. The fabric that ignited must have come from her assailant's clothing." She glanced back at the house. "Wilson's in bad shape."

"I know, and when the shock wears off, it'll be even worse for him. That's when he'll really have to deal with what's happened. I'll see him as often as I can, but unfortunately most of the time it will be on business. My mother must have priority on my time off too. I'm sure his family will see to it that he's okay," Ella added.

"If he allows anyone to help him," Carolyn added thoughtfully. "He's never struck me as the type who'd accept help easily."

"He's not," Ella admitted. "He's as independent as I am."

When Justine came up, Carolyn excused herself. "I'm going to transport the body now. I'll get back to you as soon as I can."

"Thanks." Ella's gaze shifted to Justine. "How's it going?"

"I spoke to one of the uniforms who came by to help us secure the crime scene. He's been working on the outbreak of burglaries around here, and he asked me what I thought of the graffiti sprayed on the interior walls."

"What graffiti?" Ella asked, wondering how she could have missed that.

"Exactly. There isn't any. This incident breaks the recent burglary MO on two counts, the murder and the absence of spray-paint–defaced walls."

"The style of shoes, if I'm right, seem to indicate kids though. My guess so far is that Lisa came home unexpectedly, caught them in the act, and they panicked or she put up a fight, and they killed her. They wouldn't sign their names in paint after killing someone, I don't think. Murder gets a lot more attention than burglary."

"Then our first lead will probably come with finding out

who's been robbing the houses. I'll try to learn more about the gangs in this area. I have a cousin on the Goodluck side, Thomas Bileen, whom I'm afraid is turning toward the gang influence. He's hanging around with some bad company and is giving his parents a hard time, but at least he still says 'hi' to me. Maybe I can get something from him if I don't approach him as a cop. Not being in uniform anymore will help, too."

"The Many Devils 'own' this neighborhood. When we first drove up, I saw a few of the older ones who've probably dropped out of school, and they were wearing the right style shoes, maybe even the same brand. By now, they're long gone. Too many cops are here, and the last thing the gang kids would do is stick around for questioning. Check with your cousin, and also go through the Juvenile Crime reports and see if any members of the gang have been IDed. Get a few addresses for us. I'll bet the kids know something that will lead us to the killers—if we can squeeze it out of them."

Ute came out and joined them. "I checked everywhere, but there's no cigarette lighter in sight. Wilson says that the victim didn't smoke or keep a lighter around. The only matches I found were in a kitchen drawer."

"Any flammable substances she might have used?"

"Not that we found easily accessible. Certain cleaning compounds and items like aerosol hair spray can be turned into an effective weapon, but there were no signs of those being used here for that purpose."

Ella looked at Justine. "Take lab samples for spectral analysis. Something was burned in there besides cloth, and I need to know what and how."

Ella went inside, to Lisa's bedroom and bathroom, and studied each location. There were no signs of hair gel or hair spray or other flammable material. All she could see were a few basics, like shampoo, hand lotion, and lipsticks which were scattered over the top of the dresser. A small bottle of expensive perfume stood on the far corner of the dresser. It was slightly dusty, as if rarely used.

Ella was still searching through Lisa's things, trying to get a fix on her, when Justine came in. "I'm going to go talk to some of the neighbors. Maybe one of them saw a kid or a car or something that can help us."

Ella waved her hand over the dresser. "By the way, there's no hair gel or petroleum jelly here. If that's what the goop on the wall is, it probably belongs to one of the intruders. Let me know for sure what it is as soon as you can? That might help narrow down some suspects."

"Will do. By the way, Wilson couldn't think of anything else that might help us out, so I offered to drive him home or back to the college. But he refused. I explained that he can't stay here, but I don't think he heard a word I said."

"I'll take care of it." Ella returned to the kitchen and found her friend sitting in exactly the same position she'd left him in. "What can I do to help you?" she asked, sitting next to him.

"Catch her killer." He looked up and met Ella's gaze. "That's the only thing that means anything to me now."

"It won't bring her back," Ella said gently. "I went through many of the feelings you're experiencing now when I lost my dad. But after his killers were caught, all I felt was empty."

He shook his head as if dismissing her answer. "I want them to pay for what they did. I'm sure you can understand that."

"Yes, I do. But it won't be enough. You'll still have to handle the grief and the anger."

Wilson looked up at her, anger flashing in his eyes. "There

was a time when you and I were close, but we're different people now. Stop telling me what I should feel and what I should do."

Ella felt Wilson's anger, and understood the sorrow that fueled it. "You're still my friend," she said softly. "I care about you."

"I've barely seen you in months. We used to correspond through email, though we lived only a few miles from each other. But lately we haven't even done that. We've gone separate ways and that's fine. That's, in fact, all I want now. I need time to myself. Take your cop friends and go. I'm not interested in your pity."

"I'm not offering any," she said in a hard voice. "I know that's not what you need. But I'm still going to see you and talk to you as much as you'll allow. I want to help you make it through this if I can."

Wilson met her gaze and held it unflinchingly. "Your love in life has always been your job, but, for all your dedication, you couldn't prevent this. Don't worry about calling me on the phone. Just make sure that justice is done."

The words stung, just as he'd meant them to. They'd been friends for too long not to know each other's vulnerabilities. It took a close friend to cut one so deeply.

Ella said nothing, determined not to meet his anger with her own. Whether or not he admitted it, their friendship was something that had existed for too long to simply fade away. She would honor that.

"Listen to me closely, because you haven't understood what Justine and I have been telling you. I'm talking to you as a police officer now, not as a friend. You *can't* stay here, because this is a crime scene. Until we release the house, we can't allow anyone not working on this crime investigation to wander around in here."

"I thought you were already through. People are leaving."

"For right now, but we'll be back to check on details and confirm our findings. What we find out may lead us back to look for something we didn't think of at first. In the meantime, I can't risk letting you disturb anything that may possibly furnish us with evidence. I assume that's the last thing you want to do, too."

Wilson stood up slowly. "All right. I'll go. When you're really finished here, give me a call. It won't be pleasant, but I should go through her things, and give away what I can. Her family won't be coming, and that's not just because they are traditionalists fearing the chindi. Her mother died of complications from pneumonia about three years ago, and her father is an alcoholic. Nobody's seen him for many years."

"What about sisters and brothers?"

"She told me once that she had two sisters who lived in California, but she never spoke to them. They had some kind of fight, I think. She wouldn't talk about it, so I'm not even sure where in California they're living."

"If you find out anything more about her family, let me know."

"It's unlikely. There was no one else she knew very well. Remember that she's only been at the college for a year. Most of her free time is . . . was . . . spent with me," he corrected, his voice taut. "Neither one of us had any close friends among the staff. We preferred each other's company."

The words made Ella's chest constrict. She hadn't had that type of relationship with anyone in years. During her teens years when she'd met Eugene Clah, and in the few years they were married, relationships had been easy. But now . . . Adults carried too much mental baggage.

Wilson started walking wearily down the drive, then stopped and turned around. "I heard about your mother's accident. I hope she heals up quickly and can come home soon."

Ella nodded once. Wilson had enough problems. She wouldn't discuss her mother with him now. But his words had served to shift her thoughts to her mother again, and she glanced at her watch. She needed to get back to the hospital soon, but there was still much for her to do here.

Together with Justine, Ella canvassed houses in the area. The first two she visited, those closest to Lisa's, were a disappointment. It was obvious the people there didn't want to talk to her, but she suspected that it had very little to do with the fact that she was a cop. Although the neighborhood was made up mostly of progressives, The People's response to anyone who had been in contact with the dead was so ingrained it was almost instinctive. She had a feeling Justine was coming up against the same wall.

As she knocked on the door of the next house, a young woman, about twenty and pregnant, came to the door. This time Ella was invited inside. Surprised, Ella accepted and entered the small living room.

As she looked at the woman, she noticed her light-colored eyes. Her skin was also several shades lighter than Ella's.

"My mom was an Anglo," the woman said, as if reading her mind. "I figured nobody around here was going to talk to you, and I was right. My name's Lillian Peshlakai. I wanted to talk to you because I'm hoping if I help you, you can also help me."

"What is it that you need?" Ella asked cautiously.

"My husband Michael and I just moved here from his mother's home near Holbrook, Arizona. At first I thought it was my imagination, but now I'm sure that it isn't. I'm originally from Albuquerque. I don't believe in superstitions, but there's something really weird about this neighborhood."

"Weird how?" Ella pressed.

"Well, at night there's this gang of young punks that make a nuisance out of themselves knocking over trash cans, playing loud music, breaking mailboxes, and spray painting their names all over. Nobody here does anything to stop it. I called the cops once, but when they came by, the neighbors got really upset. When I asked them why, I was told that the situation would be taken care of before too long, and I was not to interfere."

"Who told you this, and who did they say was going to take care of it?"

"That's just it. I got no answers. Both my neighbors practically told me to mind my own business after that point. But this *is* my business. Michael and I are buying this home from the tribe. It'll go to our children after we're gone. The same applies to the other residents here. That's why I can't understand why they don't fight back. I asked Michael about this, and I think he knows what's going on, but he never explained either. He told me to trust him, and I do, but things are beginning to scare me. Michael is a framer for a construction company, so he's gone for long periods sometimes, and I'm the one who has to stay here alone."

Ella considered the matter. On the surface, the answer seemed simple. Perhaps the husband didn't want his wife singled out by the gangs for retaliation while he was away. But most of the construction workers she knew weren't known for shying away from trouble. They usually had a lot of strong friends who would back them up, too. Maybe Lillian was right. It sure sounded like something unusual was going on.

"If you'd like to file a complaint—"

"I already told you. I can't do that."

"Can you tell me who some of the gang members are?"

She shook her head. "They mostly hang around causing trouble at night, and I make it a point not to be outside then. I never get close enough for a good look."

Frustration tore at Ella. This was the kind of no-win situation where civilians cried out for police protection, while at the same time insisting that they didn't want to get involved if they were called in as a witness or asked to testify. She'd seen plenty of this attitude on the outside, but not here, until now.

"Can't your officers just drive up and down the street at night, maybe in unmarked cars? You'll catch them pretty soon, and then you'll have all the answers you want."

"I'll try to arrange for the patrols to be increased. But we don't have the officers to set up a separate gang crimes unit. We only have about one officer on the force for every thousand people on the Rez right now. In the meantime, if you remember something that might help, give me a call," she said, and handed the woman a card with her office number. "I can be reached at that number day or night."

"Okay. Thanks." She took the card from Ella and placed it beneath the phone on the side table. "Hey, what happened at the Aspass woman's house? I asked Mrs. Mahlie next door, and she told me that I'm too nosy for my own good. Can you believe that?"

"What do you think happened?" Ella countered.

"Well, I know someone's dead. I saw the body bag they wheeled out to that van. I figured she must have had an accident or had a heart attack or something."

"Were you at home earlier this morning, between eight and nine, and did you notice anyone hanging around who didn't belong here?"

Lillian shook her head. "No. That's when I normally run all my errands, just after the stores open. I was at the Stop and Shop. I get most of my stuff there since the owner lets me pay for the groceries once a month, when Michael gets paid. Was she murdered?"

Ella stood up. "We're not exactly sure yet about the circumstances that lead to her death, but the house was burglarized. I would recommend that you and everyone else around here start locking your doors, vary your schedule, and keep an eye out for each other. Things are changing on the Rez. These are wise precautions now that crime is on the increase. I think you'd be wise not to confront the gang members on your own, either."

Ella walked outside and signalled to Justine. They met next to her Jeep and exchanged progress reports.

"I haven't even been able to get the people I know talking. I went to school with Vera Bidtah, but she clammed up the minute she saw me. She wouldn't even let me step foot in her house. She warned me that people in this neighborhood looked after themselves. She said nobody here wanted our help. They're scared, plain and simple, but I don't get it. Surely the Many Devils don't have that much of a hold on them?"

"Things are getting worse here, whether the people are willing to admit it or not," Ella answered. "The situation in this neighborhood has probably been going downhill for some time. My bet is that at first the residents were determined to ignore the noise and even the spray painting, figuring it would pass. But the gang got bolder, maybe breaking into houses, and now this has happened.

"Most of the residents here don't know that there's been a murder yet, but they will soon enough, when those at work who've heard it on the radio bring the stories home. Then people will really be afraid. But I'll bet they won't come to us even then. Not because they think they can handle it, but because they know they can't. If they point fingers at gang members they know they can expect retaliation, and we can't be around twenty-four hours a day to protect them."

"Murder still doesn't fit in with the youth gangs in our area," Justine said. "When someone gets killed, it's usually when a kid from a rival gang has reacted to an earlier confrontation. Even assuming the victim caught the gang kids in her house, it's more likely that they would have just run away. She must have put up a fight and made them very angry," Justine added. "Backing a burglar into a corner can turn him into a killer."

Ella's eagle-sharp gaze took in the area. "And that's what we're looking for now, a killer. Let's go. There's not much we can do around here until somebody is willing to talk to us."

As they approached the Jeep, Ella cursed softly. The tag of the Many Devils had been hastily sprayed in bright red on the driver's side door panel.

"Big Ed's going to love that," Justine muttered as she came around to look.

"They've been around here all along, watching us from hiding," Ella said softly, looking around. "Just don't react. I won't give them that satisfaction, too. This round's theirs, but the next one's going to belong to us. Count on it."

FIVE

× × ×

Ella stopped by the station to change vehicles. After filling out all the necessary forms, in triplicate, she finally got the officer in charge of the motor pool to release an impounded Chevrolet Impala, metal-flake red. It was hers to use while the people at the motor pool tried to get the spray paint off her Jeep with solvents before it cured.

Justine eyed the flashy low-rider classic with surprise. "Wow. Somehow I didn't see this as your style."

"Are you kidding? What's not to like? Probably a billion coats of cherry red paint, white leather interior with a welded chain *chrome* steering wheel, undersized tires, and about six inches clearance from the ground. The hydraulics don't work though, somebody took all the batteries out of the trunk."

"A low rider's dream, but still . . ." Justine shook her head, reluctant to put down her boss' choice.

Ella laughed. "Relax. I can't think of anything I'd want less than a vehicle that's only good for cruising back and forth down Main Street. If we had a main street, that is."

"Then why?"

"I have a plan." Ella gestured for her assistant to get in. "Come on."

Justine got in on the passenger's side and strapped on the seat belt. The buckle was chrome, and the belt red to match the exterior. "You have that determined look. Are we going to go stir up some trouble and see what floats to the surface?"

"That's right, but first we're going to stop by my house and change clothes. We have to wear something that doesn't scream 'cops driving something from the sixties row of the impound lot.'"

"Okay. So we change clothes. Then what?"

"We're going to cruise the neighborhood around Lisa's home this evening. Let's see how long it takes for the gang to come out for a look. Hopefully, we'll get lucky and they'll give us a reason to haul them in on a charge or two. Then we can question them and see if we can squeeze anything out of one of them about the break-ins."

"Good idea, as long as we don't run into my cousin. Thomas will recognize me for sure," Justine reminded with a smile. "Either way, boys will be attracted to this car like bees to honey. How did impound get this jewel anyway? It doesn't look like anything you'd see outside Albuquerque or Española."

"It belonged to Danny Pete, who lived in Albuquerque for a few years. He told his dad to get rid of it when he went into the Air Force, and Joe Pete did. He parked it off the side of the road and left it there, hoping it would be stolen, I guess. Impound picked it up, and Joe told them to keep it. Personally, I think Fred, the shop foreman, has his eye on it. He's really into vintage cars. He said this sixty-four is a classic."

"Why anyone would want to drive a car like this anywhere is beyond me. It's so low to the ground that any bump means you scrape the road. And this color." Justine grimaced. "It looks like lipstick, extra glossy."

Ella listened to the engine's deep rumble. "It's going to take lots of gas, too, to cruise in this baby. Good thing it'll be on the department's tab."

As Ella pulled up by her house, her thoughts shifted to her mother. She felt tired, and guilty. She'd barely thought of her mom all morning. Had Rose been home, laundry would have been hung on the line by now, despite the cold wind. While things dried, her mom would have worked in the herb garden, mulching and feeding the sandy soil in preparation for spring. Would her mother be able to manage all that on crutches? Emptiness blossomed and flowered inside Ella.

"You really miss her, don't you?" Justine asked softly.

"Oh, yeah. It's so quiet at home now. The house just echoes. Nothing feels right, you know?" Ella got out and crouched down as Dog Two came to greet her. "And you miss her, too, don't you, boy?"

Almost as if in response, Two rubbed his snout against Ella's chest, then lowered his head, pressing against her. "It must be lonely for you around here now, boy. I'll tell you what. Tonight, you can sleep inside with me."

The dog's tail wagged furiously, and he led the way for them back to the house.

"Sometimes, I think he really understands everything we say." Ella let Two in the house, then invited him to go with her down the hall to her room.

"We have to try and look like we're around sixteen or seventeen," Ella said, standing by her closet. She glanced back at Justine. "A snap for you. All you have to do is put your hair up with a lot of spray, and wear a ton of makeup. But it's going to take a miracle for me." Ella pulled out two pairs of jeans, then shook her head at the rest. "Nothing else here looks young enough." She tossed one of the pairs to Justine.

"You can roll up the cuffs on my jeans so you won't trip over them, short-stuff."

"No problem," Justine said with a smile. "Too bad you don't have any dark pro team jackets. That would have fit the bill beautifully."

Ella glanced back at her. "My high school Chieftains jacket should fit you fine and it'll do, I think. But I'll still need something for me.

Justine stood beside her, studying the clothes in Ella's closet. "How about that Levi jacket? That'll work," Justine said.

Outfits selected, Ella agreed to a much-needed nap, while Justine headed back to the station, promising to come back in time to get ready for this evening's scheme.

When she returned two hours later, Ella was feeling more like herself. She'd even managed to make a quick call to her mother, who was able to talk for a few minutes before she grew tired, and Ella had to say good-bye.

Two had slept the whole time on the floor at the foot of the bed, and Ella and Justine took a few moments to scratch the mutt's belly and compliment him on his guard dog qualities. It was obvious he'd missed human company lately.

It didn't take long before Justine and Ella had fixed up their hair and makeup, and were wearing combinations that suited the roles they were playing. Neither woman could recognize themselves, however. Ella took a long look at herself in the mirror. She looked like a woman headed for a nostalgic class reunion—or a Halloween party.

Justine exhaled softly as she studied Ella. "It's not going to work. Even with your hair sprayed and teased, you look like a cop playing a hooker, not a teen."

I can't be a sixteen year old again, no matter how hard I try. Certain things are impossible." Ella considered the problem. "Here's what we'll do. You take the wheel. It'll be dark soon and that'll help us. I'll wear my brother's old baseball cap and low ride in the shadows while you go high profile." Ella opened her mother's china hutch, which was filled mainly with photos and memorabilia from her children's youth, and took out Clifford's Cleveland Indians ball cap.

"The car's going to be the big attraction," Justine answered. "That'll draw them in. I'm sure of it."

Ella gave Two a pat on the head and let him back out of the house, knowing he preferred to stay outside when no one was home. She refilled his outside water dish, and put a cup of kibbles in his bowl.

On the way to the car, Ella tossed the keys to Justine, and headed to the passenger's side. Putting the cap on backwards according to current fashion, she glanced over at her assistant. "Okay, let's get this show on the road."

They drove north on Highway 666 toward Shiprock as the last vestiges of light faded below Beautiful Mountain. Before long, they reached the dimly lit neighborhood a mile or so from the Highway 64 junction on Shiprock's southwest side. There were no street lamps, but porch lights were on, a last ditch defense against the darkness and the dangers it concealed.

They cruised back and forth on the few streets that were there, the blaring car radio tuned to an out-of-state radio station featuring rap music. Rap music was Ella's second most favorite music, everything else tied for first. Still, they had an image to project.

Staring at the houses, Ella wondered how people could live like frightened rabbits, how they could allow fear to be used against them without fighting back. Wanting to understand, she tried to argue it through logically in her mind. Accepting the role of victim meant a surrender of responsibility that led to a comfortable state of self-pity. There was a peculiar sense of balance in that, insuring both wolves and sheep a place of their own in the overall scheme of things. Yet, even seeing that logic did not help her truly understand a mind-set so unlike her own.

"I think we may have picked up a tail," Justine said. "I'm going to head back out onto the highway, and then turn west on Sixty-four. We'll have more room to maneuver if they give us any trouble."

Ella looked cautiously into the rear-view mirror, making sure her face was only out of the shadows for a moment or two. "Make it easy for them to follow us and let's see if we can draw them in. I'd like to ID at least two of them, more if possible."

After they passed the brightly lit campus of Shiprock High School, there were fewer buildings to be seen on either side of the road, until eventually there was little more than a few barren alfalfa fields among the sagebrush and gently rising hills. Off in the distance to their right, the bosque of the San Juan River appeared as a dark ribbon.

"They're going to pass to check us out," Justine said a moment later as headlights flooded the rear of the car.

"More likely they're checking out the car. You're tensing up," Ella warned. "Don't do that. Remember you're a girl out for some fun."

"Here they come." The primer-paint–laden Chevy sedan pulled up alongside, matching their speed as the youngsters checked out Justine and the car.

"I hope you realize that we're supposed to be very impressed. See how they're not making any effort to go all the way around? This is meant to show us how much guts they have." Justine waved and smiled at the boys.

"And how much guts they'll spill all over the road if there's— Look out!" Ella saw the semi coming over the hill, heading straight toward the boys in the car.

Justine made a tiny sound that could have been anything

from a cry to a muttered curse, then suddenly slammed on the brakes, allowing the boys' slowly accelerating car to cut in front of them. The smell of burning rubber filled the car.

Catching her breath, Ella forced her fingers off the dashboard. The squeal of brakes still echoed in her ears. "Those idiots!"

Justine cursed loudly. "I say we arrest them, right now. I got the tag number."

"Uh-uh. We're supposed to be impressed by that stuff, so just laugh, be awestruck, and wave at them," Ella reminded. "They've slowed down to a crawl again. Now you pass *them*, but at normal speed. The road ahead is straight and there's nothing coming. I'll scrunch down into low rider position to make sure they don't get a good look at my face, but I want to ID those guys."

"You've got it." Justine pressed on the accelerator.

As they passed, the boys honked, raised beer bottles up to where they could be seen, and made lewd suggestions.

"It's just too dark. A lit cigarette here and there inside their car isn't enough to show their faces," Ella said, "especially when they're holding bottles for us to see instead. All I know for sure is that they're members of a gang, probably the Many Devils. One of the boys tried to flash a gang sign, but then he almost dropped his bottle. I couldn't make it out."

"At least I didn't see my cousin. I was worried that they might recognize us if he was with them."

"Let's go for broke. There's a gas station ahead with lighted bays," Ella said, turning her cap around so the bill would cast a shadow on her face. "Stop there and buy cigarettes. I know you don't smoke, but they don't. When the boys pull up, do your best to keep their attention focused on you. Get them out of the car, if you can, so we can get clear IDs."

As Justine pulled into the station, she gave Ella a quick glance. "Should I warn Wilbert Jones to be careful? He owns this place."

Ella thought of the frail, white-haired Navajo man. Although many believed that his thinking was no longer focused, the reality was that he was as sharp as a tack. She'd met him once while attending a Plant Watchers' meeting with her mother. They'd spoken about many things, including police work. She still remembered his advice. "Never tell all you know. Never show all you have."

"He'll know who you are," Ella said. "Don't worry about him. If there's trouble, he'll take the right course of action."

Moments after Justine walked inside the Quick Stop, Ella watched the boys pull up. Justine timed it just right and came out of the store holding a pack of cigarettes. Two of the gang members got out and began flirting with her. While Justine played it for all it was worth, Ella tried to get a clear look at the boys who'd remained in the car.

Despite her efforts, Ella soon realized that it was useless. The glass on the car driven by the teens was tinted a smokey gray. That made looking inside nearly impossible. She reluctantly settled for listening to them, trying to get a handle on who they were. As she eavesdropped, a great feeling of sadness swept over her. They seemed so lost in a world of bluster and false bravado. They hid behind gang names and created chaos because only within that did they find identity.

For a moment she shared her brother's sorrow at what was being lost. Navajo ways were of no importance to these kids. They followed a junk culture that had no past and held no future.

Strangely enough, it was through the old myths that the gangs' behavior made the most sense. In her mind, she could almost hear her mother recounting the familiar tale. When

Black God was sprinkling the heavens, creating the constellations, Coyote came up and grabbed the star-filled pouch. He flung the stars up into the skies, scattering them at random, ignoring Black God's plan. Those stars, without pattern or order, according to Navajo beliefs, remained nameless to this day. Only the stars put there by Black God had names with which to identify them.

These boys were like those random stars, without order, without definition, endowed with a potential that would never be fulfilled. Their unfocused and misdirected search for identity had doomed them from the start. They honored no one, including themselves; they were set on a course of violence that led nowhere.

Ella leaned forward to get a clearer look at the boy in the back seat. He seemed to be trying hard to stay out of sight and avoided getting close to the windows. He was wary and cautious, sitting rigidly in the seat, though all she could see was his outline. She had a strong feeling that he was the leader.

As she shifted to one side, the boy saw her. "Cops!" he shouted, then leaned over, throwing the driver's side door open for the others and diving back into the shadows.

In a heartbeat, the boys took off, running to the car. The driver leaned out the window and hurled an empty beer bottle at the windshield in front of Ella.

Ella ducked, shielding her face. The glass shattered into a spiderweb pattern but, with the exception of a few tiny cubes, the windshield remained in place.

Justine dove behind the wheel and started the engine as the boys raced down the highway.

"Don't let them get away," Ella said, urging her cousin to speed up as they gave pursuit. "We have them on a variety of charges now. If we catch them, we can haul them in and have the next twenty-four hours to question them." Ella used the portable radio unit, and called in a description of the boys' car, along with the plate number. "The boy in the back seat recognized me. That's why he recalled his troops. He must have eyes like a hawk to have spotted me like he did. I made sure my face was never exposed."

"This car's altered suspension can't handle high speeds," Justine said, her voice rising in alarm as the car began to shake like a paint mixer.

"Don't slow down. They're not that far ahead of us. We can catch up."

"They're headed back to their own neighborhood. They probably have a hiding place or a garage to pull into there."

Ella felt her blood racing with the thrill of the chase. In the dim nighttime world, colors washed out and everything became a lackluster hue of steel blue or brown. Danger, like the intensity of any life and death situation, brought back the colors. The adrenaline rush made everything feel sharper, and sensations become more focused. She was aware of the way her heart pounded against her ribs, of the cold night air that filled her lungs with every breath.

"They're going around that curve, and they'll be out of sight behind the hill for a minute. An ambush, you think?" Justine asked.

"I doubt it. They don't want a confrontation, not with cops. That's why they're running. They're only brave when they're dealing with people they can push around."

Justine had to slow down anyway for the curve, and it was a good thing. As they rounded the bend, the headlights revealed a scattered mass of broken bottles tossed across the road just ahead. Justine touched the brakes and swerved sharply. The vehicle lifted off the ground on one side, then left the road and plowed across a field thick with tumble-weeds, bouncing like they were on a trampoline. Ella hung on for dear life as the prickly branches scratched the sides of the vehicle like fingernails across a chalkboard.

As they finally slid to a stop, Justine leaned back, and glanced over at Ella. "You okay?"

"Yeah, but I hate to concede another win to those little jerks," she said, unfastening her seat belt. "They must have thrown out a case of beer bottles. The road was like a mine field for the tires."

"These punks are starting to annoy me," Justine said. As they got out and looked over their damaged vehicle, Justine shook her head. "If Fred Duncan had any ideas of buying this puppy, he's going to be sore as hell when he sees what we've done to the paint job and the windshield. But at least it wasn't a complete waste of time. We can ID at least two gang members now if we see them again."

"I'd really hoped to get a good look at the boy in the back seat, the one who I suspected was the leader," Ella said, kicking the beer bottles out of the road so they wouldn't cause an accident. "He was too cautious. That's out of character for someone with gang affiliations. Those guys are into strutting around, maintaining a tough-guy image and staying high profile. Anything out of the norm with these guys makes me curious."

Ella returned to the car and circled it once more. Surprisingly, they hadn't ended up with a flat or major structural damage. "Okay, let's get out of here. It's time to get back to the station. Let's see if our APB on the boys' car gets us anywhere."

Ella had Justine drop her by the station, then drive to the motor pool to return the Impala. Ella also gave Justine the job of finding another car for her if the Jeep still wasn't available. While her assistant covered that, Ella filled out a report. After her public comments about Leo Bekis, everything she did now would come under scrutiny. Her statements had un-doubtedly earned her an enemy or two in high places, at least in the legal community. Big Ed needed to be kept current on everything they did.

As she filled out the forms, she mentally sifted through the evidence, organizing her thoughts and evaluating what she knew. There was no reason to believe that Lisa's murder was connected to anything other than the gang and the rash of local burglaries, but something kept nagging at her.

It was common knowledge that Lisa had not allowed Wilson to move in with her, despite the fact that they were inseparable off the job, and Lisa lived alone with no family in the area. Some had speculated that it had been Wilson's idea to wait until they were married, but Ella thought she knew him better than that.

Had Lisa been protecting her virtue and reputation, or was it possible she'd had a secret she hadn't wanted Wilson to know about until after they were man and wife? The gos-sip she'd heard through her mother suggested that Lisa wasn't the kind to worry about propriety.

She ran a hand through her hairspray-stiff, shoulder-length hair and, grabbing a rubber band from the drawer, tied it back into a pony tail. What she needed to do was find answers and stop trying to formulate theories without any-thing substantial to go on.

Hearing a knock at the door, Ella glanced up just as Big Ed walked inside her office.

"Heard you've been having some interesting and hum-bling experiences," he said, a half-smile on his face as he sat down in the only chair in the room. "Is that why you're hid-ing behind all that makeup, or are you working vice tonight?"

"The punks got away, and there's been no luck on the APB I put out. Don't rub it in, Big Ed."

"Too many of our officers haven't been taking the gang problem seriously enough. When this story gets around, maybe they'll realize that these kids aren't all dumb punks."

"They eluded us this time, but I'll track them down. Two of those young hoodlums have graduated from shoplifting and burglary to murder. That puts them squarely on my home court. I'll bring them down. You can count on it."

"Watch your back," Big Ed said, standing up again. "By the way, I need you to go testify to a state DWI task force meeting in Santa Fe tomorrow."

"My mother's in the hospital, Chief. I can't go away for any extended period of time."

"It'll be just a morning trip, that's all. You can fly. The tribe will be covering it."

"Why me? I thought you weren't too thrilled with my statements to the press before. You're the spokesman for the department. You made that clear this morning."

"It wasn't my call. The Tribal President asked that you be sent to represent the tribe because you've got a personal stake in this. He wants you to remind them about the bars just off the Rez, and how liquor finds its way in here despite laws forbidding it." He placed a ticket for a Farmington-based airline on her desk. "Be there."

An hour later, Ella was surprised and happy to discover her Jeep was ready for use again. According to Justine, the new protective finish the department had been putting on their vehicles had shielded the Jeep from uncured paint. The spray paint had buffed off easily, and the car re-sealed with the new finish.

After retrieving her keys and grabbing a quick shower at the station to shed the heavy makeup, Ella drove to the hospital to spell Clifford. Her flight would leave early tomorrow morning. She'd let her mother know her plans first, then she'd have to make arrangements for Clifford or his wife Loretta to go by and make sure Two had food and water.

Her hands clenched and unclenched on the steering wheel. It was a rotten time for her to have to leave. Work was making distracting but important demands on her just at the time when she should have been free to spend time with her mother at the hospital. Frustration gnawed at her. Her brother would have said that it was her inability to embrace the two sides of her own nature that was at the root of all her problems. The *hózhq*, all that was good and beautiful, had to be paired with the *hóchxq*, the evil and ugly, in order for balance to exist.

She wondered if he would have still been able to accept the necessity of both so readily if he'd seen the effects of that darkness through the eyes of a cop. But Clifford wasn't a cop and never would be. He lived in a world where harmony was the only way.

Reaching the hospital, Ella slowed her vehicle down and parked. She was walking down the hall to her mother's room, when Clifford met her halfway. "You haven't been here all day. Couldn't you make time to see your own mother?"

She met her brother's accusatory glare with a cold one of her own. "No, I couldn't get away, but I did call. Is that a problem?"

He exhaled softly. "I'm sorry. I didn't mean to come at you like that, but I'm exhausted. I have my own patients to attend to, but there were problems here and I couldn't leave Mom."

"What's the trouble?"

"Mom isn't herself. I can't get her to cooperate with the doctors or with me. It's as if she's lost interest in everything. She sounds like she doesn't want to live. Her leg injuries were serious, but she's not in any danger of dying. The doctor says she has a good chance of walking again if she'll work at it."

"Remind her of everything she loves, like her grandson Julian. There's nothing she wouldn't do for him."

"I've done that. But she keeps insisting that it's her turn to go on. The accident was just a sign. I don't have to tell you that many of our people have been able to will themselves into a grave. Mom's scaring me. She has to snap out of this."

"What can we do?" Ella asked.

"I'm not sure," he said, a worried frown on his face. "I would like to believe that she'll work this out on her own, like she did with Father's death, but that may not be the case this time. Part of the problem is that her accident is a direct result of the Anglo world's influence on the *Dineh*. Alcoholism is an imported illness and one of many signs that the traditions and the beliefs she holds dear are slowly fading away. She's never been hurt like this before. And now, adding insult to injury, she's being asked to depend on the white man's medicine to get well. I think all that, coupled with the loss of our father, is destroying her from the inside. She feels obsolete, and too tired to continue the fight.

"And that's why she needs both of us right now," Clifford added. "Together, we're a constant reminder that the modern world and the old ways can co-exist, that she's not simply a leftover from a past whose time has come and gone."

Ella's body ached with guilt and regret. She was slowly being torn between two very different kinds of duty. "I'll be around as much as I can, but things are really flying at me in the department now. Tomorrow, I'll be testifying on behalf of the tribe at a DWI task force in Santa Fe. And I'm right in the middle of a murder investigation that's getting more complicated by the hour. There are discrepancies that are making me a little crazy."

"I know about our friend's loss. I regret not having had a chance to go see him since it happened. I tried to call him from the hospital room, but he wasn't at home." One more thing for her to feel guilty about, Ella thought as Clifford fell silent for a few moments.

"Is there any way I can help you? I'm willing to listen if you need to sort out your thoughts. You know I'll keep whatever you tell me confidential."

"I could use a sounding board," she admitted. Ella told her brother about the circular marks she'd found at the murder scene and the scene of her mother's accident, and reminded him of the other times she'd encountered them. "Of course there's no way to prove if those impressions were left by the same person who dogged me months ago. It's enough to make me mighty squirrely though." She stared at the painting of Ship Rock on the wall, lost in thought. "There were times when the cane marks I'd find seemed to be connected to incidents involving The Brotherhood and the Fierce Ones, the Anglo and Navajo groups that are struggling over the jobs at the power plant. But at other times, those prints would turn out to be linked to the evil ones." Ella avoided referring to skinwalkers directly, a custom she shared with most Navajos.

"Either way, those cane marks, if that's what they really are, always spelled trouble for you. I can see why they make you uneasy now." Clifford mulled it over before saying anything more. "A cane is something that many of the old ones use. Although it's too broad to be a clue, there's another aspect of it you might want to look into. Some believe that the *xa'asti,* those who are extremely old, can be very strong spiritually. That's why many times they are accused of witchcraft. Sometimes the accusations are completely unjustified, but at other times they're founded on the truth."

"Are you saying what I think you're saying?"

Clifford nodded slowly. "There's a chance that our old enemies are working behind the scenes, creating as much trouble for you as they can. Destroying so many of them has made them hate us more than ever, you know."

"So it's reasonable to assume that they'll strike out at us any way they can, including through our friends and family." Ella remembered the sense of evil she'd felt at Lisa's home, then brushed the thought aside. There wasn't any evidence linking a skinwalker plot to Lisa's death. She was facing two separate issues.

"We should both keep an eye out for our professor friend," Clifford said, referring to Wilson, "though he may not welcome our help. He helped me hide, then joined us to fight the Navajo witches after our father was killed. He is their enemy as much as we are."

Ella thought of her last conversation with Wilson. Her brother was right in thinking that Wilson would not want anything from them except to be left alone. "I'll do my best, but he won't make it easy."

"He has to cope with his grief right now. Give him time to come around."

As they approached Rose's room, Clifford gestured toward three women who were walking away. "Her fellow herbalists from the Plant Watchers have been visiting Mom today. Although that should have cheered her up, I don't think it helped much."

"Let me see what I can do." The idea of being able to accomplish something Clifford hadn't been able to do, appealed to her. All through her life, Clifford had been the one everyone looked to, not her, when something important needed to be done. She'd found it extremely annoying. Yet, without that unspoken competition between them, she may never have acquired such a strong drive to succeed—the one trait she possessed that was a match for his charisma and natural talents.

As Ella entered her mother's room, her confidence vanished. Although Rose was sitting up, it was as if a light had gone out in her eyes. A chill enveloped Ella. "Hello, Mom. How are you feeling?"

"About the same."

Her voice and tone were subdued, lacking the spark of emotion. Ella looked at the small green herbal plant left on the bed stand by her mother's friends. "This is pretty."

"It makes a pleasant-tasting drink, much like Mormon Tea," Rose said absently. "How is Two? Are you taking care of him?"

Ella smiled. Finally her mother was showing some sign of interest. "Yes, but he misses you."

"He has you and, if you allow it, you'll find he can be a very loyal companion."

This wasn't going well. It was as if her mother was deeding her the dog she loved. As an idea formed in her mind, Ella realized that she still had an ace in the hole. "I may be able to find a way to sneak him into the hospital. Are you interested in trying to see him?"

Rose's eyes suddenly sparkled with mischief. "They'd throw you both out, you know."

"Undoubtedly—but only if they catch us."

Rose smiled. "I wouldn't want you to get into trouble. . . ."

Ella glanced at the wheelchair that had been set near the foot of the bed. "The one problem is that you'd have to agree to meet me somewhere other than this room. You're too close to the nurses' station here. Do you think you can wheel yourself a short distance? This hall's got too many witnesses."

Rose's expression became sad. "I can't stand to even look

at that thing. Even crutches are better than being wheeled around."

Ella nodded. "I can understand that. Once you can get around without it, they'll take it out of here. But, until then, think of it as something you're using, a tool, like a car, nothing else."

"But you only use a car when you need one. The doctors say that if I don't heal right . . ."

"Don't you worry about that. In these days of lawyers and malpractice suits, doctors wouldn't guarantee that you'd find sand in the desert. Since when did you start putting so much faith in what the doctor's say anyway? Don't tell me you're becoming a progressive!"

A shadow of a smile played on Rose's mouth. "You drive a hard bargain, but seeing you get Two into this hospital is worth learning to use that contraption. You've got a deal."

"Don't tell anyone, though, okay?"

"Not even your brother?"

"*Especially* my brother," Ella answered with a wink. "He can be very stuffy at times, you know."

Before she could say more, a nurse came into the room. "I'm afraid that Mrs. Destea needs some rest now," she said, carrying in a tray of medications. As the nurse's gaze fell on Rose, she smiled. "My, you're looking better! Your daughter must be good for you."

"At times," Rose answered.

Flashing her mother a quick smile, Ella stepped out of the room. The moment she was out in the hall, Ella's expression changed instantly. What on earth had she done? In an effort to help her mother, she'd dug an even deeper hole for both of them. Two had no training except being housebroken. Even more important, he weighed at least fifty pounds. It wasn't like sneaking in a toy poodle she could carry inside a tote bag. She'd need a body bag from Carolyn's morgue and, even then, how on earth would she explain away a wriggling body to Navajos already afraid of the dead?

Ella went back out to her vehicle, glad that her mother's condition was stable and it wasn't necessary for her or Clifford to sleep in the room with her. As her thoughts shifted to her brother, she sighed loudly. She truly wished that, for once, she hadn't allowed the rivalry between Clifford and her to affect her thinking. She'd wanted to accomplish what Clifford hadn't been able to with their mom—to get her to start thinking about living instead of dying. Only, now she was stuck with the crazy plan she'd concocted.

Ella testified at the DWI task force in Santa Fe in the morning, but it was a waste of time. When she finally walked out through the massive bronze doors of the Capitol building, she wondered if she had gotten through to anyone there at all.

She'd hoped to sway them, to touch them with her own experiences growing up on the Rez. She'd told them about bars just off the Rez, where many adults spent their entire paychecks, and of parents inside drinking while their children were waiting for them outside in a cold pickup.

She conveyed the story of her father trying to console a man who'd struck and killed a drunk father of eight who had wandered onto the highway. Later, despite her father's efforts, the driver had committed suicide, a rare thing indeed for a Navajo.

Ella showed them her high school yearbook, with each page containing at least one photo of a young man or woman who had lost a family member, or died themselves from an alcohol-related death. Then she described her own mother's accident, and the possibility of her never being able to walk again without crutches. Rose was lucky, but would the next person the driver hit, when he was inevitably back on the road again, escape death? Ella was very tempted to say more, but kept her tongue out of respect for Big Ed.

As she'd studied the lawmaker's expressions, she'd seen glimmers of understanding and other emotions mirrored there that had given her some hope. But she was also realistic. Before long, maybe even by lunchtime, they'd push her testimony out of their minds and go on to the next order of business.

They were politicians who had heard it all so often they'd become jaded. In a world that had seen too many horrors, people had a way of insulating themselves, of making sure nothing touched them too deeply. These men and women had perfected that response.

In the end, the bottom line would always be money, not the lives of victims. If the conclusions of the conference called for more enforcement officers, alcohol-treatment programs, or job training to break the cycle of poverty, it would have to be done within the existing budget. Promises were easy to make, as long as they didn't require commitment, too. A lot of the politicians in power Ella knew had been elected because of their promises to spend less, not more. Getting re-elected was probably at the top of their list of priorities now.

As she walked out to the street, she hoped one or two of the lawmakers she'd spoken to would remember her words and be moved to take action. A poor constituency, and New Mexico was one of the poorest, didn't have much leverage beyond the compassion of its representatives.

Ella's trip back to the reservation was uneventful, but being stuck in an airplane for a short flight had its advantages. Here she could relax. Nobody expected anything from her. The flight ended much too quickly, however. Before long, she was back where she'd left her vehicle parked, a secure, fenced compound inside the Farmington airfield.

Ella picked up her cell phone and called the station in Shiprock the second she was inside her Jeep. No new leads had been found in Lisa Aspass' murder, but Justine hadn't finished working the evidence. Looking through school yearbooks, she'd managed to identify the two boys they'd seen the evening before.

Justine had already gone by the driver's home and cited the youth for reckless driving, littering, and a few other charges. The license number had been from a stolen tag, but had been ditched. Finding the vehicle was unregistered, Justine had written another ticket. The boy, Rudy Keeswood, was going to court for sure, if only to answer traffic offenses. Unfortunately, the boy claimed to know nothing about the burglaries, and stuck to his story.

"I'm ten-eight as of right now," Ella said, signifying she was available and on duty. "I'll make a quick stop by the hospital, then I'll be back at the station in about forty-five minutes and we can talk about this some more."

"Ten-four."

Ella disconnected the call, then dialed the hospital and left a message for her mother's doctor to call her back. Fifteen minutes later, the physician, a family friend, returned her call.

"She's in slightly better spirits," Dr. Natoni said. "The nurse reported that she has started using the wheelchair, though moving her legs is still uncomfortable for her. We're trying to get her to start some physical therapy so she can progress to crutches right away, but she's refused to cooperate."

"Doc, since you work the ER, will you be passing on care of my mother to another physician soon?"

"If I went strictly by hospital protocol I would be, but I'd like to see this through to the finish and no one's voiced any objections. We've known each other for quite a while, so trust me, she couldn't be in better hands. I was an orthopedic surgeon before I decided to specialize in emergency medicine."

"I do trust you, Doc. I know my mother has the best care on the Rez."

Ella thought about her promise to bring Two to the hospital as she hung up. Her mother was meeting her end of the bargain, now she'd have to figure out a way to get the dog to her mom. Driving on, various scenarios played through her mind, all ending in disaster.

Five minutes away from the reservation line, Ella glanced down the highway, aware of the old building that had once been the infamous Turquoise Bar. Old time drivers in the county still slowed down instinctively as they approached the Hogback, though the once-crowded tavern had been closed for years. Public pressure had forced their doors to close. There had been just too many fights, too many accidents, and too many of The People dying of exposure after passing out drunk.

Now the booze was coming from other sources off the Rez just a little further away. The route of the drunken drivers had just lengthened a bit more, placing more motorists in jeopardy than before.

SIX

——————— ✖ ✖ ✖ ———————

As Ella pulled into the hospital parking lot, serious concerns filled her mind once again. From the moment she entered the hospital, a sense of oppressiveness filled her. Some places seemed geared to crush the human spirit and, in her opinion, hospitals were a prime example. The strong disinfectant smells, the impersonal, institutional look of every hallway, and the sameness of the staff's pastel uniforms, all seemed to conspire to dampen optimism. Knowing that her mother had to remain here for the time being just made everything seem worse.

When she entered her mother's room, no one was there. An icy hand gripped her heart and her stomach sank. Did they have to take her back into surgery?

A nurse walked around her and into the room, giving Ella a distracted smile. "She'll be back in a few minutes. She's downstairs in therapy right now.

Ella drew in a long, ragged breath, suddenly aware that she'd stopped breathing. "How is my mother doing?" she managed, surprised at how calm her voice sounded when her heart had practically stopped beating.

"She's trying, but therapy is painful for her at this point with all the bruises and strain she experienced. Movement is necessary to stretch the muscles and keep them strong, but it can cause a lot of discomfort."

Ella nodded. The thought of her mother's pain, and the pointless accident that had caused her suffering, made Ella ache as well. "And mentally, are her spirits up?"

The young Navajo woman hesitated for several long moments. "She seems better, but I suspect that's because she's set a goal for herself, getting out of that wheelchair and onto crutches. I've seen this with patients before. Becoming focused helps them, but it has a downside. Sometimes patients have unrealistic expectations, and when they fail to meet their goals right away, they become despondent."

As she finished speaking, a middle-aged Navajo nurse appeared at the door, helping to wheel Rose inside. Rose's eyes lit up as she saw her daughter.

Ella gave her mother a hug. "How are you doing, Mom?"

Rose shrugged. "Your brother explained what you were doing in Santa Fe. How did it go?"

"I don't know. It's hard for me to read politicians," she said, helping to lift her mother back into bed.

As Rose settled in, Ella saw the pain mirrored in her eyes. Her chest constricted. It was hard to see someone you loved suffering and not be able to help.

"Tell me about your work, Ella. What has been happening?"

Ella hesitated, knowing how her mother liked and respected Wilson Joe. He'd been a close friend of Clifford's for years, and a frequent visitor at their home until he'd become engaged to Lisa Aspass.

"I need something to think about, Daughter, besides myself," Rose encouraged, taking a tiny pill from the nurse's hand along with a cup of water.

Ella considered it. Perhaps getting Rose involved in news outside the hospital would be a good thing. They spoke about some of her mother's friends, the latest gossip, but then when her mother specifically asked about Wilson Joe, Ella felt a cold chill envelope her. Deciding she couldn't keep the truth from her mother, Ella recounted what she could about the murder of Wilson's fiancée.

Rose listened intently, shaking her head from time to time, but she didn't seem especially surprised by the news. "You know, I don't like to speak ill of people, but I always felt that young woman wouldn't come to a good end. There was something odd about her."

"Mom, you barely knew her," Ella scoffed.

"True, but I did talk to the girl a few times when she was with your friend. There was something insincere about her, even when she was flattering Wilson. The expression on her face never seemed to match what she was saying. I think what she wanted most was to be the one to marry him, like it was a contest or something."

Ella considered her mother's words. Rose had an unerring instinct about people but, in this particular case, Ella had a feeling her mother's assessment was colored by her perception of what Lisa had taken from Ella. Rose resented the young woman who, in her eyes, had stolen the man she'd wanted for her daughter.

Aware suddenly of the silence stretching out between them, Ella glanced back up at her mother. Rose had a faraway expression on her face. "Are you okay?"

"Yes," she said, her eyes becoming focused once more. "But I have to warn you about something. My intuitions are rarely wrong, and I feel that Death follows us all now. I'm not afraid for myself, but for you and Clifford. You've got your whole lives ahead of you."

"Mom, I've got news for you. So do you. We all need you to stop talking as if you're ready to throw in the towel."

Rose exhaled softly. "Don't you remember the stories I

used to tell you when you were a child? Death is not an enemy. The reason the Hero Twins spared him was because he was a friend. Without Death, the old people wouldn't make room for the young, and without the freshness of new ideas, there would be no renewal, just an endless repeat of the old."

"I won't listen to you talk this way. Death has a purpose, but it's not one *you* can fill yet. Your grandson looks to you to tell him the stories about our people. None of us can do it as well as you can." Hearing footsteps behind her, Ella turned around and saw Carolyn Roanhorse come into the room holding a small paper bag.

She smiled broadly at Rose. "I've brought your favorite brand of chocolates. I saw them at the mall in Farmington, and thought of you," Carolyn said, handing Rose the box from the sack.

Rose looked down at the box a bit hesitantly, murmured a thank you, then opened the container. She offered a piece to Carolyn and Ella, took one for herself, then set the box on the table beside the bed.

Her mother's lack of enthusiasm struck Ella hard. She knew that Rose had few weaknesses as potent as her love for these gourmet chocolates, and rarely closed the lid on a box with only three pieces gone. Was it because Dr. Roanhorse was the medical examiner and the candy might be contaminated with ghost sickness, or was it something else? She glanced at Carolyn, and knew that the worried look etched on the ME's features matched her own.

"I'm really tired right now," Rose said looking at the women. "Thank you for coming to see me, but would you mind if I tried to get some sleep now?"

Ella kissed her mother good-bye and then walked out into the hall with Carolyn. "I thought she might be a little anxious seeing you, having come so near death herself. But it's that depression of hers, nothing else. She worries me," Ella said.

Carolyn nodded in agreement. "I dropped in earlier, and she seemed almost cheerful for a while until we saw a patient wheeled by on a gurney. Then she got tired again. Rose desperately needs something to bring the spark back into her eyes. The chocolates didn't help much. I would have suggested that you bring her grandson here, but children can find hospitals frightening, and it would only make things worse if he started crying."

"Mom would never approve of bringing Julian here anyway, even if his parents did. But I've had another idea. The only problem I've got now is working out the logistics." She told Carolyn about the promise she'd made her mother to bring Two for a visit.

"Are you crazy? What are you going to do, put a hat on his head, a coat on his back, and teach him to walk on his hind legs?"

Ella smiled. "Not quite. But you know what? If you and I work together, we'll be able to pull it off. And we wouldn't be bringing Two into her room, just someplace nearby where she could go in her wheelchair."

"Okay, let me give this some thought. I owe your mom big time as you darned well know," she said with a tiny smile.

Ella chuckled. Carolyn would help her find a way, somehow. It wasn't in her nature to walk away from a friend . . . or a challenge.

As Ella left the hospital and drove down the highway, her thoughts slowly shifted back to the murder case. Following an impulse, Ella took a right turn, and headed toward the housing area where Lisa had lived. She'd only gone about half a mile when an old compact car raced past her. She recognized the driver, Lillian Peshlakai, almost at the same time she noticed that all the car windows had been smashed.

In a heartbeat, a pickup filled with boys flashed by. The passenger in the front seat had a baseball bat half out of the window.

Ella switched on her emergency lights and siren and called for backup as she did a quick 180 and gunned the Jeep's engine. Abruptly the pickup ahead swerved and raced down a dirt road that led to the river, suddenly no longer pursuing Lillian.

Ella followed them through the shower of sand and gravel that pelted her windshield, using the dark outline of the pickup to lead the way. Her Jeep bounced along the washerboard road between two dried-out alfalfa fields, and Ella was jolted painfully against the seat belt several times. Her one consolation was knowing that the driver of the pickup was having a much harder time maintaining control at that speed. The truck was fishtailing wildly.

The boy with the bat leaned out the passenger-side window, bringing the bat up to toss at her windshield. Ella swerved to her left and ducked just as he threw. Looking up a second later, she saw in her side mirror that the bat had missed the car completely. It was tumbling down the road behind her now.

The pickup widened the gap, exploding up a narrow canyon. When it hit a soft spot, the truck nearly overturned, the left-side wheels leaving the ground. The door on the passenger's side suddenly flew open and a boy swung out, clinging to the door for dear life.

Suddenly, the pickup slid to a stop a few feet from an area filled with jagged boulders. The boy managed to hold on and jump to safety as everyone tumbled out of the cab and raced off in different directions. Ella braked hard and slid sideways, effectively blocking the road. Grabbing the pepper spray, she took off after the boy who'd been clinging to the door. He'd thrown the bat.

The boy reached the river about fifty feet ahead of her. Pushing off the sandy bank, he leaped into the icy water, and floated quickly downstream. The water wasn't more than four feet deep, but Ella couldn't see going for a swim in the forty-degree water. She ran along the riverbank, trying to keep the boy in sight, aware that he was slowly working his way toward the other bank. As Ella crashed through a stand of willows, cursing the fact that she eventually would have to go into the water, she suddenly came face-to-face with a large wire and steel flood-control barrier blocking the bank.

Ella knew that by the time she found a way around or through the rusty maze, it would be too late. The Normandy-Beach-type obstacle had defeated her for now. Losing sight of the boy, she began walking back, using her hand-held to talk to the other officers who were approaching the scene.

When Ella returned, she was surprised to see Lillian Peshlakai waiting with two officers near the abandoned truck. The moment she saw Ella, Lillian beamed her a grateful, relieved smile.

"I came back with help as soon as I could. I can't thank you enough for what you did!"

"It's all part of my job. No thanks are necessary," Ella said. "Why were they chasing you? What happened?"

"I arrived home after buying my groceries, just like normal. Usually the gang kids aren't hanging around that early in the day, so I wasn't watching. As I stepped inside the house with a bag of groceries, I heard a noise outside. I went to the window and saw four boys taking my groceries out of the car and throwing them out into the driveway and everywhere. They were joking that the Many Devils were taking over the whole neighborhood. One got out a can of spray paint. Then one of the boys saw me standing by the window watching."

Lillian's voice broke, and Ella saw the fear and anger that contorted her features. "Take your time," Ella said gently.

Lillian took a deep breath, then continued. "The boys rushed to the door before I could lock it. The one with the spray can said that they should paint my house on the inside, too. I panicked and tried to hold the door shut, but they pushed real hard. I knew I would lose, so I jerked it open real fast and the boys pushing fell to the floor. I ran right over them, and when one tried to grab my foot I kicked him right in the face.

"I reached the car first and got my key in the ignition, but they came after me," she said, her words coming even faster now. "When I saw they had a baseball bat, I ducked. It was just in time, too. Glass went everywhere. I was so scared!

"The one with the bat kept hitting the windows. I just pressed down on the accelerator and backed out of there without ever looking up. I figured I'd go to the police station. I was sure they wouldn't follow me all the way there. But then you passed by. I was really glad to see you. I figured you'd need help though, so I pulled over the first squad car I saw, but they were already on their way to back you up. I decided to come along too then, in case you needed me to identify anyone you caught."

"Unfortunately, the boys got away, so we'll need you to give us descriptions of anyone you can remember. Will you ride back to the station with one of the officers now? They can give you a ride home, too, if that'll help."

"I'm not going back. Michael's crazy if he thinks I'm going to continue living there. These gang kids are crazy. Next time they'll have a gun."

As one of the officers led her back to the patrol unit, Ella saw Sergeant Neskahi approaching. The look on his face was chilling. "What's wrong?"

"I heard your call for backup, and got over here as soon as I could. I was on my way to talk to you anyway. I'd heard a rumor about a turf battle brewing between the North Siders and the Many Devils."

Ella expelled her breath in a hiss. As if she didn't have enough trouble to handle. Now she had to contend with a gang war. "I'll meet you back at the station, Sergeant. Our team needs to get together for a strategy meeting about this."

"Juvenile crime isn't our territory."

"Murder is, and these kids have crossed that line."

Justine was waiting in Ella's office. "Good to have you back in one piece, boss."

"I assume you've heard?"

"Oh yeah. So has everyone else at the station. Big Ed is off at Window Rock, meeting the tribal honchos, but he'll hear about this soon enough, too."

"If he hasn't already." Ella went to her desk. "Anything new since I spoke to you?"

"Just that the driver of the Many Devils car that we came across, Rudy Keeswood, doesn't have any record—or didn't have one until now. Although he's going to have to go to court over the beer bottles and the broken windshield, plus pay a lot in fines, he still wouldn't tell me who was in the car with him. We already know about the other guy, but he wasn't the one who broke the windshield, so we don't have anything on him we can prove.

"I haven't been able to talk to my cousin Thomas, the gang wannabe," Justine continued. "He's never at home, and I don't think it would be a good idea to catch him at school. He certainly wouldn't talk to me there. He has an image as a bad boy to protect. But I did pick up on a rumor. The Fierce Ones, that radical group of tribal activists that caused so much trouble at the mine, is letting it be known that they will no longer tolerate gangs on the Rez. They're saying that if we don't break up the gangs and put a stop to their activities, they'll take care of the situation themselves."

Ella groaned. "Vigilantes. Just what I needed to make a crappy day even worse." Ella rubbed her temples. Her head was throbbing. Opening a drawer and taking two aspirins from the bottle she kept there, she glanced at Justine. "Any late developments on the murder case?"

"Not much. The car the boys were driving turns out to belong to Rudy Keeswood's father. He wasn't supposed to be driving it because they didn't have any current registration on the vehicle."

"Where's the car now?" Ella asked.

"It's in impound now. I thought you might want me to check it out. Unfortunately the tire prints don't match those found behind the Aspass house, and the car was spotless inside. The kids must have vacuumed it out after our encounter with them. Everything had been washed too, so no fingerprints were located.

"Oh, and one more thing," Justine added. "Several of Lisa Aspass's students confirmed that she'd forgotten her grade book every once in a while. That, plus the other evidence at the scene, like the keys still in the door, pretty much support the theory that she'd left home and then returned to get the grade book."

"Now we need some leads to the gang's burglary teams. Let's see if we can glean something useful from the incident today. The truck the boys ditched is still out there. I want it fingerprinted and a full make run on the vehicle. It's probably stolen, that seems to be another gang specialty, but the prints might give us a lead if any of the boys have records.

And the bat they threw at me should have some prints on it. Nobody was wearing gloves that I saw."

Sergeant Neskahi entered the room with Harry Ute and Tache directly behind him.

"Good. I'm glad we're all here. It looks like our murder case is getting a lot more complicated." Ella looked at Tache and Ute. "I want you both to gather all the evidence you can from the truck the punks abandoned. We might find our killers among that crowd. Treat it like one of our crime scenes. I need a positive ID on at least one of those kids. I can identify the kid with the bat, and I'll be looking at mug files soon, but, in the meantime, I'd like some hard evidence. I need something I can take to court to get a conviction on assault, breaking and entering, and maybe even attempted murder. We need an informant, but to get one we need leverage."

"We'll work on that, boss," Justine said. "And I'll track down my cousin, one way or the other. If I can get him to loosen up, maybe he can lead us to a gang member we can work on. I just hope Thomas isn't involved in what's been happening lately. My mom said his mother has been complaining about Thomas giving her fits."

As the team disbanded, Ella went into records and began searching the mug books. There was one thing she hadn't told them. Her instincts were working overtime telling her that *major* trouble was right around the corner. They wouldn't have to look far to find it.

Ella didn't find the photo of the bat boy, but she wasn't surprised. Most of the kids hadn't been involved long enough to have criminal records, though some of the hard core youths were working on it. This was a new breed of criminal on the Rez.

Then Ella took out the most recent copies they had of the local school yearbooks. The department had always sponsored the local school annuals, and purchased a copy each year. Not only did it help present the police in a positive light, it also gave the department photos of almost all the local kids. The books had been very useful in picking up truants or missing kids, and had served as a good source of photos whenever a kid who didn't have a criminal record got into trouble .

Ella was just into the sophomore class when she located the boy who'd been with the group terrorizing Mrs. Peshlakai, and who had thrown the bat at her Jeep. It was Thomas Bileen, Justine's cousin.

SEVEN

——— ✖ ✖ ✖ ———

Ella knew she should break the news to Justine right away, so she walked immediately to the small lab where Justine spent most of her day.

Ella entered the cluttered makeshift facility, noted Justine was on the phone, and caught her attention. Justine held up her hand, asking silently for a moment to get off the phone. "Thanks, Aunt. No, we're not coming to arrest him or anything, I just want to talk. I'll try again later." Justine rolled her eyes at Ella. "Yes, I'll say hi to Mother for you when I see her. Bye now." Justine hung up.

"Were you trying to catch your cousin at home?" Ella asked.

"Yes, but he's never there. And if I call first, by the time I get over, Thomas has gone out. Did you find out something I should know? You have that look in your eye, boss."

"I think Thomas ditched school today. As a matter of fact, I know he did. He was one of those who hassled Lillian Peshlakai. He was also the one who threw the bat at me."

"Are you sure?" Justine groaned. "I'd hoped he hadn't gone that far yet."

"His photo in the last yearbook matches my memory. Either he has a twin, or he's the one. Sorry, cousin." Ella shook her head slowly.

"Well, I guess we'll have to bring him in. I hope he doesn't have a burn on him. That would kill my aunt. She's going to be pissed enough as it is. Unfortunately, I think she's going to be as angry at me as she is at him. You heard me just tell her I just wanted to talk to him. Now he's going to be arrested for sure."

"Once I see him face-to-face, and we check his prints, we'll have what we need. I wish it could have been someone else." Ella knew how much un-Navajo-like pride Justine took in being a cop, and her family had always been close.

"Would you mind making the arrest, Ella? I don't want that bit of gossip to be tossed around at family gatherings."

"Sure. Maybe this will be his first and last negative encounter with the law. At least he doesn't have a record, does he?"

"No. I just hope you're right about him and the law. Thomas can be so stubborn. Do you want me to put out a pick-up call on him now?"

"Might as well. The sooner we bring him in, the less time he'll be out there getting into more trouble."

Two hours later, after making a call to her mother at the hospital, Ella was alone in her office, writing reports. Hearing footsteps, she glanced up just as Big Ed came in.

"Chief, what are you doing back here today? I thought you were going to stay over in Window Rock."

"I figured I'd better get back here. Every time I got a report it was worse than the one before. At least you have a few gang kids identified, and serious charges you can bring against one of them. What else can you tell me?"

Ella leaned back, suddenly aware that every joint and

muscle in her body ached. "I know you want more than supposition, but all I can tell you for sure right now is that the gangs seem to be right in the middle of everything that's going on. The really bad news is that I don't think they're our only threat."

"Explain."

She told him about the Fierce Ones, then added, "But it's more than that. There's something going on in Lisa's neighborhood besides gang problems or vigilantes. There's some major trouble brewing there."

"You mean the neighborhood's going to retaliate?"

"I wouldn't rule that out."

Big Ed sat back and closed his eyes for a moment, as if assimilating everything she'd said. "Besides finding and bringing in the Bileen kid, what are you going to do next?"

Before she could answer, Justine knocked on the open door and came in. "Excuse me, but the test results on the burnt cloth we found at Lisa Aspass' house came back sometime today. The state lab hasn't been able to determine what she used to burn her attackers, if that's what she did. They'd like to examine the debris I vacuumed up from the carpet."

"Have any teens come into the hospital or local clinics today with burns?"

"No."

"All right. Let me know if you and the sergeant make any progress tracking down your cousin or the other kids we're looking for," Ella added, then Justine excused herself to get back to work.

"I don't know if you're ready for more bad news," the chief said, looking at Ella, "but I don't know any way to spare you this."

Ella sat down. Something told her she'd need a chair. "What's going on?"

"An Anglo lawyer has come around looking for Officers

Michael Cloud and Jimmy Frank. He wants to interview them about that incident at the hospital the night of your mother's accident. Gladys Bekis is threatening to press excessive force charges, and Leo plans to sue you for some defamation-of-character nonsense regarding statements you supposedly made to the press that night and the next morning."

"What? Those accusations are totally false. There are witnesses who will back us up on this."

"Apparently several of the Bekis family are ready to support their side of it." Big Ed shrugged. "I'm not questioning your words, but I figure this is the spin their lawyer might put on the events. First, you go through two violent confrontations in one day, one in which you're nearly shot. By then your nerves are on edge. Then you hear your mother is in emergency surgery after a terrible accident. Upset, you come to the hospital, and the first thing you see is the driver of the other car, who has been labeled DWI. You lose control, get violent, then have to be restrained. It was natural for you to be upset, but cops aren't supposed to go over the line."

"But that wasn't the way it went down. Bekis is trying to weasel out of his DWI situation, and he's got his sister's help. They want to paint me as the bad guy," Ella said slowly.

The phone on Ella's desk rang. She picked it up, then handed the receiver to Big Ed. "It's Nadine Kodaseet over in Legal. She said you told her to call here."

Big Ed's expression was somber as he spoke to the caller. Finally, he hung up and met Ella's gaze. "It just started. Gladys Bekis has filed charges of excessive force against you."

Ella felt her stomach clench and her hands grow clammy. Bekis was retaliating against her. A cop's career could be ruined by a lot less than what she was accused of doing. "It's all a pack of lies, Chief, and I'll be able to prove it."

"I want you to consult one of our tribal attorneys. Police brutality charges have been filed, and you'll need a legal defense." He took a deep breath then let it out again. "I hate like hell to say this, but if any other charges come up against you, I'll probably be ordered to put you on paid suspension until this is settled."

"But I'm not guilty of anything!" She stood up abruptly. "You, of all people, should know I can be trusted."

"What I believe is beside the point. I'm keeping you on active duty as long as I can, but it means I'll be coming up against pressure from Bekis's friends in tribal government. We're out on that limb together right now, Ella.

"With your mother's accident making the news, and the statements you made to the press, some people are going to find it easy to believe that you overreacted. Hell, lady, you had more action that day than a lot of cops see in their whole career." Big Ed shook his head slowly.

She felt an incredible coldness seep through her. It dulled her anger and heightened her logic. "These accusations are well thought out, and meant to manipulate the department. If we let Bekis off, I bet all the charges and the lawsuit will magically disappear. If Bekis goes down, he wants to take my career with him. Well, now they've taken their shot, and it's my turn. I'm going to fight them every step of the way."

"Be careful. Everything you say, everything you do, will be watched carefully," Big Ed said, standing. "You'll be judged by the press and by the tribe long before this case goes to court. You might consider carrying a tape recorder in your pocket. A lot of cops do nowadays."

Ella watched Big Ed walk out of her office, her mind working overtime. She fought to consider the facts with cold rationality. If she couldn't prove her innocence, innuendo would destroy her career as effectively as anything else.

Picking up the phone, Ella called her mother's room at

the hospital. Maybe she could cheer Mom up a bit. If not, maybe Mom could cheer her up.

It was shortly after nine that night. After several hours of routine and boring patrolling of Lisa's neighborhood, Ella was getting restless. They had hoped to locate Thomas Bileen, but neither she, Justine, or Sergeant Neskahi had even seen a kid outside their own front yards, much less a gang member.

Obviously the gang members knew the cops were going to be watching their houses, and were staying away. Officers had stopped by the Bileen residence several times looking for Thomas, who had skipped school, but his mother didn't know where he'd gone.

"I have what appears to be a twenty-seven–seven in progress," Justine said, calling in an auto theft. "I'm on the south side of the new Chapter House parking lot."

"That's several blocks from here. How many perps?"

"I see two kids and that's it, but its dark here. I'm moving in."

"No. Hold position until I get there. Neskahi, what's your twenty?"

"I'm headed in your direction from the east end of Rio Puerco Street. I can be there in less than a minute."

"Ten-four. I'll come in from the west end of Rio Puerco. There's a wall on the north side of the parking area. It's high enough that they won't be able to scale it easily. We'll move in from three sides and force them toward it."

"There's a few cars parked outside the Chapter House, but no civilians are outside, just the two kids. Wait, make that three." Justine called.

"Four on that third kid. Sergeant, are you in position."

"Ten-four," Neskahi replied.

Ella aimed her spotlight, and immediately Justine and Neskahi did the same, trapping three kids wearing gang-style garb in the bright glow of the intersecting beams. One was carrying a car battery that still had part of the cables attached, and another teen was looking through the interior of a pickup with a broken side window. A third boy with a pair of bolt cutters was standing next to a new pickup that had its hood raised.

"Police!" Ella announced through the external loudspeaker. "You are all under arrest. Stay where you are and keep your hands where we can see them."

The boy with the bolt cutters took off running immediately, but the other two froze like deer in headlights.

"Grab him, Sergeant," Ella yelled, noting that Neskahi was closest to the fleeing suspect. The boys with the battery looked around, thinking about escape, but by then Ella and Justine were jogging toward them. They were cut off now, and they knew it.

"Don't make this even worse," Ella shouted. "Lay down on the ground with your hands behind your head."

The boys, seeing Ella and Justine both had their weapons in hand, yelled. "We're not armed!" They put their hands high in the air.

"Lay down on the pavement, and stay there," Ella ordered, moving closer, but still alert for any other teens hiding nearby.

Ella reached the perps first, checking the boys that were down for weapons. "I've got these jokers. Give me your cuffs and go help Neskahi." Justine tossed her cuffs over to Ella, then jogged off in the direction the sergeant had taken.

Ella cuffed both boy's hands behind their back, and the only resistance they offered was in curses. After reading them their rights, she got tired quickly of their language. "Save your strength for jail, guys. If you don't have a record, you've got one now."

As Ella led the boys to her waiting vehicle, she kept one

eye out for her officers. By now, a few people were standing in the door of the Chapter House, watching from a safe distance. Finally she could see Neskahi and Justine walking toward her with the third kid in tow.

"How many do we have here now?" Neskahi asked, breathing hard from the chase.

"All three," Ella said. "Any idea if they're from the Many Devils?"

"This one is. And if he wants to make up for the disgrace he's brought on his clan, he'll start cooperating a bit." Justine grumbled. "Investigator Clah and Sergeant Neskahi, I want you to meet my in-a-hell-of-a-jam cousin, Thomas Bileen."

Ella looked at the skinny young teen in baggy black pants and a red plaid flannel shirt. He tried to look her in the eye, an act of defiance or lack of respect when directed from youth to adult among Navajos, but couldn't maintain the gaze for long.

Ella suspected Thomas Bileen wasn't nearly as tough as he thought he was. Thomas was, however, in a world of trouble.

"I'll take him in, if you don't mind." Justine looked from Ella to Sergeant Neskahi, and both nodded. "Cuz has been given his Miranda, now it's time for he and I to have a little conversation."

An hour later, Ella was working on her report, when Justine knocked on the open door.

"Did any of the teens we rounded up tonight have burn marks on them?" Ella asked.

"No." Justine sounded relieved.

"All right. Let me know if you and the sergeant can get anything more from them or their families," Ella said, hoping to keep Justine focused.

Justine's eyes were moist, as if she'd been crying.

"Are you okay?" Ella asked quickly.

"Yeah," she said, refusing to meet Ella's gaze. "I just had a very hard time with my aunt Vera. She can't believe what Thomas has been up to lately, and she wants to take her anger out on the department, especially me."

A large woman wearing traditional clothes burst through the doorway to Ella's office. "This was *your* doing!"

Ella stood up and identified herself, gently pushing Justine aside. "And you are?"

"I'm Vera Bileen. One of the children you arrested is my son. He told me how he was in the parking lot talking with some friends when you put a spotlight on him. He ran away because he was afraid you'd shoot him. I know my son. He's no criminal." Tears rolled down her face, but her expression was one of rage, not grief.

Ella tried to guide the woman to a chair, but she jerked free. "You keep away from me," she repeated. "My son didn't do anything to deserve this."

Ella wasn't about to lose her temper, though in her experience nothing she could say would change the woman's mind. It was all too common for a parent, especially a mother, to defend her child in situations like this. They would even go into complete denial when faced with the harsh reality of their son's or daughter's arrest. "We caught your son and two others breaking into vehicles outside the Chapter House. We identified ourselves as the police, and told them they were under arrest. Your son, who was holding bolt cutters just used to remove a car battery, ignored our legal order and ran away. He was pursued and apprehended."

"We recovered stolen merchandise from their possession, Aunt," Justine added. "We even have their fingerprints on the items they'd taken from the cars, and the tools they were using."

"You're lying; and you call yourself my niece? Is this

what family means to you now that you're a cop? My son, your cousin, wouldn't do anything like that."

Big Ed came into the room, apparently aware of what was going on. He easily took up the entire doorway with his barrel chest. "Mrs. Bileen, we're sorry about what happened to your son, but he brought it on himself. You know we were already looking for him for earlier offenses. Officers came by your home more than once with an arrest warrant this afternoon. He's facing additional charges of a violent nature, including assault with a baseball bat against a young woman and a police officer. His fingerprints are on the bat, and both victims can identify him. You do know he's in a dangerous youth gang, don't you?"

Ella saw the look of pure hatred flash again in the woman's eyes. "You're all working together, but I won't let you get away with this. Instead of helping our kids, your solution is to arrest them." She met Ella's gaze and held it. "But this is on your head, Ella Clah. You were the officer in charge, and it's *you* I blame for what's happened. Gladys Bekis is right about the power trip you're on. Just because you're a cop, you think you can get away with anything. Someone *should* take a baseball bat to you."

"Be careful of what you say." Big Ed's voice rumbled like thunder. "I know you're upset, but I don't take any threat against one of my officers lightly. The way you're talking makes me think that the blame for what happened to your son belongs closer to home."

"My son is just a boy, now he's in jail," Mrs. Bileen whispered, then slipped past Big Ed and fled down the hall before they could see her tears.

Justine drew in a shaky breath. "They were boys all right, but they knew what they were doing was wrong. The sad thing is, they didn't seem to care. We're the bad guys, because we stepped in to try and stop it. And what's this about

Gladys Bekis? The woman is trying to ruin Ella's reputation because her brother is a drunk. My aunt should know what's going on and not believe those lies."

"Gladys is digging her own grave on this, and we can't shut her up legally. It was all come back on her later. But the bust on the Bileen boy *was* good, and we have enough evidence to make the charges stick," Big Ed said, looking at Ella, then Justine. "But often a mother refuses to see the faults of her children. This is to be expected." He moved to the doorway.

Ella swallowed hard. "I'm used to being the center of controversy. But this is going to be tough on Justine and her family now."

Big Ed shrugged. "This is where we show what we're made of." He left the room.

"I wish I'd have seen this coming with Thomas earlier," Justine said. "As it is, I doubt my aunt will ever speak to me again."

"You'll cope, it's your aunt and Thomas that have the problem. Somewhere along the way, neither of them have learned to accept that he is responsible for his own behavior, and has to pay for the consequences of his mistakes," Ella said. Experience had taught her many lessons, and that was one of them.

The next morning, while Neskahi continued to search for the remaining teen involved in the incident with Lillian Peshlakai and Justine processed the evidence, Ella spent some of her time writing down detailed notes of the encounter with the Bekis family at the hospital, including the names, words, and actions, as she could recall them, of everyone else present.

Just then someone appeared at the door, looking hesitantly around like they weren't sure they should be there. It was Lena Clani, the leader of the Plant Watchers, and one of her mother's best friends. "Come on in, Aunt," Ella urged, "and sit down a while. It's good to see you again." Mrs. Clani was a traditionalist, more so than Rose, and Ella knew she shouldn't speak the woman's name too often, and use up its power.

The sixty-or-so-year-old woman was attired in typical reservation garb for those of her generation who would be out visiting a friend: a long cotton dress, sensible canvas shoes, and a scarf over her gray hair. She sat down carefully in Ella's extra chair, trying not to let her curiosity about Ella's office show, though her eyes wandered discreetly around the room.

"Hello, Daughter," Lena said. "I heard about your mother, and we're all very concerned. I've made up some teas that I know she will like. I came by so you could take them to her."

Ella thought about Carolyn's gift, the chocolates. It had been a good gift, a thoughtful one, but those wild herbs would please Rose more because they were a part of who and what she was.

"The Plant People are the gift the Holy People give us," Lena said. "Your brother, as a medicine man, knows about the Life Way medicines that make people well. We keep the knowledge of plants, too, and share what we know whenever we can."

"I really appreciate this. I'm worried about my mother." Ella replied.

"I knew you would be, that's why I came here as soon as I could get to town." Lena reached into her purse and brought out a plastic bag with the tea, and another container as well. "Tell her you got this from me," she said, offering Ella the herbs. "This other bag has gray knotted medicine. When the plant is soaked in water, the liquid is a fine treatment for aches and pains. Tell her that you now know this thing."

Ella thanked Lena, and the old woman stood.

"Before I go, I have something for you, to satisfy the practical side of your nature, the one who wonders if you should really take time away from police work to listen to an old woman like me," Lena said with a tiny smile.

"We're taught to be observant and patient," Lena continued. "Because most of us tend to listen instead of speak, we often find out what nobody is supposed to know. I recently heard something that you may find interesting and useful. It seems that the Fierce Ones have visited some of the parents of the children you've been looking for, those in the gangs. They have been warned to control their young, or face the consequences."

Ella's eyes widened. She knew the activists were upset about the gangs, but hadn't heard anything about this. "Are you sure?"

"Oh yes. Many of the tribe's women are hurting inside, you know," she pointed to her heart. "Children sustain us, but when they go wrong, it is the mothers who bleed the most."

With Lena's words still ringing in her ears, Ella started the drive to the hospital. Mrs. Clani had declined a ride with Ella, electing to walk to another friend's home nearby the police station.

When Ella got to the hospital, her mother was asleep. Ella sat there for a while, not wanting to disturb her. After an hour, Ella left the herbs on the side table with a note, gave her mom a kiss on the cheek, then left for home.

She needed time alone to think, and the hospital was certainly not the place to do that, not unless you were a patient.

It was nearly sundown by the time Ella pulled up by her home and parked. After greeting Two by scratching him behind the ears and under the chin, she invited him inside. She walked to the kitchen to fix herself a snack and, scarcely paying attention, she split her tortilla and cheese sandwich with the dog.

The sound of a vehicle pulling up outside brought her out of her musings. Ella unsnapped her holster and went to the window, looking out without exposing her silhouette. Even here, she couldn't afford to let her guard down, now more than ever.

Ella saw Kevin Tolino step out of his pickup and wait by the running board. The small traditional courtesy, though they were both progressives, mollified her bad mood somewhat. She went to the door, and waved for him to come inside.

"What brings you here, neighbor?" Ella asked.

"Big Ed Atcitty called me," Kevin said. "He wanted the best attorney in the tribe to represent you."

Ella fought a sinking feeling. She'd called him a cockroach not too long ago, and now she'd have to depend on this man to clear her good name. "I'm not sure if that's such a great idea after the other night."

"I *am* the best attorney around," he answered.

There was no false bravado in his tone. To him, it was a statement of fact. Ella watched him for a moment. She really owed him an apology, and this was as good a time to offer one as any she could think of. "Look, I shouldn't have said . . . Okay. What I really mean is that sometimes I talk too much and . . ." She shook her head, exasperated. "Aw, hell. I'm sorry I called you a cockroach."

Kevin smiled. "That was hard to say."

"Not as hard as admitting I was wrong."

"Apology accepted, if that's what it was. But I wasn't going to hold it against you. I know that you were hurting at the time, and you said what you did out of anger, not common sense. I detest the drunken-driver situation here on the Rez as much as you do. It's a plague that's spreading among The People, and nobody seems to be able to stop it. It's going to destroy us as a people unless we find a way to bring it under control pretty soon."

She waved him to a chair, then filled a teakettle with cold water and put it on the burner. "I've been put in a position where I have to prove my innocence or I'm going to lose everything I've dedicated my life to. A criminal is innocent until proven guilty, but when it's a cop who's accused, it's the other way around. Do you realize I could be placed on suspension at any time?"

"Let's take this one step at a time. First of all, take your time and tell me everything that happened after you got to the hospital that night."

"I'm used to giving testimony and writing reports, so I've already taken notes on everything I can recall." Ella reached into her pocket and pulled out a small notebook. "The newspaper reporters who were there should help balance out the statements given by Bekis family members. They might have some photos you can use, too."

"Okay, I'll look this over, then I want you to send me a copy of this tomorrow morning. I strongly advise you not to approach any of the Bekis family, not physically, not on the phone, and not in writing, for any reason. They could very easily make up another story. If they approach *you*, tell them to talk to me, then don't say another word. Needless to say, don't touch them physically either."

"I won't go near any of them," she agreed. But if there was something else she could do to bring out the truth, she'd do that. Kevin didn't need to hear that now, though.

Kevin remained for dinner, and went through her notes again and again, questioning and asking for clarification on every aspect of her confrontation at the hospital. He was harder on her than any opposition attorney would have been, but she couldn't fault him for doing his job.

By the time he left, it was close to eleven, and Ella was exhausted. She looked at the phone, wishing she'd at least called the doctor to get his latest take on her mother's condition. Right now, the switchboard would be closed, and her mother would be asleep, hopefully. She'd stop by tomorrow morning early, she promised herself.

"Come on, Two. You can sleep in bed with me tonight. It's cold out there, and I need a friend." Sleep never came easily unless she was exhausted. In the back of her mind there was always that fear of what her dreams might become, tonight especially.

During her waking hours she didn't have to think about the hatred and wasted dreams of Navajo children who had fallen victim to the influence or violence of a gang, and of mothers who had seen the destruction of their children's innocence. The thought that she or another cop might be faced with the choice of killing one kid to save another wasn't something she dwelled upon. The responsibilities of the moment were enough to handle.

But at night, the decisions she might have to make as a cop tormented her. Serving justice had little to do with the nightmares of a cop.

Two's choices were much simpler than hers. The dog followed Ella through the house, his toenails clicking against the hardwood floor.

Ella undressed and crawled into bed, glad to have the mutt lying beside her feet. His comforting weight even kept her toes warm.

She wasn't sure how much time had passed when a low sound crept through the haze of bloody images her dream had become. The persistent rumbling reached her, nudging her senses. Ella stirred, and came fully awake as the sound intensified. As she pushed the nightmare away and opened her eyes, she realized that Two was growling. The menacing response from the normally quite gentle dog surprised Ella.

She sat up and listened, hearing the sound of a car engine. Whatever it was had to be right out in the yard. Two's ears were pricked forward and his lips curled away from his teeth in a snarl. It was a lethal warning if she'd ever heard one.

Grabbing her pistol, Ella eased over to the window and peeked outside, listening. Suddenly the glass exploded and a hail of gunfire sent her diving to the floor.

EIGHT

—— ✖ ✖ ✖ ——

Ella lay with her stomach pressed to the floor as the wall shook, ripped apart by a rain of bullets. Stucco and glass rained down on her as she pushed Two beneath the bed.

Her heart was racing, adrenalin making her senses painfully sharp. She didn't know how many gunmen were outside, but there were enough to make it impossible for her to avoid the barrage that was systematically destroying her bedroom. The blinds twanged as bullets passed through them, slamming against the opposite wall. More glass fragments rained onto the windowsill, then fell onto the floor, making it difficult to move without cutting her skin to ribbons.

Then the shelf holding her shooting trophies lost a bracket, and the contents fell to the floor with a crash.

As abruptly as the shooting had begun, it stopped and she heard two or more vehicles bouncing away at high speed down the dirt road. The silence that followed was almost as nerve-wracking as the chaos that had preceded it.

Ella checked Two. He was still angry, but he was uninjured. He stayed right beside her as she made her way to the phone. It still had a dial tone, she discovered with relief, so she didn't have to pick up the cell phone, which was recharging, or try to go outside and use the Jeep's radio.

An officer-needs-help call usually elicited a lightning fast response. Though on the Rez distances between patrol areas were great, she didn't have long to wait before Michael Cloud, his brother Philip, and two other Tribal Police units arrived almost simultaneously. The crime-scene van and Justine Goodluck's patrol car were just seconds behind them.

Ella stood on the porch, Two by her side. She hadn't turned on any of the lights, and had only checked the inside of the house, not the yard. The dog had never left her sight. She placed one hand on his collar, grasping it as the officers came up.

"Did you see any suspicious vehicles on the highway on your way here?" she asked Michael, who was the first to come up.

"The road's almost empty, like it normally is at one in the morning," he said. "But Philip and I studied the vehicle tracks leading out of here as we came up. You had at least three vehicles visit you, one most likely a pickup. Did you manage to make any IDs?"

She shook her head. "I couldn't. The gunfire kept me pinned. It was pretty intense for a while."

He nodded. "The wall around that window looks like a sieve. Is that where you were?"

"Yes. It's my bedroom. They must have been watching and noticed that's where the last light was turned off. There were no automatic weapons I could detect, but they must have fired sixty or seventy rounds in all, large and small caliber. Only a few rounds went below window level, though, so I guess all they wanted to do was send me a message."

Michael Cloud glanced at Tache and Ute, who were already working the scene, taking photos of tracks and gathering up the shell casings they'd found outside. "To me, it looks like a gangbangers' drive-by shooting," Cloud said. "There are casings from at least three different caliber weapons here, even twenty-twos."

Justine approached, flashlight in hand. "Look at the side of Ella's Jeep," she pointed the light toward three foot high red spray-painted markings. "At least they didn't fill it full of holes, too."

Ella groaned. "Not again. That's the Many Devil's tag. You can still smell the paint. Get a photo or two of that, and I'll see how much I can rub off before it sets in. I don't want to drive into Shiprock tomorrow giving those punks a free ad." She glanced at her watch. "Did I say tomorrow? I should have said today." She looked at the others. "The rest of you should just go get some sleep."

"I'll stick around, just in case they come back," Cloud said.

Ella shook her head. "You're working graveyard right?" Seeing Michael nod, she added. "Just make a pass by here every once in a while at random intervals. I really doubt they'll return anytime soon." She smiled grimly, then added, "They probably need more ammunition."

It was still early when Ella woke. After successfully removing the paint, thanks to the protective undercoating so recently applied, she'd slept with Two on the living room couch. In the center of the house there were no bullet holes in any of the walls and, more importantly, it was where she felt safest.

Ella was in the kitchen placing a slice of cheese between two halves of a tortilla when she heard someone at the front door. Ella peered out the window cautiously and saw her brother's truck.

Clifford came into the kitchen. "I came because I was angry with you for not visiting more with Mom yesterday, but I can see you've had your hands full. What in the heck happened here? Your bedroom must be a wreck. Were you injured?"

"Nah, I'm fine. How's Mom?"

"Disappointed that you didn't come back to see her when she was awake."

"I really couldn't help it," she answered, feeling guilty. "Things have been crazy and it never ends. Look around you. I went to bed exhausted, but then had a very rude awakening. This was meant as a show of force from one of the gangs. And it worked, they've got my attention."

"I'd say they were trying to kill you."

She shook her head. "Look closer. All the shots came through waist high and above, and the sound of the cars gave me a few seconds warning. All Two and I had to do was flatten until it was over. The window was the target, not me, though I'm sure no one would have gone into mourning if I'd taken a round or two," she said, and recounted the events.

"I don't like this. Are we dealing with a youth gang, or hardened criminals? We can't take them all on at once." Clifford asked.

"We've done it before, against adults."

"But look at all the firepower, Sister. Are you sure it wasn't someone like those Anglo bigots, The Brotherhood? They've tried to kill you more than once, and might just want to pin the blame on other Navajos. It would fit their concept of justice."

"I suppose it could happen. I'll ask around discreetly and see if anybody knows what they've been up to lately. Maybe they have something in the works," Ella said, then shrugged. "At least Mom wasn't here last night."

"But she'll hear about this soon, if she hasn't already. If it wasn't The Brotherhood shooting at you, do you have any idea who else it could have been?"

"From the gang tag they left on my car, which could of course been left by anyone, it suggests the Many Devils. They sure have a reason to retaliate against me after we jailed three of them for stealing from parked cars. We also have another ready to go to court with a handful of driving offenses. At least one of them, Thomas Bileen, was also involved in terrorizing the Peshlakai woman and throwing a baseball bat at my windshield."

"Your assistant's cousin? Mom will be really depressed when she learns about that. This Navajo gang flare-up is just another example of what the white world has given our children and what's happening to us as a people."

Ella slumped down in her seat. "Can you break the news to her? It would probably be better coming from you."

"You're not going to the hospital this morning?"

"Not right away. First I have to find someone to come and check the utilities and repair the house. I also want them to measure and see what needs to be done to accommodate a wheelchair, just in case. Then I have to go to work."

He nodded slowly. "Okay. I'll see Mother. But take care of yourself, and make time to get to the hospital sometime today. I can only drop by myself. I have a patient of my own. Mom worries when you can't come by more often, though she did appreciate the note and the herbs yesterday. I know how you get when you're on a case. Time seems to slip right past you."

"All right," Ella said at last. "Tell you what. I'll stop by this morning on my way in, and I'll stay as long as I can manage. I promise."

"Good," was Clifford's only response.

Ella stared across the kitchen for a while after her brother left. Clifford was right. Her work, for years, had become her center, a focus for all of her attention and dedication. And now, it seemed more like an ungrateful lover than anything else, demanding more than she could possibly give.

After calling a handyman, a Navajo man who'd done several repair jobs at the police station, Ella fed Two, and let him outside. Then she got a brainstorm and went back inside.

Five minutes later, she had Carolyn Roanhorse on the phone. Fortunately it was still early enough that Carolyn hadn't left for work either. "My brother made me feel guilty this morning, so I think it's time for me to do something for Mom. She needs me now, and I can't let her down. How do you feel about sneaking Two into the hospital this morning?"

"You know, I think it's a great idea. We all need a break, something to make us feel young." Carolyn said. "It's been a long time since I pulled a stunt like this."

"Me, too," Ella said, then chuckled. "And I've worked out a great plan. All I need is for you to fill in the details."

Two was on the front porch looking for a spot of sunlight when Ella went to get him. A shift change at the hospital was due about the time she'd get there, which would make it ideal. People going off duty would be sleepy and eager to leave, and those coming on duty would be dragging their feet until the first cup of coffee kicked in. Getting the dog's old blanket, Ella whistled and Two ran up to the car and jumped inside. "Get ready, boy. You're about to go undercover."

The dog tilted his head to one side and looked at her.

"It's on a need to know basis, but I'm counting on you to behave."

Ella drove to the hospital, an undeniable excitement spreading through her. Carolyn was right. They needed hijinks like these, not only for her mother's sake, but for all of them. Of course they weren't kids anymore, and the price, if they were caught, would be severe. If things went wrong, Ella suspected she'd be banned from the hospital, which would make matters difficult while her mother was still there. For Carolyn, the price could be higher. Ella began to have serious second thoughts about involving her friend.

Ella parked near the rear doors leading to the service elevator on the ground floor. This was the most direct way to the morgue, one floor below in the basement. Picking up Two with a grunt and covering him with his old blanket, she hurried down the hall to the elevator. A janitor gave her a curious look, but Ella was past him and inside the elevator before he could ask any questions.

As the doors slid open, at the basement level, Carolyn met her. "Everything's set. Your mother will go to the service elevator on her floor."

Ella set Two down, but kept the blanket over the dog, resisting the animal's efforts to shake it off. "Let's limit your involvement, okay? Just make sure no one else gets on this elevator."

Carolyn reached behind her and pulled a gurney with a zippered body bag into view.

Ella's eyes widened. "You borrowed a corpse?"

"No, of course not. It's mostly laundry and a pillow. But it'll do. I'll station myself in the elevator with you. Then even if someone plans on getting in, they'll gladly let the elevator go when they see this lump."

Ella laughed. "Are you sure you want to take this big a role in this?"

Carolyn nodded. "Look, in my job, you need to find ways to decompress, and this certainly fits the bill."

"Okay. We'll stop for my mom, then go all the way up to the roof and keep the elevator there. Now, all I have to do is keep Two from barking at the wrong time."

They made it up to the Rose's floor undetected, but as

soon as the door opened and Two saw Rose, he barked. Ella pushed Rose's wheelchair into the elevator quickly as Carolyn rolled the gurney in an angle, allowing her to pass.

Dr. Natoni walked by just as the elevator doors started to close and Two let out another sharp bark. The doctor's eyes widened but Carolyn began to cough loudly, leaning over the body bag.

Ella reached beneath the blanket and clamped her hand around Two's muzzle as the doors slid shut. "He knows," she said, picturing Dr. Natoni's perplexed gaze in her mind.

"If he says anything, deny it. I'll assure him it was a sound that came from the corpse passing gas."

Ella looked at her mom and seeing Rose's wide-eyed look, burst out laughing. "Don't worry, Mom, there's no corpse in there. It's just a bunch of laundry."

Two wriggled out from under the blanket and, placing his front paws on Rose's lap, barked again. His tail was thumping wildly.

"Quiet, dummy!" Ella ordered.

Rose hugged the dog. "I've missed you, boy."

Ella saw the delighted look on her mother's face and knew the risk had been more than worth it. As the doors opened onto the roof, a blast of cold air hit them, but neither Rose nor Two seemed to mind. Ella reached over and closed the doors again, and Carolyn switched the elevator off with a key so it wouldn't move, or set off any alarm.

Carolyn looked at Rose and Two, then back at Ella. "This was a very good thing we pulled off here today," she said softly.

"Yeah, I think so, too."

"I don't know how you two managed this, but I'm sure glad you did," Rose said, and laughed as Two tugged playfully at the folds of her jacket. "I can't get up right now, boy, but soon, maybe."

"If you believe that, you'll make it happen," Ella said quietly.

"I want my life back, Daughter," Rose said slowly. "I miss home and my daily routines. Though I have to admit I'm glad I wasn't there when those gangsters turned our home into Swiss cheese. Your brother already told me."

"It won't happen again. The house will be repaired this week and, by the time you get home, you won't be able to tell it ever happened. The damage wasn't major. We'll have to replace a few lamps and windows, and patch some walls, that's all." Ella said.

Rose smiled. "I can always tell when you're downplaying things for my benefit, but that's all right. I know you'll handle things at home until I can get back."

"Count on it." Ella glanced at her watch. "We have to go now. I don't want to give Dr. Natoni too much time to think about what he heard."

As they released the elevator and began to travel back down to her mother's floor, Carolyn glanced at Rose. "Do you think you can make it back to your room alone?"

Rose nodded. "Of course. And don't worry. If Dr. Natoni's still on the floor, or even waiting by the elevator, he may give you a hard time, but I don't think he'll cause you any serious trouble."

"I hope you're right," Carolyn said.

"I am," Rose answered confidently. "The biggest problem you're going to have is when you hold the elevator doors open for me while I get out. You'll be vulnerable during those few seconds."

"You're right," Carolyn said, biting her lower lip pensively. "If Two barks, or tries to go with you . . ."

The doors slid open and, before Carolyn could block the way, Dr. Natoni slipped inside.

Two barked and Ella coughed loudly.

"Nice try, but it won't wash. I know what you're pulling." He smiled at Rose. "And it's my guess that you put them up to this."

"You always say that you want what's best for the patient. Well, this is good for me," Rose argued.

"I agree," he said with a twinkle in his eyes. "And I'm not your problem. I'm off duty now, but I thought I'd come to warn you that the hospital director, Andrew Slowman, is out on an early morning inspection right now. He's looking through records that are stored in the room next to the elevator down in the basement. I saw him going over the files when I went down to the pharmacy a few minutes ago. You better not get off on that floor."

"I've got to. No way I can sneak this squirmy beast down the main hall on the first floor and right out the front door."

Rose looked at Carolyn, then at her daughter. "Put him in that body bag."

"Mom, he'll squirm, and people will run away screaming."

"No, he won't. Two understands me." She took the blanket off the dog and leaned over, whispering something Ella couldn't hear. When Rose sat up finally, she was smiling. "Just put him in there."

Carolyn glanced at Ella who shrugged. Working together, they lifted the dog into the bag.

"Lie down," her mother said calmly.

To Ella's surprise, Two did.

"Stay there now." Rose took something from her pocket, and handed it to Two. "Zip the bag up, but leave it open enough so he can breathe. And work fast!" Rose got out of the elevator with Dr. Natoni's help.

As the doors slid shut, Ella glanced at Carolyn, then back at the dog. "What did she give him?" The animal wasn't moving—much. She could detect a slight back and forth motion and the sounds of chewing.

"I haven't got a clue," Carolyn said, "but this is as good as it'll get. Do as she said and work fast."

The doors slid open as they arrived at the basement. Ella and Carolyn had just started to wheel the gurney out when Andrew Slowman appeared. He stepped back, and then moved around them quickly, getting into the elevator as they emerged from it. As the doors started to slide shut, Two sneezed.

Slowman's eyes grew wide as he stared at the bag. "What—"

The door slid shut before he could say anything else. Carolyn laughed. "Get out of here. He'll come back, but I'll dazzle him with ten thousand terms he won't understand, mostly because I'll be making them up, and then regale him with specifics about muscle contractions in corpses. By the end of the lecture, he won't eat for a week."

Ella laughed. Picking up Two and throwing the blanket over him, she hurried out the back entrance to the hospital.

Ella drove home with the window on Two's side rolled halfway down so he could stick his head out. She was freezing but nothing could mar the warmth inside her that came from knowing she'd managed to keep her promise to her mother. The best part was that, for the first time since the accident, her mother was talking about taking back her life. Ella couldn't have asked for anything better.

After dropping Two off at the house, she hurried on to work.

The moment she walked inside, Ella felt a tension in the station that made the air almost electric. As she walked down the hall, that feeling intensified. People were looking at her, and she could hear the whispers behind her as she walked past them. Now what? Didn't she have enough on her hands?

As she stepped into her office, Justine bolted out of Ella's chair. "Sorry, boss. I was just reading the paper. The headline caught my attention."

"Let me guess. I'm featured." Ella went around the desk and sat down in the chair Justine had quickly vacated. The headline read 'Good Cop—Bad Cop?' Directly beneath that was her photo and an article on police brutality. Several officers, citizens, and a local attorney had been interviewed on the topic. Although the author of the article clearly emphasized that the excessive force and defamation charges against Ella had not been proven, the attorney's comments were particularly interesting.

"I see one of the Farmington attorneys couldn't resist the opportunity to drum up a little business. He's pledging to take on any case where excessive force is the issue, and using me as a prime example of why the public needs his protection. If I was as violent as he claims, I'd go punch his lights out right now, the cockroach."

Hearing a throat being cleared, Ella glanced up and saw Big Ed standing in the doorway. Justine started for the door, but he stopped her. "Stay. This concerns you both." He closed the door behind himself.

Justine stood beside the desk, and Ella leaned back in her chair, waiting.

Big Ed took a seat across from Ella and for an interminable time, said nothing, his eyes closed.

Ella knew better than to say anything. Yet, as each second ticked by, she started to wonder if her boss had fallen asleep. That didn't seem like Big Ed, but his breathing was so steady that she wasn't sure.

Finally, Big Ed opened his eyes and he focused on her. "I'm under fire from Bekis's friends in the tribal government for keeping you on the job, but I can take the heat if it's justified. What I need from you now is some cooperation."

"Whatever I can do," Ella said, opening her hands in a gesture of acquiescence.

"I want you to take Justine along with you whenever you're out in the field. Also, get a tape recorder and use it during all your interactions with citizens. Make it a sound-activated unit, and wear it all the time, like our patrol officers. There are people who want to see you go down in flames, so you have to start covering your butt at every turn. Understood?"

"You want Justine with me everywhere? Chief, that's impossible. She's got work of her own to do in the lab, and our manpower situation isn't such—"

He held up a hand. "It wasn't a request."

Ella clamped her mouth shut. "It'll be done."

"One more thing. Are you sure the Many Devils were the ones who took potshots at you last night?" Big Ed asked.

"It sure looks like it, based upon the evidence. But my brother reminded me about others who have tried to take me out in recent months." She pointed out what Clifford had suggested concerning The Brotherhood.

"Just keep your eyes open, and don't go walking into any traps. A bullet doesn't care who fired it." Big Ed stood, and looked toward Justine. "That goes for both of you, of course."

As he left, Ella stood up and paced. "I can't believe all this is happening to me. The legal troubles as coming to me almost as fast as the bullets."

"You have real friends in this department, though, and our boss is probably the biggest one."

Ella heard the undertone in her assistant's words and knew the meaning behind what was left unspoken. "But some people in the department probably believe I did what that Bekis and his sister claim, yet they support me because they think it was justified," she said finishing Justine's thought.

Justine shook her head. "Yes, I guess not everyone believes you went by the book. They'll back you, cops stick together, but there's more than one officer who believes that you went overboard a bit physically when you arrested Gladys Bekis. When Michael and Jimmy Frank support your story, some take it at face value, others don't."

"Wonderful. So I have their loyalty, even though they think I go around roughing up prisoners."

Justine nodded. "Well, it could be worse, you know."

Ella sighed. "Anything new on Lisa's murder?"

Before she could answer, Neskahi knocked on the open door and came inside. "Sorry, I'm a bit late."

Ella waved him to a chair. "I was just asking Justine about our progress. Do you have anything to report on the murder case?"

"As you know, I've been pursuing the angle from the gang side. I decided to visit the parents of some of the kids, and what I've learned is interesting, to say the least. The families are being visited by members of the Fierce Ones."

"Lena Clani warned me about that," Ella said. "Are they intimidating people?"

Neskahi hesitated. "It's a strange deal. The parents won't identify who visited them. Heck, they won't even admit to having been visited. But Franklin Ahe's little sister talked to me. She's afraid for her brother and for her parents. Apparently they had late night visitors. They insisted that Mr. and Mrs. Ahe control Franklin, and they've demanded that restitution be made the old way."

"Old way?" For some reason the words made a chill run up her spine.

"If Franklin spray paints a wall, either Franklin or his parents must restore it. The Fierce Ones don't care about police involvement. To them, we're White Man's Law. What they want is traditional justice. If the kids won't comply, they made it clear the parents will be held accountable."

"Oh, crap," Ella muttered.

"Their son wouldn't help, but the Ahes cleaned up two walls that belonged to the neighbors."

Ella raised her eyebrows. "Well, that's going to be one major victory for the traditionalists. The community will see the Fierce Ones as heroes and support them. Our job is suddenly becoming easier, and a lot more complicated at the same time. Be extremely careful out there, sergeant. If the wrong family is held 'accountable,' we could have people at each other's throats."

Ella turned to Justine. "Have you been able to tie in any of the gang members we have in custody to the murder?"

"The kids we arrested all have an alibi for the time of death. They claim they were at the Halftime, that new cafe near the high school. The waitress who verified their story, though, is the sister of one of the boys we collared."

"Can anyone else corroborate that they were there?"

"A few other kids who were there at the time support the alibi, but I've got to tell you, I think they'd say whatever they'd been told to say. They don't want to go up against the gang."

Ella shook her head. "How did those young hoods get such a hold on our people?" Ella mused. "This problem has certainly flared up in just a short time. When I was in high school, fists were all that were needed in a fight. Now they think nothing of pulling a gun."

"Outside influences like TV, movies, gangster rap, and reservation kids coming back after living in big cities, have all contributed to this problem," Neskahi said.

Ella studied a report on her desk. "The kids we arrested

weren't wearing the same type of athletic shoes that we identified at the crime scene," Ella noted. "But that doesn't really
exclude them from the list of suspects." Ella glanced up.
"Keep me posted on your progress, Sergeant, and stay on the
gang aspect of this case."

As Neskahi left, Ella looked at Justine. "Make sure you
check whatever Thomas and the other two use on their hair,
then compare it with that substance we found at the murder
scene. I notice they all have their hair slicked back. Hopefully
we'll get a match with one of them, but not all three."

"I'll be back in my office," Ella said. "Let me know what,
if anything, you find."

Ella returned to her office and dialed the hospital, checking with the nurse's station in the section where her mother
was being tended. Her mother had made it back to the room
just fine, and her spirits were up. As Ella said good-bye, she
shifted her attention to Justine, who'd just appeared at the
door again.

"Can I come in, boss?" Justine looked as tired as Ella felt.
"I know you want a lead, something to take to Big Ed, but I
haven't been able to get anything for you yet, not on the
murder," Justine said, downcast. "I feel as if I'm failing you.
I couldn't come up with anything that will narrow down any
suspects."

"This isn't your fault. Investigations go at their own rate.
You know that."

"I just didn't want you to think that I was so preoccupied
with my family problems, especially Thomas and my aunt,
that I was being sloppy with my work."

"I don't," Ella said. "Has Thomas said anything to you
that can help us out? I know you've been to visit him in his
cell."

"Didn't you know? Robert Kauley got him released into
the custody of my aunt. He didn't even have to make bail be-

cause he has no previous record, and isn't considered a flight risk. Because of his age, they don't want to keep him with adult prisoners, apparently. Of course he'll have to show up in court on the charges, and has been warned to stay out of trouble and away from the gangs."

"Do you think he'll do that? He may not be too far gone to save if he can avoid that kind of peer pressure. I hate to see someone that age wrecking their lives like that."

Justine shrugged. "If he and his mother will face the facts and stop blaming others, maybe they can get hold of him again. He used to be a good kid before my uncle moved out. Maybe there is some of that still in him."

"We can keep our fingers crossed," Ella agreed. "By the way, did you do the follow-up yet on Jane Clah?" Ella asked.

Justine nodded. "I've asked around, but nobody's seen her in ages. The people I spoke to weren't even sure she was still alive. There are no records of her death, if she died."

"Did you drive out to her hogan?"

"No, I haven't had a chance. I could do that today, if you'd like."

"Let's do it now. I have a gut feeling that it's something we should be pursuing. Those cane prints make me think of her, for some reason."

The drive was as long as it was uneventful. Jane Clah's home was in the middle of one of the most desolate sections of the area, about thirty miles southeast of Shiprock. The paved road gave out six miles east of Highway 666, and from that point on, it became a washboard surface that sorely tested Ella's Jeep's reputation as a quiet ride.

Just when they'd come to the conclusion that their insides would never stop vibrating, they arrived at a six-sided piñon log and mud hogan built in a depression surrounded by low, eroded mesas. The blanket which covered the entrance to the hogan was ragged and threadbare, barely hanging on. The corrals were empty, and the gate swayed in the breeze. The place looked abandoned and as desolate as the surrounding desert.

Ella stepped out with Justine, cautioning her assistant to stay alert. As they stood by their vehicle, waiting for an invitation to approach, Ella felt the spidery touch of fear trickling over her, warning her of danger, though nothing seemed out of place.

"The silence out here is giving me the creeps," Justine said. "It's obvious nobody lives here anymore. Let's go and take a look."

"Not yet. Give it a while longer," Ella said, her eagle-sharp gaze studying the surrounding high ground and stunted brush.

As a coyote howled in the distance, Ella suppressed a shudder. The place was making her skin crawl, but she wasn't sure why. Uninhabited, windswept places miles from civilization were common on the Rez and that, in and of itself, had never bothered her.

"I don't even see any tracks around," Justine said, her voice taut.

"There aren't that I can see, either," Ella said quietly. "But the last time I was here, she kept me waiting for quite a long time. I want to make sure she isn't ill, and that we won't be intruding on her by just walking in."

Ella moved away from the vehicle and studied the hogan from a different angle. "It does look abandoned, doesn't it? I suspect they left that old blanket over the entrance because it wasn't worth taking down. And if someone lived here, there would be a stack of firewood around, too. The nights are still cold."

"Maybe—"

"She's dead?" Ella said, finishing the thought. "Could be, but somehow, I don't think so."

Ella understood Justine's reluctance to approach the hogan. It wasn't just an aversion to the dead. It was something about this place. The silence seemed so total that it was as if this stark area sustained itself by feeding on all the sounds.

When the time came, Ella took the lead and forced herself to go into the hogan. Brushing the dust-filled blanket aside, she sneezed hard. The dirt floor was barren of any supplies, unless tumbleweeds were included. It was as if no one had ever lived here. Yet her skin continued to prickle and all her instincts urged her to get away from the hogan.

Ella held her ground. Her brother had often said that the profane tainted the air in a way that nothing ever truly erased. That was what she felt now. There was something evil here that lingered like the stench of death.

"Are you okay?" Justine asked, stepping in beside her. "You have a strange expression on your face."

"You feel it, too, don't you?" Ella asked. "It's like there's more here than we can see with our eyes." Suddenly Ella shook her head. "Don't listen to me. I'm just reacting to memories, that's all. My husband was a kind, gentle man, but his family was something else. Not many things frighten me anymore, but *they* did . . . and still do." Ella regretted the words as soon as she spoke them. Admitting such a fear might give it power over her.

"Well, I can understand memories confusing your perceptions, but I've got to tell you, this place is really spooky and it's not just because there's no sign of life around. It's this entire area. It's in a depression, I'm sure you noticed. But it's more than its physical location. There aren't enough sounds. It's like this place exists in the middle of a void. How anyone could stand living out here for more than a few hours is beyond me." Justine shook her head.

"The old woman may have wanted to get away from the scandals, to retreat from the world. Or she may have simply wanted the freedom to do as she pleased and, out here, there would be no conventions to follow," Ella said slowly.

Without thinking, Ella kicked at the pile of ashes in the center of the hogan beneath the smoke hole, then stopped. She couldn't remember if that was a taboo of some kind. Slowly a new thought formed in her mind. Maybe the real reason Jane Clah had chosen to live here was far more complicated than they'd realized.

As they stepped back outside, a strange sensation hit her. Ella blocked it, refusing to allow her imagination to spook her. The thought that had come into her mind was that something was near, watching them both.

Justine crouched by the entrance to the hogan. "If there were ever cane marks here, the wind has hidden them from us permanently." She stood and followed Ella to the Jeep.

Ella placed the vehicle in gear, and began the rough journey back to the main highway. Silence stretched taut between her and Justine. Ella still felt the danger like a palpable force wrapping itself around her. Suddenly, as she began the turn that paralleled the cliff, the steering wheel locked. Ella yanked it hard, trying to complete the turn.

Aware instantly of the problem, Justine leaned over and pulled at the wheel, tugging at it along with Ella.

Ella slammed hard on the brakes, but on the soft earth, the vehicle continued to slide toward the drop off.

When they finally came to a stop, they were only inches from the edge. "Don't move," Ella whispered.

The Jeep dropped a few inches, and Justine yelped. "Can you put it in reverse?"

"First, we'll both get out. If the ground here gives way, I

want to make darned sure neither one of us is in the Jeep. There's about a thirty-foot drop-off."

Ella looked at Justine. "Go now, just don't rock the vehicle as you get out."

"I think it may be safer if we both get out at the same time."

Ella nodded. "Okay. On three."

They opened their doors carefully, then on the count of three, jumped out of the vehicle. Ella waited, scarcely breathing, to see if her vehicle would remain where it was. The Jeep continued running, idling in place.

Ella looked around the Jeep at the edge of the cliff. The front bumper had nothing but air below it for quite some distance. "We've got to push it back away from that edge."

Working carefully, Ella turned off the engine, put the Jeep out of gear, and released the brake. Together, they pushed the Jeep back away from the drop-off. Once on secure ground, Ella set the brake, fell back against the seat, and caught her breath. "That was too damn close."

"Yeah," Justine agreed, her voice trembling slightly. "What the heck happened?"

Ella started the engine again, went through the gears, and tried the steering. It worked perfectly well. "I don't get it. The wheel was locked tight. We couldn't budge it. And now it seems fine."

Justine shuddered. "It's this stretch of desert . . . there's something bad out here."

"It's not the place. Accidents can happen anywhere, and that's all it was; a mechanical malfunction at the wrong time." But it was the kind of mishap that, over the years, she'd learned to associate with skinwalkers. That chilling knowledge settled over her, freezing the very marrow of her bones.

NINE

✖ ✖ ✖

Ella searched the vehicle up and down. Assured no one had tampered with it, she informed Justine that they were going to return to the hogan. Justine looked slightly unnerved at the prospect, but said nothing.

Once they arrived at the hogan, Ella got out and began looking around. Justine followed her.

"I can help, if you tell me what you're looking for," Justine said.

"I'm not sure. Anything out of the ordinary," Ella answered. "We'll work in a spiral search pattern, starting with the hogan."

Ella and Justine searched carefully and methodically. As Ella reached the base of a low hill that overlooked the hogan, she saw coyote tracks leading from the rocks into a narrow wash filled with hard-packed earth. She suppressed the shudder that ran up her spine.

Justine came to stand beside her. "Anything that survives out here has to be very wily. I don't think there's much game around."

She knew what Justine was implying, that this was no ordinary coyote. "You know, if the tracks were different, I'd suspect a you-know-what, but these seem like the genuine article." Ella was reluctant to use the term skinwalker aloud, especially in a place like this. She was no traditionalist, but it made no sense to risk using the name of a Navajo witch since it was said to attract their attention.

"Odd place to find a coyote, though, wouldn't you say?"

Ella said nothing. Her badger fetish still felt warm against her skin, and she didn't take the warning lightly. She'd learned respect for traditional forces and the fetish had played a large part in that. "Let's stop at any businesses we see on the way back to the station and talk to the employees. Maybe someone can tell us where Jane has gone."

"Okay. And here's my tape recorder, ready to go. Just press the red button and it will be voice activated. Big Ed wanted you to keep one with you. I have a spare back at the station that I'll use."

Ella took the tiny device reluctantly. "Thanks. I'll keep us both in batteries."

They stopped at the first two grocery/gas stations along the route with no results. Seeing a long established trading post ahead, Justine's eyes lit up. "I've been in that place. It's the kind of old-time store that would appeal to a traditionalist."

"Okay, let's go inside," Ella said, unwilling to let even one stone go unturned.

Mrs. Willink, a woman in her late thirties, stood behind the counter and eyed them with suspicion as they entered. Her wary look intensified when Ella identified herself.

The clerk's wind-browned face held equal measures of cynicism and intelligence. Mrs. Willink stood up and Ella noted her traditionalist clothing—a long, dark blue skirt, and a red blouse. The lines that crisscrossed her leather skin spoke of years of hardship and the toughness that engendered.

Ella introduced herself and Justine, and explained where

they had just been, without mentioning Jane Clah by name.

"You're related to that woman, aren't you? What has she done that the police would come calling?"

"Nothing at all that we know about. We just want to ask her a few questions."

"If she'd wanted to speak with you, she would have made it simple for you to find her. Why don't you leave her alone? Trying to track her down won't help at all," Mrs. Willink said.

"I have to find her. She has information that might help me right a wrong. I would appreciate any help you can give me."

Mrs. Willink did not answer right away. Instead, she looked across the small room to where some Navajo rugs were folded and stacked on a table. "Good weavers are said to know enough to leave a flaw in each rug they weave. They're masters of a craft, but it's by learning that flaw that they find their strength and a sense of perfection. When you search for answers, you try to find completion and harmony without acknowledging the imperfections, the flaws."

Ella's eagerness tore at her patience. "Speak plainly," Ella said.

"To find answers, you should look for whatever doesn't fit the pattern of the whole." Mrs. Willink stood up slowly and, without another word, stepped into the back room.

Ella stared at the empty doorway for several pensive seconds then walked back outside with Justine. "Mrs. Willink just stated the obvious—which I'd somehow managed to miss," Ella said.

"I don't get it," Justine said. "I thought she was being very cryptic."

"The pattern is plain. Jane Clah's family was involved with witchcraft. Chances are that she knows plenty about it.

She's also a very intelligent woman. It's very possible she had a plan all along. Think about it. Despite the hardships it presented a woman her age, she moved out to a remote area, something that was guaranteed to make people start talking about her. She knew that sometimes elderly people are feared. Their *bíjí*, spiritual power, is strong, and that includes their power to do evil. Then, once talk died down, and speculations ceased for lack of interest, she disappears. The old woman knew I'd be coming again to talk with her, so she took the best route open to her—making sure I can't find her. But the flaw in her plan is that by disappearing, she's confirming all of my suspicions."

"It fits," Justine admitted. "And Mrs. Willink was giving you information indirectly, which protects her somewhat from Jane Clah's wrath. Does Jane resent you for what happened to your father-in-law?"

"I'd find it difficult to believe otherwise." Ella turned the key in the ignition. "Keep searching for her and quietly asking around. Don't give up. She's still in the Four Corners area. I'd be willing to bet on it."

"Even so, the Rez is a big place to hide in."

"And digging is what cops do best," Ella said.

Ella pulled into the Shiprock Police Station still feeling unsettled by the incident near the cliff and Mrs. Willink's information. She had a feeling Mrs. Willink knew far more than she'd said, but Ella also knew the woman would not give her any more help. Obviously, Ella wasn't the only one who suspected Jane Clah of being a skinwalker. The clerk was being careful not to make an enemy of a Navajo witch.

Ella drove over to the garage area of the station, planning on turning the vehicle over to a mechanic for a thorough overhaul. Everything had worked perfectly on the drive back, however. She clasped her hand around the badger fetish, noting that it finally felt cool.

"What are you going to tell the mechanic?" Justine asked, getting out.

"Exactly what happened, minus our supernatural speculations. Maybe those kids who shot up my mother's house did something to the car, and it didn't show up until now."

"What if they tell you nothing's wrong?"

Ella paused. Fact was, she expected to be told that very thing. "Well, there's a chance it was a freak thing, like sand caught in the wrong place."

"Or maybe some kind of witch magic?"

"Do you believe in such things?" Ella asked, her gaze resting on Justine.

Justine stared at her hands. "There was a time when I would have answered with an emphatic no, but I'm not so certain about things anymore. I've seen too many strange things in the past few years."

"Welcome to the club."

A young Navajo mechanic approached Ella as she got out, and Justine waved good-bye, heading inside. Learning that Ella wanted the Jeep checked, the mechanic handed her a clipboard with a form in triplicate and a rubber band attached through a hole in the form. Ella filled it out quickly, attached the Jeep's key to the rubber band, then left the paperwork under the windshield wiper and went inside the station.

Ella continued on to her office. A new thought slowly dawned on her, opening a new line of speculation. What if Lisa Aspass had been killed because she was Wilson's fiancée? Wilson had been a crucial ally, along with her brother Clifford, in helping Ella break the skinwalkers' power a few years ago.

This could be the beginning of an effort to retaliate. Revenge ran on Indian time here on the Rez. If Lisa had been killed by skinwalkers, the crime scene could have been easily manipulated by them to make it appear that the youth gangs were to blame.

What better way to punish an enemy than by killing a loved one and, as icing on the cake, they'd throw suspicion on a much despised group. It was brilliant in a sick way, and a possibility definitely worth checking out. Even the shooting at her home and the gang tag on her Jeep afterward could have been an effort at misdirection by her oldest enemies.

Ella decided it was time to try and call her old friend, Wilson. Luckily, she caught him in his college office, probably between classes. "Hello, this is Ella. I wanted to let you know I'm making progress on the case, and to ask how you're doing. Are you keeping busy? Work sometimes helps in times like this."

His voice was low, as if he'd run out of energy already, but it still held all the bitterness of their last conversation. "I don't have time to discuss your theories on stress management. Do you have anybody in custody, or at least a suspect?"

"We definitely have some leads, and hope to have a break in the case soon. But I really can't say truthfully that we know who's responsible for her death."

"What you're saying is that you really don't have any idea who killed my fiancée, right?" Wilson's voice grew louder, and took on a harsh edge.

"No. We believe the killers come from a group of maybe twenty or so individuals. I really can't tell you more than that without risking compromising the investigation." Ella didn't want to tell him that two of the Many Devils gang were their best candidates. They didn't need another vigilante out there in addition to the Fierce Ones.

"Sounds like you're talking about one of the gangs. Talk is all over campus about the turmoil boiling out of the high school. Which gang is it?" Wilson was speaking in a cool, analytical voice she'd heard before. It was when the man was at his most dangerous.

"Instead of pressuring me for answers I really don't have, I'd like you to do something for me, instead." Ella had to change the topic. Wilson had known her since they were kids, and he just might get more from her than she wanted to give if she kept talking about it.

"You want to change the subject, right Ella?"

"What I want, Wilson, is for you to be very careful about where you go and what you do. It probably has nothing to do with the case we've been talking about, but I can't risk taking any chances. You have to be warned. Our old enemies are back in town, and they may be after you and me, and my family."

"Skinwalkers?" Wilson laughed. "Not unless they've joined a gang. You're just trying a little misdirection. Leave the magic to your brother, the medicine man."

"Now you're becoming a danger to yourself, old friend. Don't for a moment ignore the possibility that they could strike out at any time. Have you forgotten who it was that was forced to kill their leader just two years ago?" Ella couldn't believe how flippant Wilson was being about such a serious matter. Normally neither one would actually use the term skinwalker out loud.

"I'll be careful, if you'll do something for me in return. Use that dammed intuition of yours to find Lisa's killers. You're more likely to find them in a low rider than a graveyard, so don't play games with me. Put all that fancy training to work and get the job done. Then we can all sleep at night again." Wilson hung up before she could speak.

She held onto the phone, shocked by his coldness. They had been best friends as recently as a year ago, now the only words he had for her were full of bitterness and, from her, strictly business. With her now in the middle of his biggest tragedy, the closeness they'd once shared might be lost forever.

Still, Ella could not lose hope. Wilson had been there for her after the loss of her father, and stuck by her despite her distrust. She owned Wilson that much in return; besides, giving up was way out of character for her.

Ella hung up the phone, staring at the clutter on her desk that had appeared in her absence, trying to decide where to begin. Just then, Big Ed walked into her office.

"Ella. I need you to drive to Farmington right now and meet your attorney at this law office." He handed her a memo with a Farmington address.

Ella sat up abruptly, taking the paper. "That's short notice. What's going on?"

"There is some good news for you, at least I think it is. Gladys Bekis has decided to withdraw her charges of excessive force and instead is filing a civil suit. I guess she wants to go for money instead of justice. I pulled a few hundred strings," he said with a sheepish smile, "talked to your lawyer, and made arrangements for Dr. Roanhorse to examine Gladys Bekis for evidence that you struck her. There was only one hitch I couldn't get past. This will have to be done now in order to accommodate her attorney's schedule. He's all for it now, because physical evidence of her 'injuries' will soon disappear. Consider yourself off duty for as long as the meeting takes. The tribe can't pay you when you're on private business."

"Thanks, Chief. I have a feeling this is going to help me out. Carolyn really knows her profession."

Ella had to use one of the department's sedans while her Jeep was being checked out. She was always on call, so the department provided her with a full-time vehicle. As she drove, she thought about all that had happened to her life in the past few days. She was under fire no matter what direction she faced, whether it be an old friend, or an old enemy. There was one thing she was determined not to do, however. She would not give her enemies the opportunity to defeat her without one hell of a fight.

By the time she arrived at the downtown Farmington address, the second floor of an old brick landmark on Main Street, Ella had schooled her expression into polite neutrality. No matter what happened, she wouldn't let anyone get to her, or cause her to lose her temper.

Kevin Tolino met her in the hall. "Come on. They've already started. Dr. Roanhorse arrived early, and everyone's eager to get this over with."

She nodded once. "This could go against me, too, right?"

"Yes, but it's not likely to. The bruise has already been documented and photographed. That's why her attorney agreed. What we need to do is find flaws or inconsistencies in the injury or her explanation for it, and if anyone can do that, our ME can. That's the one piece of information their attorney doesn't have, by the way. He knows that Dr. Roanhorse is an MD, but he doesn't know she's a criminologist, too. Somehow, that never came up in the conversation," he added with a grin.

Ella smiled. She trusted Carolyn implicitly, but more importantly, she trusted Carolyn's forensic skills and intuition. "I'm in good hands with her."

"You've got a damn good lawyer, too," he added.

She smiled. "Let's get to it."

"Don't speak to Mrs. Bekis, no matter what happens. If she goads you, or if her attorney says something out of line, just keep silent. This guy is an expert in getting people to hang themselves with their own words. He's a tricky bastard, and he's grandstanding on this one. He's the same Anglo who offered to take on any cases of police brutality in that newspaper article."

"Wainwright?"

"He's the one. Interesting sidebar: His associate, Martin Miller, is representing the bank robbers Joey and Barbara Baker."

TEN
———— ✕ ✕ ✕ ————

As she entered the room, Gladys's eyes met hers. There was no hatred there, just a look of satisfaction that sent a chill up Ella's spine. Despite a big, colorful bruise on her cheek, Gladys looked like a cat who'd just eaten a six-pack of canaries. Working hard to keep her expression neutral, Ella sat down as Carolyn began to question and examine Gladys.

"She told me to turn around just as we reached the police car, and slapped me as hard as she could." Gladys smiled at Ella. "But you didn't get away with it, even though the other policeman wasn't looking. My brother Leo saw you, and will testify to what you did, too. I bet you don't have many people stand up to you this way."

Ella said nothing, but held her gaze.

Carolyn examined the woman. "Was this bruise caused by a right- or left-handed person?" Carolyn asked matter-of-factly.

Gladys looked at Ella, then at her right waist where her weapon was holstered. "Right-handed," she smiled confidently.

"You sure?" Carolyn shook her head, shrugged, then looked at the uninjured side of Gladys' face.

"Maybe she backhanded me. It all happened so fast." Gladys added hastily, then looked at Wainwright in confusion.

"Then your cheek swelled up right away, right?" Carolyn added. "I also notice two small, curved little cuts at the edge of the bruise. Did you get those at the same time?"

"Well," Gladys reached up to feel her cheek. "I didn't really notice any swelling because my eyes were tearing and it hurt so much my face was kind of numb. The cuts must have come from her nails." She looked at Ella, who had just folded her arms over her chest, her hands tucked inside.

Carolyn nodded absently, recording her findings in the chart in front of her.

"I want a copy of that report," Wainwright said.

"That was part of the agreement," Tolino said. There was an impersonal quality to his tone, as if the matter had not been worth mentioning and in asking for it Wainwright had only betrayed his insecurity.

"Nobody's getting anything, until I have a chance to turn my notes into something coherent," Carolyn clipped, then glanced at both attorneys.

Tolino and Wainwright both nodded quickly, and Ella had to struggle not to laugh. Carolyn could be a powerhouse in her own right when she chose to be.

As Carolyn left the room, Ella followed her, Kevin close behind.

"Let's not talk here, not yet," Kevin warned, leading them outside the building. A bitter cold wind whipped against them in the parking lot.

Ella pulled at the collar of her jacket, drawing it against her to block out the icy wind that insinuated itself between her clothes.

"Did you notice how Gladys had to look at Ella's holster before she decided she was right-handed?" Carolyn asked.

"That's because Ella never hit her," Kevin nodded. "But the mark was consistent with a right-handed attacker, wasn't it? Yet you shook your head in disagreement. Why?"

"Because Carolyn is clever. Gladys didn't catch on, and tried to cover with that backhand possibility. That was just further proof she made the whole thing up." Ella smiled.

"Her lawyer really cringed at her explanation. Did you catch his expression?" Carolyn chuckled.

"Next time I question a witness, maybe you should coach me, Doctor." Kevin replied. "But back to the real issue here. Just how do you think Gladys got her big bruise?"

"I'll make a full report later, but I'm not going to stand out here any longer with you two, freezing my butt off."

"Short and sweet then. Give us the encapsulated version," Tolino said.

"It had to have happened later, and the only time she was alone was in her holding cell. It must have been self inflicted. If Gladys had been hit hard enough to cause those marks, they would have shown up during booking. We may be able to check with the mug shots taken then and establish there were no marks on her well after she and Ella parted company. There's another thing I notice Ella caught on to. Ella, show the counselor your hands." Carolyn ordered.

Ella did. Her nails were trimmed short, like a man's. "I hid my hands when I saw that coming. Gladys was the only one of us with long, polished nails. Our jobs require a little less classical femininity, I guess."

"It's a win for our side," Tolino said. "We'll check with records and have the mug shots of Gladys blown up. I'm willing to bet, like Dr. Roanhorse here, that there won't be a mark on her."

"Gladys wasn't too confident she'd be able to pull this frame off." Ella said. "I bet that's why she dropped the criminal charge of excessive force for a civil suit. She could always hope for a settlement, and meanwhile, it took some of the pressure off her brother."

As Kevin drove off, Ella walked with Carolyn to her car. "Did you get a chance to look in on my mom?" Ella had to ask.

"Yes, but she was reading a magazine, and I didn't stay long. She seemed down in the dumps, and had skipped a physical therapy session. I talked to one of the physical therapists, who said Rose has had some trouble learning how to use the crutches, and is getting frustrated. Your mom needs to put weight on those legs if she's going to get strong enough to stand. Otherwise, it'll be the wheelchair whether she likes it or not."

"I'll have a talk with her, and try to boost her spirits again. She's probably having a bit of a letdown. I thought seeing Two would have had a longer positive effect. Thanks, Carolyn, for everything." They both walked to their cars, and Ella noticed it was even colder than before. March winds could be cruel.

Ten minutes later, on route to Shiprock, Ella called Justine on the cellular. "Is my Jeep ready?"

"Yes, and they found nothing at all wrong with it. Are you coming in now?"

"Yeah, I am. I'll be there in fifteen or so."

She was passing through Fruitland, a small farming community along the way, when Ella noticed the power plant in the distance. Recalling her brother's reminder concerning the danger posed by The Brotherhood, she decided to go by there before returning to the station. After all, most of those suspected to be connected with The Brotherhood were employed at that facility.

Letting Justine know where she was going, and ignoring her assistant's reminder that Big Ed's orders required Ella to have a witness present whenever she dealt with the public, she continued on to her destination.

After all, she wasn't planning to interview a suspect, and she had the tape recorder hidden in a pocket. Taking her assistant along on this type of meeting would only interfere with what she was trying to do. The fewer people present, the more of a chance she'd have of getting straight answers.

Fifteen minutes later, she was at the enormous facility. The power plant itself was large enough, but not nearly as impressive as the open-pit coal mine which fed its fires. It was hard for Ella to imagine what the desert around there had looked like before the plant had been constructed. At least the air pollution wasn't nearly so bad nowadays, with the scrubbers on the smokestacks.

Ella wanted to see Randy Watson, one of the supervisors. He had helped them before, and if The Brotherhood was resurfacing out at the plant and becoming active again, he'd know.

The office manager, a Navajo man in his late fifties, didn't hesitate when Ella made her request. He checked for Randy Watson's whereabouts, then escorted her to the lunchroom. "He's on break, so you came at a good time."

As he opened the door Randy stood up. He was a tall, lanky Anglo in his late forties, and looked more like a cowboy than an administrator in his western-cut shirt, bolo tie, and jeans. "It's been a while since I last saw you, Investigator Clah," he said. "What's on your mind?"

Ella sat down across the table from him, glad to see that the room was empty and they'd have some privacy. Wanting to keep it informal so Watson would be more likely to talk freely, she didn't take out her tape recorder.

"I need to know how active The Brotherhood has been

lately, and, since you're close to everything that happens here, I knew you'd be the one I should speak to."

"I haven't seen any sign of tension involving that particular group, not since they butted heads with you last year. They've been lying real low. The ones who are active now are the Fierce Ones. They've been putting some serious pressure on the Navajo workers here who have teenage kids, especially those who might be in a gang."

"What kind of pressure?"

"Everything from tossing stuff out of their lockers to intimidation."

"What kind of intimidation?"

"I'm not really sure, though it hasn't involved anything physical—yet. I think it's taken the form of passing comments, innuendo, and so forth. The stories that have reached me are second- and thirdhand accounts, and not that specific. Remember, the Fierce Ones don't exactly have a high-profile image, particularly among the Anglos here."

"Generally, would you say that tensions are still high between the Anglo and Navajo workers?"

He shook his head. "No, not really. Lately everyone pretty much minds their own business. If I were to describe the atmosphere here, the word I'd use is 'guarded.' That pretty much sums it up. But if you really want to find out more about what the Fierce Ones are doing, I suggest you talk to Billy Pete. Whether he belongs or not, he would never say. I think he's one of their leaders. He always seems to have accurate information."

Ella remembered her old friend. She suspected that he was part of the traditionalist's group, too, but she'd never been able to prove it, or catch him doing anything illegal. "Is his shift working right now?"

"Yeah. Shall I ask if he's willing to come in to talk to you?"

She considered it for a moment, then nodded. Maybe putting things on an official footing would be best, at least for now.

Watson left, and Billy Pete entered about five minutes later, wearing his trademark faded Chiefs cap. His hard hat was in his hand. He looked around, saw the snack room was empty except for them, then focused on her. He appeared totally calm, but she saw a line of muscle tighten across his cheek. "Sit down, Billy. This won't take long."

He did as she asked. "Why so businesslike? I thought you and I were still friends."

"We are. It was just easier to get you here to talk to me now by saying it was official. I didn't figure it would create a problem."

He shrugged. "That depends. What do you need?"

"Information. I hear the Fierce Ones are coming down hard on the parents of the kids they think are in the gangs."

He shrugged again. "What does that have to do with me?"

"I believe they're just trying to help, but this could end up alienating the very people whose support we need most. The parents are probably the best hope of controlling the kids."

"But the problem is, they aren't doing it. That's why the Fierce Ones are getting involved. They're letting the parents know that if they don't control their kids, neither the kids nor the parents will be welcome anywhere, even in their own neighborhoods. The whole family will be treated as outcasts."

Ella knew that the Fierce Ones could pull that off. There was no other organization in this part of the Rez with more support at the moment, and on this issue, The People wouldn't hesitate to back them. "Deliver a message for me.

Tell the Fierce Ones to be very careful. I don't want to be put in the position where I have to arrest any of them. If any of the parents decide to press charges—"

"No way *that's* going to happen," Billy said, standing up. "Is that all?"

"Sit down." Her voice cracked like a whip in the empty room.

The man shrugged, and sat back down, reluctantly. "I have to get back to work."

"I'm aware of that. This letting the parents know. How much of this is talking, and how much is intimidation?"

Billy Pete looked at the clock on the wall. "The Fierce Ones reason with them," he said with a tiny smile. "If you go through the murdered woman's neighborhood now, you'll notice adults painting over the graffiti. That's restitution for the damage. There is one family, the Bileen's, whom I believe you've dealt with personally. As you know, they cannot control their son, and now he's out of jail despite the charges he's facing. The Fierce Ones will be paying them a visit soon."

"Thanks for the tip," Ella said, quickly getting to her feet.

"Don't mention it. And I mean that." Billy stood. "The Fierce Ones have a better chance of controlling the violence and the gangs than the police. You know that as well as I do. If I were you, I wouldn't interfere with them. It's not to your advantage nor to the community's."

Ella left the power plant and drove directly to Lisa's neighborhood. She wasn't worried. Her instincts weren't warning her of danger, but she knew that she had to get there right away, if she was to have any hope of identifying members of the Fierce Ones before they took action.

Ella passed by two groups of parents painting over the graffiti on the walls. As she turned the corner, she saw the

Bileen home ahead. Clothing, furniture, and bedding were scattered all over the driveway and front yard. It looked like everything they owned was outside.

As Ella pulled up, she saw Vera Bileen carrying a handful of clothing back inside. Ella surveyed the scene, disappointed that she'd been too late. Vera's son was nowhere in sight, so hopefully he was back in school.

Mrs. Bileen glanced over as Ella approached, saw who she was, then went inside with the bundle.

Ella waited until Mrs. Bileen reappeared outside. "What's going on? What happened here?"

"Nothing," the woman muttered, the anger she'd been expressing a day ago now replaced with resignation. "Please go. I haven't broken any laws."

"It looks like everything you own has been taken out of the house."

"I'm cleaning," she said brusquely.

"Where's your son, in school?" Ella pressed. "I know he's been released into your custody. Perhaps he can help you when he gets home."

Mrs. Bileen gave her a cold glare. "My son is my business. I will do my best to keep him under control. I wouldn't want you cops to lock him up again in that cage, like an animal."

Ella ignored the comment. "I'm trying to help you. No one has a right to come into your house and throw your property onto the ground."

"But it's okay for you to threaten our children with guns, and arrest them for hanging around with their friends?" Mrs. Bileen stopped and faced her. "Go away. You're of no use at all. At least the others have my respect."

Ella went back to her vehicle. As she pulled away, she saw Mrs. Bileen crying over a shattered piece of pottery. Her possessions were in disarray, some damaged beyond repair, yet she had more regard for the Fierce Ones than she did for the police.

That thought saddened Ella. The people she'd sworn to protect did not want her, and those dearest to her had been hurt because her protection hadn't been there when it was needed most. When she'd first started in law enforcement, she'd thought that enthusiasm and competence could overcome, or at least reduce, the world of crime. But that just wasn't happening, and she didn't know what to do about it.

The course ahead seemed filled with uncertainty, not answers, and that made her feel desolate, as if she were driving down an empty path, utterly alone.

For now, however, she was a cop, and that work required her attention and her continued dedication. Ella drove back to the station, checking off a mental list of things that needed to be done. Reports, the bane of her existence, had to be finished and filed. She also had to get an update from Justine. Seeing her Jeep in its usual spot, she returned the sedan to the motor pool, and went inside the station.

Justine was leaving a file on her desk when Ella walked in. "What have you got there?" Ella asked.

"The paperwork on my cousin. Despite all the physical evidence we have on him, I still couldn't get a thing from him before he was released. He and my aunt insist they won't speak to cops without his lawyer. The tribe appointed one for him. At least it's not Bekis or your lawyer, Kevin Tolino." Justine managed a weak smile.

"So how are things with you and that side of your family now? Or should I ask?"

"My aunt is still being a real—"

"Excuse me, ladies. We've got trouble," Sergeant Neskahi interrupted, appearing at the door. "I was doing some research into the gangs, trying to tie them into the murder, when I heard a call over the radio. The Many Devils and the North Siders are about to square off in the high school parking lot. That's Many Devils turf. Everyone available is being called there now, Code One."

Ella mentally acknowledged the request for a silent approach, then said, "Let's go," and started, grabbing her riot gear from the locker. "I just hope they didn't bring any guns." Seconds later, they set out, Ella driving.

"I hate this," Justine grumbled. "I went to school with the brothers and sisters of these kids."

"Do you suppose your cousin will be there? He's supposed to be staying out of trouble." Ella told her about what had happened with Vera Bileen and the Fierce Ones.

Justine shook her head. "I hope not. That boy is out of control. I'm worried he'll really hurt someone, or get killed trying."

"They're at the point where it may be too late, unless they can turn themselves around," Ella said, trying to focus on the present as she switched lanes, passing a slow-moving pickup on the bridge. "But, you know, the ones who don't break the law need our support to stand up against the ones who do. We're the equalizing force. Otherwise the kids with their heads on straight, those getting pushed around by the gangs, will be suffering too. They and their families," she said, reminding herself as well as Justine.

Justine nodded. "I know all that, but when we're up against the gangs, I see boys in baggy pants, not criminals."

"That's fine, until they start shooting at each other . . . or at you," Ella replied.

As Ella made a hard right turn, she could see the high school parking lot just ahead on her left. Ten or fifteen boys were clustered between three cars, engaged in a wild free-for-all of swinging fists and clubs.

Ella swung her Jeep into the parking lot, then slammed

on the brakes and pulled to a stop behind a department patrol unit.

Gang members were scrambling around the cars, screaming insults and swinging wildly at one another with fists, car chains, and a variety of clubs, including at least three baseball bats. Two boys already lay on the asphalt, and a third was crawling on his stomach, leaving a trail of blood as he tried to reach safety beneath the right-hand car, a beat-up Chevy sedan.

ELEVEN
———— ✖ ✖ ✖ ————

One of the uniformed officers who'd arrived just ahead of them hit the siren, then yelled over his unit's loudspeaker for everyone to set down their weapons and lie facedown on the pavement. His partner stepped out of the vehicle and racked a shell into the chamber of his riot gun.

About that time Ella and Justine exited the Jeep, batons in hand. Most of the angry young Navajos, some with bloodied faces or hands, stopped and turned toward them, clubs and weapons in hand.

"They're going to fight us," Justine said, looking toward another police unit just pulling up on their left.

"No, they're not," Ella countered, as four youths suddenly dove toward a car. "They're making a run for it!"

The officer who'd used the loudspeaker spoke a command into his radio as one of the gang vehicles spun around and, with squealing tires, raced toward the exit. Another police unit, coming up the highway, blocked their escape from the parking area. The car full of gang members swerved, bounded up onto a median, and slammed into a stop sign. The teens jumped out, each running in a different direction. Two patrolmen, exiting their unit, gave chase on foot.

"Down on the ground!" Ella shouted to the rest of the boys, who'd just stood there watching. As Ella and Justine advanced, however, the remaining youths dropped their weapons and scattered, knowing they weren't going to be fired upon by the police. A few ran toward the high school buildings, pursued by the officer who'd been directing the operation, and his partner. Ella and Justine hurried toward the wounded boys, who were down near the remaining gang vehicles.

When Ella crouched by the first boy, whose flannel shirt was slashed and soaked with blood, she felt the pulse point at his neck. He groaned. "Knife wounds, but he's alive," she said to Justine, gesturing for her to check the teen who lay about ten feet away.

Justine reached him, checked for a pulse then, looking at Ella, nodded. "Unconscious. Looks like he was stabbed, too, and struck on the head."

As soon as two other officers came running up, Ella asked them to stay with the wounded. She moved toward the beat-up Chevy, where she'd last seen someone on the ground. A streak of fresh blood showed where he'd crawled beneath the car and behind the front tire. "I know you're under there," she said. "Don't make this worse for yourself. You're going to need a doctor or a mortician, depending on how long it takes for you to come out. What will it be?"

Ella heard a curse that came from beneath the Chevy. "Slide your weapon out toward me," she said, knowing he'd had something in his hand earlier.

Nothing happened.

"I can wait here all afternoon. If you think you'll stop bleeding on your own, we can sit back and drag this out as long as you want. Or, one of our officers can drive this car away faster than you can crawl, and we can hope he doesn't run over you in the process. It's your call."

Out of the corner of her eye, Ella saw Justine trying to crouch down to see what the boy was doing. She felt her heart lodge in her throat. If he had a pistol and was looking her way, Justine could be his next target.

"Slide it out now!" Ella ordered the boy. "Your friends abandoned you. If you want to be alive to brag about your scars, do what I say."

Ella was relieved to see Justine take out her handgun and lay prone, the weapon aimed beneath the car. "What's it going to be, kid?"

A moment later, a bloody, six-inch folding knife with a carved handle came sliding out from beneath the car. Then two hands reached out from beside a tire. "I don't have a gun, just the knife. I can't move. Just don't shoot!"

Ella moved toward the weapon as Justine reached the boy and crouched down by the car.

"He's clean," her assistant yelled out.

"Who did this to you?" Ella asked, going up to the wounded lad. He'd managed to crawl out from under the Chevy with Justine's help, and now lay on his back beside the car.

The boy shook his head. "My homies will do the payback. We don't need cops taking care of our business."

"Don't add more stupidity to what you've already done," Justine said, her voice almost drowned out by the sirens of approaching emergency vehicles. "You don't owe anyone any loyalty. Face it. They bailed on you and ran like cowards." Justine continued to apply pressure to the wound in his side. "Help us out, okay?"

The boy glared at her, but a stony silence was her only answer.

Neskahi approached, radio in hand. "The ambulance will be here in another minute," he said. "Our officers identified the two other injured, and are tending to their wounds. The one with all the blood is Wilbert Garnenez. The boys called him Taco. The other, the one they called Lobo, is Gilbert Paul. He's still unconscious."

Ella recognized the last names. She knew of those families, though she hadn't met the boys. Sorrow filled her as she thought of the pain their families would have to go through, and get past, if either one died.

Then she looked down at the boy Justine was helping. At least this one had been able to talk. Maybe his chances were better. Even so, Ella could see the fear in the boy's eyes. She wondered how long it would last, and how quickly it would turn to defiance and hatred once he knew he was no longer in mortal danger.

"We've got three other kids in custody," Neskahi said. "I came in from the south side of the campus and practically ran right into them. They insist they're innocent bystanders, who just happened to be hanging out, of course. Three of our officers are still in pursuit of the rest."

Ella left Justine with the third wounded boy, and followed Neskahi to the captured teens he'd rounded up. An officer was trying fruitlessly to get names out of the youngest boy, who never took his eyes off the other two who had been arrested with him. He appeared to be several years younger, maybe still in middle school.

The older boys stayed back to back, sitting on the ground, handcuffed. Another officer was watching them carefully. The two, dressed in the black colors of the North Siders, refused to make eye contact with anyone.

Ella nodded to the officer as she took the youngest boy aside. He was wearing red, baggy pants and a white T-shirt splattered with blood, and was trying not to shiver, despite the cool afternoon. "You don't seem eager to get anywhere near those two guys. I can keep you away from them, if you want. You don't seem like friends."

"I've got nothing to say to you," he spat out, staring at her intensely.

She had been mad-dogged by much more intimidating criminals, so she just smiled. "The alternative, of course, is that you'll end up sharing a holding jail cell with them. Aren't they wearing North Sider colors?" Ella saw the fear that flashed across the boy's eyes. "Tell me what happened here."

"The Siders think they can move into our hood now that you cops are on our backs. The high school is on our turf, and they think because their homies go to school, too, they own the place. That isn't going to happen. They outnumber us, but we can stand up to them. They came to school wearing their colors right in our faces, not showing respect."

Ella noted the false bravado, and the way he stood a little straighter when he spoke of respect. "Everyone seemed to be ready for trouble today. I saw a lot of weapons. Who threw hooks first? Was it the MDs?"

"No way. The Siders have a guy they call Lobo. They pulled up beside us and started dissing us. Lobo called Taco out, and Rambo went along to back him up. The Lobo guy lost his nerve when he saw Taco holding a bat, so he pulled a knife out of his sleeve and slashed both of them real good. Taco took the blade and didn't even flinch, then hit a home run off Lobo's head. Rambo got Lobo with his knife, too, but then went down."

"Are you saying the three boys the medics are working on assaulted each other?" Ella prodded.

The boy nodded, then smiled. "Then Rambo is still alive?"

"That's right." Ella motioned to the arresting officer, who put his hand on the boy's shoulder. Before he was led away, the boy turned and gave Ella a worried look. "You'll keep your word? Don't put me in the same cell with them. I don't have my friends to back me up."

"We'll keep you separate," Ella said, then glanced at the officer, confirming the promise.

Justine, who had come up during the last part of the interview, added, "I think the boy he called Rambo is really John Begay. My mother knows his mother. He's been in and out of trouble for years."

"Let's go talk to her then. Maybe she knows what the Many Devils might do next, or could at least give us some names."

"The Begays live about three miles from me," Justine said. "Maybe I should drive. The road is pretty bad, but at least I know it."

Justine's statement about the road turned out to be the understatement of the year. Ella gave up trying to write her notes as they traveled around potholes that looked like moon craters and sections of washboard that made her teeth rattle.

When they arrived, Justine parked the Jeep, and she and Ella got out to wait.

"Are you going to tape our conversation?"

Ella hesitated. "Yeah, I guess we should, but since it's not admissible for evidence, just a way of covering ourselves, let's make sure we keep it low profile."

Soon a short, overweight woman in her mid-forties came to the door. She was wearing the traditional long skirt with a thick wool shawl over a dark-colored velvet blouse, and smelled of piñon smoke. "You're the police, aren't you. Come on in."

As they entered the small trailer home, Ella was struck by the condition of the dwelling. It had obviously been well-cared-for at one time. She could see where a torn couch had been mended, and the refrigerator door and cupboards repainted. Things had changed, however. Trash had now accumulated everywhere, and was stacked inside grocery sacks that lined the kitchen wall. There was an overturned tricycle in the hall, and toys were scattered about. Thick layers of dust covered the few pieces of furniture.

Mrs. Begay sat down near the window, and gestured for them to find places to sit.

Ella removed some dirty clothing from a chair, and sat down. Justine remained standing.

"We're here to talk to you about John," she said, delivering the news that Mrs. Begay's son had been stabbed, and was on his way to the hospital.

The woman showed no emotion. "I've tried my best with my son, but he won't listen to me anymore. He does what he pleases. I just hope he doesn't die this time. Last year he got cut up with a beer bottle in a fight over at the fair in Window Rock."

"He's only sixteen," Justine said. "He's ruining his life."

Mrs. Begay opened her hands in a gesture of helplessness. "There's nothing I can do. I went to talk to George Nahlee's mother to see, if maybe together, we could do something to get our boys out of that gang. But she won't even admit that her son is mixed up with the Many Devils. I explained why it is they dress that way, and why they cut those gang signs into their hands. I even showed her what they write in their books, practicing their own gang alphabet and names. She knew what I was talking about. She kept saying that her son was only copying what some others were doing, going through a stage. Some mothers are like that. The truth stares them in the face, but they remain blind." She took a deep breath. "In some ways, maybe that's easier. Hurts less, I think."

Ella felt the woman's despair, and wished there were answers she could offer.

"They don't belong to anything except the gang. A lot of the kids have pride in their school, but not my son and his friends. They don't even go out for sports or try to learn anything, even though the only way to escape our poverty is by getting a good education. The ones who work in class and do homework are laughed at and called schoolboys. Joining the gang makes kids like my son feel good because everybody else is afraid of them. I can tell you that being in the gang becomes more important to the kids than even their own families. I know all about it, because I've already lost my son, just the same as if he was already dead."

Ella felt her stomach tie itself into a knot. She understood what the woman was talking about. Purpose. The kids had found it through the gang and they stuck with that group that defined them, even though it would eventually destroy them. So much tragedy, so few answers. . . .

"Has anyone come by, warning you to keep John out of trouble?" Ella asked, trying to keep her thoughts focused.

Mrs. Begay's eyes narrowed, like a door closing. "I don't know what you're talking about. It's time for you to leave now."

Ella stood up and offered to take Mrs. Begay to the hospital. The offer was quickly refused. Ella and Justine left, knowing they had received their answer. The Fierce Ones had been here, too. If Ella knew anything about that group, however, it was that they wouldn't continue to accept excuses and failure. They'd take more decisive action soon, and it looked like Mrs. Begay was already expecting things to get worse.

"How can she stand to live like that? All that trash. It stunk," Justine said, interrupting her thoughts.

"She's given up. It's too much for her." Ella thought of how close her mother had come to sharing that despair when she'd realized she couldn't use her legs.

"Judging from her style of dress," Ella continued, Mrs. Begay is a traditionalist, but she's come up against the worst of the modern world in her son. Her spirit has died. She's lost hope and, without that, the struggle she faces becomes one insurmountable obstacle after another. Hope is what gives you the courage to reach out and continue trying. Without it, there's nothing."

Ella dropped Justine off at the station and drove over to the hospital for a long visit with her own mother. They also had to talk about physical therapy. The paperwork could wait.

The following morning, Ella met Justine at the office and, together, they headed out to the high school.

"I better warn you that Mr. Duran, the principal, wasn't exactly overjoyed to hear that we wanted to talk to him," Justine said. "He knew it was coming, though. I think he wants to downplay the whole incident as quickly as possible, and our presence there won't allow him to do that."

"You can't downplay three kids in the hospital, all in serious condition," Ella said, shaking her head. "A half-dozen or so more we haven't seen yet are probably bruised and cut up, too. Things weren't that much different here than anywhere else, with people passing the buck and assigning blame. Many don't want to see a reality that seems out of their control."

"Neskahi and the other officers are still trying to identify and locate the other gang kids who were involved, checking out their hangouts and their homes. I'm glad my cousin Thomas wasn't there. I heard from my mom that his mother paid him to move some furniture. He was angry when he heard he'd missed the fight." Justine shrugged. "It's a small victory, I guess."

"We need to keep a close eye on anyone who could be involved, and try to be there to stop problems before they happen." Ella said. "This gang rivalry is spiraling into a storm, and unless we stop it, there will be a lot more casualties. Soon the kids will be carrying guns, if they aren't already."

As they drove past the site where her mother's accident had taken place, Ella felt a shudder travel through her. She felt guilty already about not going by the hospital this morning, she knew she might be too busy to get there later, but the principal had insisted this was the only time he could meet with them.

Ella stared at the road ahead, trying to envision her mother's panic at seeing another driver coming at her head-on. She couldn't do it. The incident had struck too close, and the love that bonded her to her mother made the pain of nearly losing her too fierce, blocking her attempts to consider the case objectively. As Ella's gaze fell on the shoulder of the road, she remembered the cane marks she'd seen there. The more she considered the implications of their presence, the more uneasy she grew.

"You're thinking of your mother's accident, aren't you?" Justine said softly.

"There's something here that doesn't quite add up. The drunk was a real enough piece of evidence, but the cane marks . . ."

"Do you think Navajo witches played a part?"

"I want you to search carefully into Leo Bekis' background, but be subtle so they won't be able to label it harassment. See if you can find anything that connects him to the evil ones, directly or indirectly." Ella said.

"The tribe has a full background report on him. One is always done when a person applies for a position with the tribe, especially one which puts them into a courtroom. I also know his neighbors. They're friends of my older brother.

If there had been even a hint that Bekis had skinwalker connections, it would have come out by now.

"The press has been hot on the story, too," Justine continued. "They found out that Bekis.started working for the tribe when your father-in-law was still chief. I've been keeping tabs on their articles, and I noticed that they mentioned that fact once in passing but, since then, they haven't mentioned it again. My guess is that they searched like crazy, but they couldn't find anything to connect the two men."

"Look into it anyway," Ella repeated stubbornly.

"If you think skinwalkers engineered your mother's accident, shouldn't we have someone keeping an eye on her?"

Ella shook her head. "I really don't think it's necessary. Mom will be safe at the hospital. There are people constantly around her. And she's been trying out those crutches. If Mom suspected someone was after her, she'd leave that room and go for help. She sees things like that coming, remember?"

Despite her confident words, Ella decided to ask Carolyn to watch over Rose and remain vigilant for signs of trouble. If the accident had been instigated by skinwalkers, Ella could expect them to live up to their reputations as masters of camouflage.

Ella parked in the visitors parking area on the north side of the high school, the same parking lot where the gang violence had taken place yesterday, then walked through the big double doors. Classes were in session, and the halls were empty.

The moment they stepped through the office doors, Principal Andy Duran came out his office to meet them. A secretary looked up curiously, then returned her attention to her computer terminal. "Come in," Duran said, gesturing by cocking his head. A slender, athletic man in his early sixties, Duran had taken over the principal's job after teaching shop in Shiprock for many years. Ella knew who he was, but she'd never been in any of his classes back when she went to Shiprock High.

As they sat down, Principal Duran closed his door, glanced through his window at the parking lot, then took a seat behind the massive oak desk. He then reached for a sheet of paper resting facedown on the top of his in/out file and handed it to Ella. "I took a chance and compiled this for you. I figured you'd want names and addresses of the kids we know or suspect are in the gangs. You'll find them there, and their gang affiliation. I had help from my staff on this, but don't ask who. I would prefer, for legal and other reasons, that you never disclose that this list ever existed. The only reason I'm giving you this is because I'm more worried about the safety of the kids than getting sued."

Ella nodded in agreement as she looked over the list. She was grateful that he had the guts to stand up to the legal threats that seemed to be hamstringing so many public schools in New Mexico. But it was also clear that he wanted them out of there as quickly as possible. "I know you keep a tight rein on student behavior, but what's the atmosphere like here at school today? What are the kids saying about what happened?"

Duran shook his head and shrugged. "The responses are as varied as the students. Some are scared that this happened here, but most of them are taking it in stride, and I think that worries me more than anything else. It's that acceptance of the violence that stuns me and a lot of the staff. I remember what it was like years ago when you went to school here, Ella. We had our problems then, but never anything like this."

Duran stood and began to pace. "I've also heard that a few kids wanted to quit the Many Devils or the North Siders, but found out the hard way you can't do that. The other kids in the gangs turned on them. George Nahlee came in yesterday morning with a thousand bruises. I asked him what happened, but you know how far that got me. He's not at school today."

Ella and Justine exchanged glances. "Have you called his parents?" Ella asked.

"Parent. He lives with his mother," Duran said with a nod. "Off the record, she wasn't much help. She's heavy into denial. Her kid can do no wrong. George told her that he fell down the bleachers on the football field, and she refused to believe anything else." He started for the door. "Forgive me for rushing you, but your presence here is likely to escalate the trouble we're trying to control. I'd prefer if you were off campus before the classes change."

"The moment kids were assaulted with knives and baseball bats, you lost the right to handle this matter on your own and make those kind of requests. Police involvement is mandatory, and that asphalt out there is a crime scene. Let's just hope it doesn't get worse before it gets better," Ella said, and then she left with her assistant.

As they returned to the Jeep, Justine gave Ella a wary smile. "I think what you said at the end really hit home with Principal Duran."

"Good. That's what I meant to do. He and a lot of other people are living in a dream world if they think they can handle this like they would a couple of kids who got into a fist fight in the locker room. It's gone too far for that."

"Do you want to stop by Mrs. Nahlee's?"

Ella shook her head. "Not yet. I don't think it'll do much good. Let Neskahi work the street first. He's a good cop. Let's see what he digs up."

As they got into the Jeep, the radio crackled and Ella's call sign came over the air.

"Please respond to a ten–twenty-seven–one by the petroglyphs south of the Hogback Trading Post."

The three-part code alerted her before it even reached the

last digit. A homicide. Ella felt her body tense. "Who found the body, and has an ID been made on the victim?"

"Officer Michael Cloud responded to a call from Mrs. Archuleta, the wife of the trader. She'd been out there picking herbs for the trading post. No ID on the victim yet."

"Ten-four."

Ella replaced the mike. "I just hope it isn't one of the kids involved in that fight yesterday."

Justine switched on the sirens as Ella pressed down on the accelerator. When they passed the trading post, one of several in that area of the Rez, Ella slowed down. Going off road here required a sharp eye for obstacles that could disable their vehicle. The ground was strewn with boulders and sharp rocks that could rip out an oil pan.

"Up ahead, to the left," Justine pointed out the Navajo Police vehicle.

As Ella parked, they saw Officer Michael Cloud. He was standing with his back to the petroglyphs, facing away from the crime scene, and it looked like he'd just lost his breakfast. "I don't like this," Ella observed. "Something's really wrong. It's not like Michael to be squeamish."

Cloud came to meet them as they stepped out of the Jeep. "It's pretty damned bad," he said, shaking his head. For a Navajo, he was awfully pale.

"Do you recognize the victim?" Ella asked, curious about his strong reaction.

"No. I doubt his family would either. I think it's a boy about sixteen, tops."

"Gang-style clothes?"

"Yeah. He has the red T-shirt and a white web belt with the Many Devils gang sign on it."

Ella felt a sinking feeling centering in her stomach. They'd need a hefty dose of courage to view the body if it had affected a seasoned cop like Michael so badly.

Justine gave her a worried look. "I'll call the ME"

"I've done that already," Michael said.

Ella took a deep breath. She could make out a body beside the rock face but, at that distance, it was impossible to tell more.

As she approached, Ella tried to look confident, though she was mentally preparing herself for the worst. But, as she reached the victim and got her first good look, Ella felt the world start to spin. Turning away, she took several gasping breaths.

Justine, who'd come up beside her, froze to the spot. "Oh, crap."

"If you think you might be sick," Ella warned, seeing the pallor on her assistant's face, "get away from the scene."

"I'm not going to be sick," Justine said flatly. "I can—" Suddenly she took off running.

Alone, Ella wiped away a stray tear that had rolled down her cheek. The boy's kneecap and most of his knee joint was missing, destroyed by a large-caliber bullet or shotgun blast at point-blank range. Though the body was facedown, she could see bloody bones protruding sideways through the pant leg and skin. It was impossible to make a visual ID, because half of the victim's head was missing. It had been obliterated in an execution-style killing. After seeing this, Ella leaned toward the shotgun theory.

Crouching by the body, Ella smoothed the pair of disposable gloves she'd put on and looked around. Some coins had fallen from the boy's outturned pockets, indicating that if robbery was the motive, they didn't take all the money. There were mostly quarters, but the two old-looking silver dollars among them caught her attention. Ella called out to Justine. "Check the list of merchandise reported stolen during the recent burglaries for silver dollars, maybe part of a collection. One here is stamped 1873, the other is 1881. In particular, see if these were part of what was missing from the Aspass residence."

Working methodically while disturbing the site as little as possible, Ella searched the area in a precise pattern. Soon, her crime-scene team would arrive and photograph everything, and collect and mark all the footprints and evidence.

While Justine and Officer Cloud taped off the perimeter, she studied the tracks around the body. The only athletic shoe imprints here were those of the victim. The other tracks were made by three different pairs of boots.

The Fierce Ones would probably be wearing that type of footwear, most adults on the Rez did, but it didn't make any sense that they'd be responsible for a crime so violent, not unless their vigilante tactics had gotten out of hand fast. From the pattern of the tracks, it looked as if two men had led the boy to this spot, holding him from both sides. A third had followed close behind.

Hearing a vehicle, Ella turned her head and saw Carolyn driving up. While Cloud and Justine continued the search for evidence, Ella went to meet the ME. Tache and Ute would be here soon, too. They'd scour the area like the pros they were, and, hopefully, the scene would reveal something that would point them down a solid investigative trail.

Ella filled Carolyn in as they walked back to where the body lay. Being careful not to disrupt the scene any more than necessary, Ella led Carolyn along her own previous path. "I need everything you can get me on this, as fast as you can."

Ella stopped when she was ten feet away from the body, and Carolyn continued. When the ME saw the victim for the first time, her eyes narrowed. She looked back at Ella. "It looks like they tried to kneecap him first to get him to talk. I doubt he would have done anything but scream, though, after that. This can't be the work of other kids, can it? I don't see those boys as being capable of this level of brutality."

"I honestly don't know the answer to that. This is what terrorists and mobsters do to people. But on the Rez?" Ella leaned back against a tall boulder, feeling the cold of the rock seep through her clothing. Nothing made sense, and instinct told her that until she found some answers, things would continue to get worse.

TWELVE

✖ ✖ ✖

Ella was driving home the long way to give herself time to think. It was 11:00 P.M. and the day had passed before she knew it. They now knew the identity of the murdered boy. George Nahlee, the boy who had tried to quit the gang. Had this been his payback? Justine and she had spoken to those in the gang that they knew about, trying to get a lead, but it was soon clear they could expect no help from the other gang members. As usual, Justine's cousin Thomas had been out of the house, and her aunt didn't know where he was at the moment.

Though none of the officers had given out the details of the murder, the viciousness of the act had been hard to keep secret after the family had been called to identify the victim. Rumors were running rampant, and members of the press were calling the station constantly, asking for details and interviews. Particularly gruesome crimes always made the biggest headlines.

Ella was halfway home when Billy Pete called on her cell phone. She pulled off the highway to talk so she could give the call her full attention without worrying about watching the road. She wanted to pick up every nuance of this conversation. It didn't surprise her that the Fierce Ones would have heard about the latest killing. If they hadn't been responsible for it, and she doubted they were, the question was how they'd react to the news.

Billy had a question right away. "Do you think the boy was killed because he wanted out of the gang? That's the word that's going around. His own gang members had beat him up just the other day. Everyone at school saw the results."

"I don't know yet, and it's premature to even guess. Because it's an open case, I couldn't discuss it with you even if I knew." Ella reminded.

"If you don't know why he was killed, then we can rule out robbery, which narrows it down. It's a bit coincidental, don't you think, that he tried to get out of the gang, and now less than two days later he's dead, execution-style?"

"What makes you think that was the way he died?" Ella asked.

"I thought you might be handing that question back to me. It's a great way of not confirming the facts without lying. So I guess my sources were correct. I'll be talking to you later." Billy concluded.

"No, wait. Listen to me before you hang up. Righting this particular wrong isn't the responsibility of the Fierce Ones. The police will handle this." Ella pleaded.

"You're not doing a very good job so far. I bet you don't even have a suspect."

"Every investigation takes time, but we do solve most of our cases, especially murders. The only help we want or need from the Fierce Ones on this is limited to the presenting of evidence or testimony." Ella was adamant.

"Who said you're getting their help, or that I speak for them? I was calling out of curiosity."

"This late at night, on my cell phone? Don't screw with me, Billy."

"The deaths, the killings, the gang violence, they have to stop, one way or the other." He reminded her.

"We're working on it. The whole department is putting in long hours on the job. Just don't interfere. You don't want to help the killers by sidetracking us. We'll have to investigate every incident—the ones you cause included. You'll dilute our strength and muddy the water." Ella said.

"Interesting point. I wish you luck solving this quickly, then."

He hung up before Ella could say anything more. Ella got the number from dispatch and dialed the Power Plant. Billy Pete was not there at work, nor was he at his home, the number she dialed next. She decided to trace the call. The cellular phone company took a while, but was able to tell her the call originated from a pay phone at the Totah Cafe. He would be tough to track down, but Ella put out a request for any officer to hold and detain him until she arrived. She had a few more questions for Billy Pete.

At least, hopefully, The Brotherhood wasn't involved in the Nahlee killing. For that particular group of activists, trouble on the Rez from gangs would be a cause for amusement, not anger.

Ella drove through the residential area where the Many Devils hung out, but it was quieter than it had been for days. Nothing like a couple of brutal murders to keep everybody off the street. There was no sign of any kids hanging out, and the only vehicles she saw were parked and appeared to be unoccupied. The discovery made her uneasy.

Sensing trouble, despite the lack of people, Ella called in her location, and left her vehicle to check a few blocks out on foot. Her skin was crawling, and her blood racing. The badger fetish around her neck felt warm, a sign she had come to associate with danger.

Fear crept into her, touching her on a primal level that

made it hard for her to remain focused, despite her years of law-enforcement experience. Something within was warning her of the presence of evil, of skinwalkers, but there was no physical evidence Ella could detect to support the warmth she sensed from her fetish.

Clipping her hand-held to her belt, and forcing the fears down to a level where she could deal with them, she walked down the street, listening and alert to danger. Though she had a flashlight in her hip pocket, she preferred not to light up her location.

She was near the end of a cul-de-sac when a piercing, agonized scream rose in the air. Only absolute terror could have elicited that raw sound from a human. For a moment she stood frozen, beating back her own fear as she struggled to pinpoint the direction. As another, weaker sound followed, her training took over. Ella called for a backup as she ran, gun in hand, toward the house at the end of the street. She went through an open gate and entered the back yard just as a shadowy figure ran out of the detached garage and leaped over the fence. Uncertain if it was man or beast, she raced after it. The outline had been hard to define, veiled by the darkness that surrounded her. But whoever or whatever it was had possessed the agility of an animal or an athlete, clearing a four-foot barrier cleanly. Peering over the fence cautiously, she saw nothing but an open field.

Ella studied the area. To her surprise, she saw that no lights had gone on in the neighboring houses. Surely someone had heard the cry that had brought her here.

Hearing a faint metallic scrape coming from the garage, and seeing the side door to it was wide open, Ella went forward cautiously. Only moonlight coming through the doorway illuminated the interior. Ella stood by the door for a moment, noting that, from the broken wood near the lock, it had been forced open. She entered low, gun ready, choosing again not to use the flashlight.

Out of the corner of her eye, she saw movement and felt a rush of air. She stepped back just as an ax swung down. It struck the concrete floor of the garage with a loud clank and a flash of sparks. "Police officer. Put down your weapon!" She yelled, jumping to the relative safety of the other side of the entrance.

Her attacker replied with another swing of the ax, striking the doorjamb where she'd been standing only a few seconds earlier. Ella dove forward, and fired into the corner where her attacker had been standing. A faint grunt told her she'd struck her mark.

As a figure staggered forward into the zone of light coming through the doorway, she heard a loud noise behind her. Ella spun around. A paint can rolled off the garage shelf onto the floor with a thump. A diversion. She turned to her adversary again, and caught a glimpse of a second person dragging the wounded man out the door. An instant later, the door slammed shut. Ella tried to open it, but it wouldn't budge. The garage was now in complete darkness. The silence that followed had the same impact on her nerves as an ice cube suddenly pressed to the small of her back.

Ella reached for her flashlight, found nothing, then remembered hearing it fall from her pocket as she'd dived forward earlier. She felt around until she found a wall, then checked for a light switch. A few moments later she found what she was looking for, and the darkness was replaced with the bright glow of a single incandescent bulb. The first thing Ella saw was a teenaged boy lying in the middle of the oil-stained concrete, his throat slashed. She didn't recognize the victim.

Ella called in dispatch, reported her situation, and requested an APB on any gang members spotted in the area. She also asked that the hospital be put on alert for anyone coming in with a gunshot wound.

As Ella crouched next to the victim, waiting for her backup to release her from the locked garage, she began to investigate the scene. She suspected from his red sweatshirt that the victim had been one of the Many Devils. A glance at the crude MD carved into the back of his hand confirmed it.

She noticed a small wrecking bar in his hip pocket, along with a penlight and yellow rubber gloves. There was no wallet apparent. It didn't take a genius to guess what he'd been doing here. But who had surprised the young burglar? The people in this neighborhood were not offering any resistance that she knew of and, despite their apparent tough attitude with Mrs. Peshlakai, they hadn't done anything publicly to retake control.

She retrieved her flashlight, wondering about the occupants of the house next door. They must have heard the chilling screams and her gunshot. Were they home, and if so, why hadn't they reacted by now? An oppressive silence encased her. Ella went to the main overhead door, but it had been locked from the outside.

Her two-way crackled to life and her call sign came over the air. Ella answered the summons. Officer Jimmy Frank was trying to locate her. He'd found her Jeep, and now was searching for the garage. Ella called out to him and heard him respond almost immediately.

Jimmy Frank wrenched something away from the side door, then pulled it open. Jimmy's boyish looks were deceptive. He was a seasoned officer, though he looked no older than some of the boys in the gangs. He would have made a wonderful undercover officer if the kids didn't know him so well.

"Seal off the garage. I'm going to see if the owners of this house are okay. And take a look at the victim. Maybe you can ID him."

Once outside, she looked around and noticed that some of the neighbors had finally turned on their lights. If the presence of the police was what had given them courage, maybe some progress was being made in the area after all.

As Ella walked across to the house, she used her flashlight to study the ground for evidence. Athletic shoe tracks were clear but, a little further from the door, about halfway to the house, she noticed the now familiar cane-like dots and scuff marks left by moccasins. Anger filled her.

The person making the marks, old woman or not, was obviously playing mind games with her. Ella was no longer willing to assume that any or all of the trails she had found at the crime scene had been made by an innocent elderly person. Of course, it was entirely possible that the purpose of the cane prints all along had been to distract her from something really important.

Ella knocked at the back door of the house, and identified herself. Nothing happened. No lights came on and there were no sounds coming from inside. Apprehension filled her, and she aimed her flashlight beam toward a window. Perhaps there had been more than one murder here tonight.

Ella studied the lock and doorjamb, trying to see if there were any signs of forced entry. Not seeing any, she walked around to the side of the house. She soon found a window that had been forced open.

Radioing Jimmy Frank that she was going inside while he remained with the crime scene, Ella climbed through the opening, every nerve attuned to possible danger. Cabinets and drawers in the bedroom had been emptied, their contents scattered all over the floor. The mattress had been lifted, and now lay askew, but looked like it had not been slept in recently. There was broken glass everywhere. If the owners had been away when their house had been burglarized, they'd had better luck than Lisa Aspass.

The silence was deafening as Ella went through the house, room by room, feeling relief each time she failed to find blood or a body.

"You okay, Ella?" Jimmy Frank asked over the radio.

"Yes." She returned to the living room and unlocked the front door to meet the officer outside. "It's clear. Someone made a hell of a big mess, but at least it seems no one lost their lives here. We need to locate the owners and have them make a list of everything that's missing."

"I didn't recognize the body. Maybe somebody on the team will know who it was." Jimmy shrugged.

Hearing approaching sirens, she walked out to meet the additional officers. To her surprise, Justine's vehicle was the first to pull up. Tache and Ute were in the van behind her.

Standing near the edge of the driveway, she greeted them. "I should have known that you all would still be on duty, too."

"Neskahi is out looking for the Many Devils," Justine said. "With luck, he'll locate and haul in at least one of them for questioning. I told him to check at my aunt's home first."

Ella gestured toward the garage. "The body's in there. Has Carolyn been notified?"

"Yes. I took care of that. She should be here shortly," Justine answered.

As Tache and Ute proceeded to the crime scene, Ella took Justine aside. "There's something I want you to see." Ella led her assistant around to where she'd found the cane prints.

Justine's eyebrows rose. "Someone's taunting us," she said quietly.

"My feelings exactly. I want a list of all the people in this neighborhood who use a walking stick, and their relatives, too. Say it's a potential witness we're trying to identify, nothing more. And make sure we get good data on the pry mark on the garage, then see if it matches up to the Aspass break-in."

Carolyn drove up as Justine walked away, intent on her new mission. Ella went to meet the ME. Carolyn pulled out her medical bag and spoke to Ella as they walked to the garage. "The mortality rate for these kids is going up."

"Yeah, and to tell you the truth, I'm not so sure we'll be able to stop it."

Carolyn gave her a surprised look. "I know you're tired. Heaven knows neither of us seems to be getting our beauty sleep lately. But I've never known you to doubt your abilities as a cop before."

"We're not dealing with isolated murders, or even a serial killer. Gang violence has spread throughout the country like the plague. On or off the Rez, it's not a problem that's easily stopped."

"Even here?"

"It's not that much different here than it is on the outside, except in scale. Unemployment, parental neglect, and keeping bad company are all part of it. Our kids are simply emulating what they've learned from the gangs outside the Rez."

Carolyn crouched by the body, studying the victim and speaking into her tape recorder. As she pushed aside a torn spot of his sweatshirt, she abruptly grew silent.

"What's wrong?" Ella asked, aware of Carolyn's change of mood.

"This boy has recent burns on his chest."

Ella crouched beside Carolyn. "Maybe this kid got burned when Lisa Aspass was being attacked," she said thoughtfully. "Get me all you can on the burn, what you think might have caused it, and anything else you can think of. The rubber gloves and the pry bar fit right in with her case. We may have one of the killers here."

Carolyn studied Ella's expression silently. "I'll get back to you as soon as possible."

Ella left Carolyn and went next door to where Justine had just finished talking to the neighbors. "Stay sharp," Ella warned. "There's still danger around here. I sense it."

Ella went back over the fence, where she'd seen a third individual making their escape. She searched the ground every step of the way with her flashlight, yet there were no tracks on the ground. It made no sense. The ground was soft enough that some imprint should have been left behind by the shadowy runner she'd seen.

Ella crouched down, holding the flashlight closer to the ground, determined to find some trace of a shoe or boot. As she reached the fence, she saw the barest imprint right at the spot the figure had pushed off from as they leaped. The mark was so slight she could barely make it out, and it was impossible to tell much, including the foot size.

Ella knew that certain types of moccasins, worn by someone familiar with the old ways, would leave only a vague trail. But the gang kids didn't have the expertise or the interest in the old ways to have accomplished this.

Ella reviewed the things she knew. The gangs were at war, but the robberies were mostly the work of the Many Devils. The circular walking stick imprints seemed to tie her mother's accident in with whatever was happening here, but there was no reason to believe the prints were anything more than a way to make her crazy. If it wasn't just that, then she was up against an adversary whose power transcended the gangs.

Neskahi approached her. "Nothing on the boys so far. They're hiding out, and doing it well."

"We need to get the Many Devils together. There's a possibility that their burglaries have made them an enemy that they can't fight. Two of their gang have been caught and then brutally killed, though the MO on each was different. This has nothing to do with gang members killing rivals either. The worst part is that I believe more deaths will follow."

"How on earth are we supposed to find these kids?" Neskahi demanded. "They're avoiding us because they know they'll probably be taken to the station for questioning and maybe even arrested. If you think we're going to get them to turn themselves in to help us, you're not facing reality. We're the last people on earth they'd help because of what it would do to their reputation among the other kids. And let's face it, in spite of the different circumstances, it's still possible some of them killed the Nahlee boy and this kid."

"It's also possible that the kids responsible for the burglaries are in mortal danger from someone who is not affiliated with any gang at all. This kid killed tonight might well have been one of those at the Aspass house, maybe even her killer, and someone else might have found that out, too. I grant you, I have no proof of this, but we can't discount the possibility that Navajo witches were involved in the murders of these two boys."

Neskahi remained silent a long time before speaking. "I can understand your concerns, but you realize that without evidence, the police can't officially go around warning kids about skinwalkers. They wouldn't believe us, for one, and some of our guys are traditionalists. They'd rather cut off their tongues than discuss that subject."

"Put the word out that I want to meet the leaders of the Many Devils and the North Siders. I'll go alone if I have to."

"That would be ill-advised. Note that I'm being diplomatic. Those aren't the words that came immediately to mind," Neskahi said.

Justine approached from behind Ella. "I have to second that, especially after the Chapter House arrests and the battle near the high school. Some of those kids could be gunning for the cops after all the arrests we've made. That doesn't even count the ones in the hospital that are going to face charges if they recover."

Ella exhaled softly. "These kids have to be worried now that they're taking losses, and that could motivate them to take a chance with me. They're not only fighting each other. After they hear about this, I have a feeling they'll wonder who besides the other gang might be out to get them. If I can talk to them, maybe I can slow down the bloodshed, if not prevent it altogether."

"But meeting them alone . . ." Justine mused.

Ella looked at her teammate's expressions. Clearly they thought she had a screw loose somewhere for even contemplating such action. And they were right to be worried. There was no predicting what she'd be walking into.

"I'll bring that up with Big Ed when the time comes. Meanwhile, let's get back to the business at hand for now. This is going to be a waste of time, undoubtedly, but while the team continues to work the crime scene, I'm going with Justine to try and talk to the neighbors," Ella said. "Maybe someone saw something."

Ella went to the house on the other side of the crime scene, the one Justine had not yet visited, and knocked on the door. It took several attempts before she got a response and the lights came on. An elderly woman and her husband came to the door. Both were in robes.

"Woman, it's almost two in the morning," the man snapped. "What do you want with us?"

Ella identified herself. "A murder was just committed next door to you. Did you see or hear anything?"

The woman's eyes grew as big as saucers and she took a

step back. Her husband stood his ground. "We didn't see anything, or hear anything. We were asleep. Now leave us alone," he said, and shut the door in Ella's face.

The reception they received at the next few houses was similar. Finally Ella and Justine arrived at Lillian Peshlakai's and knocked. Nobody was home, the car was gone, and the curtains had been taken down from the windows. Graffiti had been sprayed on a side wall. Wherever Lillian was, it wasn't here. Ella sighed, remembering how frightened the woman had been after being terrorized by Thomas Bileen and his gang friends.

Checking her watch, Ella stopped at the end of the walkway and glanced up and down the street. Hopefully, her team would have better luck canvassing the neighborhood tomorrow. Forcing the issue at this late hour would only make people dig in their heels. She'd have a uniform come out tomorrow, someone who hadn't been around the body. Maybe that would elicit more cooperation.

When they returned to the crime scene, Justine said she needed to finish her sketch of the area, noting the places where evidence had been found. "We still don't know who he is, by the way," Justine added. "I think I've seen him before, but I just can't place him. I'll make a pass through the yearbooks we have at the station when I get back. His photo should be in there."

"Then if you don't need me, I'm going home," Ella said. "You can get ahold of me there if anything comes up."

"Get some rest. I'll be heading back to the station in a few minutes, too. There'll be an officer stationed here all night," Justine said. "I have a feeling we'll all be working longer and longer hours until these murders are solved."

Ella nodded in agreement and walked to her Jeep, wishing the department could afford to hire more people. When crimes occurred her team was asked to show almost superhuman stamina. It was true that they could have months of relative peace, without much to do except stay sharp. But when things shifted, they were expected to work pretty much around the clock. There was nothing fair about it—for them, or the tribe they served.

As Ella crossed the street, a strange sensation enveloped her making her skin prickle. She looked around her quickly. She could feel someone watching her, but none of the officers present seemed to be paying particular attention to her, and no civilians were visible. She continued to her Jeep, listening, attuning herself to Wind, trying to find a scent or a sound that didn't belong.

The sensation persisted after she'd started her journey home. Ella checked her rear-view mirror several times, but no one was following her. As she got closer to home, the sensation intensified. Ella considered not going to her house yet, but she could see no one around, and her sixth sense wasn't warning her of imminent danger. She just felt as if she were being studied, like one did with an enemy before striking. After calling in to check with the patrol officer handling the area, she went inside her home.

Ella woke up early the following morning. Dressing in a wool sweater and warm slacks, she went to the kitchen to fix herself and Two breakfast. She'd just set the dog's dish down when the phone rang. Ella picked it up. It was Big Ed.

"We have several problems. First of all, the kid they call Lobo, from the North Siders, died last night at the hospital. The other kids there, from the MDs, are going to face charges. Next, we still don't have an ID on last night's victim, and nobody has reported anyone missing. But we did get word that a young kid from Shiprock High was beaten up badly last night. It's Rudy Keeswood, the boy that was cruising around with his gang friends and encountered you and Justine. He's at home now."

"Who beat him up?"

"I don't know. Apparently he's not saying." Big Ed gave her directions to his home.

"I'll go talk to him."

"I'll have Justine meet you there."

Ella left Two outside and, grabbing some fry bread as a quick breakfast, went directly to the boy's home. When she arrived, Justine wasn't there yet. A middle-aged woman came hurrying out to her car. After checking to be sure she had a tape recorder tucked in her jacket pocket ready to record, Ella went up to the woman and identified herself.

"You officers here to see Rudy again? Go on inside. I've got to get to work. I'm already late."

"I'd like to speak to you, too, Mrs. Keeswood," Ella said, then remembered Big Ed ordering her to work with Justine. "Could you wait a few minutes until my assistant arrives?"

"Sorry, I have to go right now. He hasn't been driving again since that night, and I've tried to keep him out of trouble."

"Don't you want to be here? I have to ask him some questions about his gang affiliation." Ella tried to stall.

"I really don't get along much with my oldest son anymore. There's nothing I can tell you except that he probably won't have much to say. He sure won't talk to me."

"Do you have any idea who jumped him?"

Mrs. Keeswood stopped, her hand on the door handle. "I don't think it was anyone he knew from school. Not from that other gang." She lowered her voice. "I overheard him talking to one of the boys. They were saying something about crazy people."

That left a lot of room for interpretation. "There is one

question you can answer for me. Have you received any warnings about your son from other adults?"

Mrs. Keeswood's face grew hard. "You mean those men. . . ." She hesitated. "They were right, you know. Boys and girls getting into trouble need to be controlled. But I can't devote all my attention to just Rudy. I have two younger kids who also need clothes and food on the table. I work ten hours a day, and their father has a construction job that takes him out of town. We do the best we can. And with all those tickets you wrote him when he got into trouble, I don't know how we're going to pay for it all."

Ella had heard it all before. It was the same all over the Rez. At least the Keeswood family had been able to find employment. "Who were the men who came to see you?"

She shook her head. "They came two nights ago, and that's all I will tell you. They warned me to keep Rudy out of trouble. I told them I would try, but that he probably wouldn't listen to me."

"What happened then?"

She shrugged. "They told me not to give up, then left." Mrs. Keeswood glanced at her watch. "Then he got into that fight at school, and they must have caught him alone once they found out he'd been involved. I've got to go, I'm sorry. If you want to talk to my son, he's inside."

As she drove away, Justine pulled up and parked beside Ella's Jeep. Together, they walked up to the door. It wasn't locked. Ella led the way inside and looked around. From the living room she could see a lanky boy in the kitchen wearing jeans and a white T-shirt pouring milk into a cereal bowl. As he turned around, Ella flashed her badge and identified herself.

"I know who you are," he mumbled sullenly. He gave Justine a glance, then turned away. She'd been the one who'd written all the tickets his parents were going to have to pay.

As Ella approached him, she studied the bruises on his face. His eyes were both swollen and blackened. His lips were cut and his nose most likely broken. He could barely talk. She wasn't quite sure how he planned to chew his cereal. "Someone worked you over pretty badly. Why don't you tell me about it."

"Nothing to tell. I tripped and fell on the way home from school," he said.

"The Many Devils can't handle all the grief they're getting on their own. You should know that by now."

He shrugged.

"Will you at least tell me if adults did this to you?"

His eyes regarded her with vague interest, and she knew the answer was yes. "What do you care?" he asked.

"Why do you find it so difficult to believe the police want to help?"

"All you want to do is bust us. It's my business if I get jumped, I can take a few punches. Next time I'll be ready for them."

"You may not know it, but there's more at stake here than somebody getting beat up."

Again he shrugged. "Then we'll handle it. We are on our home turf. Nobody is going to put us down for long."

"Tell the leader of the Many Devils that I want to meet with him. I also want to meet with the leader of the North Siders. Nobody comes packing, not even a wallet chain, and no backup. Just the three of us. We'll meet in neutral territory. We can do this tomorrow at the turnoff to Big Gap Reservoir. There's no way anyone can sneak up on anyone else out there. You know the place?"

Rudy looked at her in surprise. "My dad used to take me fishing there. You're serious about this meeting?"

"Yeah. Just deliver the message and have him get back to me with a time."

"You would trust us?"

"If your word is as good as mine, I would. Since I figure we have to start somewhere, I'll have to go with this anyway. Deliver the message." Ella stood up and walked out. Justine followed without saying a word.

At the station, Ella went to her office. To her surprise, she'd no sooner settled into her chair when Justine came in with a stack of envelopes. Ella looked up.

Her young assistant handed her the mail and said, "Looks like a busy day today. We still have a body to identify, and evidence to sift through. Maybe the victim's prints will match that on the glove at Lisa's house, and we'll have us a killer. I'd better get over to the lab."

Ella glanced through the stack of letters. Everything there was routine; a letter from the Task Force thanking her for her participation, a letter from the legal department asking for her signature on some papers. Then, at the bottom of the stack, a small envelope caught her eye. It was handwritten with a pencil in a scrawl that was barely legible, and addressed to her, though her name had been misspelled.

A bad feeling spread over her. Holding it carefully by the edges, she slit it open.

The note was written on a torn piece of notebook paper. As she read it a cold chill that had nothing to do with air temperature spread over her.

You're at the top of The Brotherhood's list. Watch yourself. The bank robbery on the Rez was to raise money to hire a hit man.

It was unsigned. Ella studied the envelope. It had been mailed from a Denver, Colorado, post office.

Ella picked up the phone and dialed Dwayne Blalock's

number. FB-Eyes, as he was known on the Rez, was a good ally when he chose to be and, right now, the FBI agent's resources would come in handy.

Blalock picked up the phone on the second ring, and Ella gave him a quick rundown. "Can you check your sources and see if you can come up with more information for me? I'll send you the original note and envelope. Also, I'd really appreciate it if you would look for a connection between the bank robbers we have in custody and suspected Brotherhood members. We haven't been able to turn up anything, but the Bureau might know something we don't."

"I can tell you this much right off the bat. The Denver area is believed to be a stronghold of The Brotherhood organization. It's possible that note came from one of our contacts there."

"Maybe a result of an overheard conversation? It seemed to have been written in haste, judging from the handwriting."

"My suggestion is that you show a copy of that note to your chief, and attorney, as soon as possible."

Ella took a deep breath. "Yeah, you're right."

Ella hung up, and quickly dialed Kevin's office to fill him in. At first the silence at the other end of the line was daunting.

"Well, what's the problem?" Ella asked at last.

"I was wondering about something, and happened to stop and say hi to your brother on the way to the office this morning. We talked for a moment about the way your house was all shot up a few nights ago. He mentioned something that was on my mind, too. Do you think that this drop in Brotherhood activity at the power plant is just an attempt to lull everyone into complacency? Once you've forgotten all about them, they turn on you with an assassination attempt?

It would also serve to lower the chances of retaliation against them if it wasn't clear who'd done the hit."

Ella remembered the feeling she'd experienced the night before, the sensation that she was being studied and watched. "I hadn't considered that, but it's possible." A Brotherhood assassin could have been watching her every move, preparing to take her out of the picture.

"The reason I suggested it is because of something that happened as I was reviewing the case against you. I learned that the legal firm representing Gladys Bekis and the bank robbers has also represented several suspected members of The Brotherhood in the past."

Ella felt the spidery touch of fear walking along the base of her neck. "Things are sure getting interesting," she muttered.

"Don't let your guard down, Ella, there may be more than gang members gunning for you," Tolino said, then hung up.

Ella leaned back in her chair. So much information was coming at her. Yet there were still no real answers, except maybe with the latest teen killed. Ella recalled everything that had happened when she'd found the latest victim. She pictured going into the neighborhood and finding the crime scene, and then relived the feeling that had swept over her, warning her of evil close by. She'd felt the same way at Lisa's.

Ella picked up the phone and dialed Clifford's home number. If anyone could help her gather information about their old enemies, the skinwalkers, her brother the *hataalii* could.

THIRTEEN

✖ ✖ ✖

Ella took the note to Big Ed. After a brief discussion, Big Ed agreed with her suggestion that it would be best to pass along a warning to all the other Navajo officers about the Anglo activists. Taking advantage of Big Ed's affable mood, Ella pressed him to allow her to set up a meeting with gang members. It took some time, but she managed to persuade him, providing she arranged to have some form of security for herself.

Ella left Big Ed's office, found Justine, and gave her the note to examine and copy, asking that the original be sent to Agent Blalock.

Later, as Ella was waiting for her brother to arrive, Sergeant Neskahi knocked on her open door and came inside. His expression was so somber, Ella knew that whatever news he was bringing would not be good.

"Sit down, Sergeant."

He took the only other chair, and moved it directly across from her desk. "The Many Devils are blaming the North Siders for the death of the unidentified boy we found," Neskahi said, "and the Siders know the MDs are responsible for the death of that boy in the hospital. There's been an incredible burst of tagging everywhere, and threats of retaliation are being left all over the place. I spoke to a teacher friend of mine over at the high school, and she told me that things are really tense. Two kids there got into a fight between classes and it took four teachers to break them up. One boy was a member of the North Siders, the other one was from the Many Devils. At least neither of the boys used a weapon."

"Have the boys picked up and brought here."

He shook his head. "I've already tried. Both kids were suspended, and the mothers have already removed them from school. I checked at their homes and then where the mothers work, but the kids couldn't be found, or wouldn't answer the door. Neither household has a father living there, so who knows where the boys are now?"

Ella sat back. "Find one of the North Siders, it doesn't matter who, and bring him in. We'll take it one step at a time."

"I've got two officers on patrol searching for the kids, but so far, they haven't found any of them they can identify as gang members. They're not hanging around in the usual places, that's for sure."

"Keep trying. Those kids have got to be somewhere if they're not in school. And somebody has to know who our John Doe is. We couldn't find him in missing persons. Perhaps his parents don't want to know where he is."

As Neskahi left, Ella stood and began to pace. She needed at least one concrete lead on the killings, and identifying the last murder victim would be a start in that direction. It still seemed likely that gang kids, one of them the John Doe, had killed Lisa Aspass, and she already knew who was responsible for Taco's death in the school parking lot. But who had slaughtered the two Many Devils boys? So far what she had were hunches and vague rumors, all which could be wrong.

Ella heard footsteps and glanced up as Clifford walked into her office.

"I'm here, as you asked," he said calmly. "Now tell me how I can help you."

Ella gave him a hesitant half-smile, feeling guilty again. She was very aware that she hadn't had any time yesterday to go see her mother.

She shoved her guilt aside and struggled to focus on the murder investigation. "I'm grasping at straws at this point. Will you come and take a look at the evidence we have on the murder of two boys, and tell me if anything in particular strikes you?"

"Strikes me in what way?"

"I don't know . . . just something that captures your attention—for any reason. As a *hataalii*, you know our people. I'm trying to get a handle on the psychology behind these killings."

"You don't believe they're gang-related anymore?"

Ella expelled her breath in a hiss. "That depends on when you ask me," she said. "Sometimes I think they're all a product of gang rivalry. But at other times, I think I'm dealing with two or more killers with completely different motivations. It's very possible our old enemies are at work here." She saw her brother nod. They'd fought side by side against the skinwalkers. She knew he understood who she had meant, and would do his best to help.

Ella led Clifford into Justine's lab. As her assistant brought out everything they had on the latest victim, the teenager they knew only as John Doe, Clifford studied the evidence without handling it. When he came to the table where the contents of the boy's pockets had been laid out, he stopped short.

"That," he gestured toward a fetish. "The boy was carrying it?"

"Yes," Justine answered. "Everything from that evidence pouch came out of the last victim's pockets. I wish we knew who he was. Maybe that would give us a lead as to his background."

Clifford looked at the fetish for a long time, then, using a pencil, turned it over. "This is no ordinary fetish. Have you run tests on it?"

Justine shook her head. "For what?"

"I believe it's a coyote fetish made out of bone. If it turns out to be carved of human bone, then I'm certain it's an item of power to the skinwalkers. I can't be sure, but I have a feeling it's very old. I don't know where the boy could have found something like this."

"Maybe it's part of the loot taken from a previous burglary," Ella said, thinking out loud, "along with the old coins. The boy found it interesting and kept it."

"That would make sense. If I'm right about that fetish, the skinwalkers will want it back." Clifford affirmed.

"One of the boy's pockets was empty, and had been turned inside out," Justine said, looking at Ella. "The same was true of the Nahlee boy, though nothing was apparently taken. My guess is his killers were searching through his clothing when you came on the scene."

"Could be. There were two others in that garage when I went inside, besides the victim."

"If you don't need me here anymore, I should be getting to the hospital," Clifford said. "Mom's still having trouble with those crutches, and I'm afraid she'll give up again unless we continue to encourage her. The handyman you had fixing up the house called me because you weren't home. He said that you wanted to know what it would take to make the rooms accessible to a wheelchair. He told me to tell you all that would be needed would be two small ramps. Fortunately our father was large, and he built the doorways and bathroom accordingly. The handyman did suggest we add a handrail in the bathroom."

"I hope the entire matter about the wheelchair won't be something we will have to deal with. I know it would be hard for Mom in the kitchen, having to keep everything she needed down low, and reaching up for the sink. And what about the garden? She's just got to work her legs and get her mobility back."

"Why don't you visit today, and bring up those points?" he added with a stern look. "We need to keep her at those crutches."

"I'll do what I can," Ella said. "And I appreciate your help with the investigation." She walked outside with her brother. "I know that dealing with things of this nature is extremely distasteful for you."

He nodded slowly. "The dead and things connected to them are repulsive to me. But these killings affect the entire tribe and I have a duty to the tribe that supersedes my own feelings. If these kids have been stealing from skinwalkers they're in mortal danger, not only from the ones who'll want back what has been stolen, but also from the items themselves. You better find out who this dead kid's relatives were. They could be in danger, too." He ran a hand through his hair. "The gangs, this theft—it's a case of the worst of the new finding the worst of the old. I'm not sure how to protect any of us."

Clifford braced one hand against the top of his pickup and stood there pensively. "Tonight I'm going to do a chant taken from the Enemy Way for our family. The prayer I have in mind is one of many evil-chasing ceremonies, but deals specifically with contamination from the outside. To me, that's what the gangs typify. They're an evil from the Anglo world that has found its way here and come to harm us."

After saying good-bye to her brother, and promising to do

what she could as a cop to help, Ella returned to her office and called for Justine and Neskahi, who was still at the station, to join her. They arrived within a few minutes.

"Justine, have you been able to determine if there's a match between the fingerprint found on that glove at the Aspass scene and the print lifted from John Doe?"

"Sorry, boss. It looks like we're on the right track, but that fingerprint lifted from the rubber glove just wasn't very distinct. There just aren't enough points of concurrence, and we need at least ten to establish a match in court." Justine shrugged.

"Then we'll have to hope the ME will be able to help us out on that burn, and that the other evidence, like shoe prints, will support the case."

She then told them what Clifford believed, adding, "We might have a bigger problem than we first thought, though the possible motives for the crimes are becoming clearer, and the John Doe might have been one of those responsible for the Aspass killing. If that fetish was taken in a burglary, it's likely that other skinwalker items were stolen as well."

Ella continued. "My brother is seldom wrong about these things, so I think his assumption that the skinwalkers will want these items of power back is probably right on target. The way I see it, we're dealing with several different sets of criminals, each intent on different goals. The Many Devils are responsible for the burglaries, and there *is* a gang war going on, but the skinwalkers may be responsible for the death of at least one of the boys involved in the burglaries, possibly both."

"Which means that deaths will continue until harmony is restored," Neskahi said. Seeing the surprised look Ella gave him, he shrugged. "I'm not a traditionalist, but sometimes their way of looking at things fits."

"You're right," Ella conceded. "Here's what I propose.

We do our best to find out if John Doe was involved in Lisa's murder, and who might have been with him. I also want all of us to do some serious digging into the religious lives of all the theft victims. This is an extremely sensitive matter, so we'll have to handle it with discretion. None of the families will thank us, and if word of what we're doing gets out, we could ruin the lives of some of these people. We all know how fast gossip travels on the Rez."

"This type of investigation will require that we ask each victim's neighbors some pointed questions," Justine said.

"I know. Just tread softly. Choose your words carefully. And Justine, see if you can track down your cousin, Thomas. I know you're having problems because he's a relative, but it would be a real help if you could get him to talk. At least, see if he can identify our John Doe. That wouldn't compromise any of his gang loyalties that I can see."

"I'll certainly make an attempt," Justine agreed.

"I suppose you'll want Lisa Aspass' religious background included?" Neskahi asked.

Ella nodded. "Just don't approach Wilson Joe on that. I'll handle that interview myself." She glanced at Justine. "Don't worry. I'll clear going solo for that with Big Ed."

Justine nodded.

As her investigators left, Ella sat back, mulling things over, but soon the telephone rang, interrupting her.

Ella picked up the receiver and recognized Carolyn Roanhorse's voice. "I've got something useful for you," Carolyn said. "Our John Doe was burned with a flammable powder of some kind. Though I haven't been able to identify it specifically, I've extracted a few grains from the blistered area on his chest. I also extracted some tiny fibers from within the wound. We can see if they match up with any from the scene. That would help place him there."

"I'll have my team check Lisa's house again for a powder that would do that, and also see if the tests on the carpet debris we vacuumed up are ready. Thanks for the info."

"Did your people ID him yet?"

"No. Justine ran his prints, but we didn't get a hit locally or with the FBI database, and they didn't match up enough with the one on the yellow glove to be conclusive. She's going to see if Thomas Bileen, her cousin, can identify the victim. Do you have anything else that might help?"

"I'm checking dental records." Carolyn paused for a moment. "Off the subject. Are you coming in to the hospital today? I think Rose really missed not seeing you yesterday."

"My brother said she was feeling down again."

"It's the physical therapy, I think. She's finding excuses for skipping sessions. It's uncomfortable for her, and the crutches are rubbing, but she has to continue it regardless of how frustrating it can be. Unless she keeps at it, her legs won't maintain enough strength to allow her to stand at all, much less progress to a cane."

Ella said nothing for several long moments.

"Hey, are you still there?"

"Yeah, I'm just thinking of something my brother told me once, a long time ago. He said that when a patient lived with a condition for a certain amount of time, the patient made his peace with it. It then became easier to accept the infirmity than it was to fight to get well. I think that's what Mom's doing. Physical therapy involves pain for her, and is very tiring. On the other hand, she's comfortable when she stays put. Since the nurses take care of all her needs, it's simpler for her to do nothing for herself. What we have to do is make things a little more uncomfortable for her."

"How? You can't ask the nursing staff to ignore a patient, or force her to use the crutches." Carolyn said.

"True, but we can try and give Mom more incentive to want to leave the hospital, even if it means sore muscles and discomfort for her with the crutches. And she'll have to convince Dr. Natoni that she'll continue physical therapy, or he won't consider releasing her."

"You've got another plan, I presume?"

"Yes, but I'll need your help with this." Ella heard Carolyn sigh, and knew she was probably rolling her eyes. "Can you get the floor nurse to call you whenever my mom has visitors?"

"I think so. Why?"

"I want you to go to her room and join her guests as often as possible."

"Why? Her friends aren't going to want me anywhere near them. Don't you remember? I'm still known to the traditionalists as the Death Doctor. The tag has become a way to describe what I do."

"That's precisely why I want you to go. Her friends will find reasons to leave in a hurry if you're around. And if they keep running into you whenever they visit, they'll cut back on their visits, or stop coming altogether. That's going to really aggravate Mom. She'll never tell you not to visit, and risk hurting your feelings, but it'll make her crazy. And it'll sure give her incentive to get out of the hospital in a hurry, even if it means working at those crutches."

Carolyn chuckled softly. "You've got an evil mind, girl."

"Yes, I do, don't I?" Ella said. "And I really do want what's best for Mom. Well, let me get a few things straightened out here, then I'll be free to go pay her a visit myself."

Thirty minutes later, Ella drove to the hospital. With each passing day, everything seemed to get more complicated. If her mother was released from the hospital while still in a wheelchair, she might need more than the ramps. Rose might also need someone at home to help her out, at least for a while.

Ella considered what taking an extended leave of absence

would do to the cases she had pending. There was no way she'd be able to ask for one with a clear conscience, not with three unsolved murders on her desk.

She thought of her duty to the tribe, then of her responsibility as a daughter, feeling like a failure on both counts. No matter what she chose to do, it would result in letting someone down. Her mother might understand if someone besides her daughter stayed with her, but would it be the right thing to do?

She wondered what it would have been like if she'd gone into another career field, with set hours and the chance to take time off for family responsibilities. But what kind of job would it be? She'd been a cop practically all her adult life. She'd never wanted any other career.

Later, as she walked down the hospital corridor, she watched the nurses. That was one job she'd never be able to do. She despised hospitals, but not because she was in any way a traditionalist. She hated the smells and the atmosphere of impending doom that surrounded hospitals. Of course that was her perception, and probably entirely psychological, but it was the way she felt.

As she entered her mother's room, Ella noticed that Mrs. Pioche and Mrs. Clani were both there. The two women, part of the Plant Watchers group, greeted her warmly, then continued the story they were telling Rose, filling her in on the latest gossip.

Just then Carolyn Roanhorse entered the room holding a jar of jelly beans. "I thought you might enjoy these," she said, offering them to Rose, who took one. Carolyn then offered some to the other women, but they declined, scooting back in their chairs and putting a little distance between themselves and the ME.

As if oblivious to their reaction, Carolyn proceeded to

monopolize the conversation, not allowing even Ella the chance to get a word in edgewise.

"I've managed to decorate my new trailer with some great antiques. I found a great little store in Farmington that has wonderful prices. I bought a trunk that dates back to the 1800s that still had some of the owner's clothing in it!"

Ella almost burst out laughing. These women would consider antiques of a personal nature repulsive and dangerous. The clothing of one who had died would be seen as contaminated by the *chindi*. She saw the horror on their faces, and realized that hearing this from the Death Doctor made it even worse for them.

It wasn't long before Mrs. Pioche and Mrs. Clani excused themselves and hurried out.

Rose gave Ella a bewildered look, but Ella pretended not to notice. "Those antiques sound beautiful. I'm going to have to make time to come by some evening. Maybe tomorrow? I can come right after work. Oh, wait. I'll have to stop and feed Two. On second thought, I'm sure he can hold out for an extra hour. I'll just set out extra chow at breakfast."

"You most certainly will *not*," Rose snapped. "That dog needs his food, particularly in this cold weather. Don't you dare neglect him like that. You *have* been making sure he has food and fresh water?"

"Sure, I feed him every morning and evening, regardless of when I get home from work. He might have skipped a few night feedings here and there though. I've got so many things going on right now it's hard to keep track of everything."

Rose's eyes blazed with anger. "You *make* time for him, regardless of your job. He needs to eat on a regular schedule, and deserves some of your attention every day. I don't want excuses. Is that very clear?"

"Well, yes, Mother. I'll do my best. By the way, I was talking to my brother, and we're making arrangements to add ramps in case you decide to keep the wheelchair instead of the crutches. The handyman can also pour a big concrete patio where your herb garden is. You can go out there in the wheelchair without getting stuck in the sand. We know how you like fresh air."

"You tell your brother and that handyman to stay away from my house. Nobody's touching my herb garden. I'm walking out of this place on my own two feet, not that stupid chair." Rose's face was animated now, her face flushed with anger.

"I'll tell him exactly what you said, Mother. Does that mean I shouldn't be looking for someone to take care of you when you're released?" Ella was on a roll.

"Nobody is going to follow me around in my own home like some baby-sitter. I'm already sick of not having any privacy here. If I need your help, I'll ask for it. Now you two leave me alone. Don't you have work to do?" Rose turned away and looked out the window.

As soon as they were out of earshot, Ella and Carolyn burst out laughing.

"What a team we make!" Carolyn managed, laughing. "First the antiques, and then her herb garden."

"Everything worked like a charm. And if you keep your end up, pretty soon nobody will be staying long when they visit. Between us, we'll have her cooperating with the doctors and literally on her feet in no time. Mom will be fighting to go back home."

Ella drove back to the station, worry clouding her features. Now that they were actively working to get Rose ready to come home, she wondered if she really would need to find someone who could come in and take care of her mother. Guilt assailed her until she remembered the hospital also had a social worker. Maybe they could find somebody Rose knew to come in and check on her from time to time. With Ella's irregular hours, there wasn't any other choice.

From the moment she walked inside the station, she knew something was up. The mood had lifted somehow. She was walking past Big Ed's office when he called out to her.

"Ella. We've finally got a break on a case, one that links up with that note you got in the mail," he said waving her to a chair.

"What's going on?"

"The preliminary hearing for the bank robbers is set for later this afternoon. FB-Eyes called me about five minutes ago. In exchange for reduced sentences and new identities, Joey and Barbara Baker will testify that the heist was arranged by The Brotherhood, and the operation was an organizational 'fund-raiser.' The one hitch is that they'll only give their statements to you."

"Me? Why?"

"I don't know, but they're behind bars and no threat. I say you go over there and play this hand out. Maybe we can get enough information from them to follow up on the threat to you."

Ella nodded. "Enough to find the hit man before he finds me," she said. "I'll give Blalock a call and set up the meet."

Ella phoned Blalock and then got underway. They'd both agreed that the Bakers' stipulation that she be present was unusual, but the payoff would be worth it. As an extra precaution, Ella decided to have Justine tail her, rather than ride along, but the trip was uneventful.

Ella parked next to the courthouse. Blalock's car was only two rows away. As she made her way around to the entrance, she saw a drunken street person leaning against the side of a store front that was adjacent to an alley. Hearing the dirty-faced Anglo woman retching loudly, people walked by quickly, turning away and trying to ignore her.

As Ella approached, a strange feeling spread over her. Her skin tingled, her heart pounded, and she felt the certainty of danger. Her badger fetish was warm, almost hot against her flesh.

Instead of looking away, like the other pedestrians were doing, instinct told Ella not to take her eyes off the woman. Something wasn't quite right, though the smell of alcohol and the bottle of cheap whisky seemed consistent with the image being projected.

She studied the vagrant carefully and realized what it was. The woman had one hand in her pocket, and the other was covered with well-made, skin-tight leather gloves. The pricey accessory didn't fit with the old, moth-eaten coat and worn scarf, and it was too warm today for gloves, even for someone who'd been outside all day.

Ella also noticed that the woman kept looking in her direction, but always avoided making eye contact. Most street people she'd come across used eye contact to keep others at a distance, because they trusted no one.

Hoping Justine would have the sense to keep back, Ella took a step into the alley to see what would happen. The woman suddenly spun around, pulling a silenced automatic pistol from her pocket. In a fluid, reflex action, Ella grabbed her attacker's wrist with her left hand, forcing the gun down and away. Simultaneously, she stepped across the woman's path, bumping into her heavily and, throwing her off balance, pushed against her while she grabbed the gun with her right hand. Using her assailant's body to gain extra leverage, Ella was able to wrestle the weapon from the woman's grip. It fell to the sidewalk.

The woman retaliated quickly, landing a hard left to Ella's stomach. Seeing the right hand coming as she tried to catch her breath, Ella dodged and grasped the woman's arm as it passed by. Moving quickly, she forced it behind the woman's back in a lock.

The woman continued to struggle and kick, though the pain must have been considerable. "Keep it up, and you'll break your own arm," Ella warned.

The woman didn't seem to hear her, or maybe just didn't care. She jerked back, hitting Ella on the chin with the back of her head. Ella tightened her grip, forcing the woman down almost to her knees. The woman tried once again to jerk free. Ella heard and felt a snap, and the woman groaned.

"You just broke your arm. Don't make this harder on yourself than you already have. Quit struggling so I can get you some medical attention."

The woman leaned forward and kicked back again, catching Ella in the stomach. As Ella staggered back, losing her grip, the woman fumbled around with her left hand inside her blouse, reaching for a backup gun in her bra.

"Leave it," Justine said.

Ella turned around. Justine had her pistol aimed right at the woman's chest. "Took you long enough," Ella muttered.

"I couldn't find a parking space."

Ella removed the backup pistol, handcuffed the woman despite the probable broken bone, then read her her rights. The woman never gave any indication that she was in pain, nor in any mood to talk. Her single-mindedness frightened Ella. Justine quickly took the names and addresses of the startled witnesses for later followup.

Blalock met them as they came through the courthouse/police station door, took one look at the prisoner, and gave Ella and Justine a surprised look. "What's this?"

"One second." Ella turned their prisoner over to a pair of Farmington cops at the booking desk, and explained briefly what had happened. Surrendering custody, after they agreed to lock up the prisoner and have a doctor look at her injury, Ella returned to where Blalock stood.

"Okay. Now we can talk," she said.

"What the hell was that all about? Did the woman throw up on your Jeep? She looks awfully pale."

Ella scowled at him. "Save it." She recounted what had taken place, showing him the backup gun and silencer-equipped pistol, both of which Justine had wrapped in a handkerchief, pending further investigation.

"Well, with those weapons in custody, and several witnesses, this won't turn into another excessive-force suit," Blalock muttered. "You think it was a set up from the beginning?"

"Yeah. The promised statement from the Bakers was probably just a way to throw me off. This must have all been part of the contract The Brotherhood put out on me."

"Let's go have our little talk with Joey and Barbara Baker," Blalock said.

"Right. I'll bet my last dime that they were the ones who put me in the path of that assassin. How else could the killer have known I was coming?"

"Let's push them with a murder-conspiracy charge and see if they crack."

"I have another idea. Shepherd seems to be the weakest link in this chain. Leave the Bakers out of the loop for a while longer. Have Shepherd brought in to us."

"Done."

Blalock led them to a conference room, just off the judge's chambers, then left to make arrangements for the prisoner to be brought in. As soon as they were alone, Ella requested a Farmington officer join them and turned to Justine. "I want you and the officer to make sure those guns are entered into evidence. Then you should go back to the booking desk and find out everything you can about the woman who attacked me. And make sure she's getting medical care. I don't want another brutality suit coming my way. Then track down the witnesses and get their statements. Blalock and I will work on Shepherd. If you find out anything that'll give us an edge, let me know right away."

As soon as the Farmington officer arrived, Justine hurried out. Blalock returned, accompanied by another Farmington officer leading Shepherd, who was handcuffed and had a chain connecting his handcuffs to leg irons. The prisoner had to walk in short, shuffling steps. Shepherd's court-appointed attorney, a young man who appeared to be fresh out of law school, entered the room a moment later, out of breath.

Shepherd sat down at a small wooden table, his wary eyes darting back and forth from Ella to Blalock.

Ella sat across the table from him in the only other chair, a tape recorder in front of her. "You're in a lot more trouble now than when you were first booked, Mr. Shepherd," she said. "You're now involved in a conspiracy to murder a police officer."

Shepherd groaned, saying nothing, but his attorney's eyes grew wider. "This is news to us. I want to hear all the charges against my client, pronto. When did all this come about?"

"Late-breaking news, counselor," Ella said. "The murder attempt took place less than an hour ago."

Shepherd leaned forward. "Wait a second. I'm no killer. A convicted thief, yes, but not a murderer, and I certainly would never be stupid enough to go after you."

Ella smiled slowly. "I didn't say there had been an attack against me."

"But I thought . . ."

"No, you didn't, you know. That's why you're in this new mess." Ella watched the prisoner squirm.

The young attorney glared at her. "Do you intend to offer

my client some kind of a deal, or are we just playing games?"

"If he's willing to turn state's evidence, we can arrange to drop some of the dozen or so charges against him, I'm sure," Blalock said.

"You're in this up to your neck, Shepherd," Ella said. "The best thing that can happen, unless you cooperate, is that you'll get twenty years in prison."

"The worst is that the judge will consider your latest trick as a third offense and that'll mean life without parole," Blalock added.

Shepherd turned one shade paler, and looked at his attorney.

The young attorney gave him a tired shrug. "That's only *if* they get a conviction. We haven't seen what they've got on you yet, so I'm not willing to assume they can."

"How can you blame me for what happened when I've been in jail all this time?" Shepherd said, looking at Ella and Blalock.

"Knowing about it makes you a co-conspirator, or at least an accessory. Where you were when you obtained that information isn't relevant."

Shepherd cursed. "I had nothing to do with trying to kill you," he repeated stubbornly.

"But by your own words, you've established before witnesses that you knew what was being planned," Ella said.

The young attorney moved closer to his client. His voice was whisper-soft, but Ella managed to hear enough of what he said to get the gist of it. "Their evidence against you, as far as it pertains to the bank robbery, is solid. Your chances of beating those charges are slim. If they can pin conspiracy to murder on you, you probably won't get the third strike, but you'll go away for a very long time. If they offer you a deal you can live with, take it."

"If I talk to you straight, you'll get me out of jail?" Shepherd asked Blalock.

"I can ask the DA to offer you a deal for a reduced sentence, and I can *guarantee* you won't be kept anywhere near the Bakers," Blalock said.

Ella saw Shepherd hesitate. "I'd take that if I were you. I don't think you've got much of a choice, really. Once we prove that you're involved in this conspiracy, your future prospects are in the hands of a local jury. People in Farmington are very unforgiving toward criminals nowadays, I hear."

Shepherd shifted in his chair, his gaze darting around like that of a trapped animal looking for an escape. "I knew about it, but I wasn't part of the plan, okay? Barb and Joey do whatever they please. They don't consult me."

"The Bakers hired the assassin?" Blalock pressed.

"Oh, hell no. They don't have enough money to buy popcorn at the movies, let alone enough to contract a hit."

"Then who?" Ella prodded, fighting the urge to shake the weasely Shepherd until his teeth rattled.

"Barbara hated you from the moment you screwed up her plan to spring Joey. She contacted Martin Miller, the lawyer who is connected to The Brotherhood. Joey said they made a deal with him to set you up in exchange for him representing them. The Brotherhood wants you dead, and they were more than happy to use Barb's help."

"Was the robbery a way to raise funds to hire the hit man?" Ella asked.

Shepherd shrugged. "I don't know about that. All I knew for sure about the robbery was that I'd get my cut after expenses. What Barb and Joey chose to do with theirs was their business as far as I was concerned."

"You'll have to testify to all this in court," Blalock said.

"I'll do it, providing you get me moved someplace back east where I know they won't be able to get to me."

"Deal," Blalock said. "Assuming the DA goes along with it. And I think she will."

"The Bakers will deny everything, though," Shepherd said, "and so will Miller, their attorney. It'll be my word against all of theirs, and Miller will argue that I'm just trying to save myself. Miller has no record, and he's one smooth cookie. By the time he's finished, wanna guess whose side the jury will be on?"

Ella didn't answer him. It wasn't necessary. They all knew Shepherd was right.

FOURTEEN

✖ ✖ ✖

Once Shepherd was taken back to his cell, Blalock glanced at Ella. "He's right, you know. His testimony won't get us a conspiracy charge unless the hit woman corroborates his story, and that's pretty unlikely. So, now what? Any ideas?"

"I'd like to get that legal cockroach, Miller," Ella said thoughtfully. "I don't see any reason to talk to the Bakers now, but can we tap his phone?"

"Not without a court order, you know that, and that's something we'll never get, not without a lot more evidence than we've got now. Miller has an established reputation as a trial attorney. He'll claim we're trying to harass him, file a lawsuit, and make it very public. That is, unless we can get the assassin to talk to us."

"Shall we question her?"

He considered it. "I'm not sure I want you along on this. You were her intended victim, and since it happened off the Rez it's out of your jurisdiction. Also, because of the brutality charges that have been leveled against you, you have a personal stake in the results of her testimony. Your presence during questioning may jeopardize the case when it comes to court."

Ella nodded slowly. "I have a feeling my attorney would probably agree with you."

"I'm a damned good agent. Trust me to do this, okay?"

She nodded. "I do, but I still would have liked to be in on it."

After a few more words with the FBI agent, Ella drove back to the reservation. She stopped at Kevin Tolino's office, which fortunately was in Shiprock instead of Window Rock, the seat of tribal government. She wanted to fill him in on this latest development. Maybe with his connections, he'd be able to question the assassin alone, or at least sit in on the questioning.

She found Kevin behind a stack of manila folders that almost blocked him from view. In that respect, his office was a lot like hers. The paperless office of the computer age had been a hoax.

Tolino waved her to a chair. "What brings you by here?"

Ella filled him in quickly. "I thought you'd want to know about this as soon as possible."

"Thanks. I'll get over to Farmington and persuade Blalock to let me in to question this woman."

"Is there some way you can get me in on it, too?"

Kevin shook his head. "I can understand you wanting to be there, but Blalock's right. It's a bad idea. You're too close to the case after what happened. If you really want to do something useful, why don't you follow up on those booking photos on Gladys Bekis? Check again with everyone who was at the jail when she came in and may have seen her. Maybe there were onlookers there besides police personnel. See what you can get me."

Just then, the phone rang, and Kevin picked up the receiver. Ella was about to leave, but Kevin gestured silently for her to stay. Though she couldn't hear the other side of the conversation, Ella caught enough to surmise the call was about Leo Bekis, the drunk responsible for her mother's accident. Tolino's expression was grim when he hung up the phone.

"Bad news?" Ella asked.

Kevin nodded. "You might say that. At least some things never change in the justice system."

"Let me guess. That cockroach is out of jail." Ella's voice was strained.

"At least his license was pulled this time. Until there's a hearing, he's been forbidden to drink or drive." Kevin shrugged. "His friends could only do so much when faced with the bad publicity you gave him."

"I wish I could have done more than that. What are the odds he'll follow the court orders?" Ella knew the only way to insure his compliance was to have someone follow Bekis around, and that would never happen. They just didn't have the manpower. "Alcoholics drink no matter what they promise."

"Let's hope his family will look out for him. Their name has been dragged through the mud, too. Just see that you stay away from him, Ella." Kevin warned.

"I'm not making any promises," she said, stepping out the door.

As Ella headed back to the station, she thought about everything that had happened recently—her mother, Lisa Aspass' murder, the gang violence. The world she knew was being torn apart by hate and violence. Her efforts to prevent that seemed no more effective than stomping out a forest fire with her boot.

As she pulled into the station, she saw Neskahi running out toward his vehicle. She called out to him.

He hurried over to her car. "We got word that the leader of the Many Devils, Franklin Ahe, wants to meet with you across from the storage tanks south of town in an hour. I'm heading out now to check out the place, to make sure nobody else is trying to set you up. I know the area, it's near where old man Nez runs his fruit stand in the fall."

"What about someone from the North Siders? Any word from them?"

"I've been told their leader won't meet with you or go anywhere where the Many Devils might be. He thinks it's a trick."

"Then let it be. I'll meet with Ahe."

"Big Ed insists you wear a vest and have backup close by. I agree that a little caution wouldn't hurt."

Ella nodded, then went inside to her office. She generally hated to wear vests, but Big Ed was right. Besides, this was why she'd purchased her own, a lightweight, more comfortable model than police issue, that was still highly effective. It had cost her a month's salary and it was worth every penny. Ella fastened it on beneath her loose-fitting pullover sweater. As she walked back toward the door, Justine suddenly appeared.

"I'm riding backup with you," Justine said.

Ella shook her head. "You'll have to keep your distance. I'm going in alone so I won't spook anyone. That was the deal."

"At least meet him out in the open; that way Neskahi and I can watch," Justine said. "It's the only other logical choice."

Ella considered it. If Big Ed found out that she'd been without protection after he called for backup, he'd be furious, and the last thing she needed right now was to shake her boss's confidence in her judgment. "Okay, but make sure you don't get close enough to be seen," Ella warned. "These guys are likely to start blasting at the drop of a hat."

"Call the sergeant back then, and I'll ride along with him," Justine said. "The fewer cars, the better."

Ella watched the clock, waiting for the proper time. Then she drove south of Shiprock several miles to where the storage tanks were standing, making no attempt to hide her approach. The oil facility was west of the highway, and there was a small shack across the road on the east side where old man Nez sold fruit and vegetables after the harvest. It was impossible to sneak up on that location unless one approached from directly west of the oil tanks, using them as a screen. This would have to be done on foot, though, and whoever approached would still have to cross the road at close range to reach the shack.

Ella used the cellular to communicate with Neskahi and Justine, just in case the kids had managed to get ahold of a police-band radio. Instructing them again to stay at their selected vantage point on a low hill farther north, she drove off the road, close enough to the shack for anyone inside to see her.

She stepped out and called out to Ahe. "You know who I am. I want to talk to you."

Ahe shouted at her from inside the cabin. "I'm not going out there where any sniper can blow me away."

"If I'd wanted you dead, we wouldn't be talking now. I would have sent a SWAT team with tear gas and automatic weapons."

Silence was her only answer. Finally, Ahe replied. "Go around behind the shack, out of sight from the road. We'll both have cover there from drive-bys."

Ella understood what he meant. Gang strategy was usually limited to driving up and blasting away indiscriminately until the targets went down or the shooters ran out of bullets. At least this way, he was protecting himself somewhat.

She walked around the shed cautiously, knowing that Neskahi and Justine were probably not thrilled about this new development. She wasn't even sure if they could still see her through their binoculars.

She was standing about ten feet behind the light wood frame structure when one of the wide boards swung up and Ahe appeared. As he came through the opening, she heard metal scrape against the wood. This told her he probably had a pistol stuck in his belt at the small of his back. Her own weapon was in its pancake holster at her belt, and Ahe could see it clearly. She wasn't about to go into a dangerous situation unarmed. She didn't watch enough television detectives to be that stupid.

Ahe was a sturdy-looking eighteen-year-old, almost her height, and he outweighed her by a good fifty pounds. He had a trace of hair where a beard would be on an non-Navajo, but probably wouldn't grow much more due to his heredity. His face bore scars of recent fights, and his black eyes seemed expressionless. It was that cold lack of humanity that told her he was destined for prison, or an early grave. He was undoubtedly the one in the back seat the night she and Justine went 'low riding.'

"Okay, I'm here. What do you want?" he snapped.

"I want to talk to you about the murder of another one of your homies last night. We don't know his name, so we haven't been able to tell his family about his death. Do you know who it might be?"

"I think it could be a new guy, we call him Shopper, because he likes to go 'shopping' in houses when the people aren't home. He comes from over by Holbrook somewhere, I think. I don't know his name."

"Did he have a burn on his chest?"

"You tell me. I just look at girls' chests." He leered at Ella. She took comfort in the knowledge that she'd been trained to gouge an attacker's eyes in hand-to-hand combat, and continued with her questions now that he was talking.

"This Shopper, if that's who it was, had some evidence on him that leads us to believe that neither his killing nor the death of George Nahlee have anything to do with the Siders. There is someone else, not a gang, responsible for taking out the two Many Devils."

"We're at war with the North Siders now, and nobody's gonna stop fighting till it's settled. If anyone gets in our way, we'll take them on, too. We're not afraid to die, and threats don't work on us."

Ahe spoke like a terrorist, willing to sacrifice as many lives as necessary in order to gain attention and respect. That knowledge frightened her. "You're in the big leagues on this one, and talking tough won't impress anyone. When you started burglarizing homes, you made the mistake of picking the wrong victim, and somebody is punishing the Many Devils for that. You've probably already heard how brutal your adversaries are. They don't fight, they just catch you alone and take you out. You don't have a chance against them unless you pay some attention to what I'm telling you."

Ahe laughed. "You're jerking my chain, right? The Many Devils taking advice from the cops?"

"Do you have any idea what you're up against?"

"It's that skinwalker crap one of our guys found, right?" Ahe shook his head. "That scary stuff is for old people. I heard they just smoke loco weed, mess with dead people, and run around naked."

Ella's eyebrows rose. This boy was so out of touch with Navajo culture she was surprised he even knew the word 'skinwalker.' Ahe didn't have a clue about the forces he was up against. Maybe she could relate to him on another level. "Crazy people are often the most dangerous."

"We'll deal with grandma and grandpa if they ever get

in our way. Right now, the North Siders are looking for guns, and the Fierce Ones are getting in everybody's face, making threats and all. They want us to be schoolboys or something. If they keep it up, I can guarantee that some of the Fierce Ones will go down, too. In the end, the Many Devils will be standing tall. You better learn to respect us."

As he walked around to the front of the shed, Ella stood there, shaking her head as she noted the .32 pistol stuck in his waistband. There wasn't going to be any easy way to stop this. The gangs had their own agenda. More kids would die in the power struggle, and for what? The right to paint their names and slogans on somebody else's walls? Worst of all, after the smoke cleared, not even the survivors would be able to escape the payment their chosen lifestyle would exact. Kids joined a gang for life—which often turned out to be miserably short.

Ella got back into her car and drove out to meet with Neskahi and Justine. Joining them, she played back Ahe's conversation on the small, voice-activated tape recorder she'd carried in her pocket. "As you heard, it was a complete waste of time, except for this Shopper gang name. Those kids want to square off, and Ahe is enjoying the control and power. The more deaths there are, the more he'll use the kids' anger and thirst for revenge to continue the fight."

Neskahi exhaled softly. "That's what I figured you'd be up against. I've heard a lot about this kid from a uniform who knows him and his family. He's about as far gone as a kid his age can get. Even his family doesn't want to have anything to do with him. They're afraid of him, and he knows it."

As Neskahi started back to his vehicle, Justine turned to follow, but Ella called her back. "Ride back with me. I have some work to do at the station, but I'd like you to find Thomas one way or the other, and get him to identify Shopper, our John Doe. I know you've been trying, but I suspect his mother may be covering for him. If he's not at home, have someone stake out the place and detain him if he shows up."

Ella and Justine were back at the station in ten minutes. Justine got on the phone, trying to locate her cousin Thomas, while Ella stopped by the booking desk. It only took a quick look at the photo in Gladys Bekis' file to bring a smile to Ella's face. The image, a sharp close-up, failed to reveal any marks on her face at all. After making arrangements to have the photo enlarged and a copy faxed to Kevin Tolino, Ella went searching for Justine. Just as Ella spotted her assistant near the front desk, hanging up the phone, she received a call on her hand held.

The call was from Neskahi. "Can you switch to channel six?"

"Ten-four." Ella switched frequencies. "Whatcha need?"

"I heard from Principal Duran at the high school. One of the teachers overheard that the Many Devils have called out the North Siders this afternoon. Ahe says he wants to hold a council, but nobody is buying it. They know it's his way of calling for a final showdown. All available officers have been ordered on duty or standby, but even so, there won't be enough of us. Additional units have been requested. The problem is that it'll take time for some of them to get here from Window Rock and farther west."

"Then the Siders are really going to show?" Ella asked.

"Yeah, it looks that way, and you can bet they'll come ready for a fight."

"Okay—when and where?"

"The fair grounds, sometime today—maybe after dark. That time is only a guess, though. The way I'm figuring it is that the Many Devils are outnumbered so they'll want to hide that fact from the Siders, and they can do that best at night."

Justine, having walked up during the conversation,

shifted, facing Ella. "Should we go over there and take a look?"

Ella nodded, her body tensing. She knew trouble was coming, she could feel it with every beat of her heart. Ahe was into power, and he'd use anything at his disposal to create the tension needed for a confrontation. He didn't care about the boys in his gang, nor about the cost of his actions.

"Why don't we just stake out the entire area? If they see us there, they'll back off," Justine said as they ran to her Jeep.

Ella shook her head. "If we do that, they'll just switch the location or the time of the fight, and then we may not find out about it until it's over. We have to take them by surprise after everyone is on the scene, and arrest as many as we can before they start shooting. If we can fill up our jail for a day or two, that will buy us and them some time. With luck, some of the boys will have the chance to reconsider their actions."

Less than five minutes later, as Ella pulled into the fairgrounds, she caught a glimpse of a familiar figure by the rodeo arena, talking to two men working on a fence. "Billy Pete! I've been trying to find that guy ever since we had that cryptic phone conversation." She pulled to a stop, and hurried over to the group.

Billy saw her and leaned back against the wooden railing, regarding her with polite disinterest. "It's good to see you, Ella."

"Don't give me that." Ella said, gesturing for him to leave the others so they could talk privately. "The Fierce Ones got wind of what the gangs were planning, right?"

"I'm here because I knew you would be come, too, eventually. I'd like to talk to you."

"What about?" Her skin was prickling. Billy was acting way too cool, too controlled, and it made her nervous because it wasn't like him.

"I heard something interesting—that there's a chance the skin . . . evil ones are involved in the murders of those last two boys. Is this true?"

Ella considered her words carefully, knowing that, despite all his evasions, Billy Pete was here on behalf of the Fierce Ones. "We have some evidence that indicates Navajo witches are involved. But the gangs are still responsible for a lot of the trouble that's been going on."

"The Fierce Ones can handle the kids and their parents. They could also protect your family. You and your particular skills are needed to take care of the tribe's old enemies."

Ella shook her head. "The Fierce Ones can't help with the gangs, not without interfering in police business," Ella said, struggling to keep her temper, "and that will only muddy the waters more."

"You don't see it, do you?" Billy said, also exasperated. "The police department doesn't have a chance to stop the gangs. You don't have the manpower, and the law prevents you from making them see the light."

"You think the Fierce Ones can do all that?"

"We have more options, and more ways of controlling them. We can put pressure on the community, because we are part of it. The problems won't be solved overnight though."

Ella met his gaze. "All societies have ways of putting pressure on individuals, I know that. But when that involves using fear and intimidation against others to achieve a goal, the solution starts becoming part of the problem."

"Groups that are a threat to our tribe have already declared war on the *Dineh*. Gangs of kids, or more ancient foes—it doesn't really matter which source we're talking about. Either way, The People have to take care of it. The Navajo police can do just so much and, so far, that hasn't been very much at all," Billy commented.

"The Fierce Ones can help us, but not by taking matters

into their own hands. Let us know when you hear of trouble and keep your eyes open. Pass us whatever information you uncover that might help us identify the kids behind the burglaries or solve the murders. Peer pressure is one thing, threats are another."

"What about the other threat? The one we both know exists but will never make the evening news? Who will deal with the evil ones?"

"People like my family, and the others who have fought them before. But first I have to identify our old enemies and find out what they have to do with all this." Ella exhaled softly. "Now tell me, will the Fierce Ones help by keeping clear of the trouble, or will we have to keep looking over both shoulders?"

"I'm sure your words will be considered, but I can't speak for anyone. Who knows what will happen?"

Ella heard her call sign come over the radio at her belt. Picking up the call, she spoke to Justine.

"There's no sign of any kids yet. Neskahi is at the highway turnoff and, although several cars have gone by, the gangs are nowhere in sight. Get my binoculars out and keep a sharp watch.

"We'll look on it as luck turning our way. Now we have time for our extra officers to arrive and position themselves." Ella looked around and, except for a half dozen empty cars and pickups and the old fairgrounds dump truck and backhoe, the vast parking area was empty.

Ella focused on Billy Pete as he turned and walked away, heading toward the exhibit hall. "Take my message to the others," she called out, "and do your best to sway them."

Ella was walking back to her Jeep when Justine stuck her head out the window, binoculars in one hand, and yelled. "I think its about to happen. One car is coming in on a back road, and another is moving toward it from across country. Both vehicles are full of teenagers. The cars should meet just north of the main exhibit building unless they veer off. I've called in all available local backup from the station, and Neskahi is coming our way."

Ella jumped into the Jeep, gunned the engine, and raced across the parking lot to intercept the incoming vehicles. Suddenly the dump truck roared to life, and swung out in front of her. She swerved to avoid a collision, and rammed a large plastic waste bin, sending it tumbling across the gravel lot.

The dump truck picked up speed, moving away from Ella and Justine with black smoke billowing from the twin stacks like dragon's breath. Two vehicles full of kids turned parallel to each other, oblivious to the approaching dump truck. It was apparent that they intended on pulling up alongside and blazing away at each other.

Ella raced toward the action, but she was too far away to interfere with what happened next.

The massive truck skidded around, crunching into the rear fender of the closest vehicle. The car spun like a top, then rolled slowly over onto its side as it slipped into a shallow drainage ditch.

The truck circled, turning toward the remaining car like a bull going after a farmhand who'd wandered into the wrong pasture.

"Who's driving that dump truck? He's using it like a battering ram!" Justine's fingers clutched the edge of her seat as Ella sped toward the action.

"We've got to stop that truck first. Then we'll worry about the rest."

The kids in the second car did their best to get out of the way, heading out across the desert. One boy stuck a handgun out the window to fire at the approaching truck, but the weapon bounced out of his hand as the car fishtailed and pitched across the uneven ground.

"Neskahi. Where are you?" Ella called out into the mike.

"Coming around the exhibit hall from the south. Is the dump truck chasing that car?"

"He's trying to ram them. See if you can cut off the car before it reaches the highway, but stay away from that truck. He'll squash you like an old beer can."

Just then the fleeing car reached the fairgrounds road. It quickly increased the distance between it and the slower, lumbering dump truck, which continued its relentless pursuit, undeterred.

The gang car reached the highway and swung out onto the pavement right in front of an oncoming pickup, which skidded off onto the shoulder, fortunately remaining upright. The dump truck slowed down and, instead of following, veered in the opposite direction, driving into the parking lot of the Stop and Shop. There, it came to a stop.

"Break off pursuit, Sergeant," Ella ordered Neskahi over the radio. "Call the paramedics and go back to the rollover. Just be careful when you approach. I think the kids inside are armed."

By the time Ella reached the highway, the other gang car was out of sight, heading across the bridge. Calling for a unit to try and cut them off, Ella pulled into the Stop and Shop parking lot.

A quick check confirmed that the dump truck, still running, had been abandoned. While Justine reached in to turn off the engine, Ella checked the two cars parked next to the front sidewalk of the market. They were both unoccupied.

No one in the store would say if the driver had entered, so, after taking the names of all the shoppers and employees,

Ella and Justine left to check on the gang car that had been struck by the truck.

Neskahi and another arriving officer had eight young men facedown on the ground. The kids, whose colors suggested they were North Siders, were bruised and scratched, but otherwise appeared unhurt. In the open trunk of Neskahi's unit were three pistols and a sawed-off shotgun, plus ammunition and a collection of knives and clubs.

"Where's the rescue unit?" Ella asked.

"It's on it's way."

Ella felt the air around her grow heavier. Her worst nightmare had come true. The kids were carrying guns now, and it would only be a matter of time before innocent bystanders were caught up in the lawlessness of the gangs. Today, they'd made some arrests but, unless any had previous records, they'd all be out on bail within a day or so.

Ella took another look at the weapons in the back of Neskahi's unit, then slammed the trunk in disgust. Then she heard the paramedics approaching.

Ten minutes later Ella was able to talk to one of the EMTs. "What's the story on these kids? Do any seem seriously hurt?"

"No, they'll live. They're bruised, mostly, and a few have some minor cuts. None will require a hospital visit, it appears. They were packed in like sardines in that car, and that must have kept them from being bounced around too much."

"Maybe we can squeeze one of them and find out where they got the firearms," Justine said.

Ella doubted it, but she didn't say anything. No sense in letting her own frustration dampen her assistant's optimism.

Ella turned the scene over to another arriving team of officers, then returned to the Jeep with Justine. "I have to stop for gasoline before we head back to the station."

"While we're there, I think I'll get a cup of coffee for myself. I'm freezing. Can I get something for you?"

"Yeah, some hot chocolate. It beats that place's coffee hands down."

While Ella pumped the gasoline, Justine went inside. She returned a short time later and handed Ella her styrofoam cup of chocolate and a tribal newspaper. "The press is giving us a break finally."

Finished filling the tank, Ella read the headlines. "Secret Society Brings New Era of Hate." The article that followed linked both the bank robbery and the assassination attempt to The Brotherhood. "Oh, those boys are going to have fits when they find out their secret organization is front page news."

"The Farmington and Albuquerque papers also ran the story."

"Which means the local TV stations won't be far behind. This publicity will not only discredit The Brotherhood, it will make them well known to the public." Ella smiled mirthlessly. "Of course they'll blame me for this, and will strike out somehow. Only now, they can't hide behind a cloak of secrecy. Things are going to change. We'll just have to see if it's for the better."

FIFTEEN
------ ✖ ✖ ✖ ------

Ella arrived at her office at dusk, harboring the hope that today she'd get out in time to visit her mom. But as she walked in, the phone was ringing. Grumbling under her breath, she picked it up. It was her attorney, Kevin Tolino.

"Thanks for the photo. This will be very helpful in blowing the Gladys Bekis suit clear out of the water. I plan to use it wisely. And in return, I've got interesting news for you," he said.

"I like good news, but I'm not so sure about 'interesting.' What's up?"

"I've been told by one of the Bekis attorneys, Robert Kauley, that they are calling a press conference in about an hour concerning the accusations both have made against you and the department. I'll be there personally, of course, and you may want to catch it on Channel Thirteen, if you can grab a free moment."

Ella thanked Kevin, then hung up and dialed the hospital. She hadn't checked on her mother since this morning, and even though she felt terribly guilty about it, she simply hadn't been able to find five minutes to call her all day. On a hunch, Ella asked for Carolyn Roanhorse's extension. The ME's tone was definitely cheery.

"Have I got great news for you!"

"I sure could use some. What's going on?"

"I've been making sure to stop in on your mother as often as I can. The nurse there calls me whenever Rose has company. This morning as I was about to interrupt a visit, I heard Mrs. Pioche telling your mom that the Plant Watchers wouldn't be back, but that they would visit her often once she was home. She said that the women from the Weavers Guild felt the same way."

Ella smiled wryly. "So Mom's working those legs and using the crutches?"

"Better. She made a bargain with Dr. Natoni. If she's allowed to go home, she'll come back for therapy as often as he wants."

Ella sucked in her breath. She hadn't counted on this, and wasn't at all sure how she could swing it on her work schedule.

"I know what you're thinking," Carolyn continued. "You're scared to death that you won't be able to drive her in for the therapy. Well, get this. Dr. Natoni thinks she'll be able to drive herself if she gets a vehicle with an automatic transmission."

"That's great. Leo Bekis' insurance company hasn't settled yet, but when they do, I'll make sure mom gets a car or truck with automatic. In the meantime, her own insurance provides for a rental car, and hardly any of them are standard. Things just might work out. My schedule's been crazy, and Clifford has patients all over the Rez."

"If Rose can't drive, how about your sister-in-law, Loretta? Isn't she still at home with the baby?"

"Yes, but she doesn't drive at all. Never learned." Ella leaned back in her seat. "I'd like to know I'd be around to bring Mom in whenever she needs, but criminals refuse to follow a set schedule. Certainly I'll try."

"I've noticed the same with patients at the hospital. Nobody seems to get sick or injured at convenient times. Fortunately, those I work with personally aren't *ever* in a hurry. But don't worry, I have an idea. Alice Willie is the social worker, and they have drivers who transport patients who don't have vehicles or can't drive. All Rose would have to do is schedule a hospital visit a day ahead. And if she's able to drive herself, that won't even be necessary. Do you want me to catch Alice and ask if she can put your mother on her list?"

"Yes, do that. I'd really appreciate it. I'll be there in another thirty minutes or so. Then I can give Mom the good news."

Ella told Justine where she could be reached, then set out for the hospital. Ella drove into the hospital parking lot, and after checking her watch, walked quickly into the building.

As she reached her mother's room, Ella saw that Rose had already packed. She was sitting with her crutches beside her and a paper sack of belongings on her lap. "I'm ready to leave as soon as you are."

"Did Dr. Natoni release you already?"

"Well, not exactly. I mean, not in so many words. He agreed to my plan for therapy, and I'm getting around fine on the crutches now, so I figure it'll be okay if I leave."

"Let me have him paged. I can't just take you out of here, then find out that there's been a misunderstanding." Ella looked at her watch again.

"Are you in a hurry, Daughter?"

"A press conference is about to start on TV. The man who caused your accident, and his sister, are going to be there with their lawyers. I heard they're going to make a statement."

Rose gestured toward the TV set mounted on the wall.
"Turn it on. Whatever concerns you, also concerns me. Let's
hear what those liars have to say for themselves."

As Ella switched it on, she noted Rose's calm expression.

"I think this is going to be good news for you," Rose said.

"One of your . . . feelings?"

Rose nodded slowly. "But I can't guarantee that my positive attitude isn't being influenced by the newspaper articles the hospital staff has been talking about. Things are
getting brighter for you. The paper has been investigating
The Brotherhood, trying to prove its existence. Now that it's
been confirmed, The People are angry that they've dared attack one of our own—you."

The significance of that wasn't wasted on Ella. When
she'd first returned to the Rez over two years ago, she'd
longed for that acceptance, although she'd despaired of ever
getting it. Now she was begining to see that it had been given
to her sometime after she'd stopped reaching for it. She no
longer heard the term "LA Woman" murmured behind her
back, or used directly when people spoke to her. The joy that
realization might have given her, however, was lost under the
weight of her present responsibilities.

"Turn up the volume," Rose said.

Ella did, noting Gladys Bekis had already appeared on
screen in front of several microphones. "I've dropped the
lawsuit for excessive force against Special Investigator Ella
Clah of the Navajo Police Department." Ella noted Gladys
was reading from a written statement. "Don't get me wrong.
The incident happened just as I said it did but, after careful
consideration, I've accepted the fact that I won't be able to
find justice in a community where police are allowed to harass and abuse law-abiding citizens without fear of reprisal."

It was then that one of the local television reporters asked
the question foremost in Ella's mind. "Your comments sound

like the sort of rhetoric we would expect from someone who felt they would be unable to prove their case if it went to trial. As a matter of fact, members of the press were just shown a photo taken at the police station twenty minutes after the alleged incident, and your face was unmarked. How do you explain the discrepancy?"

Gladys's attorney, Wainwright, stepped up from the side, and spoke before Gladys could respond.

"We haven't seen any photo, though I understand Officer Clah's attorney has made one available to reporters. I have to tell you though, it wouldn't surprise me at all to learn that the tribal police had one doctored up to protect their own rogue cop."

Robert Kauley, Leo Bekis's attorney stepped up to the microphones next. "My client, distinguished tribal attorney Leo Bekis, has advised me that he is willing to drop his defamation of character suit against Investigator Clah as well, on the condition that Investigator Clah make a public apology concerning her unfounded allegations concerning my client. If such apology is not made within twenty-four hours, we will continue to pursue this litigation in court."

The same reporter as before had a question ready immediately. "Do you think Mr. Bekis's prior arrests on DWI, and the blood alcohol results on his recent accident will influence Investigator Clah's decision concerning the appropriateness of an apology?"

"I'm sorry, I can't answer any questions related to a pending legal action." Kauley responded quickly. "Investigator Clah can bring all this to a satisfactory conclusion with an apology."

"He expects *me* to apologize. That son-of-a—" With effort, Ella clamped her mouth shut.

"Don't be upset, Daughter. Some will believe this nonsense, but the majority won't. At least you won't have to face the ridiculous claim that you hit that woman. And once Leo Bekis is convicted of DWI again, and I'm sure he will be, his lawsuit will no longer be a threat. I think he's bluffing, hoping you'll apologize before he appears in court. He's trying anything to save his reputation."

"I think you're right. I'll have to ask my lawyer what he thinks, but I bet Kevin Tolino already knows I'd never apologize to that drunk. Once Leo's twenty-four hours run out, he'll probably drop the suit just like his sister did."

"Then let's talk about something else more pleasant, like getting me out of here?" Rose laughed.

Dr. Natoni came into the room, and seeing Rose packed and ready to go, laughed. "Boy, you don't waste any time."

"You said I could leave as long as I came back for therapy, Doctor."

"Yes, but I never said you could check out today."

Ella felt her stomach drop when she saw the disappointment on her mother's face. "Don't you think Mother is strong enough to use the crutches and get around at home? I'd heard she was doing much better. I can try and take a day or two off, and I'm sure my brother and our friends will help keep an eye on her when I can't be there."

"That's not necessary," Rose said. "You'll keep searching for criminals, just like you've been trained to do. I will look after myself."

"Is she ready for that?" Ella asked Dr. Natoni.

Dr. Natoni looked at Rose, then back at Ella. "Let me examine her one more time before I say anything else. Come back in about twenty minutes."

As Ella walked out into the hall, she saw Carolyn approaching.

"I was just on my way to talk to you," Carolyn said.

"Did you catch Alice Willie?"

"Yes, I sure did, and she's glad to help out with transportation. Apparently she owes Rose quite a few favors, and was happy for the chance to repay her."

Ella breathed a sigh of relief. "Well, that's one worry off my mind. I'm pretty sure I can get Clifford or Loretta to look in on her often during the day, and I'll be there as much as I can. But if Dr. Natoni tells me that she's going to need someone to stay with her full time, I'm not at all sure I can take off work, with things being the way they are now. Who can I get?"

"Alice has a list of volunteers who can spend a half day or more at a time helping around the house. She posted that list in every department of the hospital, even mine. I can recommend some people to you from that list."

Hearing footsteps behind her, Ella turned her head and saw Dr. Natoni. "Is Mom ready to come home?" she asked.

"I think so. She gave a demonstration on those crutches that makes her look like a pro. I think keeping her here for another day would do more harm than good at this point. Her frame of mind is extremely important, and the boost she'll get from being released will help her far more than an extra day here."

"Can she take care of herself without help?"

"I think so, but I'd like someone around for the first several hours, at least. Then, maybe you or someone could drop by once or twice during the day, just to make sure she hasn't hurt herself somehow. Crutches can trip you up, too. Pushing a full-time companion on her now would probably be a mistake. She needs to know that she can cope when she's by herself."

"All right. I'll take care of everything," Ella replied.

"Good. Then I'll go ahead and sign her release papers, and you can take her home. If there are any problems, day or night, have her call me immediately."

Ella said good-bye to Carolyn, went to help her mother

with her things, and found that Rose had already walked out into the hallway. "I hope you're ready," Rose said. "I've been stuck here long enough, and some of the Plant Watchers promised to come visit me this evening."

A nurse came up and, brushing aside Rose's protests, escorted her down the long hallway in a wheelchair as Ella walked beside them, carrying her bag of possessions and the crutches. "I don't want you to overdo it, Mom, or you'll end up back here."

"How can I overdo? I'll have these sticks to lean on," she said, pointing at the crutches. "But at least I'll have my privacy, and Two will keep me company when no one else is around." She sniffed. "You'll be stopping by once in a while during work, I expect."

Ella felt her chest tighten. "I thought about asking Big Ed for some time off."

Rose's eyes grew narrow. "And what would you do, sit around and watch me like I was some toddler?"

"I could catch up on my paperwork, I guess," Ella said with a tiny smile.

Rose burst out laughing. "We'd both be better off if you were at work. You're not much good at goofing off."

"I am serious about getting some leave." Ella said. "Let me know if you'd like me to."

Rose studied her daughter's expression as they went out to the Jeep, but she remained quiet until they were underway and alone. Then Rose took a deep breath. "Police work is the job you've given your life to, and it's part of who you are. If you get away from it for more than a few hours, you get restless."

"I know," Ella admitted, "but I have a responsibility to you, too." She was about to explain how guilty she's felt over not visiting the hospital more, when she heard her call sign over the radio.

Ella picked it up, identified herself, and received the report of a 10-25.

"What's going on? I couldn't make out a word through all that static," Rose asked as Ella placed the mike back.

"It takes practice. They're asking me to go meet a neighbor of Wilson's murdered fiancée," she said, avoiding Lisa's name out of respect for her mother's beliefs. To speak of the recently deceased by name to a traditionalist like her mother would be inappropriate, and according to many, dangerous. "Apparently, my teacher friend went inside the house this morning, and hasn't been seen since. I'll go check it out as soon as I get you home."

"No. Don't worry about me being with you. Let's go now. I'll wait in the Jeep. Your friend may be in trouble," Rose said in a tone that broached no argument. "He shouldn't have gone in there again anyway."

"All right, we'll go," Ella said, and called in her response.

At the speed she traveled, it didn't take long to arrive. As reported, Wilson's truck was in the driveway. As Ella parked in front of the house, she saw her mother tense up. "Are you sure you're okay with this?" As a traditionalist, the last place Rose would want to be near is the home of someone who had been killed in a violent way. That she had insisted on coming was an indication of her fondness for Wilson.

"Go inside and do whatever is necessary. I'll be fine out here."

Ella saw Lisa's neighbor step out onto her front porch. Before Ella reached her, the middle-aged Navajo woman gestured toward Lisa's house and Wilson's truck, then went back inside. Ella understood the signal. The woman had helped all she was going to. She was also afraid of the house.

Ella tried the front door of Lisa's home, and found it closed but not locked. Opening it, she went inside. There was still something about this house that felt wrong. She looked around, unable to identify the source of her uneasiness, wondering if it was just a case of imagination mingled with nerves.

"It's Ella," she said loudly.

A moment later, Wilson stepped out of the hall closet, a handful of folded clothing in his hands. "I'm here."

Ella felt her heart go out to him. He'd lost weight over the past few days, and he looked as if he hadn't slept in a very long time. She smelled what she thought was liquor, and wondered if Wilson had been drinking. She dismissed the thought immediately. Wilson never drank at all. It was probably cleaning fluid or rubbing alcohol that had spilled somewhere while he was going through the closets.

"What are you doing here?" She spoke softly. "You've got the neighbors worried. They saw you come in hours ago, but no one's seen you since then."

He gestured to several large boxes stacked against the wall. "I'm going through her things. I figure I'd give the clothing to an Anglo church group outside the Rez, so they can distribute them to the poor. Since you're here, why don't you go through the cupboard and put the non-perishables you find there into a sack for me to take along with the rest. No Navajo would touch that food if it was known where it came from."

"Okay, just let me go tell my mother everything is all right. I also need to let dispatch know the same."

Ella was back in three minutes. She went to the kitchen cupboards and looked inside. They were barren except for a dozen or so cans of vegetables and fruits, mostly sliced peaches. "There's not much here. How about putting these in one of the boxes with the clothes?"

"Sure. Go ahead."

Ella looked inside the small built-in pantry. Except for one plastic bag of herbs, and an unopened can of coffee, there wasn't anything else in there. Curious about the herbs, she opened the bag and sniffed the contents. The sickeningly sweet aroma seemed to squeeze the oxygen right out of her lungs. Closing the bag quickly, she clung to the door for support.

"These herbs," she asked, managing to find her voice, "What is this stuff?"

"Oh *that!* Throw the bag out. It's one of Lisa's home remedies, a blend she made up. She was convinced it was good for everything from poor circulation to indigestion, but it tastes like swamp water when it's brewed. She made tea for me with it every time I came over. The stuff is foul, but I didn't want to hurt her feelings."

Ella placed the coffee can in one of the boxes, then put the tea in the trash. Herbs were common on the Rez, and people who knew enough to mix their own teas usually had their own specialty blends, like her mother. Rose, in fact, had her own blend for just about everything. With the exception of her mint tea, though, most of it tasted and looked like water that had been scooped out of a mud puddle.

"Okay, the food is in the boxes," she called out, and then went to join him. "I better go now, though. Mom's still waiting in the Jeep. She's finally gotten released from the hospital today."

"Why didn't you ask her to come—" He shook his head. "I'm not thinking. I was about to make a very dumb suggestion."

"When she heard you were here, she insisted on coming to check on you, before I could even get a chance to drop her off. She was worried about you. We both were."

"I'm sorry I haven't been by the hospital for a visit, but I don't think I could cheer anyone up right now."

"Then just come out and say hello to her," Ella suggested.

Wison shook his head. "Not when I've been handling the personal effects of someone who's passed away," he said.

"Normally, I'd agree with you, but I think she'd like to see you anyway, just so she could confirm that you're okay."

Wilson shook his head again. "I have to finish this now, while I still can. Some other time. Do you have anything new to tell me concerning the crime?"

"We have a dead gang member we think might have been one of the killers, but we still haven't been able to confirm his identity. Once we do that, we hope to find out who his partner was. I'll let you know when we make an arrest."

"Thanks. I just hope whoever it was doesn't kill someone else in the meantime." Wilson's voice was starting to take on that harsh edge again, and Ella knew it was time to leave.

"Promise you'll give my mother a call soon, or come by. I think it would be good for both of you."

Wilson agreed.

When Ella finally joined her mother back in the Jeep, Rose seemed more tense than ever.

Rose gazed at the house in silence, then looked away. "There's something bad coming from that woman's house," she said, avoiding the mention of names. "You must have felt it, it's so strong."

Ella nodded. "I know what you mean." The feeling had been strong, all right, though she wasn't sure she'd attribute it to anything more than the knowledge that a particularly violent crime had occurred there.

"How's your friend? He really shouldn't stay in that house."

"He's packing up his fiancée's things," Ella answered.

Rose shook her head. "He should walk away from it all," she said. "It's not our way to handle things that belonged to the dead, and he knows that, whether he's a progressive or not. This house should be abandoned, too, or sold to an Anglo. Wilson is behaving very dangerously because of her. I knew that woman was trouble when she started keeping Wilson from visiting his old friends."

"You mean when she didn't let Wilson see *me*," Ella clarified for the sake of logic. "It really was understandable. Everyone thought that there was something going on between Wilson and me, and she must have heard the gossip. Under the circumstances, I don't blame her for not wanting Wilson to visit with any of us."

Rose shook her head. "It was more than that. I'm sure of it now. There's evil in that house."

Ella considered her mother's words as she drove down the highway. "If you want to know the truth, that entire neighborhood gives me the creeps. You wouldn't believe what we found in the pocket of one of the murdered teens," Ella said, then explained about the bone fetish.

Rose looked down the road for a while, then finally spoke. "You know enough about the gifts our family possesses to trust your instincts. It's only when you ignore what you can't explain that you get into trouble. Take Clifford back there with you and have him check that woman's house and yard for things associated with witches. A *hataalii* can sense evil and knows what signs to look for. He may be able to help you recover objects that she's kept hidden from everyone, including your friend."

"You're that sure there's something there to find?"

Rose nodded slowly. "I think you know that, too, but for whatever the reason, you're blocking the thought."

Ella considered it. Maybe she had shied away from this aspect of it for personal reasons. She still hadn't questioned Wilson about Lisa's religious beliefs, as she'd told her team she would. She didn't want to find out that Lisa was involved with skinwalkers, or worse, *was* a Navajo witch.

Learning that the woman he'd loved had been no more than an enemy casting a spell against him would destroy Wilson.

"I'll take my brother over there as soon as I can," Ella said at last, as they pulled in front of their home, noting from Clifford's car and the interior lights that he was waiting for their arrival.

Ella wasn't at all sure how Wilson would react if he happened to still be there when she returned to Lisa's home with Clifford. If he thought about it, he'd guess the reason for sure. Once, the three of them had put their lives on the line, standing together against the skinwalkers. This time, the line between enemy and friend would not be as clear.

Two ran up and barked furiously the moment he saw Rose. When her mother opened the car door, he jumped up on his hind legs, licking at her face furiously.

"Two, no!" Rose laughed, then gave the dog a big hug before pushing him down off her lap. "Have you been feeding him on schedule? He looks a bit thin to me." She gave Ella a stern look.

"He's fine, Mom. He even sleeps with me at night."

Ella stood by in case her mom needed help. Rose maneuvered herself out of the car and onto her crutches without much trouble. As they approached the house, her eyebrows rose. "You never told me how bad the attack was."

Ella looked at the pockmarks, clearly visible because the stucco used to patch the wall was a shade lighter than the old. "It looks worse now, because the new stucco doesn't quite match the faded old stucco," Ella said, minimizing the incident, though she knew her mother hadn't been fooled for one second.

As they entered the living room, Rose sighed contently, leaning on the crutches as she turned slowly around. "I'm home, I really am," she whispered to no one in particular.

Clifford emerged from the kitchen, Loretta half a step behind him. "Mom called from the hospital before you left. We've been waiting forever. I thought you two were coming straight home," he said, glaring at Ella. "Julian is asleep on your bed. He just couldn't stay awake any longer."

"I wasn't planning on a detour, but things got a little complicated," Ella said.

"I asked Ella to make a stop," Rose said, putting an end to the discussion before it became an argument. "Now, why don't you two go off and talk, while my daughter-in-law and I get something fixed for dinner. Later, Loretta can show me my grandson when he wakes up from his nap."

As if sensing that his mother's words were not a request, Clifford gave Ella a puzzled look, and followed her into the next room. "What's going on?"

Ella filled him in on their mother's intuitions about Lisa's home. "Mom thinks you'd be able to sense and maybe locate things the lab techs and I missed. She may be right. You want to go over there with me now?"

"Let's get Mom settled in, then we'll go later this evening, when we can be sure Wilson has left. I hate the idea of going where someone has died, especially their home. But this is for our friend, and I can do that for him."

It was dark when Ella and Clifford arrived at Lisa's home. "Where are the gangs?" Clifford asked. "I didn't see any teenagers at all hanging around here tonight. Have you arrested everyone?"

She shook her head. "Some are in jail, but most are hiding out. They're afraid they're easy targets out in public these days, not just from the police, and they're right."

As they left the vehicle, Clifford stopped and looked up and down the street. "There's fear here, a lot of it," he murmured. "It hangs over this area like a dark cloud. The neighbors don't even look out their windows to see who we are."

They went inside Lisa's house, using a duplicate key Ella had picked up at the station. She stood back and allowed her brother to walk through the house, room by room. Wilson had emptied the closets, and most of the things that he could give away were now gone, but the place still smelled of death. Ella tried to block it from her mind as she followed Clifford into the kitchen.

Clifford walked past the trash, and seeing the discarded bag of herbs, picked it up and opened the cellophane bag. Before Ella could warn him, he sniffed the contents.

His face suddenly contorted into a deep scowl.

"Oops. Sorry, brother. I should have spoken faster. That stuff stinks. It made me a little sick."

Clifford face was set. "I know this foul concoction. It's a evil mixture that's supposed to be given to confuse and control an enemy."

"Are you sure?"

"Don't you remember the smell in the tunnels where the three of us fought our old enemies? The herbs they used were similar to this. Separately, these herbs aren't harmful, but together, mixed to a certain strength, they induce a sense of complacency. It's much like a powerful sedative. In fact, one of the herbs is valerian."

"I'll take it to Justine and have it analyzed."

"You'll find nothing spectacular. It won't help you make a case, I don't think, except against one who is already dead. They're common herbs. The effectiveness of the mixture is completely dependent on the skill and knowledge of the person making the infusion. I'd advise you to bury it. Give it back to Mother Earth to purify."

"This was prepared for our professor friend on a regular basis," Ella said, avoiding the mention of names and watching Clifford's reaction to the news.

His eyebrows rose and he expelled his breath slowly. "Then the bone fetish you recovered may have come from here, too."

"We found a small, empty metal treasure box the day of the murder. I wonder if she kept the fetish in that. The box, I think, was what triggered the attack on her. She may have been fighting over it." Ella paused, trying to recall the details. "Our friend's fiancee managed to burn one of her assailants. Then later, when we found the body of one of the murdered Many Devils, a kid we know only as Shopper, the ME's report confirmed that the body had been burned with some kind of powder. Are you familiar with a chemical capable of doing that?"

"The burning powder sounds like something the witches use. Remember that they learn to distill all kinds of powders from plants and minerals. It's part of their bag of tricks. You've encountered some of those in the past yourself. Remember the red powder the witches used against us in the tunnels?"

Ella nodded slowly. "I strongly suspect that they are searching for a particular item of power that was taken from the metal box I mentioned." She looked across the room lost in thought. "Whatever it is, it's got to be fairly small."

"An item of power could be just about anything," Clifford said, walking around the room. "including something taken from an enemy's body."

Ella considered that. "There's another possibility in all this. Maybe our friend's fiancée was under someone else's influence," she said, and reminded him about the cane prints she'd found.

"And you haven't been able to find the one who has been leaving that trail?"

"No, and not for lack of trying," Ella heard a slight rustle in the bushes outside the house. Quickly she opened the back door and ran outside. The yard was empty.

Ella glanced around, searching the area with her flashlight. As she aimed the beam at the place beneath the window nearest to where they'd been standing, she saw a fresh trail left by someone using a cane. Ella followed the tracks until they disappeared on the pavement, a dozen yards away.

She muttered a soft curse. "I can't track anyone down an asphalt road on a moonless night," she said, glancing at Clifford, who'd come outside.

Clifford crouched, studying the tracks. "If you find the person who was here, you'll have the answers that have been eluding you. I'm sure of it."

"Whoever it was is gone now." Ella leaned back against the side of the house. "You realize that we can't discuss any of this with Wilson. The suggestion, without solid proof, that he was about to marry one of the tribe's mortal enemies, would destroy what remains of our friendship with him."

"That's exactly the type of plan you'd expect our enemies to come up with. It's a divide-and-conquer strategy," Clifford said.

Ella exhaled softly. "Once I do have evidence to back up my suspicions, I'll talk to Wilson. No matter what the consequences, I'll have to warn him. His life could depend on his staying alert. But here's another thought. If he was being set up, and his fiancée was part of the plot, you can bet we're also targets. We'd all better start watching our backs. Our enemies specialize in treachery and deceit, and those are powerful weapons."

SIXTEEN

——— ✕ ✕ ✕ ———

Ella went to the station the following morning a little late. Her mother had insisted on everyone, including Loretta and her grandson, Julian, who'd both spent the night, eating a proper breakfast. Rose was learning to get around the house in her crutches, and was already doing more than Ella had ever dreamed she'd be doing this soon.

As she walked inside her office, her intercom buzzed. When Ella answered it, Big Ed's voice said, "Ella. Come and see me."

Usually if there was bad news, Big Ed came looking for her, so she took the summons as a signal that Big Ed had good news. She hurried to his office. Maybe things were finally turning around for her. Ella started to knock on Big Ed's open door, but he waved for her to come inside.

"Sit down," he said, gesturing to a chair. "I wanted to let you know that since the brutality suit against you has been officially dropped, you can stop taking Justine with you. I still want to caution you to be very careful. And I want you to stay away from Leo Bekis and his family now that he's out on bail, clear?" Seeing her nod, he continued. "Just use your common sense, like always, and you'll be fine."

"Thanks for that, Chief. I needed a vote of confidence around here."

He nodded. "I think I know how you've been feeling, like everybody is pulling at you from every direction. Sometimes nothing you do as a cop seems to make the slightest bit of difference. I've been there, so has every other senior officer in the department. The Rez has changed in the past few years, and the same troubles that plague law enforcement everywhere else have caught up to us here. To make matters worse, when we take action to protect the ones we serve, they sometimes create more problems for us than the criminals."

"It's more than that, Chief. My problems . . . go beyond that."

"You have some personal concerns at this point, too, I understand that. We all do. But you'll get through it, and the cases you're working on, too. If you ever have second thoughts about making a difference, just remember The People need your expertise and your instincts," he said. "You're an asset to the tribe, one that would be hard to replace."

Ella knew that Big Ed was trying to ease the pressure she was feeling, and she appreciated his concern. "You can count on me to do my best, Chief."

Ella had just left his office when Justine flagged her down.

In Ella's office Justine dropped wearily into a chair. "We've been grilling the boys involved in the Fair Grounds situation for hours, and we've got nothing. We've used every trick we know, questioning them separately, intimating that we know far more than we do, but they're saying nothing. We have no idea where they got the guns or ammunition, either. The only thing they insist on mentioning is the Many Devils, blaming them for absolutely everything, including the neighborhood robberies and the murders."

Neskahi came into the room, nodded to Ella, then sat

down in the empty chair next to Justine. "I did get one thing from the youngest kid. He's twelve, do you believe it? And he hates school, his parents, and just about every thing I mentioned, especially the Many Devils."

"But you still got something!" Ella said. "What is it?"

"The kid wanted to make it even tougher for their rivals. He said he'd heard one of the Many Devils bragging that they're going to start roaming around between midnight and two A.M. They want to tighten their hold on their neighborhoods by making sure everyone is afraid to go to sleep. They want people too scared to complain, and too tired to stand up to them."

"Those kids just don't get it, do they?" Ella commented. "They're going to get hunted down and killed one by one by the Navajo witches. They've stolen from a group that has far greater power at night."

"Yeah, well, you try telling them that," Neskahi said. "They'd just laugh in your face. And now that the North Siders know when and where the MDs are hanging out, they might come looking for them. Everyone will be in danger then. This gang thing is going to explode, and soon."

Ella sat back and stared at an indeterminate point across the room. "I'm afraid you're right, Sergeant. Let's stick close to their area tonight. We want to keep the lid on the powder keg, if we can. We also need to get one of the MDs to tell us what else was stolen that was skinwalker in origin."

"But anyone who knows that could also be the one who was Shopper's partner in killing Lisa Aspass. I doubt that boy will be too cooperative." Justine said. "I wish I could get my hands on Thomas, my cousin. I know my aunt's been lying about not knowing where he is. We've had a stakeout on the place, but he hasn't shown up. But even if I found him, I doubt he'd talk."

"We'll have to do what we can, and without a warrant, you can't search their home. I'm afraid the next time these two gangs meet, what we've seen in early encounters is going to seem like a school dance in comparison." Ella shrugged.

Ella patrolled the darkened neighborhood in a souped-up sedan from impound. It was a lackluster vehicle, not one meant to attract attention, unless gray primer paint could be considered an asset.

So far she hadn't seen any of the Many Devils or North Siders cruising, but she had a strong feeling some of the kids were inside their homes, watching her. The Many Devils who were not in custody were scared, but when these boys were frightened, they sometimes acted rashly to try and prove themselves. Machismo wasn't just a Latin thing with gangs and that worried her now.

Minutes turned into hours, but there was no sign of any teens, much less a gang. As she turned the corner and drove past Lisa's home, she felt a shudder travel down her spine. She couldn't rid herself of the sense of evil she felt whenever she was on this street.

Ella shook her head, trying to push back the thought. As she turned the corner again, she saw a truck ahead, driving down the center of the road, weaving from one side to the other.

Visions of Leo Bekis and her mother passed through Ella's mind. She picked up her dome light, and placed it on the dashboard. Lights flashing, she pulled the driver over. She was parking behind him when she recognized the truck, despite a muddy splotch over the license plate. Ella put down her mike, choosing not to call the incident in just yet, and approached Wilson Joe's vehicle.

The driver's side window was rolled down and Ella clearly smelled liquor on her friend's breath. She didn't need a sobriety test to know that he had been drinking too much to drive safely.

"What are you doing in this neighborhood at this time of the evening?" she asked. "Don't you know this area isn't safe?"

He gestured to the rifle rack behind him, where his weapon was resting. "Let the little punks come after me. I'll give them the same chance they gave my Lisa."

"Is that why you're out here? Are you hoping to find some trouble, anything to give you an excuse to take the law into your own hands?"

"I've been waiting and waiting for you and your FBI training and fancy crime team to come up with answers, but you haven't been able to turn up anything except a couple of dead kids. I'm out looking on my own now. I know that when a killer isn't found right away, the chances of ever catching him decrease with each day. I'm not going to let that happen," Wilson said, his speech slow with the effort it took for him to enunciate clearly.

Ella felt her throat tighten. She'd never seen Wilson drunk before. As far as she could remember, Wilson had never touched alcohol. He hated the problem plaguing the Rez as much as any of them. Then she remembered her suspicions the other day at Lisa's house. This wasn't the first time Wilson had turned to the bottle.

Sadness filled her as she saw the anger and hatred in her old friend's eyes. "She's gone, and nothing you can do will change that," Ella said quietly. "Don't throw your life away by doing this."

"Doing what? Your job? Someone should be looking for the killer, and who better than me?"

Ella knew that if she took him to the station and they did a breathalizer test, his career as a college professor would be jeopardized. He'd saved her and Clifford's lives more than once, and had stood beside them like a rock when no one else had wanted any part of them. Whether or not he still thought of her as a friend, that's exactly what she was and would be to him now. It was time to repay their long friendship, and see that he got home safely.

"Come ride with me. We'll go to the Totah Cafe and talk."

"Talk about what? There's nothing more to say."

"There's plenty, believe me. You're not the only one in pain, you know. My mom was like a mother to you, too, and now she needs someone else's help to cope with her new challenge. You haven't even come by to say hello. Mom misses seeing you," she said harshly.

The truth must have penetrated Wilson's alcohol haze, because he looked instantly contrite. "I'm sorry, Ella. You know that I love her, it's just that . . ."

"Let's go. You can tell that to her once you sober up."

He climbed down out of the truck, managed to lock the door, and followed Ella to her vehicle. Ella radioed her team and canceled the operation. It was too quiet tonight. The remaining gang members must have opted to stay home and avoid a confrontation, knowing they'd be ill-equipped to handle it. That, or they'd noticed the police were patrolling heavily. Switching frequencies, she contacted Justine and told her she could be found at the Totah Cafe.

"I'm going back to the office, then," Justine said. "I need to finish a few reports before I call it a night, and I want to stop by my aunt's to see if Thomas is home. I think she's been hiding him from me, and I want to catch her unawares."

Neskahi called in next. "I'm going to stick around here a while longer. I have a feeling about tonight."

"What kind of feeling?" Ella pressed, never one to discount a colleague's gut reaction to anything.

"I don't know. Maybe we're missing something, maybe

we're not. Anyway, you won't be far, and there are extra patrols in this area. I'll be okay."

"Stay in radio contact," Ella advised, then signed off.

Throughout the drive to the Totah Cafe, Wilson remained silent. Ella allowed him time to mull over his thoughts. Maybe, the alcohol fog that had clouded his brain would lift, and he would see that she'd done him a very big favor tonight. She was his friend, and would always honor that.

Ella parked and led the way to a booth in the back, the one which would give her the clearest view of the room. Without asking Wilson what he wanted, she ordered an entire pot of coffee. "That should hold us while we talk," she said.

He remained morose, staring at his hands.

Finally, after his second cup of coffee, Wilson began to come around. Ella saw him take a sip of water, then pour himself another cup of coffee. His hand wasn't shaking so much anymore, and his eyes looked red, but clear.

"It looks like I owe you one," Wilson said quietly, sipping the strong coffee. "I don't know what the administration at the college would have done had they learned that I had been out driving around like this. Hell, a while before you came along, someone almost hit me broadside. I pulled out into the street, and all I ever saw was his lights as he swerved. I was lucky. Considering what happened to your mom, I'm surprised you didn't throw the book at me."

"I think you're forgetting how many times you've saved Clifford's life, and mine."

"We were all pretty close once." He met her gaze. "We were facing trouble from every corner, hunted by everyone, including the cops, and yet, when I look back on those days I don't regret one single moment. We knew where we stood then, and what we were fighting against. Things don't seem so clear-cut now. Was it really simpler then?"

"Things were never simple. But we always knew that no matter how tough things got, none of us stood alone. It's that way now, too, even if you don't realize it." Ella reminded him.

"Things have changed in all of our lives. We've changed."

She nodded slowly. "That's true enough. But not all change is bad. For one thing, I never expect to see you like this again—not if you want to stay out of jail."

He looked into her eyes. "You won't." For a long time Wilson stared into his cup then, finally, he looked up again. "Something's eating at you, Ella. Something that goes beyond your job. Is it your mother?"

Ella was glad that he'd given her an out. She wasn't ready to talk to him about Lisa and the skinwalker connection. That was the last thing he needed to hear while he was still coming out of his alcoholic haze. "Mom's doing better now, and she can take care of herself again, but I've got to admit, she had me scared silly for a while."

Time passed quickly, and as Wilson relaxed Ella was glad to see that their conversation became more natural and easy-going. They hadn't spoken this freely with each other in months, but of course, there were still many issues she couldn't broach with him. She wondered how she would ever be able to bring up the possibility of Lisa being linked with skinwalkers.

She was about to suggest they call it a night when Justine came into the cafe. In her hand was a thick manila folder, and the red tab let her know it was an active case file. Her face was set, a sign that some progress had been made.

Justine smiled at Wilson, then at Ella as she sat down. "A report from the ME was in my office when I got back. It's a breakdown of the chemicals used in the flash powder that burned the first victim's attacker," she said, avoiding Lisa's name for Wilson's sake. "None of the components are unusual, so their origin would be difficult to trace."

Wilson stared at a photo that had slipped partially out of the folder as she set it down on the table.

Ella looked at him, concerned by the strange expression on his face. "Are you feeling okay?"

Wilson nodded. "I was just thinking of the last time I saw that little fetish."

Ella kept her face expressionless, but it took some effort. "This one?" She brought it out all the way so he could see it clearly. "This was hers?"

He nodded. "Sure. I remember the first time I saw it. I discovered it underneath her pillow by accident one afternoon when I was helping her carry the laundry and make the bed. It surprised me that she had one at all. Then again, a lot of Navajos carry Zuni fetishes for protection. You do, too, though yours is a badger," he added, looking at Ella.

"Yeah, but the one Ella carries isn't made of human bone," Justine muttered.

Wilson's eyes grew wide. "What did you say?"

Justine looked at Ella, who stiffened, then nodded. "It's been tested. It's human bone," Justine answered.

Ella watched as Wilson realized the implications, his expression turning from confusion, to surprise, then finally anger.

Wilson met Ella's gaze with a cold one of his own. "Do you think Lisa was a skinwalker, and that gang members are being killed because they stole her ritual items?"

Ella paused, trying to figure out the best way to answer. Wilson knew her too well. He wouldn't accept anything but the truth.

"Your silence tells me all I need to know," he said, getting up abruptly and heading for the door.

Justine looked at Ella. "I hope you're not angry, but I thought if Wilson knew, he might be more inclined to help us. He's the only one who might know where Lisa got the powder, or who taught her to make it. This way, too, he didn't have to hear it from you, and I know you've been worried about how to do that without destroying your friendship."

Ella tossed a few bills on the table. "This may not have been the best time. But, either way, it's done. We'll discuss the new evidence later. Right now I've got to go after him."

"I'm coming with you."

Ella left the cafe with Justine right behind her. Wilson was walking along the side of the road, staring at the ground. His face was tucked down into his jacket, shielded from the wind. He was headed back toward where they'd left his pickup.

"Wait a minute," Justine said, stopping abruptly in mid-stride and taking a quick glance back toward the cafe. "What the heck is *he* doing here?"

"He, who?" Ella asked.

"Don't let on that we're on to him, but he's to your left, parked near the window. It's my cousin, Thomas Bileen."

Ella turned casually, catching a glimpse of the boy as she pretended to look down the road in the opposite direction. She took a moment to study him out of the corner of her eye.

"Was he here when you arrived?"

Justine considered it for a moment. "There was a car there, the space wasn't empty, but I don't remember seeing him in it at the time. Maybe he had ducked down.

"Forget about Wilson for now. He'll be okay. Pull your car around like you're leaving, but cut off Thomas's exit instead. I'll go over there and talk to him once you're in place."

Justine completed the maneuver within a few moments, and Ella strode over to where Thomas's car was parked. He'd ducked down from the moment Justine had got into her car, and was obviously trying to avoid being seen.

As Ella drew near, the boy looked up, and his eyes grew wide. In a heartbeat, he bolted out of the car, and headed into the brush behind the cafe.

SEVENTEEN

——— ✻ ✻ ✻ ———

Ella ran back to her Jeep, then headed out across the open terrain, keeping the boy in her headlights as well as she could. The way the Jeep was bouncing, the searchlight would have been impractical. As Ella increased her speed, hoping to catch up to the boy before he reached a place where she couldn't follow, she heard Justine request backup over the radio.

The boy kept his wits, running over uneven ground that slowed her down. As he took off up a narrow canyon, Ella was forced to leave her vehicle and continue the pursuit on foot.

Despite his baggy pants, Thomas was fast on his feet and Ella was sure she wouldn't be able to catch him without help. Hoping backup would arrive soon, she continued after him, managing to keep him in sight.

As Ella raced uphill, she cursed the many cups of coffee that were now sloshing inside her. Suddenly a vehicle swerved into action just ahead, cutting the teen off. It wasn't a marked unit, and she had no idea who was inside.

Before she had time to consider it, the driver fired twice at the running youth from inside the vehicle. Ella saw Thomas dive for cover.

"Stop shooting!" Ella yelled, unsure if the driver was an ally or an enemy. It wasn't Wilson's truck, and something told her it wasn't an off-duty cop responding to the call in his or her own private vehicle either. Stopping for a second, Ella drew her pistol and crouched, expecting trouble.

The driver turned his pickup around, his identity hidden by the bright headlights, and fired in her direction, forcing Ella down to the ground. Ella returned fire, but it was a nearly impossible shot from her angle, and she missed the truck altogether. Ella crawled over to better cover behind a boulder, keeping her head low. As she peered out from behind the edge of the large rock, she saw Justine zig-zagging forward on foot. Her vehicle was at an angle to the hill, probably bogged down in the sand. A heartbeat later Neskahi's vehicle pulled up next to Justine. She jumped inside, and they moved on toward her position.

The driver who'd attacked her and the boy kept his headlights aimed their way, blinding them as he fired two more shots toward where the boy had taken refuge. From her position, Ella couldn't see Thomas. Afraid that their enemy in the truck might be able to see well enough to target the boy, she fired back, putting out first one, then the second headlight with direct hits.

Ella continued firing and emptied her gun, trying to cover Neskahi and Justine's approach. When the slide came open, signifying that her clip was empty, Ella crouched back down behind her boulder. She braced herself for return fire as she felt around in her pocket for a second clip. In the seconds it would take her to reload, the shooter could do a lot of damage, and she had no idea where he was at the moment.

A shotgun blast got her attention. Ella looked out around the base of the rock and saw that Neskahi had dropped Justine off behind cover. She'd fired that shot, while he had stayed in his vehicle and pursued the shooter, who was now fleeing in his truck at high speed.

Ella came out into the open and ran toward the spot where she'd seen the boy take cover. "Are you okay?" she yelled.

She heard the sound of someone gasping for air, but no one answered her. "You really don't want me to leave you here all alone now, do you? Let's face it, whoever that was shooting at you could come back, and I doubt you're carrying a gun."

She heard the rustle of cloth against the brush, then a boy wearing the dark baggy pants and the red jacket of the Many Devils, stood up. "What are you going to do to me now?"

Justine arrived just as Ella approached Thomas Bileen, and he looked warily at her shotgun. "Hi, Cuz." Thomas managed weakly.

"Be glad that we're the ones who ended up with you tonight, Cuz." Justine sighed. "I'd hate to have to explain *your* death tonight to your mom."

"Get in my Jeep, Thomas. We're going to drive to the station and have a long talk." Ella ordered.

Justine glanced at Ella. "It looks like you've got this covered. How about if I back my car out of here and see if Neskahi can use some help?"

"Go," Ella answered.

Two hours later, Ella sat in her office. Justine was in the lab, but Neskahi was still out in the field. He'd chased the driver and vehicle into an area familiar to him before the attacker had disappeared. He'd opted to continue the search on his own.

Sixteen-year-old Thomas Bileen sat in the chair across from Ella, apparently hoping to somehow intimidate her with his mad-dogging. His parents could not be located, and he had turned down an offer from Justine to be there with him.

"You realize that so far you've given me nothing, including any incentive to help you stay alive," Ella said, her expression impassive. Hostile stares didn't frighten her after years working for the FBI.

"So, you're going to put me in jail, like you did before. I don't care." the boy said, his tone cocky.

Ella knew that was exactly what he wanted. Jail time was a status symbol in the gangs, and it would also be nice and safe at the moment to be locked up. "No, not at all. True, you ran away from a police officer, but I'm not going to hold you on that. You're free to go, but if I were you, I'd keep an eye out while walking back to your car. Someone is trying to blow you away."

Thomas lost his hostility in a second, and it was replaced with uncertainty, then fear. His voice raised an octave. "You're just going to let me go? You can't do that. They'll find me!"

"Who'll find you?" Ella never looked up, feigning disinterest while making a show of searching through her files.

"Don't you know what's going on?" His voice rose even higher.

"Does it have anything to do with this young man?" Ella brought out a police photo of Shopper, the gang member she's found with his throat slit.

Thomas crumbled in his seat, and his face turned pale. When he finally spoke, his voice was crumbling, and moisture was forming in his eyes. "Yeah. He was my homie, Shopper. His real name is Glenn Shorty. He came from Tuba City about four months ago. I think he ran away when his parents tried to put him in the D-home. He was the one that witch tried to fry when we broke into her house. He managed to hit her with that box, then whacked her on the head with some horse statue. But now the other skinwalkers are after the Many Devils. They've gotten two of us already, and I'm next. If you don't keep me locked up here, they'll find me again. Those skinwalkers are cold."

"If you decide to make a statement, we'll protect you."

The boy slumped in his chair, looked around the room one more time, then finally nodded.

Ella called in Justine and Big Ed. Both brought tape recorders. Once everything was set up, she nodded to the boy. "Okay, we're ready. Tell us all you know about the crimes we've been discussing."

"And you'll keep those witches from getting me, like they did to Shopper, right?" The boy looked at Ella, then the chief.

Big Ed nodded. "We'll put you in protective custody, and do all we can, if you'll cooperate."

"My homie Shopper, Glenn Shorty, I mean, belongs to the Many Devils. We needed money to get some guns for protection from the Siders so we started breaking into houses and selling the stuff we got. Sometimes we'd find a pistol or shotgun, and we'd keep those. Hunting rifles are no good up close. Then we hit that witch's house right after she left for work. We didn't know she was a witch at the time, though. Shopper and I were trying to open this small metal box we'd found when she suddenly came back to the house. She walked right in on us. Instead of yelling or running away, she got real angry and ordered us to put the box down. Her voice was really strange, spooky-like. We thought she might be crazy or something.

"We laughed at her, I mean what could she do? She was a skinny woman, and there were two of us." Thomas shook his head. "We didn't know she was a witch."

"You said that. Then what happened?" Big Ed pressed.

"She muttered some strange Navajo-sounding word, then she pointed her finger at me. My legs just buckled and I fell back against the wall, hitting it really hard with my head. Shopper freaked out and threw the box at her. He lucked out and it hit her right above the eye. She went down, and was bleeding pretty good. We thought she was knocked out. I wanted to get out of there fast, but Shopper laughed and called me a wimp. He went to get the box. It had come open and he wanted to see what was in it that was so important. I told him to forget it, but he wouldn't listen. The box was on the floor beside the witch and, the second he got close, she blew some yellow powder all over him. She'd been faking, you know? Shopper started choking and sputtering. He told me to get her. I saw the witch crawling away, but I just couldn't move. It was as if she had glued my feet to the floor with some kind of magic trick.

"Then Shopper grabbed a metal statue, a horse I think, and really whacked her on the head with it. Blood splattered everywhere, even on me. She fell down on the carpet and didn't move. That's when the yellow powder on him started burning. Man, it was like fireworks. Shopper started screaming, and I pushed him down on the carpet and helped him smother the flames. I guess when the witch got hit by the statue, it must have broken her spell, because I could move again."

"So the woman was dead?" Ella asked.

"It sure looked like it. She wasn't moving, and there was blood everywhere. Shopper was really pissed. He wanted whatever was in the box she'd fought so hard to keep, kinda like a lesson to her who was toughest. We found the fetish of a wolf or a coyote first. I couldn't really tell which. It looked really cool, so we figured we could sell it easy. The other thing just looked spooky, but Shopper decided we should take it with us, too. He put it in his pocket, then we took the TV and VCR out to our car and split."

"Tell us about the second object. Can you describe it?" Ella asked.

"It looked like a really ugly rag doll, and I mean *really* ugly. Kind of like one of the voodoo dolls you would see on TV, only worse. The cloth was yellow and dirty and the hair looked almost real, but half of it had fallen out." Thomas shook his head. "How could anything that disgusting be worth that much? But Shopper thought it might be real old, like from a museum."

"What did you do with it?"

"Shopper kept the fetish as a trophy, but decided to hide the doll and sell it to an Anglo trading post operator in a few months. Then Shopper got his throat cut, and I knew the same would happen to me if I didn't watch my own back. I told some of the homies, but they thought I was just chicken. I figured I'd keep my mouth shut, and stayed home mostly. My mom had me hide and told the cops and Justine that I was out roaming around. Then, two nights ago, things went really crazy. I heard a noise outside, and there by the back door was Shopper's body. Someone had dug him up, and they'd pinned a note to his shirt. The note said that unless they got their stuff back, I'd be next to die."

"Where's the body now?"

"I put it into a trash bag, and dumped it into the river down past the water treatment plant."

"Where is the doll now?" Ella asked.

"Shopper and I had a hard time deciding where to hide it. He finally said we should put it back in the witch's house after the cops were done there. We figured that would be a real safe place. It's in a heating vent right over the kitchen door."

Ella left the room with Big Ed, while Justine stayed with her cousin. "I'll go back there and see if I can find the witch doll. Once we have it, I could let the word out and that may help us stop some of the bloodshed."

"The gangs will continue to fight for the usual reasons," Big Ed said wearily, leading the way back to his office.

"I know, but at least we can cut down on the number of deaths—if we're lucky."

"Most of the boys will be out on bail in a few more days. We can't keep them all until their hearings." Big Ed reached his office chair, and sat down wearily.

Ella nodded and started to say more, when Justine stepped up to the door. Thomas Bileen was with her, handcuffed. "Your sister-in-law is on the phone on your direct line," she said in a quiet voice. "She says it's an emergency."

Ella ran back to her office while Justine took their prisoner to a holding cell. She grabbed the receiver before she'd even reached her chair. "What's going on?" Ella asked Loretta.

"There are people up on the mesa overlooking your mother's house. I caught the glimmer of something like a small fire, or maybe a mirror." Her voice was just above a whisper. "I'm not sure what's going on, there's only the moon for light outside. I don't want to alarm your mother, and I can't call my husband, because he's with a patient some distance away. He won't be back until tomorrow. My son and I were going to spend the night with your mother, but I'm not sure what to do. I don't know whether to try to leave or stay in the house."

"Stay in the house. You're all safest there. I'll send people over there immediately. Stay away from the windows, and lock the doors."

Ella grabbed her jacket and ran down the hall, but Big Ed

blocked her. "Someone's watching my house," she explained quickly. "My mother, sister-in-law, and my nephew are there alone. I need a unit sent over there *now*."

"You've got it."

Sirens filled the air as Ella pulled out of the station, Justine close behind her.

"Michael Cloud is patrolling south of your home, about fifteen minutes away. He's responding now," Justine informed her on channel six. "Sergeant Neskahi was on his way home, but he's also responding. He'll be coming up behind me."

"Ten-four."

She knew Michael should arrive first, and he would do whatever it took to make sure her family was safe. But she had no idea what they'd be up against. Maybe the skin-walkers had lost their patience, or what was left of the Many Devils, or The Brotherhood, had decided to get payback.

Ella felt her hands go clammy. She had too many enemies. The glimmer that Loretta had seen could have been headlights, or special binoculars, or even a shot fired from a silenced weapon. She just didn't have enough information to even speculate accurately. About five minutes from her home, Ella instructed Justine and Neskahi to switch off the sirens.

She then contacted Michael. "What's your ETA now?"

"I'm at your place. I approached without lights or sirens. Unless whoever's watching the house has top-notch equipment, they probably don't know I'm here. I figure that while other officers move in on the people up on the mesa, I should stick by your house. I'm at the northwest corner where I can keep an eye on anyone who approaches from the mesa side. I've already spoken to your sister-in-law, and everyone's okay inside. She's going to help keep watch."

"Good plan. Stay there."

As they reached the turnoff, Ella gave Justine and Neskahi their instructions. The three of them would approach the mesa from three different directions, driving in as far as they could before continuing on foot.

They moved in slowly, lights off. Ella was circling around to the north, and Justine would take the east side. Neskahi, arriving last, would approach from the west. The going was slow and rocky, but if it meant that they could close in on whoever was up there, so much the better.

Ella maintained radio silence as she left her vehicle and moved up the northern face of the mesa. At least this was territory she knew well enough not to need a flashlight. She chose her way carefully in the dark, and made no mistakes.

Suddenly a voice came out of the darkness from up above. "Don't come any closer. We are not your enemies. We are here to protect you and yours."

Ella didn't recognize the voice. "I haven't asked for help."

"But you need it. You fight the tribe's oldest enemies. We will watch your family while you hunt the evil ones. Accept our help. Don't become our enemy."

There was a sudden explosion of light that blinded her, and the concussion almost knocked her down. She felt rather than heard a vehicle speeding past her on the left, but she couldn't get her eyes to clear. Ella reached for her radio.

"My night vision is gone, and I can barely hear!" Justine called out, "but I think there's a car out there."

"Just wait until your sight clears. If you push it, you'll just fall and break a leg, or worse."

Ten minutes later they met at Ella's Jeep. Ella saw the anger on Neskahi's face. He had never liked giving up, or losing. Justine's expression was just as easy to read. Frustration was etched on her features.

"We were so close!" Justine muttered. "That flash-bang did its job well."

"At least the concussion didn't do any permanent damage. We were all far enough away from it."

"Who'd use that kind of thing around here?" Justine asked. "Not that it couldn't have been worse. Lately, we've been getting bullets instead of warnings."

"I know who they were," Ella said. "It seems the Fierce Ones are now insisting on watching over my family while we take care of the skinwalkers."

"Oh, wonderful," Neskahi said. "You realize that the Fierce Ones will be in your corner only as long as you don't do anything to annoy them. If, at any given point, they feel you've stepped out of line, they'll happily put you on their enemies list."

"They're unpredictable, I'll give you that, and dangerous. That number they did with the dump truck could have easily cost lives instead of saving them."

"Do you think my cousin Thomas could have been wrong about who was trying to kill him?" Justine asked. "The Fierce Ones have been escalating their activities against gang members."

"Maybe, but the skinwalkers would want him pretty badly for what happened to Lisa Aspass. They also want what was taken, and would rather see Thomas dead than in our hands." Ella considered the matter. "To be honest, I don't know if the Fierce Ones would deliberately try to kill a kid, but Navajo witches wouldn't let the age of the victim stop them."

"Don't underestimate the Fierce Ones," Neskahi said.

"I don't, believe me. But, for now, there's not a thing I can do about them. I have no IDs of any of them, except for Billy Pete, and he can be as scarce as hen's teeth when he chooses to be. You might try to pick him up at his job tomorrow, but I have a feeling you'll find that he's gone on vacation or something like that." Ella paused, then added, "By the way, were you able to dig up anything interesting on Bekis?"

"If he's connected to the skinwalkers, he's hidden that link like a master. Of course, that would have to be expected. All I can tell you for sure is that I found no evidence to support or negate a possible tie. I did find out that he's been keeping a very low profile since he made bail. His lawyer is worried he might be disturbed." Justine answered.

"Couldn't happen to a more deserving man," Ella said. "I'm going home to try to get some sleep. I suggest you two do the same. Our plate has been full tonight, and tomorrow could be just as busy."

As her team drove off, Ella went over to meet with Michael Cloud, who had not left his position beside the house. She filled him in, and saw the look of concern that crossed his features.

"You want me to stay close?"

"Yeah, I do. What the Fierce Ones don't quite realize is while *they* might know when a threat approaches, I won't, because I won't be able to tell a real threat from one of my self-appointed guardians." She paused. "I wish I could get them to understand that, but I can't talk to them because I can't even find them. I could broadcast the word, but if I do, I'm also notifying my enemies."

"For now, we've got to work with things the way they are," Michael said. "If I see anything, I'll call it in and check it out. We can't afford to assume anything at this point."

"I wonder if they'll realize what's going on, and back off, or decide that I'm really their enemy."

"That's out of your hands. You're doing what you have to do," Michael said.

"You're right. I just don't have a choice."

As Officer Cloud drove off, Ella returned to the house. It

was closer to dawn than midnight, but Loretta was waiting for her as she walked in.

"Is everything okay?" she whispered.

"Yeah. How are things here?"

"Julian's asleep and so's your mother."

"No, I'm not," Rose said, and came into the room on her crutches. "Did you catch whoever was up on the mesa?"

Ella shook her head, and explained that the Fierce Ones had decided to protect her, but didn't mention any of the complications that would cause.

Rose nodded slowly. "They'll try, but it's just a matter of time before they're overwhelmed by the pressures of the fight they've chosen. Their methods—their principles—may change as they realize what it will take to win. Sooner or later, the line between right and wrong will blur for them, and they'll become a law onto themselves. But that's in the future. For now, they aren't a threat and we're okay. You two get to bed. That's where I'm going."

Rose turned around, and returned to her room.

As Ella looked at Loretta, she saw the fear in her sister-in-law's eyes. "It's okay. There'll be patrols in the area. You and Julian will be safe here tonight."

Loretta nodded, her tight-lipped expression betraying the fact that she resented everything that was going on.

"I wish that things could be different for you . . . for all of us," Ella said, "but you knew about our family before you married Clifford."

"I never realized that it would be like this. I don't like violence."

"Neither do I, but I'll do whatever's necessary to protect our family."

"Where are you going now?" Loretta asked as Ella started putting on her jacket. "It's three in the morning?"

"There's one more thing that needs to be done."

Ella drove to Lisa's home. She'd be lucky if she managed to get any sleep at all tonight. She rubbed her neck with one hand, wondering when the Rez had started falling apart, and if anything would ever be able to stop the process, much less reverse it. Lately, things just kept getting worse.

She took a deep breath. She'd think about such things later. Right now, she had to concentrate on finding answers to the murders, not to the future.

As she entered Lisa's home, she felt its now-familiar sense of oppressiveness almost engulfing her. But maybe she could define it better now. It wasn't a sense of evil alone. What she was reacting to, what touched her and left her so unsettled, was an inescapable sense of futility, a sadness that came from acknowledging the final results of a life wasted on revenge. The skinwalker's apparent plans to destroy Wilson in order to hurt Ella's family seemed, in retrospect, nothing more than an ill wind that had passed through their lives, its power dissipating as its own evil consumed it. Yet that realization was not one she would share with anyone, in hopes of changing what was yet to come. Reason could not touch certain people. They were immune to it, hiding behind beliefs that gave them the illusion that they were powerful, not just pawns in a game they didn't understand—life.

Ella pulled a chair out from around the kitchen table and stood on it, using her pocket knife to unscrew the vent. The foul-smelling doll fell right into her hands. Revulsion filled her. It was a caricature of evil, something meant to oppress and corrupt, a tool of fear. She resisted the urge to throw it on the floor, to rip it apart until nothing remained.

The artifact might yet produce some good. It could turn out to be her ace in the hole, and she wouldn't risk losing it. She stepped down and stared at it blankly, trying to figure out what to do with the thing now. She wouldn't bring the doll into her own home and dishonor her mother that way.

She also couldn't carry it around. To keep it at the police station would place it at risk. She still remembered when two of the skinwalkers had been cops. Who could say that none still remained, undetected?

Ella walked back to her Jeep, and picked up a large brown, padded envelope from the floor of the vehicle. She'd meant to use it to mail a wedding gift to Wilson, a weaving her mother had made. It would no longer serve that purpose, but it would be useful in a different way now. It even already had priority mail postage on it, and the weaving weighed much more than the doll that was taking its place.

Feeling awkward about removing evidence from a crime scene in such an unorthodox way, Ella snapped several Polaroids of the doll with the camera she kept in the Jeep for police work. These would serve as her backup, recording what she'd found and when. She then wrote a note explaining what she wanted done with the doll and stuck it in the envelope along with the doll.

Lastly, she addressed the envelope to Blalock in Farmington. He'd probably dislike holding onto the thing, because he'd also encountered skinwalkers in working with her, but this way he'd have no choice and it would be safe with him. His office had a closet built like a safe.

Ella drove directly to the post office. The lobby was open all night. Of course, with the gang problem, there was no telling how long that would last.

Passing the envelope through the special rotating package depository, she returned to the Jeep and drove home. Everything was quiet now. As she entered the house, she felt the peace that came from finally coming home after long hours of work.

She went to her room and lay down on her bed, surprised when Two jumped up and lay by her feet. "I'm going to have to get up in another minute and undress, so don't get too comfortable," she warned, but, before she knew it, she was sound asleep.

The phone ringing next to her bed woke her, and Ella sat up abruptly. The sun was already shining through her windows, and it was bright outside. She'd meant to be up before dawn, but she could see that it was at least eight o'clock. Tossing the covers aside, she bolted out of bed and reached for the receiver.

She recognized Neskahi's voice even before he identified himself. "After our run-in last night with the Fierce Ones, I went back to the area where I lost the driver who took a shot at the kid."

"Did you find him?"

"No, but I have a feeling he's still out there, hiding. I'm going to stick around a while longer. There's a truck that might be his parked next to a vacant house here that's still under construction."

"Have you gotten any sleep?"

"No, but maybe I'll catch up tonight."

Ella knew the burst of energy that often came after complete exhaustion. She also knew about altered moods and perceptions that were an offshoot of that state, too. "Sergeant, I'm coming over. Even if you're sure you've IDed the suspect, do not initiate any action on your own. Is that clear?"

"I'm tired, but I'm doing okay. Don't worry," he said.

"Fine. My order still stands."

Ella hung up with one hand and reached for a clean pair of jeans with the other. She washed up quickly. As she walked down the hall to the kitchen, she tripped over Two. "Sorry, mutt, but you're in my way."

The dog looked up at her, wiggled his tail twice, then with a beleaguered sigh, placed his head back down on his paws.

"Rough life," Ella muttered, then stopped in mid-stride, wondering suddenly why Two wasn't with her mother.

Rose appeared at her bedroom door as Ella came by. "Mom, you're up. Did I wake you?"

"I've been awake for hours. It just takes me a long time to dress," she said wearily, as if the task had sapped most of her energy.

Guilt filled Ella. "Sorry. I wish I could stay this morning, but I've got to run and help Neskahi."

"What's wrong with the sergeant?"

"He hasn't had any sleep at all, and is running on adrenaline. I'm afraid that he'll be a danger to himself and others unless he gets some rest soon."

Ella picked up her jacket and slipped it on while grabbing a slice of bread to munch on. The house really seemed cold this morning. "Mom, are you warm enough?" Ella noted that her mother was wearing a long-sleeved velvet blouse, a shawl, and a long skirt. The traditional outfit was something her mother wore often, but it had never seemed as warm as a pullover and a thick sweater to Ella.

"I'm plenty warm. If you wore our traditional clothes from time to time, you'd know that."

Ella shook her head. "I'd feel clumsy in the skirt, and naked without my slacks and jacket."

Rose smiled. "And your badge?"

Ella pressed her lips together, hating to admit it, but knowing it was futile to deny the truth. "Yeah, and the badge."

"It's what you were meant to do. Don't let anything keep you from that, Daughter."

Ella shook her head in bewilderment as she reached into the refrigerator for the milk. "I don't get it. I thought you'd rather see me doing something else, anything else, than to be a cop."

"Yes, but I've grown to accept it because I've learned that it's a part of you. Just don't ever stop seeing that yourself. No self-doubts."

"I do see it," Ella said slowly, pouring herself a glass of milk, then setting it down to check her weapon. "But I see a lot of other things, too, like responsibility to family and friends."

Rose shook her head. "Just don't worry about me, or our teacher friend. Things will work out, you'll see."

Ella took a deep breath. "I hope you're right, Mom. But I don't have time to think about it right now. Let me wake Loretta to help you with breakfast, and then I've got to go." She gulped down her milk in a few swallows.

Rose shook her head. "It's too early. Let her and Julian sleep. We'll know soon if your brother is going to return this morning, as he said, to take his wife and son home. And remember, I can take care of myself. I don't need a baby-sitter."

Ella hurried to the door, grabbing another slice of bread to eat on the way. "I've got to go, but we'll talk later, okay?"

Ella sped down the dirt road, wishing she'd known that Neskahi had made an all night stakeout before now. She intended to read him the riot act about following procedures later, but right now she wanted to make sure he was covered.

Ella notified Justine at the station as she raced down the highway. She wanted more backup in case of trouble. Assured that at least one patrol car would be dispatched to the area, she began to feel the first burst of optimism. If Neskahi had managed to track down the gunman's vehicle, there was a good chance they'd find the driver, too. The prospect made a burst of adrenaline race through her. This was the best part of being a cop. It was an indescribable rush when things started to come together.

Ella saw Neskahi's truck parked just down the street. This was a strange neighborhood. A dozen or more houses were in various stages of construction, but only four looked like they'd been finished. The new dwellings had been laid out in clusters of four and only the central cluster was inhabited. The only house that looked lived-in was older, and a different style from the rest. Many other lots had been staked out, and construction trailers and fenced areas with materials still stood, though it looked like it had been months since anyone had used them. The area had the feel of a ghost town in the making, despite the presence of one paved street.

Ella remembered hearing about this section of Shiprock. It had started with a few new houses going up around a very old one, one which the resident refused to have renovated. But then, after the first three new houses were constructed and people moved in, the tribe discovered that no one was willing to remain there for more than a few months. The houses would be found abandoned. No explanations were ever given. Most of what she knew came from gossip, but, seeing the place now, she'd bet it was accurate.

As she looked around, she silently commended the shooter's instincts. Had she been trying to escape pursuit, this was just the area she would have picked. First, there was the mystique, and secondly, there were enough arroyos and half-completed buildings here to hide or confuse any cop in pursuit.

Ella parked her Jeep, then walked over to meet the sergeant. "I've called in backup," she said.

"It wasn't necessary. This is my collar."

She gave him a hard look. "You're exhausted, and if you want to make a collar at all, you're going to need help. A two-year-old could get past you right now."

He squared his shoulders, blinking to keep his eyes focused. "You're wrong. I—"

Suddenly a pickup shot out of a closed wooden shed. The building burst, wood flying everywhere. In a heartbeat,

Neskahi jumped behind the wheel of his truck. Ella jumped into the passenger's side as he started to pull away. "Okay, so maybe you're less tired than I thought."

"I knew he'd wait until morning, then hit the highway and try to blend in. I just didn't expect him to use another vehicle. I bet he saw you arrive, and figured that others would be joining you for a house-to-house search." Neskahi pointed out.

Ella called in their position. "We'll try to head him off," she told Neskahi. "I've ordered a roadblock set up at the intersection ahead. He'll be trapped between them and us."

Justine was too far away to take part, but had managed to get two patrol units in place, one a cop who was on his way to work and another who was in the area on a routine patrol. "We've got him, now," Ella said, confidently.

"No, not yet," Neskahi said, as the driver turned off the highway and headed across an open field.

"Where the hell is he going? This leads nowhere."

"Maybe that's exactly where he wants to take us," Neskahi suggested.

Ella studied Neskahi's expression. He was alert, but after this was over, he'd sleep for hours. Adrenaline would only carry him so far.

Ella released the men manning the roadblock, but as Neskahi headed across an arroyo, the transmissions began to break up.

"I don't know the roads in this area. Do you?" Neskahi asked.

"No, but it's obvious he does, so stay sharp, and watch for holes and rocks."

The chase continued for another twenty minutes, and they moved farther and farther south, away from the Shiprock area. At times they were traveling at fifty miles an hour, despite the absence of any road more defined than an occasional dirt track. Ella could feel her tension rising. This wasn't a chase, they were being led somewhere on purpose. And there'd be no backup there for a while, because any other cops would have to find them first.

"Should I take a chance of losing him and cut across that wash ahead? If it works, we'll head him off."

"Stay with him for now. This is familiar ground to him, so he's got the advantage. If we try to cut him off, we may lose sight of him permanently."

"I'm worried about a reception party waiting at the end of this chase," Neskahi said after several more minutes.

They were traveling at speeds unsafe to both vehicles, but neither of them had ended up with so much as a flat tire. Ella shared Neskahi's uneasiness, but remained silent, knowing it would do no good to voice her concerns now. Whatever happened, they were committed to seeing this through.

"Keep alert for an ambush of any kind," she warned, her eyes darting back and forth, searching for danger.

"I don't think that's what's on his mind," Neskahi said, his voice taut.

"What then?"

He shook his head. "Look around. This isn't the type of terrain one would pick for an ambush. It's uneven, sure, but it's barren of vegetation, too. The canyons are too few and too wide to afford any real cover."

"Then where the hell is he going?"

"I wish I knew."

Ella tried to picture where they would be on a map. Things like the solitary microwave tower ahead were looking vaguely familiar. Her skin prickled, and a feeling of dread spread all through her. "I know where we are," she said.

"Where?"

"Jane Clah, my father-in-law's aunt, lived in a hogan around here somewhere."

"Lived? Past tense?"

"Justine has been asking around for her, and we came out looking for her and checked with local businesses, but she seems to have disappeared. The one thing we're fairly sure about is that her hogan was abandoned."

They passed within sight of it, rimming part of the natural depression where it rested, but the person ahead of them continued at his breakneck speed.

"What else is around here?"

"Nothing, except what you're seeing, I guess, but we didn't conduct much of a search," Ella answered.

The driver ahead accelerated as they reached the road Ella had taken days before when looking for Jane's hogan. It was on that hill, farther along, that her steering had failed and they'd almost gone off the side.

A trail of dust filled the air as Neskahi negotiated a tight curve and they moved up the same hillside. Suddenly, the vehicle ahead went out of control. It flew over the edge, and slid down the embankment, smashing headlong into an enormous boulder.

Ella leaned forward, bracing herself on the dashboard. "Hurry!"

Before they could stop, the truck below erupted into flames.

Neskahi hit the brakes and Ella jumped out, sliding down the slope toward the vehicle, hoping to get the driver out before the flames engulfing the engine reached the cab.

In a heartbeat, Ella threw the door open and pulled out a middle-aged Navajo woman. Her face was embedded with glass, and blood poured down her forehead, but Ella recognized her. It was Mrs. Willink, the clerk at the trading post along Highway 666.

"Where were you going? What were you hoping to do?" Ella asked.

"I've done what I intended," she whispered. "Out here alone you will get no more help. This is *our* land. You won't make it back to Shiprock alive."

"But why did you do this? I barely know you."

"You know me as someone who takes care of a trading post . . . but that's not who I am. I'm one of the many witches you've sworn to destroy . . . and part of the family you've tried to forget."

Ella tried to take it all in, but her mind was reeling with all the implications. She hadn't forgotten any of her family. Surely this woman was crazy. "And you hated that boy, Thomas Bileen, too? Why? What did he do to you to merit your wanting to shoot him?"

"He serves no purpose . . . to anyone," she said, her voice growing weaker. "He even hates himself, though he's afraid to die. We want . . . to teach a lesson the youth gangs won't soon forget. We rule here, and they exist because we allow it. Our 'gang' came from the earth in the very beginning, and we'll be around long after people like you and that boy are dead and forgotten," she added, her breathing labored.

Ella studied her features. Slowly an idea formed in her mind. "You're related to Randall Clah, my father-in-law, aren't you? You're part of his other family, the one he kept secret."

"I'm his oldest daughter, one of many who hate you for what we never had, because he was too busy raising your husband."

With effort she raised a bloody hand to her lips, then gasped.

Ella realized a second too late that the woman had just taken some kind of poison. As she held the lifeless body, Ella looked up at the skies and raged in silence against the bitter hatred that had destroyed yet another life.

EIGHTEEN

✖ ✖ ✖

Ella stood up slowly. Neskahi was waiting by his vehicle. His gaze remained on the wrecked car, not on the body.

Ella looked down at the corpse. She understood hatred, but not something this powerful. This woman, whom she scarcely knew, had been willing to die in the hope of taking Ella with her.

"Do you know who she is?" Neskahi asked Ella.

"Yes. She worked at the trading post over on Highway Six-six-six. She's also our former police chief's daughter."

Ella walked away from the body. There would be time for the dead later. Now their own survival seemed far more important. "You heard what she told me?"

He nodded once. "I honestly don't understand it. We should have no problem getting back to Shiprock. The truck's undamaged, and even if we had to hike out to the highway, I can't imagine either of us dying out here." He paused, then added, "Unless there's something else that we don't know about waiting for us," Neskahi said.

Ella nodded. "My thoughts exactly."

As a coyote howled in the distance they exchanged quick glances. "Nothing to do with us," she said.

"Yeah."

They got back into the truck. As Neskahi started up the engine, Ella saw the gas gauge was nearly empty.

"That can't be right. I should have at least a quarter tank," Neskahi said, turning off the engine. They both got out to check for holes in the fuel line or tank.

Squatting down, Neskahi looked under the truck and saw a steady drip of fuel coming from the tank. He got underneath, and held his finger over the hole until Ella could find a stick. Neskahi took the piece of wood and wedged it into the hole, almost stemming the flow. Then he crawled back out and stood, dusting off his clothes quickly. That should hold it for awhile," he said, looking weary.

"Let's hope a while is long enough," Ella replied.

Before long they were on their way, driving west toward the highway. "I spent most of the night staking out her neighborhood, but I guess she was watching me just as carefully," Neskahi said. "I must have been groggier than I thought if she was able to get past me and poke a hole in my truck's gas tank. It looks like we've been pumping gas onto the ground ever since the chase started. She lured us farther away from the roads, knowing we would run out eventually and that, out here, radio transmission is poor because of the terrain."

"But she didn't know about my cell phone," Neskahi smiled. "Maybe we can still get through." He reached for the phone, then groaned at the low battery light.

"Try it anyway. I left mine in my Jeep," Ella said with a shrug.

Neskahi punched out the station number, but the phone failed to respond. "Sorry. It's been almost twenty-four hours since I charged this thing."

"It's okay. Justine knows where we turned off, and so do the others. They'll come after us soon."

Ella took a deep breath. "It's okay. You had to keep your eyes on the road. Justine knows where we turned off, and so do the others. They'll come after us soon."

Neskahi felt a blast of air and sand hit the truck, slowing it down. "Luck's not with us. We're in for a dust storm, and driving against the wind will cost us even more fuel."

Ella didn't believe in luck, good or bad, but she wasn't sure what else to call the storm that was building. "We'll drive until the gas gives out, then walk the rest of the way to the main highway. The sand's unpleasant, but it has a plus. It'll hide us from our enemies."

"And them from us," Neskahi said.

The gas gave out after only a few miles. After considering waiting out the sandstorm inside the truck, they decided to head for the highway instead. Neither wanted to waste time waiting to be found when there was work to be done. Once they reached the highway, help would be quick to reach them.

Ella left a note inside the truck explaining what had happened in case a patrol car found the vehicle. They hadn't been able to reach anyone on the radio, but they took their handhelds anyway, hoping that as they narrowed the distance to the highway that would change. Seeing Neskahi reach for his shotgun before getting out, Ella nodded in approval.

The moment they stepped out of the vehicle, they got pelted by a blast of stinging sand. Ella zipped up her coat and stuck her hands in her pockets. The wind was icy, and she found herself wishing she'd eaten something more substantial for breakfast. At least then she would have had more calories to burn to warm herself up.

Keeping some distance from each other, in case of an ambush, yet remaining within sight of each other, they kept quiet, listening, trying to make out sounds over the howl of the wind. Ella felt the danger all around them, she knew her enemies were near, but she couldn't see anyone. She wasn't at all sure if they'd have to go up against her father-in-law's family, skinwalkers, or both. Her father-in-law had been the former police chief and the leader of a group of Navajo witches out to seize power on the reservation. Her own father had been their first victim.

After a short time, they found themselves in a low area that seemed to go on forever. "We're getting near Jane's hogan. I remember it was in a large basin. Her home gave me the creeps before, but I'd be willing to go along if you want to take shelter in her hogan until this storm passes," Ella shouted. "It's worse than we thought it would be."

"I'd rather not, if we're voting on this." Neskahi yelled back.

"Why?"

"I don't like the idea. We don't know what happened to her," Neskahi said.

"Are you worried about the *chindi?*"

He shrugged. "I don't know about that, but I don't like the idea of being on their ground. If it gave you the creeps, that's enough for my thumbs down." Neskahi quickened his pace until she had to hurry up to keep him in sight through the dust.

She knew he wasn't really so far away, that it was just the blowing sand that made it seem so. Finally, she spotted something to her left that gave her an idea. She checked it out, then caught up to Neskahi, who was waiting after he had lost sight of her.

"There's a shallow cave back there, and it looks like there's nothing inside except spiderwebs. Let's hole up there until this wind dies down a bit. Is that okay with you?"

It seemed like a good solution, and Neskahi quickly agreed. As she slipped through the tall, narrow opening cut into the hillside itself, she felt a sense of destiny. Something inside her assured her that she'd been meant to find this place.

Neskahi brought out a pocket flashlight, illuminating the interior. "Someone's used this place before."

Ella fought the urge to turn and run as she saw the two wedding bands resting in a bed of ashes beside the rock wall ahead. One had been cut through to allow the second band to become entwined within it.

Ella recognized the bands. They'd been custom-made out of turquoise and silver. Eugene, her husband, had worn one, and she had worn the other. He'd been buried with his. Hers had been put away, along with the memories that it had carried, in what she'd thought to be a safe place. It had been placed under a rock on a hillside where they'd first made love.

Yet now both bands were here, intertwined, as if the *chindi* of Eugene was calling out to her. It was meant to unnerve her, or if you believed the traditionalist's views, to bring on her death.

"You've seen those rings before," Neskahi observed.

"They belonged to my late husband and me—a lifetime ago."

"Do you think our enemies meant for you to find this?"

Ella considered it. "I think they were hoping I would. It's their way of reminding me that my enemies are everywhere, and will never give up." She went to pick the wedding bands out of the ashes, determined not to allow them to remain here, but a sixth sense stopped her from reaching for them. "Hand me that stick," she said.

As she slipped the slender reed inside one of the rings, she heard the distinctive dry shake of a rattlesnake's tail warning her to back off.

Ella dropped the stick quickly, and the bands fell to the

ground. As she stepped back she saw the head of a torpid snake peering out from beneath a ledge in the rock face. She stood still and the reptile slithered farther back into the shadows.

"You cheat death often," Neskahi said quietly.

"It's the gift I'm most fond of," Ella said. She snatched up the rings and put them in her pocket. They represented memories best laid to rest, so she would bury them later once she was alone again.

"Look, I know it's miserable out there with the blowing sand, but I'm willing to risk it, if you are," Ella said. "What do you say we continue toward the main highway? We'll have officers out looking for us soon enough, and we might reach someone on our hand-helds once we get close."

"Okay by me."

As she moved back to the mouth of the cave, she noticed the barely perceptible imprint of a cane in the sandy cave floor. Ella smiled slowly. "You lost that round, too, Miss Jane," she said. Her whisper-soft voice was drowned by the angry howl of the wind.

Ella wasn't sure how long they'd been hiking, but she knew that after a night without sleep Neskahi was ready to drop. "We can stop and rest here," she said.

Neskahi shook his head. "I'll be okay. The wind has died down quite a bit, so it's just a matter of getting there."

"And avoiding any traps between us and our people," Ella reminded him.

As they sat down upon a big chunk of sandstone, she tried her radio again. Interference was still too pronounced to allow a transmission to come through.

"I can't afford to rest for too long," Neskahi warned. "I'm so tired at this point I could doze off. If you want me to stay alert, we have to keep moving."

"Let's go then."

It took another two hours before Ella and Neskahi saw Highway 666 off near the horizon. She was about to try the radio once more, when she saw a dust trail rising in the air. A moment later a patrol vehicle approaching from the west came into view.

"Justine, I bet," Ella said, relieved beyond words.

As the vehicle drew near, Ella saw her assistant behind the wheel.

Justine smiled as she pulled to a stop beside them. "Boy, I'm glad to see you two! I thought you'd probably be okay, but you sure had everyone worried."

Ella and Neskahi quickly got into her vehicle, enjoying the warmth of the heater. Ella filled her cousin in while Neskahi dozed in the rear seat. "I'll need an ID on the body, and anything else you can tell me about her. And I'll want that as soon as possible."

"Naturally." Justine smiled. "And your Jeep is back at the station. Two of our officers coming on duty dropped by and picked it up, along with the shooter's pickup. But there's another bit of news you need to know right away. Leo Bekis was killed in a car accident last night, and his sister Gladys is in the hospital."

Hearing about the death filled Ella with a black sense of satisfaction. Justice, in its own way, had been done. "Is Gladys going to be okay?"

"According to what I heard, she's in satisfactory condition. She was wearing a seat belt, and Leo wasn't. They say he was thrown out of the vehicle when it rolled."

"What happened?" Ella sat up straighter in the seat as a thought occurred to her. If it turned out to be a homicide, she could well become one of the suspects—that is, if certain Farmington lawyers had their way.

"Gladys says someone pulled out right in front of them,

and Leo had to swerve to avoid a collision. He lost control, and they went over an embankment. She doesn't know how many times they rolled. When she regained consciousness, it was dawn, and Leo had been dead for hours."

"He wasn't supposed to be driving at all. They pulled his license." Anger filled Ella, though she wasn't surprised to hear the news. Bekis had been an arrogant man.

"He wasn't supposed to be drinking either," Justine added. "Gladys admitted that was why she had her seat belt on."

"And the other driver never stopped?" Ella knew how common hit-and-run accidents were in New Mexico, with so many drivers uninsured.

"No. But you can bet his family isn't going to pursue that suit against you anymore, considering the way he died. Maybe there's some justice in this world after all," Ella's assistant added.

"I suppose, but I wish my mother hadn't been his second to the last mistake."

After they were back at the station, Ella arranged for Neskahi to get a ride home for some much-needed rest, and then made out a full report for Big Ed. Leaving the file on his desk, she proceeded to Justine's lab.

Justine took a deep breath. "I've got bad news. There are two patrol units out at the accident scene along with the ME, but they haven't found Mrs. Willink's body."

"What? I told you exactly where they should look!"

"It's not there," Justine said. "Tache and Ute went straight to the pickup. Except for the burned-out wreck, and a few traces of blood, there was no evidence that anyone had ever been there."

"Someone must have hauled the body away then," Ella said. "I know the woman was dead."

"If they did, the duststorm covered their tracks, so there's no hope of following their trail."

"What about the cave? They found that, right?"

"Yes. Tache's in there now, but he hasn't discovered anything except the rattler you told them about."

Ella dropped down in a chair, reaching down into her pocket to assure herself that the rings were still there. "What about the neighborhood where the woman was hiding? Have you heard anything, besides gossip, I mean? And what about her truck?"

"I haven't had a chance to look into it yet," Justine answered. "Every time I start, something more critical comes up, like today. We did find a pistol in the car—a thirty-eight revolver. It had been wiped clean—even the empty shell casings. The truck was stolen a week ago from Farmington."

"I'm glad you were there today to give us a ride back," Ella said with an apologetic smile. "You have enough to do. I'll take care of checking that neighborhood myself."

Ella went back to her office, her thoughts racing. Sitting at her computer terminal, she pulled up all the tribal records she could find on the housing area where the chase had started. The people living in the one home that had originally been there had remained, undisturbed by whatever was happening around them. The Benallys, the owners of that home, had moved from near White Rock, not too far, by reservation standards, from Jane Clah's hogan.

The connection made her skin prickle. Skinwalkers. That explained why the houses continued to be abandoned almost as quickly as the tenants moved in and why the tribe had never received any plausible explanations. The People hated talking about skinwalkers, and why make an enemy of them when it was simply easier to leave?

Ella leaned back in her chair. It was time to take the offensive. If the skinwalkers were trying to get the doll back, then that was her trump card. All she needed now was a plan.

As she mulled things over, Justine came into her office. "I've got bad news," she said, her face was pale.

"Go ahead," Ella said, waving her to a chair.

"It's my cousin, Thomas. He was being taken to a safe house at Teece Nos Pos. On the way, the two officers escorting him had to stop at Beclabito because they were having car trouble. They found out they were low on oil, for some reason. One, Officer Dodge, went inside while the other stayed in the car with the boy. When Dodge returned, he found his partner out cold, and Thomas was gone."

Ella sat up. "Did anyone see anything?"

"No, just a fresh set of tire tracks. This happened almost an hour ago, but I just got the report. All the radio traffic went through Window Rock, for some reason, and they just forwarded the message here. Apparently, Officer Poyer was taken to the Teece Nos Pos clinic. When he came around, claiming to have been drugged by some kind of red dust, both officers hurried back to Beclabito. They tried to pick up the kidnapper's trail, but were unsuccessful. They put out an APB, but because the request went through Window Rock, it was slow getting here. So far, nobody has found any trace of the kid. According to them, it was as if he'd vanished off the face of the earth."

"I'm going to call my brother and see if he'll meet me at the place where your cousin was abducted. He'll know what to look for more than we would, under these circumstances."

"I don't know what to tell my aunt. Do you think he's still alive?"

Ella pressed her lips together. "I honestly don't know, because I think the evil ones were responsible, not the North Siders. What bothers me, is that they took him right out of our hands in broad daylight. That's a big victory for them, and it's going to boost their confidence and morale."

"Would you like to talk to Poyer and Dodge?"

"Yeah. Tell them to meet me where it happened, then get your things and come out to the Jeep. I'd like you along."

"I consider Thomas my responsibility now. I'll do whatever you think will help get him back alive."

Ella dialed Clifford's number and arranged to meet with him at the gas station where the incident had occurred. She could feel his tension as she explained what she needed from him.

"If that boy is found dead, you're going to have a morale crisis at the station, and not just because he's a relative of one of your officers. No matter how modern the Navajo, ancient fears persist just beneath the surface. This victory by the evil ones is going to cost you a great deal."

"I'm aware of that. I'll meet you there at Beclabito, and hopefully you can tell me something I don't know," she snapped. As soon as she hung up, she regretted losing her temper. Taking it out on him had been pointless, particularly when she needed his help. Fatigue and stress were taking their toll on her. It was only a little after noon, and already the day seemed endless.

She didn't have time to waste, however. She gathered her equipment and headed for her Jeep, where Justine was already waiting.

Ella beat Clifford to the gas station and, as Justine had arranged, the two officers were waiting to report. "We were alert," Poyer said almost instantly as he met her gaze, "but we were ambushed. Our unit was parked out in the open, and I was keeping watch. Whoever it was must have come from the front. The hood was up, and my view was obstructed. All of a sudden there was this awful-smelling reddish smoke that seemed to engulf the car. I tried to yell, but I couldn't even draw a breath. The kid managed a cough, that's all. I remember trying to reach for my weapon, but my hand felt as if it had been turned to concrete. I couldn't move. I guess I passed out, because all I remember was Dodge shaking me hard and asking me what happened." His face was flushed with embarrassment.

Dodge shrugged. "I parked the vehicle right beyond the gas pumps. I was inside for only a few minutes getting three quarts of oil, but when I heard a car drive off it was already over. Whoever sneaked up on foot was picked up by the vehicle, along with our prisoner. All I saw was a blue sedan going over the hill. There was no license plate. We're sorry, Investigator Clah. We screwed up. I should have guessed somebody had tampered with the oil, knowing we'd have to stop."

"Okay, I need answers fast. Talk to everyone in the area who might have been around or seen any strangers. Do whatever you have to, but I want to know where that kid is. Clear?"

"Understood," Poyer said, then turned and strode back to his patrol unit with Dodge at his heels.

Ella watched them drive off, knowing that they were embarrassed by what had happened, and would be doubling their efforts to make up for it. Just a moment's complacency was all it took for a cop to lose his or her life. She doubted they'd be fooled like that again.

After the officers left, Ella turned to Justine, aware of her assistant's mood. "I understand how this has upset you, Justine. We're going to do all we can to get your cousin back alive."

Justine exhaled softly. "I know; it's just that Thomas had started to trust us a bit, once he realized what he'd gotten into. I thought there was a chance for him to turn things around. Now he may be dead. I see this as a double failure on our part, and it goes against everything I intended to accomplish when I became a cop. If we can't help these kids— if we can't do more than just arrest them—then we've failed ourselves and the tribe. I'm not ready to quit being a cop, don't get me wrong, but I'm just not sure how I can get back the feeling that I'm doing something positive for the tribe when I can't even protect my own family."

"If you come up with any answers, make sure you tell me," Ella said. "I felt the same way when Mom was hit by that drunk driver."

The gas station was nestled in the low piñon and juniper pine hills just east of the Arizona state line. As Ella scanned the area, she saw Clifford had arrived while she was questioning the officers and talking to Justine. He stood by his truck, parked on the southern shoulder of the road across the highway from the gas station.

Ella went to join her brother, while Justine went to question the station employees. "Sorry. I was tied up when you arrived. Did you find anything that could help us out?"

"Not really, but from the description you gave me, I thought it would be sheer luck if I did," Clifford said.

"You found nothing at all?" Ella insisted. Something told her that he was holding back.

Clifford took a deep breath, then let it out again. "Well, let's just say I found nothing that you can use for evidence."

Ella looked at him curiously, then asked the obvious question. "What aren't you saying?"

He said nothing for several moments, staring at Justine, who had come back out of the gas station and was walking around, looking for clues on the ground. "I saw vehicle tracks, like you probably did, but I also noticed something I haven't seen during daylight hours in many years. There was an owl perched on the roof of that gasoline station, not a burrowing owl either. It was a Great Horned Owl, one of the largest I've ever seen."

"Something terrible is on the way, is that what you're telling me?" Ella pressed.

"I'm just saying that evil attracts evil. Whatever happened here is the start of something, not the end," he said. "I've already sung an Enemy Way, like I said I would, but I'm not sure . . ." He shook his head gravely, took a pinch of pollen out of his medicine bag, murmured a brief prayer in Navajo, and released it on the wind. Then he walked to his truck and drove away.

Ella met Justine, who had finished questioning the station staff. They had seen nothing except the two cops. Ella and Justine walked the area silently together for another ten minutes, finding no evidence except a set of car tracks to support Poyer's story. Finally, they headed back toward Shiprock.

"Where are we going?" Justine asked, as they failed to make the turn for the police station.

"I want to make a stop by Agent Blalock's office in Farmington. I need to talk to him," she said.

They were still lost in thought as they passed through Kirtland. Abruptly a large bird swooped down in front of the Jeep. Trying to avoid colliding with it, Ella slammed on the brakes and swerved, but the bird still hit the window hard. Ella veered off the road onto the shoulder. When they finally came to a stop, she drew in a long, ragged breath.

"It was an owl," Justine said in a shaky voice. "A really big owl. You saw it?"

"Yeah. It's back there on the road, dead, right?"

They both looked back. The road was empty. Ella left the vehicle and looked around, walking back to where she gauged the impact had taken place. There had to be at least some feathers around! The sharp, cracking sound of the bird striking the windshield still echoed in her mind. She was surprised the glass hadn't shattered.

Justine searched the shoulder on both sides of the highway. "I know you hit it, I was sitting right there. But it's nowhere around, and there are no traces of blood or feathers either on the windshield or on the road."

"We were startled by the impact, and we must have magnified it in our minds," Ella said, trying to explain it to herself as much as to Justine. "It wasn't nearly as bad as we thought. The bird managed to fly away."

Justine held firm. "It was bad."

They got back into the Jeep, shaken and quiet. As they continued on to Blalock's Farmington office, Ella told Justine what Clifford had said.

Justine shifted to face Ella. "Something is really wrong here. It goes beyond the problem with gangs. The skinwalkers want *you*. I bet that's what your brother was trying to warn you about."

"That's no news. They've wanted me and my family for a long time," Ella shrugged. "I think what's happening is that they want the item I've recovered." Ella explained about the doll. "They may be hoping that, through it, they can destroy me. But I've got to tell you, it's going to take a lot more than a stuffed rag doll to finish me off. They're ticking me off, not scaring me."

Ella stopped by Blalock's office in Farmington, and asked if the package she'd mailed him had arrived. It hadn't, the mail came later in the day, so Ella showed Blalock a photo of the doll and explained that she needed him to keep the artifact for her until she asked for it.

Blalock looked disgruntled, but agreed.

He gestured to the photo Ella had given him. "It's an ugly-looking thing, isn't it," he observed with distaste. "I'll go ahead and keep it in my safe, but outside the Rez who would want to steal it?"

"If the skinwalkers track it to your office, they'll come for it."

"Skinwalkers? Here? I doubt that. They'd be off their home ground, and I know bullets will stop them. I shoot as well as you do, almost."

"They may consider raiding your office an acceptable risk in exchange for the chance to retrieve this object of power."

Blalock shook his head. "Are you ready to take these people down? Do you need backup?"

"No, on both counts, at least not yet. Thanks for the offer. I'll let you know when I'm ready to make my move."

As they left, Justine looked through the remaining photos of the doll. "This thing is really sickening," she commented. "Are you going to fill me in on your plan now? Do I have a part in it?"

"You're in," Ella assured. "I want you to cover me. We're going back to the neighborhood Neskahi was in last night, where I joined him this morning, and that's not a place I intend to venture in alone."

Justine shuddered. "Shall we wake the sergeant and have him come along?"

"No. There'll be plenty of time for him to get involved later, but give Big Ed a call and let him know where we'll be, in case we need backup."

Ella stopped across the street from the Benally house, shuddering at the empty echoing feel of the abandoned neighborhood. "I want you to keep your distance and stay out of sight as much as possible, but try to keep me in view. I'm counting on you to watch my back."

"You've got it."

"And watch your own, while you're at it," Ella warned.

"Always."

Ella left the Jeep and walked slowly toward the door of the innocuous-looking wood-frame house, giving Justine a chance to slip out of the Jeep and get into place. Everything was quiet. She didn't even hear birds chirping. She stopped in mid-stride and looked around. There was no other living thing in sight.

She knew too much about her instincts to blame an overactive imagination for her uneasiness now, but there was no obvious logical reason for the way she felt. The house was ordinary, a simple one-story stucco, that looked like many other thirty-year-old homes on the Rez.

Ella knocked on the door. Since this neighborhood wasn't a stronghold of traditionalists, she had opted to approach directly rather than wait for an invitation. An elderly Navajo man came to the door. His weathered face looked as unyielding as a cliff face. His eyes gleamed out at her like dark coals.

Ella pulled out her badge. "I'm looking for a relative of mine, Jane Clah. Do you know her?"

The man's face registered nothing. "I don't know any woman by that name," he said and started to close the door.

Ella stepped forward, putting her foot out to block the door, just like an annoying salesman. "I have something that I believe belongs to her," Ella continued, and pulled out one of the photos she'd taken of the doll.

There was a brief flash of shock in his eyes and his expression changed, becoming hopeful. Yet that benign emotion somehow twisted his features, giving it an ugliness that unsettled Ella.

"If that *is* hers, be assured that she will find you and get it back," he said.

"Then you do know her?"

He shrugged, and started once again to close the door.

Ella kept her boot in the way. *"Do you know her?"*

"She will know that you are searching for her. That is enough. She will find *you.*" He smiled slowly. It was not a nice smile. "Maybe she's already paid you a visit." He swung the door, and Ella stepped back to protect her foot. The door banged shut.

A cold wind whipped against her. It was her imagination of course, but she felt as if icy fingers had stroked her cheek— the greeting of Death. Pushing that creepy thought to the far recesses of her mind, she walked back to the Jeep.

Justine joined her a moment later, slipping through a fence a couple of houses farther up the street. "There's something weird going on in that house. I stood where I could see both front and rear doors, and the moment you left, a potted plant was set out on the back step, and the porch light was turned on. It's daylight."

"I expect this is a skinwalker's place, and a contact point for many others. Whoever killed George Nahlee and Shopper might live at that house, or at least visit there often."

"They would all know who the murderers are." Justine shuddered. "What are we going to do?"

Ella looked carefully in all directions before she pulled out onto the highway, glad to leave the neighborhood behind. There was something easily identifiable about a place of evil. Even the Anglos in their pragmatic world felt it, though they seldom admitted it openly. Nobody wanted to buy homes marred by tragedies or violence.

To combat what lay ahead, Ella knew she'd have to out-think her enemies and use every trick she had in her arsenal. "I'm going to find Clifford."

"Why?"

"I won't turn over the doll to the skinwalkers under *any* circumstances, but they're sure to want it back. Maybe we can trade, in exchange for learning the killers' identities. My brother is the only person I know who could make a duplicate of it for us that might actually fool them into thinking it's the original."

"You think he'll do it? It's got to be against all his beliefs."

"It'll take a lot of convincing," Ella admitted, "but I've got to get him to agree. I want whoever murdered those boys, and the only thing I've got to trade is the doll."

"They won't sell out any of their own."

"That depends how badly they want the doll, wouldn't you say?"

Justine considered it. "Yeah, you're right. A lot of them got their power by selling out a loved one—maybe even killing them. One more life or two, if the price is right, won't make that much of a difference to them."

As Ella drove up, the wind blew against the blanket that covered the hogan entrance, and she saw Clifford working inside. "Wait for me here. I have a better chance of convincing him if I go in alone."

Ella left the vehicle as her brother stepped out of the hogan and waved for her to come in. Ella entered and sat down on the sheepskin rug. "I've come to ask you a huge favor."

"Whatever you need, all you have to do is ask," he said, sitting across from her.

Ella fished a photo out of her shirt pocket. "I need you to make a duplicate of this."

He took the photo, looked at it, then bolted to his feet, throwing it back at her. "Get that filthy thing out of this place. How can you ask something like that of me?"

Ella stood up. "I'm truly sorry, but it's my only chance to stop the bloodshed. I need the ones who killed the gang members, and this is my only trump card. Even if I can't get them to give me the killers in exchange for the doll, I can at least stop the killings. If they think they've retrieved the doll, they won't have a reason to murder the kids. They want the real doll back, of course, but I can't give that to them. It's evidence." Before her brother could speak she added, "I know, it's more than that, too. There are principles that go beyond the ones I'm sworn to uphold."

"I'm glad to hear you say that."

"You're the only one I know who can make a duplicate that might look and feel real to them. You'd think of things that no one else would even consider, because you've dealt with skinwalkers before."

"I know our enemies, that's true enough, but you're practically asking me to partake in their rituals. That's real hair on that doll and the blood stain in the center is human blood from a vanquished enemy. I couldn't ask anyone else to give me the samples I'd need to construct a duplicate. The hair, the blood, all would have to come from me. And, if they knew that, their magic could be more effective against me."

Ella's mouth dropped open slightly. She hadn't anticipated this. "Can't you use horsehair and animal blood?"

"They would know in an instant, as I would, if the positions were reversed."

"If I can pass it off as real, for even a short time, I might be able to ID some of the skinwalkers. That's all I'm asking for."

"If they get their hands on an obvious fake, they'll know immediately. It won't feel right, and one glance will confirm their suspicions. Don't underestimate them."

"What about using my hair and blood? I don't have the kind of power that could be used against me."

"No, little sister. Whether you believe or not, what you're asking would make you more vulnerable to them than you already are. That would be too dangerous when you're depending on being able to deceive them."

Ella knew she couldn't ask Clifford to consider using

blood and hair from a corpse. It was too close to skinwalker magic. Defeated, she reached out to pick up the photo. "Forget it then. You're right. I didn't realize what I was asking."

"Wait."

Ella turned around.

"What about your father-in-law's relative, the old woman? Have you found her?"

"No, but she's involved and, the way I figure it, she's my relative, so it's up to me to stop her. The problem is that I can't close in on her. Trying to get to her has been a bit like trying to carry water in your fist. The more pressure you exert, the more slips through your grasp."

Clifford held her gaze for a moment, then said, "I will construct the doll you need. But afterwards, you must promise to do your best to bring it back to me."

"I'll do everything in my power to retrieve it. You've got my word," Ella said, silently acknowledging the sacrifice her brother was agreeing to make. According to his beliefs, Clifford was allowing some of his power to fall into the hands of his enemies. He was risking a great deal for this chance to stop the killings.

More worried than ever, Ella drove back to the station and rounded up the last member of her chosen team. Neskahi seemed well rested and was eager to take part in the operation.

"It'll be only the three of us. The fewer who know, the greater the chance we'll have of pulling it off," Ella said. "But I've contacted the Cloud brothers and they'll be patrolling in the area. If we need more backup, we'll have it."

"We're going to stake out that house?" Neskahi asked.

Ella nodded. "I'll be positioning myself in one of the unfinished buildings behind the home, and Justine and you will find hiding places on either side of the front of the place. You'll be in two adjacent abandoned houses, probably. I want to have a clear view at every side of that house. We've made our move, now they'll make theirs. If there's any kind of ceremony or gathering there tonight, I'm sure Jane Clah will show up."

"What makes you so certain?" Neskahi asked.

Ella recounted her meeting with old man Benally at the house. "I believe they're the ones who have taken Thomas Bileen. The Fierce Ones would have left him alone, once he was in our custody, so it couldn't have been their operation. I believe Thomas is still alive, and that they plan to use him as a bargaining chip to get back what was stolen from them."

"So, we're looking at a potential hostage situation," Justine said, "with my cousin in the hot seat."

"Yeah," Ella answered. "Get infrared scopes and everything you think we might need for an all-night stakeout."

"Of course all night," Neskahi said with a grin. "Nobody on this team ever sleeps at night."

"Hey, where else could you get all this excitement?" Justine muttered cynically.

As Ella filled out the paperwork they needed for the equipment, Justine's words stayed in her mind. She'd joined the FBI for that same sense of excitement, though she'd tried to couch it under a lot of nobler sentiments. She had hoped to make a real difference through her work, that was true enough, but she'd also known that, to her, a nine-to-five job would have meant dying by inches. She needed the adrenaline rush that came with uncertainty that was so much a part of police work.

Ella picked up the phone to call her mother and check on her, but then set the receiver back down. She had time. She'd go and visit instead. If only she could figure out a way to balance her business and personal life!

Leaving Justine with instructions to do whatever was necessary to get things ready, Ella drove home. A weariness that had nothing to do with physical sensation seeped through her. The gray clouds that filled the skies above added to her low spirits. It was so clear-cut on television—cops followed their professions with the kind of clarity of mind and singleness of purpose that only religious zealots possessed. But the reality of the job was measured more in losses than in wins. The trick lay in the ability to keep going in spite of overwhelming pressures, and impossible odds.

As Ella walked inside the house, she saw her mother sitting alone near the window, staring outside. Rose's loneliness touched and enveloped Ella.

"Mom, are you okay?"

Rose nodded. "Why are you home so early? What has gone wrong?"

"Nothing. I just came by to see how you were doing since I'm going to have to work late tonight," Ella replied, noting her mother's crutches were on the floor beside her. "How have you been getting around today?"

Rose shrugged. "I've been doing fine, except that Two has been a bit nervous around my crutches. He tried to haul one away while I was having lunch. I can't wait until I get rid of them completely." Rose met her daughter's gaze. "But something is bothering me. It's more than a mood created by the dreariness and cold outside, too. There's something bad brewing out there, Daughter. You feel it, too, don't you?"

Ella nodded. "There's going to be a lot happening before the night is over, Mother. Will you be all right tonight without Loretta or me to help you?"

Rose waited for an explanation, and when none seemed to be forthcoming, she sighed softly. "I can fix my own supper, and take my bath without anyone else's help, thank you very much. But since I can't watch over you, you'll have to watch yourself. Keep your badger fetish close at hand, and trust the instincts you've inherited. We've made powerful enemies throughout the years. Although they're out to destroy all of us, you're leading the way, so it's you they want to take care of first."

"I know." Ella admitted. "But I'm not alone. I work with some good cops."

"I still worry about you, Daughter, but this police work is what you were meant to do. We need you to stand and fight for us."

Stunned by her mother's words, Ella went into the kitchen to make some coffee for her thermos bottle. She'd never thought she'd live to see the day when her mother would actually advise her to continue being a cop. Ella mulled it over as she made sandwiches to take along on her stakeout, then she said good-bye to Rose and walked out to her Jeep.

When Ella arrived at the station, Neskahi was on his way out carrying two rifle bags. "Any problems getting the equipment we need?" Ella asked him.

"None at all. Everything's set. Justine has your gear ready and waiting in the office."

"That's great. I made us sandwiches and coffee. But we'll all have to slow down some. I want it to be completely dark before we move in to take our positions."

"We'll be ready whenever you say the word."

As Ella walked down the hall toward her office, Justine rushed out to meet her. "We've got big trouble. The Many Devils heard that Thomas is missing and blamed it on the Siders. They ambushed them at the Valley Elementary basketball slabs, and two of our officers are pinned down in the crossfire."

"Let's go. It sounds like the powder keg between those two gangs just blew up." Ella's face was grim.

NINETEEN

—— ✕ ✕ ✕ ——

Ella drove the Jeep while Justine followed in her own vehicle with Sergeant Neskahi. They had all armed themselves for a firefight. Hopefully, the boys would realize that they were outgunned and outclassed and give it up. Somehow, Ella doubted that would happen.

The only advantage she could see to this situation was that at least now they had most of the remaining active gang members together in one place. One of the first officers on the scene had positively identified Ernest Redhouse, the leader of the North Siders.

As Ella approached, she evaluated the tactical situation. One cop was lying facedown on the pavement beside his unit, and the other, across the road from him, was crouched behind the hood of his vehicle, which was parked sideways on the road.

The two officers had converged on the scene, blocking the escape of the old sedan between them with three boys inside. The neighborhood was on North Sider turf. It was easy to guess that the Many Devils had come in the old sedan for a drive-by, targeting the North Siders' meeting place, the outside basketball court.

The Siders must have spotted the car and ducked inside

the cinderblock public rest rooms adjacent to the road. They were firing through the doorways and two small windows which had been knocked out.

Ella swung the wheel, hopped the curb, and parked perpendicular to the downed officer's car, placing him in the shelter of the L formed by their two vehicles. Justine pulled in from the other side, making the L into a U. They now had protection on three sides.

By the time Justine and Neskahi were out of their vehicle, Ella was in position behind the engine block of her Jeep, ready to provide cover fire with her shotgun.

Justine, crouching down, made her way to the fallen officer's side. "It's Dodge," she yelled. "He's been hit in the lower arm and leg by small-caliber bullets. I'll try and stop the bleeding." Justine opened her first-aid kit.

"The EMTs are on the way, but we can't let them come in until it's safe," Ella shouted. "Do what you can for him." Ella glanced across the way and saw Neskahi had taken a position near the other cop, Officer Poyer.

Ella reached for her hand-held, keeping low. No shots had been fired in her direction yet, but the car with the gang kids was bullet-riddled, and pockmarks around on the rest room doors showed that those inside had also been targets. "We've got to get the leaders to cease fire," she called to Neskahi and Officer Poyer. Any ideas how to get them to do that?"

"Just don't offer to go over there and talk to them. Your career will be over in a hurry," Justine warned.

Ella nodded. "I need ideas. If we don't stop the shooting soon, Dodge could bleed to death."

As Ella hooked her radio back to her belt, she realized the boys in the car had stopped firing. The only shots were coming from the house. "I think we just got a break. Either the Many Devils have run out of ammo, or they're out of action. They're not returning fire."

"The boys in the house haven't slowed down though," Justine said as a burst of gunfire from the bathrooms struck the Many Devils' car again.

Ella grabbed the car mike, and used the loudspeaker to identify herself. "If the wounded officer here dies, you're all going to be locked up for as long as the law allows. Give yourselves up. We have you outgunned, and more officers are on the way. Play it smart."

"We can't come out," a voice called from the car. "If we do, we'll be gunned down."

Ella recognized Franklin Ahe's voice. This time the bluster was gone. The kid was scared. What he'd planned as an act of revenge had really backfired.

Ella called out to the North Siders' leader, Redhouse. "Lay down your weapons and come out on the far side."

"No way. I don't trust you cops either."

"Don't make us use force," Ella countered.

A burst of gunfire struck her Jeep, shattering the driver's-side window, effectively ending the conversation.

As three more units pulled up, Ella was able to have Dodge carried to where the EMTs could treat him. Meanwhile, she organized an assault team. She sent two shotgun-armed cops with gas masks to positions where they could cover the windows and doors of the rest rooms where the Siders were holed up.

The boys in the car didn't need much persuasion to leave once they saw the additional units, realizing their best chance lay in surrendering to the police. They left their weapons behind and slipped out of the car on the side away from the building, while the police gave them some covering fire. They were quickly taken into custody.

Ella then turned to Justine. "Fire the tear gas through the rest room windows. It's time to fumigate."

Justine sent a round of gas through each window. The North Siders surrendered within a minute, choking and coughing. Working with Philip Cloud, Sergeant Neskahi led the boys behind the line of patrol units and turned them over to Sergeant Hobson. The by-the-book cop had the gang kids facedown on the ground instantly.

Ella smiled grimly. The old cop was like a gnarled cottonwood. His presence alone was enough to command respect. None of the boys so much as moved as they were handcuffed and searched.

Once the scene was under control, Ella had the two leaders brought over to her. The war wasn't over, she knew that from the defiance and hatred in their eyes. The gangs would continue to fight each other and the police as long as they were allowed to exist.

"Listen to me carefully, boys. I know speeches don't work on hardasses like you two, but you do seem to understand force—and fear—so try this on for size. You're wasting your lives fighting each other when you have a much more powerful enemy to worry about. You both know by now that there's more going on around here than your little turf war. Don't make things easier for the ones who want to destroy you. If you try to kill each other, you're playing right into their hands."

Ahe looked at her. "You're back to that skinwalker thing? They're fakes, like magicians on TV."

"Whether or not you believe skinwalkers have power is completely irrelevant. Learn from experience. Two out of the three gang members they went after are dead already. Whether you want to call it magic or not, they are more effective at killing their enemies than you, and they don't waste time strutting around playing macho games. What you have to accept is that *they* believe in what they're doing. They believe in the power of relics. Stealing from them was a *big* mistake."

"That's not our problem," Redhouse said. "They're after the Many Devils, not us. We didn't take anything from them. And if they want to kill the Many Devils, that's just fine."

"They're not taking any more of *us* out," Ahe argued. "If anyone should worry, it's the Siders. They aren't going to grab one of our homies without paying the price."

"You still don't get it," Ella interrupted them. "Thomas Bileen wasn't taken by the North Siders, he was taken by the Navajo witches. But they're my problem. I'll deal with them. And Redhouse, don't be so sure that when the skinwalkers are through with the Many Devils, they won't turn their attention to you and your homies. They've killed with less reason before, and you guys are a pretty easy target."

She looked at both gang leaders with disgust. "All you boys are going to be cooling your heels in jail. And while you're there, I suggest you think hard about this gang war. If you continue it, the tribe itself will come down on you. That's worse than just having a cop pulling you over. Remember that the law we enforce is an invention of the Anglos. Long before there were cops out here, the *Dineh* had their own ways of dealing with threats to the tribe."

Redhouse scoffed. "The People won't go up against us. They're too scared."

"Ask the MDs how scared the Fierce Ones are, they know firsthand about that. And now that they know *your* names, how long do you think *you* can last? Your families will be driven out, and the pressure will start coming in from all sides. The tribe's patience doesn't last forever."

As the boys were taken away, Neskahi and Justine joined Ella. "It's getting dark now. If we're going to make our move, we'll have to make it soon." Neskahi advised.

"Let's get rolling," Ella agreed. "You know the plan, so stay in radio contact. I'll meet you there."

Ella strode back to her Jeep, passed out coffee and sandwiches to her team, and got underway, heading toward her brother's house. Through the thickened cloud layer, the thin sliver of the first quarter moon was dimmed. That muted light would come in handy tonight. Darkness was a powerful ally. Even the gods had looked to him for help, since Darkness went wherever he wished. Even Wind couldn't boast of power like that.

Without thinking of what she was doing, she clasped the Badger fetish in her hand. It felt warm, but not overly so. She held on to it for a moment longer, willing it to give her courage to face whatever lay ahead.

Lying on the cold concrete foundation of a half-finished house, Ella brought out her infrared scope, using it like binoculars. Fifty yards away, people were gathering behind the Benally house. She'd seen skinwalker gatherings before, and something wasn't quite right about this one. She tried harder to make out the faces but she was too far away.

Ella glanced at the duplicate doll beside her in disgust. Her brother had done an exceptional job. The responsibility for using it to trap their enemies, and then bringing it back, now weighed heavily on her. No matter what it took, she would make sure it was never used against her brother.

Minutes later, when it seemed as if everyone the group below expected had arrived, Ella saw a boy being brought out the back door. He was blindfolded and, although she couldn't make out his features, she didn't have to guess at his identity. The person holding him turned Thomas directly toward her, as if he knew exactly where she was hiding.

Ella gasped, the boldness of the action taking her completely by surprise.

"What's that all about?" Justine asked, her voice crackling through the static of the radio.

"I'd say they're offering me a trade—the boy for the doll."

"So, it's moving according to plan," Justine said.

"For now," Neskahi warned.

Ella took the doll and prepared to go down to face her enemies. "I want you both to cover me with your rifles. I've got a vest on, but I'll feel safer with trusted eyes watching."

"You've got it," Neskahi said. "And if you have to bail, we'll make sure you have all the backup you need to get out."

Ella checked her nine-millimeter pistol and the backup derringer in her boot, then went in. Skinwalkers preferred more traditional weapons, like their flint-edged knifes and arrows, or magic, but they were quite capable of using serious firepower. Young George Nahlee had been utterly destroyed by one of their shotguns.

Skinwalker magic worked best against those who believed in their power, and Ella knew this. But she also believed in the power of good, something her family had demonstrated in abundance in countering evil. Ella knew she had to depend on that power tonight.

As she approached the gathering of witches, the badger fetish around her neck seemed to increase in weight, as if it didn't want her to go any closer.

Acknowledging the warning while continuing her advance, Ella approached the circle, where a piñon fire burned brightly. The paint on the faces of those present obscured their identities, while the shadows cast by the flames made them seem more supernatural than human. The rifles and shotguns held by a few of the skinwalkers brought a touch of modern reality back into the situation. "Come no farther," a man's voice commanded.

The skinwalker who held the boy stayed in the shadows

by the back door, with a revolver stuck in his belt. "Put the doll down on the ground, then move back."

"No. The doll for the boy. We trade at the same time, or not at all," she said firmly.

"We will trade," he answered.

"Good. Let him go." At the same moment the boy was released, Ella placed the doll down on the ground and moved back a few steps from it. The boy started to come toward her, still blindfolded, and the skinwalker who'd been holding him began moving toward the doll. Ella could sense the boy's fear as he hurried forward toward the sound of her voice. "Just a few more feet. That's good. Just keep coming."

"It's okay," she said as he reached her. Taking the blindfold off Thomas, Ella pulled him behind her and began moving away from the group, never turning her back on them.

Suddenly the witch who'd picked up the doll screamed in rage and threw it to the ground. "It's a trick."

Ella fought the urge to retrieve the doll right then, but to make a move now would put her among the armed kidnappers and leave the boy undefended. She'd have to retrieve it later, after the skinwalkers were arrested. Her team would move in just as soon as she and the boy were clear.

"It doesn't matter. We were prepared for treachery," a shrill woman's voice called out.

Ella turned her head and saw Jane Clah approaching from the house, with another small group of skinwalkers. She had a cane, but scarcely seemed to need it now. Wilson Joe was walking behind her in stiff, halting steps. Ella's jaw dropped. She could see his eyes were dull, despite the glow of the fire, so she knew he hadn't come there on his own power. If he recognized her at all, he made no indication of it. Her heart turned to ice.

"You see?" Jane said, pointing her cane at Wilson. "I planned a surprise for you. I knew you couldn't be trusted."

She gestured toward the doll, and the man who'd held Thomas earlier brought it to her.

Jane studied it, then looked at Ella, her gaze probing and cold. "Interesting. It isn't the real one, of course, but it may yet prove useful." Her smile was feral. "But, right now we've got other matters to discuss. As you can see, I control your friend, the college professor. Bring me the real doll, and you may have him back. If it isn't here with us before sunrise, your friend's mind will be lost forever. I will make sure of that. Right now, the effects of the herb mixture we've given him only make him compliant. But in greater quantities . . ." She shrugged. "The effects won't kill his body, but not much of the man you know will remain."

Ella nodded, not trusting her voice. Jane Clah was as evil as Ella's father-in-law Randall had ever been, if not more. Right now, she wasn't at all sure if the woman before her had been Randall's follower, or his leader.

"This other doll will also remain with me. I sense it has . . . possibilities."

"You know it's a phony, yet you would keep it?" Ella said, forcing her voice to remain steady. "You must have a plan to trick your own followers someday."

Jane Clah laughed. "You're hoping to foster suspicions among us and create division? Don't waste your time; it won't work. They know enough to trust me completely. I've led them through far worse than anything you can threaten them with." Jane studied the doll in her hand. "This is no ordinary copy, I can sense that." She paused, then added, "You made a mistake tonight, and I believe I know what it was."

Ella backed away, pulling Thomas Bileen along. "The real doll will be yours, provided my friend is returned unharmed. Don't waste both our time discussing the copy," she said, forcing herself to sound disinterested, though the prospect of what that evil woman might do with her brother's creation made her sick. She'd given her word to Clifford. If she failed him, she'd also be failing herself in the worst possible way.

Jane laughed, the sound full of derision and contempt. "Go quickly, now. You only have until sunrise to trade for your friend."

Ella hurried Thomas along until they reached Justine. Sergeant Hobson was there, too, having responded to Justine's call for backup. Ella turned the boy over to the sergeant.

Thomas was so frightened that he was shaking like a leaf, his speech unsteady. "They're all crazy down there," he said, his words rushing together. "You were right all along. You'd better give them the real doll, or your friend won't have a chance."

"I'll handle it," Ella said gently. "Leave with this officer now."

"No, they'll find me again!"

Sergeant Hobson turned the boy around and looked him right in the eye. "Nobody is going to snatch you this time, Nephew," he said, using the term to denote tribal ties, not actual kinship. "It's easy to take someone by surprise when they're not expecting trouble. But they've used up all their tricks. Now *we're* armed and dangerous, and if anyone gets near us before we reach safety, they're history."

Ella knew Hobson was tough, but so were the skinwalkers. Yet the boy responded to the sergeant's confident words, calming down.

Once Thomas was safely away, Ella left Justine on watch and walked back to the Jeep with Neskahi.

"What do you need from me?" Neskahi asked.

"Hang tight. I'll give you instructions in a minute."

Ella called Blalock on the cellular and breathed a huge sigh of relief when she learned that the real doll had arrived safely in the mail. "Will you meet one of my people at the Flare Hill turnoff with the doll? I'm facing a hostage situation here. That doll is the payoff, and I don't have a lot of time."

"You've got it. And I'll be there to help, too. I'm walking over to my weapons closet right now."

Ella nodded to Neskahi and handed him a note with detailed instructions. "Take care of my shopping list, then meet Blalock and bring him and the doll here. Get going."

"What's going on?" Blalock asked.

She'd wanted to end the conversation, but Blalock refused to be put off. He wanted details, and Ella knew that if she refused to give them, he'd only continue to press for information, and he might dig in his heels and refuse to bring the doll.

"Wilson Joe is being held hostage," she admitted finally, giving him the details of the situation, but not her own plans for resolving it. That would have been too risky over the air.

Blalock snorted in disgust, and asked if there was anything else she needed. When Ella said no, he ended the call to get underway.

Ella hung up the cellular. Blalock would be a plus to have on her team. She'd need all the well-trained manpower she could get to carry off what she had in mind. That . . . and a lot of luck.

Ella knew she'd need to summon her brother. A medicine man was the best defense against the evil ones, and Clifford had helped her before. But first, she dialed the ER at Shiprock Hospital next and asked for Jeremiah Crow. His cooperation was absolutely the key to the operation.

It was close to four in the morning, and bitterly cold. Taking her cue from the bank robbers, Ella had staged a phoney accident near the turnoff to the neighborhood. The screech of tires, followed by shouts of pain and cries for help at the site, had all combined to make it very convincing. The road was close enough to be easily seen from the Benally house, and she knew the skinwalkers were watching their every move.

According to plan, the cops watching the house had left for the accident, making no attempt to hide their departure. Ella had left too, joining the general exodus, but as soon as possible, she sneaked back with her assault team, taking a roundabout route that hid them from view.

As Angel Hawk made a wide circle over the staged accident scene, now filled with emergency vehicles, she knew she'd successfully diverted the skinwalker's attention. Through her nightscope she could see figures at the front windows, watching from behind the curtains.

Clifford, unofficially armed with a .38 revolver and wearing a bulletproof vest, crouched beside Ella. "You could lose some of your people tonight," he whispered, "despite the Enemy Way I sang, maybe we'll lose our teacher friend as well."

"I know, but I have no other choice. You can back out, though, if you'd like," she said.

"No, I'm in. You have your own abilities, but I'm the only real equalizing force you have against the metaphysical weapons the skinwalkers will throw at you. I can counter any of their illusions, or at the very least, warn your people when they're being tricked. And there is that item I made for you. I want to find it."

"At least our enemies won't get what they're after," Ella muttered. Big Ed was reluctantly taking care of the real skinwalker doll now, having locked it away in his office safe. He'd proved to be trustworthy, unlike his predecessor, and was standing by at the station, waiting for the arrival of officers from all over the Rez. If Ella needed reinforcements, he's be leading them himself.

"It's almost time," Ella said, and gathered the officers around her. She'd pulled in Philip and Michael Cloud, Jimmy

Frank, and Sergeant Hobson, in addition to Justine and Neskahi. Blalock had also joined them. They were all in full SWAT gear, with bulletproof vests, helmets, gas masks, sidearms, and shotguns.

Ella had opted not to use assault rifles because the officers were much more familiar with their own weapons. There was also less chance of being struck by friendly fire with the guns they were using. Shotgun pellets, for one, were less likely to pass through walls.

The assault team checked and rechecked their gear, awaiting her go-ahead.

"Angel Hawk will pass over in another minute and drop the flash-bangs in the front yard. The minute Angel Hawk comes into view, we'll move. The chopper noise will mask our approach. Once the flash-bangs detonate, Justine will send tear gas through the back. The ones inside the house will expect us to attack from that direction, but we'll circle around and go through the front instead. Surprise should give us a temporary advantage. But they won't be fooled for long. We have to move fast and take them down hard."

Ella glanced at the determined faces crouched around her in the shallow ditch, less than a hundred feet from the Benally house. Not one of the officers beside her would hesitate for a second once the assault began. Wilson Joe was well-known and respected by all of them. They all knew his life depended upon the effectiveness of this attack.

"We work with partners, covering each other's backs. Keep the masks on because of the gas. I know they're old, but they'll have to do. If a mask failure puts you in danger, get out, then cover a door or window in the back yard. Justine will be out there, too, backing us up with a rifle and night-scope, so you won't be on your own."

"Are you sure you can't delay this an hour until I can get some better masks here?" Blalock asked. He was armed with an HK submachine gun, a weapon favored by anti-terrorist forces.

"We can't afford to wait any longer, and I didn't dare ask you for them over the phone, in case someone was listening. That's why I had to mention the doll. We're running out of time to help Wilson," Ella answered. "I hope it's not too late already."

As everyone checked their gear one last time and put on their masks, Clifford approached and gave her a small *jish*, a medicine bundle. "There's sacred pollen in this. I know you don't believe in it, not really, but our enemies do, and you may find it useful. It may also help break the hold the witches have on our friend."

"Thanks."

He smiled, then put on his own gas mask as he had been instructed.

Angel Hawk roared overhead and Ella scrambled out of the ditch and ran toward the side of the house, the assault team at her heels.

A muzzle flash appeared at a half-open window at the same time a shotgun roared, and one of her team fell backwards, struck on his chest. Behind them came the blast from Justine's rifle, and the window shattered. The officer's partner stopped to cover the fallen man, but the rest continued running, splitting into two groups as they circled around toward the front door.

The night suddenly turned to day, and two groundshaking explosions told Ella the flash-bangs had gone off. There was another blast that came from the back of the house. Ella hoped it was the first tear gas round smashing through a window.

Hobson, who'd volunteered for the job, rushed forward and hit the front door low with his shoulder. Ella's eyes widened as the door broke in the center and fell inward, separating into two pieces as Hobson tumbled into the house. Neskahi, serving as his partner, was right behind him, shotgun ready. Ella and Clifford followed, covered by Blalock.

As they entered, Ella saw one of the skinwalkers lying on the floor, stunned apparently by the door striking him as it crashed inward. Hobson had his pistol at the man's throat. Neskahi gathered up a rifle and threw it outside.

Suddenly another skinwalker holding a pistol rose up from behind a sofa, and with a curse, threw a handful of yellow powder toward Ella. Clifford responded immediately with flash of light from his hand, and the powder fizzled toward the ground where it burned with a pale blue flame. Blalock fired a three-shot burst from his submachine gun, and the skinwalker clutched his chest, falling to the ground.

Neskahi and Hobson cuffed their prisoner hand and foot, then signaled that they were going to check out the kitchen. Clifford waved them off, and instead, threw a cushion from the sofa into the entryway. A rain of yellow powder from somewhere inside the kitchen struck the cushion, and it burst into flames before it hit the floor.

Ella drove through the doorway, rolling as she entered the kitchen. She surprised a woman, who was hiding in the corner, coughing from the tear gas. Before the woman could swing the revolver she was holding into line, Ella fired two shots, striking her in the chest. Blalock and Clifford were in the room at almost the same time, but there were no other skinwalkers present.

A shotgun blast, followed by a flurry of gunfire, came from the back bedrooms. "Go, you two. Help the others!" Ella shouted to Blalock and her brother. Blalock complied instantly, but Clifford stayed, pointing to a utility room.

"She's in there. Want me with you?" Clifford whispered.

Ella shook her head as a bright light flashed from somewhere in the back of the house, and another series of gunshots rattled the walls. Some of them she knew were from Blalock's automatic weapon. "You're needed in the back."

Clifford uttered a word of blessing, and disappeared.

Ella grabbed a cup from the counter, then swung the utility-room door open, throwing the cup into the darkened space. She followed right behind it, crouched low, before the broken pieces stopped rattling.

Ella smelled the suffocating stench of kerosene almost immediately and realized her gas mask had slipped. The odor overwhelmed everything, including any traces of tear gas that might have penetrated this far into the house. Before she had time to think, a burning lantern suddenly arced across the darkness, striking the doorway right behind her, and shattering with a splash of fire.

One entire wall of the little laundry room ignited, illuminating the room. Ella took off her gas mask, and shoved it into her jacket pocket, hoping it would stay. She had to warn the others in her team.

"Fire!" Ella shouted the word as loud as she could, moving away from the heat.

Turning, Ella saw Jane Clah limping through the doorway that led into the garage, pulling a robot-like Wilson along with her. She closed the door before Ella had a clear shot.

Ella jumped across the room, but it had already been jammed from the garage side. Without hesitation, Ella placed four rounds into the hinges and kicked the door open.

Ella slipped into the darkened garage quickly, escaping the growing wall of flames behind her and keeping her back to the wall. "Give it up," she ordered. "You're not taking him anywhere."

"Shoot her," Ella heard Jane Clah yell from one of the dark corners of the garage.

Ella slipped farther along the wall. The far side of the

garage was in shadow, despite the flames from the utility room. She'd thought of going for the light switch, but light would make her an easier target, too.

Straining to see, Ella worked her way along the wall toward the darker side of the room. Something brushed her cheek, and she instinctively swatted it hard, thinking it was a spider. It was a pull chain to an overhead light. Suddenly the light came on.

Wilson Joe stood about twelve feet in front of her, shielding Jane Clah with his body. He was holding a lever-action thirty-thirty Winchester, and it was pointed at Ella.

"She wants to kill me. You can't let that happen, my love," Jane Clah purred to Wilson from behind her human shield, pointing her cane at Ella. "I'm your bride. When you look at me, you know I'm your Lisa."

Ella looked at Wilson. His eyes were so glazed that right now she was sure Jane would have been able to convince him that she was the cover model from a sports magazine's swimsuit edition. Jane was playing with Wilson like a cat with a cockroach.

"That's not Lisa, old friend," Ella said. "Reach inside yourself and fight. You know me, you know my voice. I'm Ella. Feel the power of my name. We've fought their kind together in the past. This witch has no power over our friendship. Shut her voice from your mind, and let your heart lead you to the truth."

"Listen to her. She's jealous, don't you see? She's trying to split us apart. You can't let her destroy our love," Jane whispered.

To Ella, the woman's wheedling voice had the same unpleasant resonance as fingernails on a chalkboard. As Ella stood her ground, she felt heat emanating from her badger fetish, extending in a line of fire from her neck to her waist. Suddenly she remembered Clifford's gift. Reaching into the *jish*, she opened the bag and threw the contents toward Wilson and Jane. Sacred pollen scattered over all them.

With a scream, Jane jumped back quickly, brushing the pollen off herself frantically, as if on fire. Her cane rattled to the floor.

"You're still the man I know," Ella said, reaching toward Wilson with her pollen-dusted palm up and open. "You don't have it in you to kill a friend. The drug is powerful, but so is your spirit."

Wilson breathed in the pollen heavily, then slowly turned, looking at the frantic Jane Clah as if seeing her for the first time. "Who are you?"

Jane recovered and stumbled toward the burning utility room, ignoring Ella's order to stop.

"You won this battle," the old woman shrieked, silhouetted by the flames. "But, for you, the fight is not over. My death will insure that you will never know who your true enemies are."

Seeing Jane place something into her mouth, Ella dove toward her. Jane reacted by throwing some shiny powder into the air, and it exploded into a cloud of flame, knocking them all to the floor with a powerful blast of hot air.

By the time Ella scrambled to her feet, the woman was lying beside the scorched utility-room door, seemingly dead. Ella pulled her up, though she could feel Jane's strength ebbing away with each passing second.

"Wilson, I need your help!" Ella's voice cracked through her friend's drug-induced stupor, and he picked himself off the floor, stumbling forward. "Help me drag her outside," Ella ordered.

Choking smoke from the burning utility room engulfed the garage. Ella took her gas mask and placed it over the elderly woman's face. She intended to do everything in her power to make sure Jane lived to rue the day she'd declared war on those Ella loved.

Ella grabbed one of Jane's arms and placed it over her shoulders and, with Wilson's help, carried the elderly woman away from the fire. The utility room behind them was in flames, and smoke billowed everywhere. There was only one way out. Ella shot away the lock, then forced the spring balanced garage door up with a desperate shove.

Smoke choking them, Wilson and Ella made their way onto the driveway, then out onto the front yard, dragging the old woman with them. The entire neighborhood was now illuminated by the flames from the burning house.

Ella felt her chest tighten as she saw that two members of her team were down on the ground. She recognized Blalock and Phillip Cloud as the officers tending them. She breathed a little easier as she spotted Clifford there, too, helping to give first aid. Turning around, she saw the other officers walking around the house, keeping the perimeter safe.

As the emergency vehicles from the phoney accident scene approached, and Angel Hawk hovered overhead, waiting to carry away the wounded, Ella swallowed back bitter tears.

Pushing away her grief so she could function, Ella laid the woman she held responsible for this tragedy down on the ground beside the street, a safe distance from the heat of the fire. When Ella and Wilson released their hold on her, Jane jumped up with an agility that surprised both of them and, tearing off the gas mask, stumbled back toward the house. Ella was after her in an instant, determined not to let the evil woman escape or take her own life.

Pressing her sleeve to her mouth, and struggling for every breath, Ella stepped back into the smoke-filled living room and saw Jane reaching for a pouch underneath the sofa. As

Jane's fingers closed around it, the ceiling above her abruptly collapsed, and flaming timbers came crashing down on the old witch.

Coughing and gasping for air, Ella picked her way through the rubble to where the woman was pinned, but it was already too late. Jane Clah was dead, her skull crushed by a massive beam.

Ella stuck the pouch Jane had tried to retrieve into her own belt. There was no time to check the contents now, but it felt as if the doll her brother had made was within.

Ella was making her way to the door when two firemen wearing masks arrived, and helped her back outside.

As they stepped out into the lightening horizon of a new day, a paramedic ran toward her. Ella accepted the oxygen mask he offered gratefully and, a short time later, was finally able to stop coughing. As Clifford and Justine approached her, Ella removed the mask.

"Are you okay?" Clifford asked, crouching in front of Ella.

She nodded. "I think I've got your doll," she said, reaching for the pouch she'd stuck in her belt. "She went back for it—" Ella felt a sudden burst of fear as she realized that the pouch was no longer there. Only a small piece of cloth remained where the pouch had been, as if someone had yanked it off her. But no one had. Surely she would have felt that. "Help me look. It has got to be around here someplace."

They searched the ground outside the front and back of the house, but the pouch was nowhere to be seen.

"It probably came loose when the firemen pulled you out," Clifford said, pointing to the house, now completely engulfed in flames despite the efforts of the firemen. "Don't worry about it now. It's gone forever in the flames. I would know otherwise."

Ella was still bitter. "But she still won, in a way. She died, and with her passing goes our only link to the remaining members of my father-in-law's secret family—our sworn enemies."

"This may not be much of a consolation," Clifford said slowly, "but you won't have to search for them."

Ella nodded. "Yes, I know. Sooner or later, they'll come after me."

"Why don't you go home, boss? You look like hell. I can handle the wrapup." Justine said.

"I can't go, not yet. There's still work for me to do here." Ella stared at the black smoke, and the flames that flared up almost every time the firemen appeared to be making progress. Their fight paralleled her own. There was a war raging between her family and those enemies of the tribe who were willing to use the old ways against the *Dineh*. She was needed here, and, for now, this was where she belonged.

TWENTY

✕ ✕ ✕

The bodies of five dead skin-walkers were recovered and taken away, and the one survivor who'd been knocked out by the door was taken to jail. Although Officers Hobson and Michael Cloud had sustained injuries, they were not life threatening, thanks to the body armor and helmets they had worn.

Ella helped load both into Angel Hawk—thanking them for their dedication. Her team had reason to be proud of the job they'd done today. They'd fought bravely, and stood together against a fearsome enemy.

While Justine took care of the after-action logistics, Ella turned her attention to Wilson Joe. He stood immobile, staring at the burning building as it slowly collapsed. Though still a bit groggy, the spark of life was back in his eyes, a trait she'd missed the past few weeks.

"Come home with my brother and me. You need us now, and we need you," she said softly.

Wilson nodded. "Yes, you're right. I wanted to forget the dangers in our world, but I almost paid the ultimate price for that foolishness."

Clifford stood by them. "We scored a victory for our side

today, but there'll be a price to pay later for it. That's inescapable." Clifford reached for his keys, and handed his borrowed revolver back to Ella. "I'll meet you at Mom's in a little while."

Wilson was quiet for a long while as Ella drove. When he finally spoke, he said, "I've been meaning to talk to you about something. In fact, I was getting into my truck to come see you when those . . . people took me."

"What's on your mind?" Ella asked.

"I heard about Leo Bekis, and that his sister said someone pulled out in front of them. They went off the road, and the resulting crash killed him." Wilson's voice had dropped to a whisper. There was a deathly pallor on his face.

Ella looked at him, and the intuition that Wilson had been the other driver who'd caused the accident hit her like a bolt of lightning. She remembered the night Wilson had been drunk, when she'd taken him to the Totah Cafe. She also recalled hearing about Gladys' statement, that the pickup she'd seen had been mud-splattered—it was the same recollection Ella had of Wilson's truck that same night.

"Did you know he was at the wheel again, and drunk?" Ella said, interrupting Wilson. "We'll never know whether he died because of his drinking or not. He lost control of a vehicle he wasn't supposed to be driving in the first place. I don't think it matters if we ever find out who the other driver was. Leo was living on borrowed time, and fortunately Gladys will be all right. That's all that's important now, right?" Ella looked her friend in the eye, hoping to convey the message that his confession would serve no purpose at this time.

"Don't you think that the truth is more important . . . ?"

"What I think, is that sometimes justice is more important that the truth, especially when the truth will only damage the living. We should get on with things, and live our lives the best way we know how." Ella said, hoping Wilson would drop the subject, once and for all.

"I have a lot of soul-searching before me, I can see that. What lies ahead for you now that this is all ended?" Wilson asked, acknowledging what she'd done without the need for words.

"I've thought a lot about my responsibilities to my family and to my job, and the guilt of knowing that I've been putting the job first for a long time," she said. "Mom said that I was doing what was right for The People, and that I shouldn't feel guilty about making the right choice. There's not a selfish bone in her body. Sometimes I think she knows each of us better than we do ourselves."

Wilson glanced over at her. "You've helped me, and stood by me. Let me offer you some advice now that I hope will help. What you really need to learn is how to balance things. You neglect yourself constantly because your duties demand so much of you. To take care of the needs of others, you first have to look after yourself. Guilt shouldn't even be a consideration."

She nodded. "I know. I have to try harder for that balance, or someday I'll look back on my life with regret for all the things I haven't done. I don't think I could stand that. If there's one thing I've learned lately, it's that life is way too short."

Ella pulled up by her home and walked inside with Wilson. Crutches or not, as Rose came to the door to greet them, it felt like old times. Happier memories gave Ella comfort now.

"You're just in time. I've made breakfast," Rose said.

Ella looked at her mother in surprise. "How on earth did you know when we were coming?"

"I knew," Rose answered with a shrug.

Clifford drove up a short time later, and the three of them sat together in the kitchen. Rose, refusing their help, kept busy, as usual, setting plates filled with fry bread and eggs in front of them. The aroma of fresh green chile and the warmth of the kitchen filled Ella with a wonderful sense of peace.

Content, Ella looked aimlessly out the kitchen window watching the early morning sun dappling the Sacred Mountains in a beautiful reddish glow. To the naked eye the desert could seem stark and lifeless, but within that was a gift of unsurpassed splendor waiting for those who cared enough to see. This was a difficult time for the *Dineh,* but Ella knew that, somehow, the tribe would survive and continue, just as they'd always done.

"What are your plans now, old friend?" Clifford asked Wilson.

"I'm not going back to teaching at the college," he said.

Ella looked at her friend in surprise. "You're a born teacher. What are you going to do?"

"The Rez is changing. My teaching skills are needed, but they have to be focused differently in order to be useful to The People. All of us here have seen the effects of the gang problem, and the drinking as well. There's just not enough for the kids to do, no constructive way for them to channel their energies. I'm going to do my best to change that. I intend to pull every string I can to raise funds for a youth center. I'm going to make alternatives for the kids while they're still young, so they won't be quite so tempted to join the gangs."

"Let me see if I can get the department involved," Ella suggested. "That should help things along for you."

"That would be great," Wilson said.

"I'll take part, too. Instead of fees, I'll have some of my patients donate time and skills to either building the center for you, or renovating an existing building to house it," Clifford offered.

Rose smiled, pride etched on her features. "Despite all they've done, our enemies have not been able to destroy the ties that bind us together. Friendship is our greatest strength."

Ella looked at Wilson and her brother, silently acknowledging the truth her mother had just spoken. Life was short. It was what one did with the time one was given that mattered most. "Let's rough out some plans for that youth center," she said. "The sooner we start on it the better."